Mutations

Kevin C. Popp

Copyright

Print ISBN: 978-1-7323211-0-6

 Written by Kevin C. Popp
www.TheGarrisonSeries Instagram www.instagram.com/popp.kevin or Facebook at www.facebook.com/TheGarrisonSeries

Editing and Interior Design by Nita Robinson, *Nita Helping Hand?*
Cover by Kelly Martin, KAM Designs

Forward

*L*ewis knew he was in his own private hell. He knew what to expect regarding his fate. For the past twenty years he has had to fight off the worries of becoming what he feared the most, which was becoming one of them; becoming a monster that is half human, half animal. He was now in a constant battle with both sides of the human world and the animal kingdom. This strange realm of continuous schizophrenic conflict of what is human and what is animal requires the victim to constantly balance their emotions. It forces one to merge the two worlds so the one can exist in peace. Once this is mastered, a special, unknown world is revealed and the victim becomes blessed. The only price one must pay is an altered physical appearance and the knowledge that the blessed one will outlive all that he encounters throughout his existence. For these unnamed beings, the experience of death will become one's most frequent incident that they will only share through the eyes and words of others. Death would remain the most distant and unknown companion through the journey of the unidentified. Sometimes in life, death, for some beings, is the only way to total freedom. For the blessed, they will have no description for this state of being that is placed on this rarest of species. Death will be a strange and unchartered concept to their personal world.

Lewis thought about all that he once had that had now vanished. He knew death was the only answer, but would Wolfgang be so kind as to grant him this option? Lewis had spent almost half of his life in the quest for answers to something that apparently doesn't have answers. There is no cure; there is not an antidote to this strange metamorphic transition from one commonly known world into a dark, demented underworld where only a handful of beings exist. He was at the threshold of a world that has no hope for normalcy. He was entering a world that, for him, was frightening, a place that was dark on so many levels. What confused him the most was that the few occupants of this dark and seedy world viewed this form of life as a wonderful and lovely place to exist. This concept was lost on Lewis. He couldn't accept or understand their way of thinking. How would one cope with such restrictions on one's destiny? He didn't want this 'blessing'. Thoughts of suicide went through his mind, but this window of opportunity was only open for a few months. After this window is boarded up forever, he knew he would never die once the transformation was complete. Forever is a lonely and powerful word for the victims of despair.

CHAPTER 1

Agnostic

I often wonder if god is concerned about me achieving a certain level of perfection in all areas of my life. I wonder if god, if he exists, wants his creations to be perfect like he is supposed to be or does god just want to remain in constant control over his imperfect subjects? Does he just want us to play by his rules with our limited intelligence and ability, thus always having the upper hand in all battles throughout our existence? Does god want his subjects to be like him or does he just imply that to be the case? If he wants us to be more like him then why won't he allow us to be as perfect as he? Why aren't there more people out there in this world like him or me for that matter? Which leads me to another question: Why me?

Lewis looked at me and said, "I know, Garrison, that you have always doubted the existence of God. I will say, I highly doubt that God is concerned about any of His creations being as perfect as Him."

I raised my eyebrows and spoke with stronger conviction. "I propose that god is jealous of his creations, especially when these creations perform repeated acts of perfection at certain times throughout their lives. We all have experienced these moments during our lifetimes. These moments are rare, but they do exist. We usually experience these moments of perfection from extremely gifted people from this world's past. We experience these moments by either listening to our most gifted musical composer's works or by benefiting from inventions from our most accomplished inventors of the past. There are moments in these extraordinary humans' lives that, during short respites of time, these creatures came up with a great idea or stumbled upon something that helped create a more perfect world. There are rare moments during the human lifespan that perfection was achieved, either through an act of mental reasoning or physically doing an act."

I continued, "Our great leaders and geniuses of the past have proven this concept to be true. They all, at one time or at multiple times, have had this incredible mental breakthrough that allowed just enough insight so these pioneers of music, medicine or science could come up with or could piece together different threads of knowledge from strange, unexplored and undiscovered thoughts that, when applied properly, made a profound impact on humanity. It is that certain moment in time where everything fell into place for the creator, the inventor or the composer. That moment of awe or that moment when you knew you created something special. The feeling at that moment of perfection when everything in the world was just perfect enough, is what god feels and experiences every moment of his existence. That is, if this god exists."

"We have learned this concept of perfection from our great leaders and geniuses of the past that make our world a better place today in all of life's endeavors. The common problem all humans share is that they only experience brief glimpses of this perfection throughout their lives. They cannot sustain their perfection. The moments of greatness happen so sporadically and are not consistent. This inconsistency is a trait that is common among all us humans, which are flaws and imperfections that impede or mask our true genius in one or a handful of subject matters that we excel in during our short lifespan. To my knowledge, there haven't been too many humans alive since they inhabited this planet, that is perfect in all areas of life's activities; none, in fact. So, the questions that are raised are profound ones. Is god a fan of man who wants the best for his subjects or does he have a sick and twisted mind that enjoys seeing people struggle with disease, physical restriction, or mental limitations? Is god jealous of others who are or might only experience a small taste of perfection? Think about that for a moment. If god does exist, why is he the only one perfect? Why not us?

7

Why does he have to corner the market on the rarest of commodities, the product of perfection?"

Lewis quickly said, "It is absurd to think that God is jealous of His creations. I would like to think that He wants all His creations to do well. He gave us free will and I would think He would want to see all of His creations succeed."

I said, "You mean to say for all of his creations to obey him, right?"

Lewis answered, "No, that is not what I am saying. I believe that God is a good God and wants the best for everyone. I believe He wants us to make the right decisions that would benefit us."

"So, you believe there is a god?"

Lewis said forcefully, "There has to be. If you look at all of what is around you, something or someone had to create the trees, grass, animals, humans... everything."

"So, where is your proof that he exists, Lewis?"

"You have to take it on faith, Garrison. Not everything is black and white in this world. I have been trying to tell you that since we met."

I smiled as I laid my head on the back of my leather chair and said, "I find it quite strange that not once has god appeared before me or shown himself to others, for that matter. The lesser-minded people of this world will tell us that god acts through the actions of others. If god is so all powerful then why does he need to act through others? Why are you so vague, god? Are you afraid to stand before your own creations face-to-face and tell them they are doing wrong and they are disobedient? That maybe you just might like to aggravate them out of your own sadistic pleasure just to see them hurt while you are enjoying every painful minute? I am probably out of line in questioning his great powers, but it does seem very illogical when one thinks about his existence. Even if this god does exist, one must admit that his actions, or rather his inactions, do seem to call into question his character. He hides and doesn't interact with his creations. Why? I think it might be a control issue for him. He wants to control his creations and doesn't want them to get out of line. In addition, I believe he wants to keep us at arm's length."

Lewis said, "At arm's length? You know, for someone who questions God's existence, you sure talk like He does exist."

I playfully responded, "He wants us to have free will, but he doesn't want us to accomplish too much success, especially in certain areas like science, religion, music or medicine. Knowledge is a very powerful weapon to any enslaved group of people or even to any enslaved group of animals. The smarter an individual becomes, the more that individual begins to question. More questions tend to create a potentially dangerous situation for the master of the incarcerated. The more intelligent and informed the enslaved becomes, the more the enslaved wants to escape from its master. Therefore, it is in the master's best interest to eliminate those who are the most educated. If you look at some of the most learned individuals in our past, many of them have died at an early age or they were ridiculed beyond comprehension. I believe this is god's work. He doesn't want his enslaved occupiers to learn too much or achieve too much success."

Lewis said with a smirk, "So, do you think God is jealous of you?"

I looked at Lewis and also felt a smirk form on my face. I thought to myself, *Of course he is jealous of me, if this self-proclaimed god was to exist.* "I believe he is, to some degree, but what I don't understand is that if he is all powerful and he is jealous of me then why doesn't he just eliminate me from existence? Then he doesn't have to worry about me achieving perfection. Free will is the answer many will throw back at me. For example, I know that at any moment I could pick up a rock and at any moment I can throw that rock and hit anything in my sight with a high degree of accuracy."

"Others could attempt this exercise, but all would probably fail. This is what god wants and this is what he has been used to since the beginning of time. He is not accustomed to the idea that one of his enslaved creations has the power to challenge god's powers. Again, it is not that god is afraid of someone being his equal, but the fear of losing control over his creations. God doesn't want his creations to be free. God doesn't want his creations to achieve levels that are close to his achievements."

Lewis said, "For such a young individual, you have a warped and jaded view of God. You also have a very high opinion of yourself."

"Well, I am better than most, correct?"

Lewis raised his eyebrows and nodded in a forced agreement.

I continued my rant. I felt my heart beating faster as it pulsated my blood faster throughout my body, causing my thoughts to be clearer and my senses sharper. "I don't have a jaded view of this deity that no one has seen. I only deal in reality and scientific facts. I believe that through his creations, failures bring joy to god. It gives him comfort knowing that he still controls them. With me, though, I believe it bothers him that I take that joy away from his viewing pleasure. Hmmmmmm! I've speculated many times in my life how it must feel to be like him, and I know it must bother him in the worst way because few people have my abilities. I bet that if this god does exist, my ability must annoy him because one of his creations can perform a certain level of perfection that his other creations cannot perform. This action that I can demonstrate with a high degree of regularity and accuracy makes god nervous. The last development god wants is for me or any of his enslaved to achieve some or any piece of power that might rival his own ability. This frightens god and creates, for him, a feeling of discomfort."

Lewis looked down at his glass of Devil's Cut dark bourbon. I could sense that he didn't want to push this god issue any further, but I wanted to toy with my old doctor friend, and I continued. "Just the other night I was watching a documentary on this autistic, blind gentleman. He had the ability to listen to a piece of work played on the piano of any genre of music. He only listened once to a piece being played. He obviously couldn't see the notes or watch the piece being played, he only listened to the work. He then sat down and played the piece with a 95% accuracy rating. After he passed this test, the people that were studying him took him to a place that looked like a bar in downtown London. In this bar were people that studied rare and seldom-heard music from obscure composures. This prodigy had only heard these pieces once, many months ago. Some of the works were old and some were new. The students then tested the man by requesting he play a few bars or a few measures from a wide array of the musical selections that he had heard months ago. On some occasions they requested a piece be played in a different key from what he had heard. Without fail, he correctly recalled and played all their requests with uncanny precision."

"When I was watching this documentary, the first thought that popped into my head was what a blessing for this young man to be able to demonstrate such a feat. Then I must ask: Why did god have to make this man blind and make him intellectually inferior when it pertains to anything other than music? Is this the price he had to pay god for his musical genius? Did he even have a choice to want or accept this gift? Would he trade this gift for his eyesight? Why could he not just have been born normal, per se, and still possess the musical gift? I also wonder: What does he have going on in his brain that people with lesser abilities don't possess? Why is a certain section of his brain so advanced as compared to someone who maybe has talent somewhere besides music? Do you have the same power that his musical genius has? Is there a way you can play like him by just tapping into a certain area of your brain that you haven't used previously or knew how to use? Can you imagine the power that you potentially have, if this resource was available to you like it is for this prodigy?"

I stopped for a moment to catch my breath. I waited for Lewis to make eye contact with me and as soon as he did I said, "Lewis, I am going to let you in on a little secret. I can tap into my brain any time, on any occasion, and I can release this stored information as quickly as I can think. The price that I must pay is a lifetime of pain. As you well know, I have suffered both physically and emotionally. To add to that price is the loss of my parents. I saw them suffer in the most inhumane ways. I have the awful memories of a monster who was my brother. I have these memories to play around with in my head every day of my life. On top of this, I will live forever. I will never die, and those horrible and most

11

unpleasant memories will haunt me for the rest of my life. All the friends I will meet in my life, I will outlive them all. I will constantly have to make new friends every decade or so. How will I explain my body not getting old like theirs? How do I explain this phenomenon to my friends or to anyone that will end up knowing who I am? This is god's punishment to me for being as close to perfect as anything he has created."

I stepped over to the large glass window in my great room overlooking the large pool. I glanced at the dark green grass that lay like a blanket at the feet of the four large trees that were using my dead brother's rotting flesh and decaying bones as fertilizer.

As I looked at those trees, a wirily grin formed across my face. I said softly, "I often ask god the question: 'Why me?' But, of course, he never responds with an answer. I didn't choose to be born. I didn't choose this way of life. So why am I being punished for something I didn't choose? As a result, there goes that free will of choice thing that the almighty has been brainwashing his subjects with since the beginning of time, when men discovered the ability to think and reason for themselves. People say that god knows all. If so, how can we have free will? If he knows what he will end up deciding for us in the future, then how is that free will for us? I know many scholars on the subject will have a field day with me on this opinion. I chose not to listen to the garbage they articulated by way of their mouths on Sundays or by what their fingers produced with a pen. Either way, I think if there is a god, he tends to influence your decisions in certain directions throughout your life. I think he forces his own decisions on all of us, either by changing the rules in the middle of the game constantly or by just killing off the subject completely. Take, for instance, the worlds of art, music, and science. How many times has he killed off some or many of the greatest composers, musicians, artist, sculptors, and painters of the world before their time was near?"

"I wonder if god wants anything to be perfect in his own little, precious world. Why did he allow such a monster like my brother to be born and end up letting him kill my father when he was just beginning to live his life in a more perfect way of living? The same goes for my mother. I often wonder what this god, which so many people pray to throughout their lives, have in store for me in my future? God has punished me by creating me different from others, thus making it so I have virtually no friends. I watched both my parents die before me in a very gruesome manner, and I was forced to kill my own brother. My god, man, what a price I have paid in just as little as nine painful years on this planet. I am told that I should live forever or at least, in theory, that I could. I have no solid proof that this will be the case, but at this juncture of my life I believe this to be true."

"I carry these unpleasant memories around in my head always, Lewis. I think about these events every day of my life. It is god's fault that I have this cross to bear in my life. What irritates me the most is that I am forced to listen to others talk about how great, all powerful and merciful he is to us lowly subjects that he has created for his own amusement."

I looked at Lewis and sensed that he was starting to understand at a deeper level than when we started our conversation. I continued, "Maybe he exists and maybe he doesn't, but it is very hard to tell either way since he has never shown himself to anyone."

Lewis quickly injected, "Some people believe they have seen or felt Him around them. I don't know if I necessary believe that, but many people say that He is pure love."

I said, "To be honest with you, I highly doubt that to be the case. He seems to like to cause pain for people, and to me it doesn't seem to be very loving to inflect pain on people and watch them squirm. I should know, now shouldn't I? I enjoyed the pain that I inflicted on my brother – maybe too much – but I never called myself the ever-loving deity that he self-proclaims."

"I believe that as you grow and learn about life, you end up taking all the experiences you have gone through and respond accordingly to those experiences. You take what you know and then act upon those decisions. The more you experience, the more you begin to understand the many different situations life offers and how to respond to those situations. These experiences can be in the form of art, music, literature, television, friends, or any vehicle that forces you to think differently or to reflect on the issue of love. Through these different vehicles we have at our disposal, we can begin to understand what we want and what we are looking for in love."

Lewis said, "I have to say, Garrison, it is always a pleasure listening to you talk. Your insight is very informative." Lewis glanced at the large trees in the back of the estate and asked, "Where do you find love, Garrison, or does love find you? I mean, do you think there are a set of rules to finding love or does it just happen?"

I wondered to myself why Lewis was so interested in love. He had never demonstrated to me that he was ever interested in love. I felt he was hiding something from me, but I couldn't figure out what. Usually I can read him like a book, but on this subject his mind was strong. I opened my heart to my friend, but my thoughts were dominated by the invisible one. "I discover love through music. Music is what makes me tick, it is what makes me feel alive and, after all, isn't that what love is all about? The feeling of being alive, being a new and regenerated person, a person that feels clean, free, and happy. Love is not meant to be smothering or forced on you to obey a certain set of ten rules that were allegedly carved in some stone many years ago. No, love is freedom; it is exciting and it is where the rules are the same on both sides."

"Speaking of rules, why does god get to make up all the rules? What about our rules that we should place on god? Why are we not permitted to place rules that would favor us like his rules favor him? To be frank, this concept is beyond my understanding. I would assume that many don't approve of my stance toward god. Many would probably think it is a sin for me to express the strong opinions that I have of this creator of all things. I stand before god to challenge him, not to disregard him. The mistake that people make with god is the failure to question him. We must question his existence and his reasoning to better understand him and what he is trying to accomplish."

"Throughout humans' existence, people have blindly supported him because someone older than themselves told them to love him unconditionally. The old followers of god have installed in the younger followers of god that he should not be questioned. Why? To not question something shows a lack of desire to understand it. To blindly follow with no question is not education of the divine being, it is mindless support out of fear of the holy being and what he might do to his followers that question him. If one ponders the existence of god, he does more than someone who just accepts the fact that god exists and should be worshiped. One must understand why they are worshipping god first then they will understand and appreciate him more as time progresses. It is not that I do not believe in a god, but I want to know what I believe in first, and I dismiss any notion that forces me to believe in god and accept someone else's version of god. God should be experienced and questioned, not taught and forced on someone. I just want the answers to simple questions, but he does not want to listen unless it is on his terms and his terms only. That is my main issue with the divine being."

"The problem with many humans is their mind is what governs and controls their heart. The mind is based on experiences and reasoning. The heart is based on emotions and the sense of what is natural. Therein lies the problem. If you can train your mind to focus on emotion, you will be a truer and happier person. It is difficult for a human to love unconditionally because that would require no reason. Reason is something humans must rely on for their basic existence. This is their downfall. They base everything on reason, not emotion, thought over instinct, thought over passion. Since day one, humans were taught to control their feelings and emotions, which basically says to ignore what is natural. Society forces upon the human a blueprint to act in certain controlled ways in different situations. Our society in the past has frowned on humans being centered on their basic instincts. They prefer their fellow humans to rely more on their sense of reason."

Lewis said, "You speak as if you are not human. Do you consider yourself human?"

I contemplated Lewis's question for a moment. My heart raced and I grew angry but I controlled my emotions. I wondered why he would ask this type of question. Of course I am human. I am not an animal. As I stared at Lewis, I suddenly realized that I do separate myself from others when I talk about our species. I calmly said, "I feel that I am so superior to other humans that I don't fit into that grouping." I looked across the room and began to explain why I feel that I am different from all other humans. I continued, "Some scholars say that ultimate love is god's love because it is unconditional. The problem rests in the fact that humans find it very difficult to love unconditionally, and many humans think it is impossible to love unconditionally. Many people love each other through their minds instead of their hearts."

"You see, Lewis, humans fail to utilize all their senses. They act on reason instead of acting on their senses. There is no reason when it comes to love. Love is a sense, not something that can be dealt with in cool, hard reality. In other words, humans attempt to use their minds to assist them in figuring out how or why they love a person instead of just allowing themselves to let the basic, natural, caring, and nurturing process run its course. One's senses rule this natural process. Some will say it is the heart or the soul. The passion in one's soul is the driving force that guides the person to demonstrate their love for another person. Reason is absent from the process. Only brutal, natural, animalistic desire of what comes innate is performed. This is true love."

"Pure, unconditional love has no reason. Pure love is an instinct. It is based on all five of the senses working together as one. You demonstrate your feelings, your smell, your sight, your taste, and your hearing by the experiences that you have practiced throughout your life. Therefore, the secret to love, in my opinion, is to find a balance between your mind and your instincts. The mind is based on your experiences in life. Your instincts, there from day one of our existence, are inside all of us. They are constantly being developed throughout our lives. It guides the human being toward what is natural and right. The mind gives us knowledge and the heart gives us the passion and desire to want more of this knowledge. With the help of both forces, it will produce pure love."

"True love rests in the fact that love must be created and worked on every day, and not something that just happens. I do not believe that one just falls in love at first sight. I believe that is called infatuation, which is an essential ingredient for love. Infatuation is not love, but it is vital for one to capture this feeling because we must experience some sort of infatuation to get to the level of pure love. Infatuation lights the fuse of interest that one person has in another being. This infatuation controls the receiver for a short period of time until the subject is no longer interested. When the receiver has its total attention controlled and the subject's interest is generated, then the attention of the subject develops to another level. We do this very thing when it comes to love. One must first be captivated with someone else, and that infatuation grows from there, over time. One must attract a mate first, then once the subject's attention is achieved, further analysis can develop to see if this subject is worth the extra time and devotion that will be needed in the future. So, infatuation is a necessary stepping stone that one must take to achieve and experience pure love. We do this every day of our lives. When we eat, we choose what we put in our mouths by first seeing if it looks appetizing. If we have multiple choices of food laid out in front of us, we tend to stare at the food that looks good to us for longer periods of time than the foods that do not look as good as our first choice. The more we stare, the more interest or hunger develops, and that interest or hunger tends to grow from the contemplation. One must develop an interest first in the food before it is consumed. Thus, we must be somewhat interested, thus infatuated, with that certain type of food before we can really begin to enjoy its taste."

Lewis asked, "So you believe that love is built and created on experiences of and through the world around you?"

I answered, "Yes, and the reason I say this is that to be happy and find love in the world, one must feel the emotion these worldly experiences give off. Hopefully this emotion will trigger something inside the observer, force them to recall a previous experience in their lives that they can relate to. It gives insight to a subject that is unexplored by the person. When we experience something, that knowledge will give us more experiences and, with some hope, we will learn from them. In my opinion, this is what love is or should be about when we are living our life."

"One must feel the emotion of another individual. Through that emotion, one relates past and present experiences with the emotion they had previously discovered to gain a better insight of oneself and the other individual. Through that insight, one can find pure love. This is the reason I have a problem with the almighty. He is not there for us; he stays silent in his reported adoration of us lowly animals called humans. He does not respond when called upon. Many say he does in 'acts' throughout a person's life. Just because something happens to you in your life in an odd or strange way or just because some stranger haphazardly walks up to you on the street and tells you something unexpected, that does not mean god is speaking to you. Maybe it is just life speaking to you. Just because you pick up some book that has been passed down from centuries upon centuries and was written by men from those many generations past, does not make those words god's. The words in that book, which can be interpreted a thousand different ways, cannot be proven or disproven to be about one lowly man's life. Did he perform those things while he was on this planet if, in fact, he really did exist?"

Lewis smiled, looked down and suddenly his facial expression changed. He questioned, "Do you believe in everlasting life?"

I responded, "What about this everlasting life thing? How does that work again? Where does your 'soul' go? Some place in the sky? What happens if you don't like it up there? Can you leave of your own free will? I don't know about you, but I am a little worried about spending my life to make someone I have never met or something that might not exist, happy by doing all the things that his followers instruct you to do. Then, moreover, you must blindly be led into this floating palace in the sky where you receive the 'honor' to be with him for eternity. Kind of pretentious of this potential mythical creature now, is it not?"

"One day I am going to find out the secret to living everlasting life, the life that I possess, not the pretend everlasting life that exists in some fantasy land."

I could tell that Lewis was increasingly becoming annoyed. I wanted to push his buttons just to see how far I could take this conversation. I said, "Apparently only two others possess my gift. One day I am going to find out the secret behind being perfect and to be able to understand how to control and channel all your senses into one working unit like I've been learning to do over my lifetime. When I do, I will tell the world about it, profit from it, and make as many people as perfect as I believe I can be. I am close to my goal. It is now my responsibility to develop all my senses to the peak of efficiency so I can demonstrate the power of my senses so I am able to operate at levels no human being has ever accomplished. I am close to this when I play my violin, when I study, and when I think hard about many issues in life. I believe this is my calling, and the one thing that I might have over god is my everlasting life. I just need to keep myself out of troublesome situations so no one will end up killing me or ending my life abruptly."

I noticed Lewis possessed a concerned look as he attempted to process what I expressed. He knew beyond any doubt that I was going to be dangerous over the many years of his remaining existence.

CHAPTER 2

Notes

My name is Garrison Winthrop Seawick. I am only nine years old. I have been educating myself over the past few years by reading and studying books from my parents' library and from books my teacher and good friend Carolyn has bought me over the years. I do not understand why I was chosen to be so intelligent or why I was the one that had to have this gift bestowed upon me.

I have never been sick a day in my life. I have no clue how being sick would feel or how it would attack my senses. All I know is that I have seen this sickness, like a common cold, and it appears that this common cold can be very painful or at least very discomforting. I am a nice boy. I have done some things in my life that I am not proud of, but I feel that my soul is clean and pure. I have good intentions and hopefully someday I can help others cure certain illnesses that they have and make people better humans than they were at the start. As a result, to follow is the biography of my life from the age of nine to where I have grown into an adult. These experiences are from my own words as well as from others that have been or are a part of my life.

God has not been good to me during my short life. I have witnessed the murder and mutilation of my father. I have seen my own mother kill herself in my presence. I have been forced to murder my own brother in the name of humanity. On the other hand, god has sent many blessings my way. I manage multi-billion-dollar businesses. I have more knowledge stored in my brain than most college professors would have if they lived a multitude of normal life spans. I can memorize, reason, and comprehend better than anyone I have met, either in person or by reputation. I can play the violin better than anyone could or has on this planet. I can memorize an entire violin concerto in just a couple of sittings and play the work better than the composer who created the piece could ever imagine it being played. I have this ability to call upon my senses to make all the instincts that god has allowed us to have, to operate at such a high level. I can complete feats, mentally or physically, that no man can achieve or, in some cases, has ever accomplished. I am not as perfect as this god most people admire and worship, but many times I have come close to being able to perform perfection, even on a whim. I am better at it than any human I have known in my life. I am a very special young man.

I stay up late every night because I only require a couple of hours of sleep daily. I find it to my benefit during this peaceful time of day to read, study, practice music and contemplate situations and life in general. I often wonder if god has punished me for the very gifts that he has blessed me with during my lifetime. I have wondered if, in the back of god's mind, he had to do it over again, would he have created a being that, when it wanted to, was able to perform close to or just at the highest level of performance known to man? That level of performance being having the ability to achieve perfection. Did god have this in his plans from the very beginning or did this ability to demonstrate perfection take god by surprise? This goal of perfection is the primary objective of many men throughout time. Some men, like my favorite composer, Wolfgang Amadeus Mozart, reached that level many times during his life through his musical talents. They were not interested in being special, it was just part of their lives. They strived to be great all the time. Great men and women of our time want to achieve perfection in what they are either creating or inventing.

For example, a quest for a cure of a disease is not to cure only half of the symptoms, but all the symptoms of the disease. A composer doesn't write a piece of musical work then halfway through trash the remaining sections on purpose. No, the composer attempts to create the piece to the best of his abilities, and his goal is to achieve perfection. A bowler strives for the perfect game; a golfer, a hole in one or to hit that perfect shot. An archer's goal is to shoot for a bullseye; a basketball player's goal is to make a basket; and a football player's goal is for the perfect pass or the perfect tackle. When you cook something, you want to make it look and taste a certain way and you will not be happy if it is not... perfect. Again, the goal for all humans is to strive for perfection and to achieve it. It is what makes us better and different from plain animals of this world.

I believe we all have reached perfection many times in our lives, and most of us are not aware of this fact. There are moments in everyone's life that we have created something that could not be improved upon or created better. Rather, it was the perfectly thrown ball or a perfectly written signature or a perfectly read sentence from a book. It might have been an event where you have operated at the highest level, where all your senses worked together as one to perform a perfect act. This act might have occurred during a sporting event during your life or you witnessed someone else doing this act. If you can bottle that moment, that very moment of knowing that you have performed or acted out perfection, that is what I experience daily. In my life, I can achieve perfection at almost any time I want. I have tremendous control over my gifts and I seem to fully comprehend its power. Some days are better than others and some days I am on my game to a point where I sometimes get frightened about what I am capable of during those special moments. I have learned throughout the years to be able to control these moments and have these moments become more readily available for me to manage and use. The more I practice, the better I become at my endeavor. I can perfect a skill to a level where I cannot improve on it any further.

In the beginning, I helped create my mind, soul and physical body into a being that is as close to perfect as it could be. Although I am not completely perfect in every aspect, I am close, very close to that perfect structure that most of mankind hasn't even thought of achieving. This is not what god wants me to accomplish, but I am on the verge of developing some of my skills so I am close to being as good as any human that has ever lived. I just need to continue to improve on what I have already perfected and then I need to discover other ventures in my life to attempt to develop and perfect. At least I will try, and through my efforts, maybe I will find the secret to everlasting life, or at least find the secret to a better life.

I have seen many people that were crippled, cannot see, hear, or speak. I truly feel sorry for these people. What kind of god would do this to his creations? It is a shame, if you ask me. I don't know why I have been chosen to have this perfect eyesight, hearing, and sense of smell and taste, but I must take advantage of my good fortune.

I have often wondered if god is, at times, jealous of me. Did he ever intend for any of his creations to come close to being perfect or come close to performing an act perfectly? I sometimes contemplate if it angers him. It seems to me that when god gets upset, he lashes out in anger by either 'allowing' something in one's life to happen that would cause them pain, or just killing the person all together to eliminate the problem. This would explain why god didn't allow some of the greatest men in the history of mankind to finish the work they started here on earth. Men like Mozart, Beethoven, Schumann, Chopin, and Michelangelo, just to name a few. It seems to me that all the great military leaders of the past died young or died before their time should have ended. What keeps me up at night is the thought, *Am I next?* I don't mean to be so arrogant, but I can do things that others just cannot do. I am very special. I wonder if I torment god at times or maybe I have not tormented him enough.

I know I will never die a natural death. Therefore, to some degree I am protected, but not protected from someone who would want to murder me. I guess if I stay awake and can be on the lookout, I can safely say I might be the largest thorn in god's side. Between you and me, I kind of like that idea. The pain and suffering that he allowed my parents to experience was so unnecessary. It is something I can never allow myself to forgive him for; his actions or his will that just had to be done in his own little twisted way.

It still amazes me that Lewis, Carolyn, Loren, or anyone for that matter, cannot experience the things that I experience in my everyday life. I will offer you a simple example of a squirrel eating an acorn. I can hear a squirrel as it runs up a tree. I hear their mouths as they bite into an acorn. I hear the acorn as it falls onto a limb. I even hear the half-eaten acorn as it whistles through the air on its long descent from the squirrel's powerful grip far up into the tree. I hear it hit the soft ground below. This is just a small example of what I go through in my daily life. This is just one of thousands of examples of things I experience throughout the day that other people do not experience. Every day of my life I see, hear, taste, and feel things that others don't. For the life of me I cannot understand why others are not allowed this privilege as I am allowed to partake. My friends cannot hear this and I don't understand this to save my life. Only one other person has heard this, and that was my father.

I have attempted to study myself privately to come up with some reason I have this power that I possess. It is very difficult for me because I don't know what it means not to possess these gifts. I don't take my gifts for granted, but it is difficult not to appreciate them because these gifts are innate. They are a part of my nature, my instincts, and part of my soul. I knew I was different from a very young age, but I couldn't understand why I was different or what made me diverse.

I have learned in many books that I have read throughout my short life that most people only use a small percentage of their brainpower. Maybe I use more of my brainpower than most. I think this is an obvious assumption on my part. My mastery over knowledge of any subject presented to me just comes naturally, which leads me into the subject of Formula L. As time passed, Lewis informed me of the history of the formula. He told me how I have this formula flowing throughout my body. In an unexplainable and strange way, this formula has caused me to use all my senses and forces them to work as a unit. Each one of the senses builds upon the others to form a perfect understanding of an object that I am focusing on or thinking about at any given moment.

For example, just a simple act of throwing a ball is a total sensatory experience which provides me tremendous pleasure out of doing this very remote act. When I pick up a ball I can hear the wind in the air from where I am to where my target is located. I first recognize the smell of multiple odors in the air, while at the same moment I feel the wind and the sun on my skin. If I concentrate long and hard enough, I can force the ball to go wherever I want it with a high degree of accuracy because I use all five of my senses together, which allows them to work as one. I can use my eyesight, my hearing, and my sense of touch or awareness, to force all my actions into one neat little pile of energy, so to speak. Then I release the ball toward the target. I cannot fully explain it, but I hit the target that I am aiming for most of the time. When I was younger and didn't concentrate, I was usually off the mark, but over time I have learned to control my thoughts and concentration level and have them work for me. Over time I have discovered that in most situations, when I am angry I tend to concentrate better and have supplementary accuracy of performing a particular act.

My ability doesn't stop with athletic skills. My control over my intellect is even greater. My mind is full of information and I can recall any part of any subject matter that I digest. I always feel great, alive, and well, and never sick or sluggish. I see everything, I hear everything, and thus I process everything to the eth degree. I want others to feel the way I feel, see what I see, and hear what I hear. If I can find what makes me the way I am, I can make people's lives more rewarding and easier than they are today. I want to share what is in me with the world. Maybe then I will be the earthly god to the masses, the thought of which brings a smile to my face.

It has been a few months now since we buried both my mother and her additional offspring. The grassy area where my mother bled out when she killed herself in front of me, is getting larger by the day. The grass is not only as green as any spot of grass that I have ever seen before, but the grass is so thick I can hardly get my fingers to touch the soil. The grassy patch of dark, rich green is rapidly growing. Therefore, I can only assume now that whatever is flowing in my blood makes the grass grow wild. I assume this formula would make any living plant grow faster, stronger, and healthier than one could ever imagine. I wonder what is going to happen when the roots of those four trees we planted with Adam's body parts start to mix with his blood. I guess the trees will grow very large and fast. Again, more reminders for me of a terribly horrible moment in my young life.

Lewis is still tirelessly working in his lab, trying to find the secret to Formula L. Loren continues to work with me on numerous business activities. She is teaching me every day about all our interests that we have in many different business sectors. I know my grandfather's passion was real estate and he got his start in that area, but I prefer the mining industry. I love gold and we own a multitude of gold mining companies in our conglomerate. I have met with all the heads of the many sectors of the holding company since the death of my father. I am pleased, for the most part, with our leaders' level of intelligence and business sense. While I am only nine years of age, it remains difficult for me to accept the fact that I am more intelligent than everyone that works for me, although it still gives me great pleasure and amusement. I know I intimidated and impressed many of our leaders from the first moment we met. Usually they treated me like a normal nine-year-old boy, then after the first few minutes, I see how their opinions of me changed quite rapidly.

Carolyn is taking over the control and care of the estate, as well as the grounds of the estate. On top of these responsibilities, she has also been cooking our meals. I keep telling her that we can hire that out, but she wouldn't think of it. Personally, I think she wants to feel important since she was hired to educate and tutor me. Since I have surpassed her intellectual level years ago, she feels like she is out of place in this household. I tell her often how much I love and respect her. Carolyn has always been there for me, just like Loren, and neither woman will ever be without a home here on the estate as long as I am alive.

Meanwhile, I am still studying as hard as I can on as many subject matters as possible. I have developed more of an interest in chemistry over the past few years. I want to assist Lewis someday so we can get to the truth of what is in my blood system that has made me into what I am today. If, somehow, we can duplicate this formula and make hundreds, if not thousands, of gallons of whatever this substance is, we can recreate the human race. This opportunity is immense if we can discover the formula's secrets.

I have noticed something over the last few years of my life. I have not been sleeping well at night. In fact, I believe that I only sleep a few hours a night. Sometimes on rare occasions I might get about five hours of sleep, but more times than not I average about three hours. The rest of the time I just lay there in bed, tossing and turning, and I just cannot get myself to sleep. I do just fine throughout the day on this limited amount of sleep and I rarely feel tired or worn out. I have recently discovered that if I rest throughout the day, I feel better than if I do not. Sometimes a short ten-minute nap does wonders for me. I use this oddity to my advantage. The rest of the time while I am awake and others are sleeping, I use the time to study and learn about anything and everything. I read books, I study thesis on the Internet, and I check out many books from the library. I not only recall what I read, but it usually makes sense to me and I can put things together in my head the way the inventor, author, composer, or creator of whatever I am studying intended the receiver to grasp.

I have been playing the violin all my life. I practice every day and I am getting better. I sometimes play for a couple of hours straight without stopping and rarely make mistakes. When I first began I was making errors, but I soon corrected that problem. I have been contacted by numerous colleges and universities, offering scholarships for my violin playing. I know most of these institutions are after my money and that is what I expected from the beginning. I don't mean to be cocky, but I am very good with the classical violin. I thought about composing my own type of music, but I love Mozart's music so much that whenever a piece would pop into my head, it tended to sound like the melodies Mozart created centuries ago. Therefore, I gave up.

Just recently, I ordered a copy of a piano concerto, his 24th to be exact, and I followed the notes along with the music. I could see why

Mozart is regarded as one of, if not the best composer of all time. His music makes you smile one minute and then cry the next. Mozart's music has the ability to touch all emotions of an individual and heightens all the senses throughout the human body. Maybe that is why I love his music so much, because of his ability to touch me in all phases of the human emotion. He attacks most of the senses; the hearing, the sight, and the feeling of the music.

Mozart's music, for me, is what true classical music is all about. I have listened to many other composers, but Mozart touches my senses more than any other composer can. My father was correct when he said that with Mozart's music, you could either listen intently or listen casually. Either way, his music touches your soul. I have always said that one who does not like the music of Mozart is one who does not understand the passion of life and what life can potentially offer. Those individuals will never find inner peace or happiness.

Mozart is like an opera; if one does not like opera, one is incapable of passion. Passion is a cute little word with many properties. Passion is a love, a desire, a yearning for something you are either missing or something you need in your life or in your soul. Passion is not lust or sex, it is a pure meeting of the soul and the mind coming together to work as one. This is why Mozart's music speaks to me readily; because all my life I have been working with all my senses to function as one. When that happens, I feel, see, hear, and experience things that apparently only a few humans have experienced. I seem to enjoy life more than others do. I think it is because I have a small glimpse or a link between this world and the next. We, as lowly humans, are not allowed to see or understand the next world, but we can feel its ever-looming presence. Some say we live in order to die. We live to prove our worthiness to our god. For some, Mozart helps bridge the gap between the worlds that we are all currently trapped in, to the world of all the answers. I believe this is just sick and demented on god's part. Why not let us see what he is trying to sell to us? Mozart is like god to some degree. He does not always answer your questions and, in fact, he raises more questions than answers. The difference is that Mozart understands which questions to ask at the right moment, whereas god remains silent on all issues. Mozart forces you to think, whereas god leaves you guessing.

If there is a god, he gave Mozart a talent that Mozart developed at such a great level. In fact, Mozart was developing ideas and creating such music that even god had to be envious. What god would not be envious of their own creation that went beyond the boundaries of his work and possibility god's own understanding of how his creation could bring a small glimpse of heaven to earth? This could not have pleased god. Therefore, god called Mozart away from us. Maybe this is our true punishment that every man and women must suffer the thought of what could have been, that god has teased us with a small amount of perfection. God has only allowed one man, Mozart, a glimpse into the Garden of Eden. Mozart saw and experienced paradise in his mind. He then created the scene onto paper so the less fortunate could see, hear, and feel the paradise that he experienced.

Mozart was getting too close to revealing the complete and total picture of paradise. This had to be the only reason god took Mozart's life at such a young age. Any other reason is unthinkable. Could god have been jealous of his own creation that he did not want one of his creations to give away the secret of paradise? Maybe Mozart was too close to revealing the secret and god stopped him before it was too late.

By way of his music, Mozart is the only one that saw the secret to what awaits us in the after-life. It took Mozart more than thirty years to describe the idea of heaven. Through Mozart's music, we only experience a taste of what is something truly magnificent. You can feel it in his music. Mozart's music makes you comfortable with what heaven might be like when it is our turn to enter paradise. Mozart reached a level that no other composer before or after his time has ever been allowed to reach. No one composer has ever created so many musical masterpieces in so many different genres in such a short time period. No one ever had, or will have, the innate sense of counterpoint, melody, and the ability to change the mood of his music at the drop of a hat. Mozart can make you cry one minute then turn your tearful world into instant happiness. One can never fully explain Mozart's music, they can only experience it in its true brilliance. The power of music that Mozart created is beyond any description or understanding, even god's. That must be the reason why he killed him at such a young age. I wonder if god will attempt to kill me in my pursuit of perfection and the secrets behind my attempt at perfection.

CHAPTER 3

Edification

One day, I thought about the idea of taking up playing the piano. I called one of the local companies here in Louisville that sells some of the best pianos money can buy. They had a few of these high-priced beauties resting in their store. I attempted to play a few of the pianos at the store's location, and after a couple of hours, I decided on the one for me. I had the piano delivered to my estate the next day. I placed the piano in the great room and everyone in the house was very pleased with my purchase. Loren loves the piano and she offered her assistance from the start. "Garrison, I could teach you if you would like." Then she laughed to herself and said, "Oh, what is wrong with me? That would only last for a week and then you'll have the thing mastered."

After a week, Loren could not show me anymore than she had. I surpassed her teachings. I said, "I believe I need a more advanced teacher now."

I contacted one of my friends with the Louisville Orchestra. They knew of a piano teacher that was retired but still tutored on occasion. After a short time, I was informed that the lady would love to tutor me. I thank my reputation on such an offer, as well as my money. Without my reputation and money, the tutor would not be available to me. After a few days passed, the woman stopped by the estate for my first lesson. Her name was Kim Whistel.

When she rang the doorbell, Loren answered. "So, you must be Mrs. Whistel. It is a pleasure to meet you."

Kim said, "Thank you. So where is our special student?"

Without batting an eye, Loren said with a stern look, "Don't underestimate him. He will master your teachings in just a couple of weeks."

Kim smiled and laughed, thinking she was joking, but after a few seconds she noticed Loren was not amused. She thought to herself, *This is going to be one of those clients that believes their kid is a prodigy.*

When Kim entered the room, I walked up to her and extended my hand. She accepted my greeting. "What a handsome young man you are, Mr. Seawick." I told her to call me Garrison.

Kim was a short, older woman with a prune-like complexion. Her hair was silver in color, short in length, and she smelled like old newspapers. Kim looked over her surroundings as she entered the house. The size of my dwelling amazed her. I showed her around the house and then we got to work. She taught me how to sit, where to hold my hands, and how to read the various notes. It helped being knowledgeable from having played a musical instrument like the violin.

"I am impressed with your knowledge of the keyboard in such a short time. Miss Loren has taught you well." I showed her what I could do by playing short pieces that Loren had taught me. Kim was very impressed and told me that my reputation of having mastery over music was simply unworldly, to her pleasant surprise.

"Kim, I want you to push my limits. Show me everything you know. Don't hold back." We began on a very advanced level for a beginner. I struggled at the opening part of the lesson, but when I got control over my hands, the playing became more comfortable for me. We both quickly discovered that I was better than we originally thought. After a couple of hours, I noticed she was getting tired, but she was very interested and amazed at how fast I was catching on with my lessons. I stopped and told her that she could leave and to come back tomorrow. She was disappointed at first, but I knew she was tired.

As the short month went by, I was playing extremely well, so well in fact that I was catching up with Kim in talent and ability. Kim was astonished with the speed at which I picked up learning the piano.

She knew of my violin talents, but she didn't think I would have the same level of excellence with another instrument.

She regrettably told me, "Garrison, you have surpassed my teaching abilities. I need to refer you to one of the best teachers in the Commonwealth. His name was Lyle Korgan."

Lyle agreed to speak with me on the phone, as a favor to Kim. When we were first introduced on the phone, he was rather blunt and extremely condescending. "I have a rule that I always refuse to teach inexperienced kids at this stage of my career, no matter how famous they might be in other instruments. The piano is a complicated instrument to play. I am beyond that sort of thing, but as a favor to Kim, I will make this one exception. I typically don't make it a habit of surrounding myself with performing monkeys. Meet me at my studio and prepare yourself for a small demonstration so I can see what level I have to deal with and if you are truly worthy of my instruction."

I could not believe my ears. Normally I am never treated with such disrespect. I am a very kind and approachable person and rarely use my money or prestige to my advantage. The exchange we had did not sit very well with me. Usually my reputation with the Louisville Orchestra, my financial status in the community, and my limited but substantial fame tends to have people stumbling over themselves to meet or do business with me. The fact that I had to travel to his house made me very angry. I am usually very nice and treat people with a great deal of respect. Throughout my life I have always been given a certain level of respect because of who I am and what my money can buy.

Carolyn drove me to his studio, which was small, old and a rather messy landscape. The neighborhood matched the area's old and somewhat tired part of town. I was rather disappointed in his dwelling. I expected more from such a figure in our society. With Carolyn by my side, we knocked on the old, wooden door. After what seemed to be an abnormally long wait, the door opened.

There he stood in front of us, rather short and on the obese side. His uncombed and very long white hair, mixed with gray, was moving all around his head as he stood there motionless. Lyle's shortness was difficult to ignore as well as his cockiness. He did not like people in general and thought very highly of himself, to a point that he rarely spoke to someone he didn't know. He was bossy, loud, and extremely arrogant.

He didn't say a word and, in fact, after he opened the door he didn't move a muscle. I had to introduce myself. I extended my hand as I looked him directly in the eye. "It is a pleasure to meet you, Lyle."

At first, he seemed to be rather put off by my presence, but when I addressed him by his first name only, he seemed to be upset. He was not very friendly and refused to shake my hand. He said, "I must make you aware that I don't take on the role of mentor. I am only doing this as a favor to Kim. Therefore, I will grant you my precious time to listen to you play for only a few minutes."

This old man was getting on my nerves with his pompous attitude. After listening to him, I just laughed, which it seemed to offend him. I walked over and sat down at the piano and said, "I want to play the piano part of Mozart's Piano Sonata No. 17 in B flat major, K 570."

The crusty old man laughed while he raised his hands and told me, "Go right ahead and knock yourself out for the few minutes that you have."

I said, "But this piece lasts for eighteen minutes." He stopped laughing. Within seconds, I began to play.

I was feeling a great anger inside of my being. I allowed myself to step outside of the comfort zone that I had chained myself to since the Adam incident. My senses were now all flowing together and working as one. They were all lit up to a level that I hadn't experienced since Adam's death. Everything felt perfect and the notes came easy to me. The coordination between my mind, eyes, feet, and fingers was something I could not explain. I memorized the notes from all three movements of the concerto and as my mind recalled the notes, they appeared to me as clear as they ever had. I just let my fingers move across the keyboard, and I think I could not have misplaced a note of the music even if I had wanted to. I heard the orchestra in my head and I paid no attention to the awkward silence when the piano was not speaking.

I had been practicing for many days for my skills to be as finely tuned and perfected as possible for this piece of music. I knew I had the old man when he slowly lowered himself onto the couch to listen to me while watching my fingers move across the keyboard.

Several times I spoke during my playing. "Notice how perfect my fingers glide over the ivories and how Mozart must be so proud right now." What seemed to be a few minutes were more like eighteen and I came to the end of the piece. I stopped playing after the last note. I looked over at Lyle and said, "Would you like for me to play another piece of music so I can prove myself worthy of your magnificent instruction?"

Lyle was not pleased with my attitude toward him, but on the other hand he had never heard someone play so beautifully in his life. I continued, "Pick out any piece of music for me to play. I will show you more of my abilities."

Lyle coughed, stumbled over to a desk and pulled out a large stack of sheet music in a book. He handled me a Beethoven piece. I quickly responded, "I am not fond of his music but, of course, I would further demonstrate my skills for you through Ludwig's music." To make matters a little more uncomfortable I requested, "Lyle, I would like for you to be the page-turner because with this piece I have to follow the sheet music since I have not memorized this lesser piece of work."

Lyle obviously didn't like my attitude or being told what to do, but I didn't care because soon I would no longer need his services as a teacher. I could immediately tell that I would only use him for a couple of months. After a long, uncomfortable moment or two for Lyle, he begrudgingly sat down beside me and I began to play. I made a few mistakes but nothing major. I finished the piece with his help as the page-turner. I told him, "I know my timing was off. I came in late on a few bars and early on some others, but after a few goes I would perfect the piece."

Lyle sat there stunned and when he got up he said, "Come back tomorrow for the next lesson." That response was unacceptable to me. I noticed Carolyn had a little smile on her face, knowing what was about to happen.

I said to Lyle, "If you want to tutor me for a few months, you will come to my house and I will decide on the time and for how long the lesson will run."

Lyle stood there in shock. I enjoyed his outward display of anger as I watched him move away from me. He was shocked that I was so direct with him, as it was obvious that he had not been spoken to in this way for a while. "I don't think you understand whom you are talking to. I am the most sought-after piano instructor in this area of the country. I refuse to be told by some boy on where and what time I should show up. No one does that to me."

I responded, "You are aware of my reputation." Of course, he was quite aware of my repetition. "I want you at my house tomorrow at noon," I said as I walked out of the house. Lyle knew he was defeated from the start, and this added to his anger. He knew that word would get out amongst his peers that he turned down an opportunity of a lifetime to tutor one of the greatest child prodigies in centuries. Carolyn followed me with a large grin on her face.

Throughout the next day, I heard nothing from Lyle. I sensed that he would eventually show up at the house at my stated time. When the time of our appointment came, I heard a car driving up the long, winding driveway. After a few minutes, I heard the doorbell ring. I sensed it was good ole Lyle. I could feel it inside of my soul. I hurried to answer the door out of sheer gloating because I knew that I had forced this pompous twit's hand.

When I answered the door, he looked at me and then quickly looked away, staring at the marble floor on which I proudly stood upon. He began to nervously speak, "I am sorry about my attitude toward you, Garrison. I can be an ass at times. If it is okay with you, I would like to teach you all that I know about the piano."

I knew without him saying a word that he had thought better about not training me. He knew he could add to his already impressive reputation if he was the main instructor that helped me through the difficult schooling of piano. I let him inside without uttering a word and started as soon as we reached the piano.

Over time, Lyle and I became good friends. I learned a lot from him, especially on timing, which was my largest and most difficult hurdle to climb during my piano training. We worked hard when we could find the time to practice together. After a couple of weeks, I was playing almost as well as Lyle. He was very amazed, and from time to time he offered his apology to me for being such a twit at the start of our engagement. I accepted his apologies, but to be honest, I was just as big a twit as he was, although I never let him know that fact. I paid him well for his valuable teaching. I even provided him prime seats at the Louisville Orchestra where I was again the guest solo violinist for the season's opening night.

I performed a Mozart violin sonata and a Mozart fifth violin concerto. Lyle was surprised by what he heard. I even invited Lyle to come backstage to meet many of my friends from the orchestra, as well as the maestro. Lyle was on cloud nine and could not stop talking about the experience he just witnessed. He also told members of the orchestra that he was teaching me piano and how fast I had learned the instrument. He said, "I have never seen such vast improvement in someone in just a few months of studying. Most people would take twenty or so years to develop the skill that Garrison has developed in just months." As Lyle dropped this little gem on the orchestra, most of the members either stood or sat in their places without a sound. They were all shocked beyond belief hearing this news.

The maestro of the Louisville Orchestra is Colin Steinwig. Colin has been the leader of the orchestra for about ten years now. He knows me quite well and, in fact, is the main reason I am invited to play as often as I do. Colin and the entire orchestra were very impressed and surprised to hear the news about my newfound endeavor. Colin wanted to hear the music flow from my fingertips. He respectfully insisted I play the piano that was on the stage. I reluctantly agreed and began walking out onto the stage with Colin. Since I had been the last performer of the night, there were some people still standing and talking in the aisles of the auditorium. While I was walking toward the piano, I heard many footsteps behind me. As I looked back, I saw about a third of the orchestra following me. I approached the piano, sat down, and immediately began to play a Beethoven piece that Lyle and I had been working on for the past few days. I played with a lot of emotion, and again called upon all my senses to act as one. I played rather well, then after about ten minutes, I abruptly stopped because I noticed Colin was in tears. I asked him, "What is wrong?"

Colin responded, "I am so blessed to be in the presence of such a talent, a talent I have never seen the likes of in my career."

Lyle was nodding in agreement with every word Colin spoke. I then heard clapping in the aisle. As I looked in that direction, I noticed a couple hundred people were standing around and had heard me play. I realized a crowd had been gathering while I played, but I didn't know there were that many people listening. While playing the piece I heard, "Boy Wonder is playing the piano and you have to come and see this." It made me proud. I love to perform in front of people and I love to wow them as best I can. No one could believe that I was now playing the piano almost to perfection, just like the violin. It was a surreal experience for all us.

As luck would have it, one of the local writers from the Louisville newspaper was in attendance. After I finished playing, he said, "Mr. Seawick, may I have a moment of your time, sir? I would like to interview you, if you don't mind." I agreed to the interview and told him the story of me taking up piano, but that the violin was still my first love. The writer interviewed many members of the orchestra and they were all highly complimentary, not only of my playing, but of my overall understanding of music in general. Many of these members really liked me, and in their eyes, they believed I was one of the greatest musical prodigies of our time. Little did they know that I possessed more than just musical talent.

The next day my picture and story were in papers around town. Loren received many phone calls requesting an interview with me from other newspapers in the Commonwealth, as well as from local television shows. They all wanted to know how I possessed such talent to be able to play piano on a concert level in such a short time of study. To be honest with you, I was not perfect with the piano. I needed more practice to get to the perfect level. Colin wanted me to play a piano piece as part of the orchestra's program later in the year, and I told him that would make me very happy. Colin has always liked me for me, not for my money, so I knew when Colin said something nice to me, it was genuine.

Over the next few days, I continued my piano lessons and practices. I improved on my timing and rhythm at an astonishing rate. I also continued with my violin playing, and Carolyn had to tell me a few times not to forget my studying. The piano came very easy to me, in fact, easier than the violin. I had three special rehearsals with the orchestra and believe I improved each time. Colin told me, "Please carve out some time on your schedule to play at a local church. Every month we have a guest performer, and this month we would be honored if that person was you." I ended up playing a violin piece, followed by a piano piece. The performance was recorded live on a local public radio station. I believe I played well, and judging from the response I received from everyone, the audience thought that as well.

Lewis took great interest in my piano playing as well; not as a fan of classical music, but as a scientist trying to find answers to the Formula L secrets. Since I first discovered I had Formula L in my system, Lewis had always told me, "The adrenaline in a human's body is what accelerates Formula L's effectiveness." Lewis wanted to run a few tests by putting me under pressure, and in other cases no pressure, to see how I performed in both case studies. What was astonishing was that the more pressure placed on me, the better I performed. My birth father told Lewis that as the adrenaline glands work harder, they became more efficient with the formula, thus making my skills better. The higher the adrenaline, the better my senses work, and the better I perform. Funny thing about this is that I knew this before the start of the experiments. Whenever I was to perform for an audience, I would work myself up into a ball of stress, and the violin playing improved over when I was not stressed. The same results were achieved when it came to my piano playing, and certainly to my studying. The more interested I was in a subject, the better I comprehended the subject matter. I noticed the more stress and excitement I felt toward something, the better I felt. My ears and eyes were more receptive under this condition and seemingly my senses took in more information than before.

I did a few exercises with Lewis, trying to get our arms around this Formula L chemical. We wanted to know how the formula reacted to my adrenal glands. These exercises varied from throwing darts at a dartboard to throwing rocks or baseballs at objects in the yard. Lewis even went out and purchased a set of golf clubs. He used to play the game in college and was quite good at the sport. I remember when I first picked up a club. Lewis told me how to hold the club, where to put my feet, my shoulders, my hips, etc. I was terrible in the beginning, so I did research on the Internet and read up on the sport. I studied the golf swing closely and read about the mental makeup of the game. I then went out and, after a week or so and hundreds of balls being hit, I started to get the 'swing' of things. I would practice mostly with a pitching wedge and do half swings in the back yard. Lewis then took me out to the driving range and asked me to hit a bucket of balls with different sized clubs. I did what was asked, per his instructions. Again, at first I didn't do so well but after a few attempts, I started to swing the club properly. I was becoming accustomed to having the ball hit the middle of the club. Meanwhile, Lewis was busy taking notes on every swing and documenting every one of my shots. The game is a very frustrating game to play and it was getting me a little angry. Of course, when that happened, I noticed that I was hitting the ball better than before I was angry, which has been a common theme throughout my life. As I swung the club more under the feeling of anger or stress, the straighter I hit the ball. Before long, I could hit the ball where I wanted with a high degree of accuracy.

We continued with other exercises, or experiments, if you will. I practiced throwing darts and somehow I was able to throw a bullseye at least every other time after some practice. Lewis and I would go out into the backyard and walk past the four trees where Adam now lays. We would walk into the woods and I would find a rock, pick it up, and throw it toward birds or squirrels in the trees. I would guess that I hit them at least once every three throws, and on some days, I would hit the animals half the time. I also practiced with some of the lawn darts. I was good with those, hitting inside the circle at a high rate of accuracy. Once more, the common theme in all these experiments was I got better under a more stressed or angered state of mind.

Another exercise Lewis had me do was with a baseball and bat. Lewis would throw me a ball and we would see how often I would make contact with the ball. I remember one day before our exercise, Lewis took out a handkerchief then used it as a blindfold on me. He positioned me in a batter's stance then walked about fifty feet or so in front of me. Obviously, the goal was for me to hit the ball. As Lewis walked away from me, I heard every one of his footsteps, even some small twigs that were broken as he stepped on them. I felt the ground vibrate from the weight of his steps. The next sound I heard from Lewis was the rustling of his shirt as he was going to throw the ball towards me. I heard his fingers sliding off the ball as he released it from his hand. I heard the ball as it came closer and closer, while at the same time I could hear Lewis's right foot hit the earth at the end of the release. I could hear, and actually feel, the ball getting closer to me. I couldn't physically see the ball, but I felt the ball coming closer, which is very hard to explain. I felt the ball like someone would feel the sun on one's skin. I knew I had to swing at the ball, and I allowed my natural and pure instincts to take over the swing. In one almost unconscious movement, my arms and hands worked as one as I swung the bat and it connected with the ball. I did not swing hard because that was not the purpose of the experiment. The ball went up in the air and I heard it hit just behind where Lewis was standing. I did not hit the ball squarely, I hit the bottom portion of the ball, making the ball go higher in the air.

Lewis was not surprised that I hit the ball, but he was surprised when I told him, "I can hear your body movements. I can hear your feet, legs, and arms as they move, cutting the air like a knife through warm butter. I can hear your fingers release the ball from your hand. I can hear the ball as it speeds through the air, and can somehow feel or sense the ball getting closer to me. I mean, I can count in inches how close the ball is getting to me. It is like the ball is traveling in slow motion."

He went over and picked up the ball and threw it towards me, about seventy or so feet from where I was standing, all while I was still wearing the blindfold. This time I was not in a batter's stance, I was standing there with both hands on the bat but facing in the direction of Lewis with the bat in front of me. Again, I heard the ball in the air and I noticed it was higher in flight and was thrown underhanded. The ball was going slow and high in the air, so I moved around quickly as I brought the bat back to prepare for my swing to start. I waited calmly for the ball to reach me and then gently swung, attempting to hit the ball back to Lewis. I made contact, but I was off in getting the ball back to Lewis. The ball fell about ten feet short of where Lewis was standing. I heard Lewis walk up to the ball then tell me that was very good, but his tone and rhythm was a little off. It rather caught me by surprise. I then heard him pull a few blades of grass out of the ground as he picked up the ball. He continued to talk to me as I heard his arm rear back then release the ball from his hand. He threw the ball over handed and the ball was coming toward me at a high rate of speed. I didn't have time to move my body to the side to hit ball, but I put the bat up in front of me as a shield. I placed my hands on opposite ends of the bat as I quickly moved the bat up to my chest. As the ball came closer to me, I contacted the ball. I pushed the bat toward the ball in the direction of where Lewis was standing. The ball came off the bat, went high in the air, and landed about five feet to Lewis's right. He just started to laugh and told me to remove the blindfold. He said, "I think we can do this all day long, and I wouldn't be able to get the ball past you, Garrison." We laughed as we went inside. Lewis interviewed me and wanted to know exactly what I heard, what I was thinking, and how I felt when we were going through the experiment. I told him I felt I was in total control. I could see him in my mind as he was going through the motions of picking up and throwing the ball. I even knew where he was standing after he released the ball. Lewis made countless notes on this experiment.

There was another time when Lewis wanted to see how fast I could learn and type on the computer. I knew the keyboard but I rarely used all my fingers. Lewis taught me where to place my fingers and I practiced for a couple of days. Lewis then told me to type, but not to be excited or angry in any way, just be in a normal state of mind. He wanted me to keep my adrenaline down when I attempted the first typing test. When I finished the test, which consisted of about five full minutes of non-stop typing, I was given another typing test, but this time Lewis wanted me to get the juices flowing, so to speak. I thought about my parents and how they died. I used those thoughts to get the adrenaline pumping through my body then started typing, surprised at how fast I typed. I was told that a good typist can type anywhere from 60 to 100 words per minute. My first go at typing I averaged about 130 words per minute. The second time was around 220 words per minute. Lewis again entered all this information in his logs. Each time he made countless notes on each experiment, and continued to be shocked.

One of my favorite tests came by way of a computer chess game. The same procedure was performed as in the previous tests. I would play a series of games in what we commonly called the low-key mode then I would play a few games in the high-key mode. Again, the angrier I got, the better I played. I rarely lost a game of chess to the computer. In fact, I was quite surprised by some of the incorrect moves the computer made. I also worked crossword puzzles and other more complicated mind and word games on the computer. Repeatedly, Lewis documented everything and took numerous notes on my facial impressions, speed of the completion of the tasks, and any body movements, just to name a few.

During the time of our tests on myself, my business interests had been going extremely well and had been very profitable. I got more involved in all facets of the business. At first, many people did not respect me because of my age, but I gained their respect after they got to know me and saw what I was capable of from a business perspective. I never allowed my emotions or my anger to interfere with any of my business decisions. I seemed to impress many of the business leaders by remembering their names, and memorizing all the important numbers in their presentations and the different branches of the respective divisions they managed. I proved to them that I had total control over the many businesses we operated. This was a very difficult task because it is not often you see a child run a multi-billion-dollar conglomerate. What tended to aid in my acceptance was that I would allow my people to do their jobs and I very seldom offered any advice unless I was asked. Loren, on the other hand, tended to talk a lot in the meetings and offered her point of view on numerous occasions. From time to time I offered my opinion, but because of my age, many times my opinions were not well received. Thus, I let Loren speak to circumvent this prejudice.

Through the following years, I studied for hours on end. I read so many books my head was filled with many different genres, structures, and styles from a multitude of countries. I read mostly documentary-type books, as well as autobiographies. I've read most of the popular books over the many centuries. I developed the ability to speed read and finish a large volume book in a very short timeframe. I had the ability to sit for long periods and study without many breaks. As time went on, I concentrated mostly on chemistry and the cell structure of different kinds of chemicals. I was very interested in furthering the study that Lewis had dedicated part of his life to over the years. I have hopes that someday, with my knowledge and his experience, we can duplicate the chemical structure of Formula L with some minor changes.

I am extremely satisfied with the way I am, from my personality to my physical appearance to my intelligence level. My dream is for mankind to experience what I experience daily. I want people to be free of disease and the common cold, and I want people to be able to complete tasks to as close to perfection as possible. But this blessing comes with some drawbacks that I need to correct. I do not want the general population to be feasting on animal's tendons and muscle tissue; I want others to be more normal than me.

Can you imagine what this world would be like having a large-scale population that never gets sick and will live forever? Moreover, their knowledge of anything they desired would be so great that the comprehension of their discipline of choice would be mastered in a short time. In just my limited number of years on this planet, I have been able to master the violin and piano, know as much about chemistry as most college professors, and have knowledge of how to run a multi-billion-dollar company. I have read almost as many books as anyone alive has read. I must say, that is very powerful, maybe too powerful for most to handle in a proper way.

As time passed rapidly during this section of my life, I took many standardized tests that I needed to take for me to test out of grade school and high school. I scored so high that I impressed the local and national press. I took the ACT and the SAT tests and got a perfect score on both tests, missing not one question on either exam. Many school administrators did not believe my tests scores so I was asked to retake the tests again, in their presence. I ended up retaking the SAT test and, with high level monitoring, I again got a perfect score. My non-related family thought I was too young to go to college, and I reluctantly agreed with them at the time. What I wanted to do was to study what I wanted to learn about and not what some old, crusty professor wanted me to study. I had the freedom to examine and think on my own, and to study whatever I wanted. It was not easy because so many college administrations really put the pressure on me to go to college. Some got so pushy that they were told not to call back.

At this juncture of my life, it did not take long for me to get to the core of what I wanted to do with my life. After seeing the physical, chemical, and emotional changes of my dead parents and brother, as well as myself, I knew I had to study chemistry or some aspect of the field. Through my studies of chemistry, I also developed a great interest in biology. I loved how biology related to the chemical aspects of my studies. I thought at the time that no college could offer what I had at my disposal. I had the public library, my own personal library, and the Internet, which made for very valuable avenues of learning. Also, with my wealth behind me, money was never a problem so I just bought books upon books, and established a second library in the basement. I had carpenters build bookcases next to bookcases for all the books I bought. I read every book I could get my hands on and, with Lewis's help, I memorized the most important and basic concepts of both chemistry and biology. I had found out a long time ago, as with other areas of my life, that when I felt pressure and stress I really did well in my studies. I tended to memorize things to a point that I could almost reread the book that I was reading. I attempted to memorize everything I could, including the periodic table, different chemical formulas, their makeup, and the way they interacted with other chemicals. I found this to be very interesting and fun. Lewis was astounded by my ability to not only comprehend, but also to reason. I love complicated chemical formulas and I would stay up very late attempting to figure them out. I purchased many college textbooks from any college bookstore I could buy them from, and I thumbed through the multitude of pages.

Lewis and I grew so close through these years. After my parents died and the extermination of Adam, Lewis was the only strong male figure I had in my life. He taught me so much about life, about myself and about his work. I taught him some things as well, and I made him think about situations in a different light. We worked well together, but I was getting bored with being confined to the house all day long. I was around eleven years old when I decided I really wanted to go to college.

Loren was very much against me going, and when I told her that I wanted to attend Harvard, she just about lost her mind. Lewis was not supportive of the idea of me going to Harvard either; he wanted me to attend one of the local universities so he could have control over me. Lewis was always concerned about me losing control over my emotions and doing something similar or worse than what I did to my brother when he was alive.

I wanted to attend Harvard because of my adopted families' history with the school, and I believed I needed to leave home for a while. I needed to clear my head and experience a few things on my own. Of course, my age was a major hurdle for everyone except me. To make a long story short, I contacted the admissions people at Harvard and they all wanted to speak to me. Loren made the necessary arrangements for us and set up the interviews then, with much regret, Loren and Lewis accompanied me to Harvard for the interviews. What I heard and sensed from the other end of the line with the Harvard administrator was a great sense of excitement about having this boy wonder join them.

The Dean, Jack Smallon, called me and asked, "Mr. Seawick, I would like for you to answer several questions from some music professors about the possibility of being in the School of Music here at Harvard."

I said, "That would be fine, but I was more interested in the fields of Chemistry and Biology."

The Dean answered, "That could definitely be arranged. I will get back with you in a few days, Mr. Seawick."

As soon as Harvard received my application, I began getting phone calls from not only the Chemistry and Biology departments, but sure enough, I received many calls from the School of Music. My reputation was very strong amongst the musical world. Most considered me to be the next Mozart because of my ability to play with such ease at a young age.

Heads of both the departments of Chemistry and Biology called me, and I told them I wanted to meet with both and wanted to major in both disciplines. I sensed they were apprehensive over the phone. The professors knew of my violin and piano virtuosity but knew nothing of my entire intellectual capability. I knew they were thinking, *Who is this kid that is making such a demand to two very powerful and well thought of professors in the country?* I held my ground and was anxious to prove to them that I possessed quite a bit of knowledge on both subjects. After much discussion, they finally agreed to a meeting with me.

47

Lewis, Loren, and I loaded up the suitcases and drove to the airport. We flew into Boston and drove to our hotel room. The next morning we met the Dean of Students, Jack Smallon, who began our day. There was a great deal of concern about my age, but after meeting with the Dean, he seemed to get over the age factor. We were then introduced to the head of the Chemistry department, John Elliot. I knew everyone had been briefed on the money I had because they were all very guarded in what they said to me.

I asked Dean Smallon, "Please stay with us while we meet Professor Elliot."

Smallon said, "Mr. Seawick, we will accommodate you to the best of our abilities. Your family, especially your father, was a very generous man. I am so sorry to hear about his passing."

Professor Elliot let out a small snort as if he was trying to hold back a snicker. Smallon quickly noticed the reaction. "Professor Elliot, I am sure you have many questions for our young lad?"

The Professor looked at me and said, "I hear you are a good violinist and just recently started dabbling with the piano." I immediately knew we were off to a rocky start. I could sense that he thought I was some spoiled kid who was not as smart as many had said. I showed him copies of my tests scores, not only the ACT and SAT tests, but other tests that I had completed to show that I was home schooled and passed all the necessary requirements asked of me. I knew I was going to be put through some tests there on the interview so I was very well prepared.

The Professor respectfully told me, "I must be honest with you, Garrison, I don't want some preteen child in these classes. This is a place for serious thinkers and not a place for some privileged musical prodigy walking in from the streets trying to buy their way into my classes."

Smallon quickly said, "Professor Elliot, you are out of line."

I said, "That is quite all right. If I was in the Professor's shoes, I would be thinking the same thing, Dean Smallon." I then looked at

Professor Elliot and said, "So, quiz me on some subjects in the field of chemistry."

Elliot started out questioning some of the basic chemical abbreviations, which insulted me because that was so elementary. Not only did I provide him the information he wanted, but I also told him the makeup of each chemical of that particular element. In addition to that information, I told him how those elements would react with other elements that he had tested me on previously. We continued with this for over ten minutes. The professor didn't seem to be impressed, but I sensed that down deep he was and might be getting somewhat frustrated. He wanted to prove that I was not ready for Harvard, especially his classes, at this age.

I abruptly stopped the quizzing because I was getting everything correct and we were not getting anywhere. "Look, I have studied a multitude of chemical books from Harvard's bookstore. I have read ten to fifteen books, studied them, and feel comfortable with most of the material. I believe I have mastered the information in those books."

After hearing this he said with a laugh, "Well, that would be impossible."

I then told him to quiz me on any subject in the Organic Chemistry book or the Experimental Chemistry book, both of which were required textbooks for some of his classes. The Professor then asked me a few questions and after several minutes of questions, I began to give my answers. Luckily, the questions he asked I remembered well enough to demonstrate my knowledge. I brought up more information from other chapters in the book, as well as from other books related to some of the questions he had asked. I attempted to link as much information together as possible. The Professor was very shocked and finally took me seriously. He told me that he wanted to test me so he could gauge where I was in the scope of things. I obviously agreed.

After many hours of meeting with the Professor, we broke for lunch. In the afternoon, I met with Professor Bart Thiemann who was the head of the Biology Department. Professor Thiemann was a very nice man and welcomed me warmly. I could sense that he had just spoken with Professor Elliot and was briefed about what to expect. I believe he spoke at length with Professor Elliot about my abilities. We talked and I explained why I was interested in Chemistry and Biology. I told him I wanted to know how things worked, both naturally and chemically. I was interested in the cell make-up of all living things and I wanted to devote part of my life to its research. Professor Thiemann was very excited and started talking to me about some of the experiments he had conducted through the years. I remembered many of those experiments from the books I had read and purchased from the Harvard bookstore. I completed many of his thoughts and explained many of the experiments to him before he even started. He was just amazed. He, too, wanted to test me on my knowledge of the books that I had studied.

I remember staying in a hotel room near Harvard for about a week. I took test after test to prove my knowledge of certain material. I ended up testing out of many of the intermediate chemistry and biology classes. The Professors were amazed at my ability to take the tests, one right after another without any rest. In fact, they needed the break more than I did at times. They questioned me not only on the material, but how I grasped the material in such a short period of time. What also astounded them was my understanding of what I learned, read, and memorized. I could connect the dots and put two and two together, as they said.

To make a long story short, I finished my admissions into Harvard and was going to start the next semester. I decided to take as many courses as I could to get to the meat of the subjects that I wanted to study. I wanted to have the degrees behind my name and the experience of college. Because of my youth, they would not allow me to board on campus so we spoke with Carolyn about the possibility of renting an apartment near the school and having her live with me while I went to college. She happily agreed to do this for me. I know she was getting bored at the estate and wanted to do something new and different. While we were there, we considered some apartment complexes I could call home for the next few years.

We got home from the Harvard visit and I noticed that Carolyn was very excited. She had always wanted to spend more time with me and this would give us time to bond further. I knew that Loren was not pleased with the decision of me going away to school and I knew she was a little upset that Carolyn would be spending more time with me than she would. I reassured Loren that we had grown so close with running the business together, but now it was Carolyn's turn to help me out. In the process, we would have an opportunity to reunite. I assured her that I would not play any favorites. Loren understood my position, just as she had since my birth. She also understood why I wanted to board away and why I chose Harvard. Harvard had been part of my family for decades, but they also have one of the best Biology and Chemistry programs in the nation.

As the months went by, I chose the classes that I wanted. I waited out the summer and when it was close to the fall semester, Carolyn and I went to Boston and got the apartment ready for our living purposes. Most of the classes, like English, History, Psychology, and others, I already knew. As a result, I thought I wouldn't have to study much so I took not just five or six classes like most students did, I took double what most students took. I was taking ten to twelve courses each semester. My reputation spread in the first week while I was on campus. I had so many people come up to me, telling me that it was an honor to meet me. They all wanted to meet this prodigy from Kentucky. I was more popular during my first week on campus than most students were that had been going there for years.

During my undergraduate years, I befriended many of the Chemistry and Biology professors. Whenever I had any questions I would stop by and all welcomed me. They told me they were looking forward to teaching me or, as most of them said, teaching them a thing or two. I already knew, from my past studying, most of the one and two hundred level Chemistry and Biology courses. What I wanted to learn was more advanced studies in the fields of biochemistry and cell biology.

I ended up graduating in just two years with the help of summer school and testing out of many courses. I never made less than an A in any subject. My undergraduate work was easy and very boring. I will not go into specifics of my everyday life, but it was a boring time for me. I knew the material, I kept my mouth shut, and I even studied material I already knew. I double majored in basic Chemistry and Biology. I graduated with the highest honors from Harvard at the tender age of thirteen.

CHAPTER 4

Education

During my Harvard days, I still had my love for music. The news about my ability to play the violin on an elite level spread throughout the campus. The news hit the papers and the news stations in Boston. Everyone in the local area was very excited that I was there. As the news grew, I was even invited to Carnegie Hall as a guest violinist within my first couple of months on campus.

I knew the main reason for most of the fanfare surrounding me was to profit off my reputation and, of course, my wealth. Everyone wanted to make me feel special in hopes of possible generous donations coming their way in the future. Many of my fellow students heard about my upcoming performance, and most of them were excited and told me they were going to be there to listen to me play.

I met with the maestro of the Boston Symphony Orchestra and we went over the program. He wanted me to play a violin piece and I agreed to the request. What I also wanted was to add a piano piece, namely a piano concerto. This really surprised the maestro, and I knew at first he was not willing to fulfill my request, so I asked him for a dry run with the orchestra. A friend of mine from the Louisville Orchestra used to play for the Boston Symphony and he called the maestro to help further my case. Within the next few days I got my wish and played for the Boston Symphony Orchestra. I played on their most grand of pianos, which was like the one I had at my house. I played beautifully and surprised everyone in attendance. The maestro was very happy with what he had heard and agreed to my terms of adding a piano piece to the program by bumping other work he had chosen previously. I told the

Maestro that I would set the world on fire and create such a buzz for the orchestra that the attendance would set records.

I requested to play Mozart's Violin Concerto No. 5 in A Major, K. 219 and his Piano Concerto No. 20 in D minor, K. 466. When the news got out that I would be playing these pieces of music, all my professors were absolutely dumbfounded. Most of them knew of my reputation and my history with guest appearances with the Louisville Orchestra, as well as other orchestras. Many of my professors had been blown away discovering for themselves my high-level mastery of chemistry and biology for my age, then to also have someone at my age play for the Boston Symphony was just too good to be true. I was creating a stir for Harvard and they seemed to love 'special' young men and women. Many still could not believe at the time that I had not reached the teenage years of my life.

The night of the performance, Loren and Lewis came up from Louisville. Many of the college professors, especially the ones that I knew, attended the performance. Many of my fellow classmates told me they were there, although I did not see many of them since they were all seated in different areas of the auditorium. I got very nervous, which was good for me since that is when I play or think my best. My senses were on overdrive that night. I was to play the Violin Concerto first, break for intermission, and then start out the second half of the performance with the Piano Concerto.

I can remember the conductor telling the audience about having a very special guest, a student from Harvard that they had heard about but many had not seen. When the conductor waved his hand for me to come out, I heard this loud standing ovation. As I walked, I heard my footsteps above all the clapping and talking. I even heard my heart beat inside of my chest as if I had just run a marathon. My juices were flowing and my adrenaline was at a peak that I had not been at in quite some time. As the crowd settled in, I nodded to the conductor to begin the piece. I played my heart out for this Concerto and as I played, I didn't hear a sound from the audience. My level of concentration was at its highest level. I made no errors, my bow strokes were perfect in very detail, and my finger placement was so perfect that even Mozart would have been jealous of my capabilities.

When the concerto was completed, the crowd rose as one as they clapped for what seemed to be forever. I had a similar experience with the piano concerto after the intermission. The crowd was louder than they were after the first concerto. I had not demonstrated my piano playing skills too often so this was a treat for many in the audience. I really surprised many of the people in attendance because most people didn't know I could play the piano. The Piano Concerto, Mozart's twentieth in D, is a dark and stormy Concerto when played properly. While I was playing the piece, a warm fever-like sensation hit my soul, and I was playing at an extremely high level of perfection. Every stroke of the ivory was as close to perfect as was humanly possible. Then the last movement came, in which the Concerto breaks out into a more fun-loving yet serious piece of art. I personally think it was one of Mozart's best works, and so did Ludwig Van Beethoven. After numerous curtain calls, I was finished for the night. I really caused a stir, not only at the Boston Symphony, but also with the people at Harvard.

The Boston Symphony had taped the performance after I gave the producers my permission. The production people created a music CD from my performance that night. I was fine with the taping because of the added attention it brought to my playing skills. I guess you can call me rather vain, but I do like the attention, and the potential financial fallout from the taping is a nice bonus as well.

I had a wonderful and action-filled time during my first two years at Harvard. During this juncture of my life, I made many appearances at little musical gatherings that Harvard's Music Department organized for its students. The students would submit a piece that they wanted to play and the professor of the Music department would pick which of the performances would be played. The short performances were free and open to anyone on campus. I was always approached by many of the music majors, as well as the music professors, to participate in these short afternoon performances. I did a number of these performances; most were short works or just a section here and there from many of Mozart's works. I had requests to play other composer's works, but I only played Mozart. Every one of my performances was not only well attended but standing room only was the norm when I took the stage.

My social life was rather limited because of Carolyn being at my apartment, and many times knowing that I had to come home and explain my whereabouts to her controlled my social behavior. Overall, she and I had an understanding and we gave each other space. Of course, I was an underage child and never had sexual relations during my college years. Most of the women at the college treated me as a little boy and not a young man. Many gave me their number and contact information, asking me to contact them when I got of legal age. I knew they were all after my money and to potentially increase their social standing.

I knew many important people across the country through my father's endeavors, and of course through Loren's involvement with the business. I made numerous connections with many influential alumni, families, and professors during my stay at Harvard. The Harvard alumni especially wanted to get to know me well from a social and a business point of view. I played along with their social games because one never knows when one might need to have strong contacts in this world. Of course, my fellow students knew this and wanted to act like they were my best friend so they could leach onto my good fortune. For me, this time at Harvard was rather boring outside of my socializing since the class material I had to take was quite boring and rudimentary.

After two years my undergraduate degrees were complete, so I decided to take on two other concentrations; high-level Biochemistry and Cell Biology courses. I worked with other professors that I had befriended over the years and I was really starting to enjoy college for the first time. My mind was expanding and I was finding it more difficult to grasp all the subject matter, unlike in my first two years. I loved the challenge and the opportunity of being forced to think a little harder than at any time in my life. I studied and worked almost every waking minute of every day. I didn't play the piano or the violin for audiences like I did in the first couple of years; I was totally dedicating my life to my two new majors. I studied hard and often, especially with the professors who all loved to speak with me about the subject matter at hand. I learned so much from them and they treated me like I was one of them, to a limited degree. I felt as if they were an extension of my family back home, which I missed terribly. Those few years spent studying and completing my Biochemistry and Cell Biology majors felt like just a few months. I never made less than an A, but I did miss a few questions on some tests, mostly because I did not pay attention to the test question. This was very new to me since I had never missed test questions before.

In about five years of college study, I had four degrees to my name and I was only sixteen years old. I received job inquiries from every chemical and biological company in the world, it seemed. I didn't have any interest in working for anyone but myself. My only goal at the time was to learn all that I could from the greatest minds the world had to offer about cell make up and the structure of a living organism. I wanted to learn and know everything I could about cells of the living, both human and animal, and how they could affect each other.

I loved the chemical and biology courses I took. I relished and thoroughly enjoyed all the course work they entailed. I continued to go to school after my four degrees, working on furthering my education, with an emphasis on biochemistry and cell biology, for about two more years. I went to as many classes as possible and racked up an obscene amount of college hours. I received a Master's in both of my disciplines over a two-year period. These accomplishments were not bad for an eighteen-year-old man. I didn't have a plan for how much education I was going after at the time, but I was taking as many courses as I could take, if I thought they would help me with my quest.

As time passed, school became somewhat of a bore. I went to class and absorbed everything taught to me. I worked endless hours in the lab and learned as much as I could learn from all my professors. I studied during the night and have been blessed with the ability to study something once then knowing it forever. Since I didn't require a lot of sleep, I had the nights free outside of studying. I read quickly and comprehended everything I read. I made it a point to read as many textbooks and published articles that pertained to cell research or any subject matter that could help me gain more insight into my desire for more knowledge of cell mutation. I enjoyed working with my professors, which was usually in the evening hours. I learned a lot while at Harvard, but I had a few thoughts brewing in my head about the human cell and chemical makeup, which made the end of my Harvard days more difficult to endure.

Through those five years, I made it back to Louisville only a handful of times. Usually Lewis found his way up to Boston and we visited when we could. Lewis was very proud of me and although he was just a doctor, all these years working and studying the formula made him very knowledgeable of chemicals and their structures. He self-taught his way through how various chemicals reacted with other chemicals. I sent him as much information as I could back home, especially when I thought it pertained to my condition and to Formula L. My goal was to learn as much as I could, anything that might lead to a kind of breakthrough regarding the formula's secrets. Then hopefully I could have enough knowledge to reproduce Formula L without the unpleasant side effects. I helped Lewis in his studies of the formula and many times we sent information back and forth to one other when an idea formed in our brains.

I felt bad leaving Carolyn in the apartment all day long through the first couple of years. Carolyn ended up getting a job early in my college career and told me she was happy with what she was doing. I sensed she was telling me the truth so I let things continue as they were. She got an accounting job at a nearby doctor's office, working there full time. This worked out well for both of us since I spent little time at the apartment and we never really saw much of each other anyway.

Meanwhile, Lewis moved out during my years away. He stepped back into his private practice, but only for a select few patients. He looked forward to working with me but didn't know, and neither did I at the time, how long I was going to be away. He obviously kept working on the formula when he was not with his patients. Lewis seemed to enjoy this part of his life which, for the most part, was relatively stress free. He didn't have to worry about anyone else's problems, all he had to worry about was his life and his interests.

Loren continued to run the company and would send me reports every month on how our interests were doing. My companies were mostly doing very well, but the gold companies were doing the best. Gold, which was a large part of my portfolio, hit multiple all-time highs during my college career. Loren had absolute control over the entire judgment making, and rarely did I ever disapprove of her decisions. She continued to live on the estate and took care of everything that was important to me in my life.

CHAPTER 5

Vital

O ne night while studying, I received a call from Lewis. He told me that Loren had had a heart attack, but she was doing well and resting in the hospital. Carolyn and I took the first flight out of Boston back to Louisville. We visited her in the hospital and she was very happy to see us. Loren had really aged over the years since I had left for college. As soon as I received the phone call about her heart attack, I knew it was time for me to come home. I could have stayed at Harvard for decades, but when is enough actually enough? I loved Harvard and everything about the school, but I had responsibilities now at home. I spoke with Carolyn over dinner at the hospital cafeteria about wanting to come back home. She liked Boston, but really wanted to get back home to Louisville which, for her, was a place she liked and she wanted to spend her remaining days in a place she felt comfortable.

Loren was doing fine at the hospital. I stayed for about a week to visit and take care of business. I had multiple live video teleconferences with the directors of all the companies I owned. I told them the direction in which we would be heading. Loren would still be the main leader of the organization, but I would take her place for the time being.

Carolyn and I went back to Boston to take care of some business and gather our possessions. Carolyn quit her job and I stopped my studies at Harvard. It was hard for me to leave my professors and others I had studied and worked with, but everyone understood why I had to leave. Most of the professors told me that I was welcome back at any time. They all told me I had a job waiting for me, either as a professor or as a research person at the University. We exchanged contact numbers, said our goodbyes, and I packed up my personal things for our trip home. In less than three days, we left on a plane for Louisville. I had the movers pack our belongings in boxes and had them shipped back to the estate.

Loren, in the meantime, came home, and Lewis forced her to take care of herself. Loren still worked, but only on a limited basis. I really felt bad because I think she was just overworked and that probably brought on the heart attack. Loren was the type of person that never rested and was a workaholic. She didn't need to work so hard because we had terrific managers that were very good at running our many interests within the organization. Actually, most of these interests ran themselves. Our part in all this was to be an overseer of some sorts. We are a holding company that allows our many companies to function and make decisions on their own with minimal supervision. Loren tended to take things a little farther than she needed, which was why I was so confident to have her as the main controller of the conglomerate, Seawick Enterprises.

After a few days passed and things started to calm down from all the excitement of the past couple of weeks, Lewis and I met in his office. I spoke to him about the multitude of subjects that I had learned from my studies at Harvard. Most of the material he had previous knowledge of and we had already covered in our past conversations and correspondences, but there were some issues that were foreign to him. I wanted to confer with him and compare what he and I both knew. From the very beginning, the main purpose for me going to Harvard was to further my education on how human and animal cells interacted with each other. I have read countless books on animal and human cells and chemical structures. I had studied a multitude of experiments regarding these areas and wanted to know how the cells reacted with certain chemicals. My other main objective was to meet with some great minds to cover these issues and have someone that I could ask questions when I didn't understand an issue. They might not have the answers, but their discussions or theories might trigger something in my brain that I hadn't yet thought of. At least that was one of the main reasons I went to college.

The other reason I wanted to go off to college was that I wanted to know how it felt to be a normal student. Of course, with my high intellect I was never going to be a normal student, but I grew tired of reading and studying on my own. I grew tired of using my father's contacts at Harvard, having them buy textbooks for me so I could read and study the material. I also wanted to get out of the house and live on my own, to be more independent. I wanted to be like other students, especially college students. I never wanted to be normal, but I have always wanted to be treated as normal. While away, Carolyn and I grew closer and it was the best for all concerned when I look back on the situation. I missed both Lewis and Loren, especially Loren. She had always been there for me and was more like a second mother to me. I loved her so much. Lewis had always been a father-figure to me, even more so than my own father. When I think about everything we have all been through, I am surprised they stuck with me through the years.

My main goal in trying to educate myself was to find the chemical structure of Formula L. My long-range plan was to be able to mass-produce this formula or at least have the ability to do so. I wanted to be able to control the market for this product. I cannot imagine the potential value of this formula on the open market. Just think about the possibilities of being able to sell this product to the masses. Think about being able to purchase a formula that, when introduced to your body, you will not only live forever, but you will never be sick a day in your life. Imagine if you could take a pill or drink something that would make you smarter than you could ever dream of being, and to be able to hear better, see better, and think better than ever before. On top of this, you would be able to sense your entire surroundings and use that knowledge to your advantage. Your hand-eye coordination would be better; everything you do would improve a hundred-fold. The potential of this discovery would be one of the greatest breakthroughs in the history of mankind.

To push the matter even further, we could possibly break this formula down even more and isolate some of its qualities from the other remarkable traits the formula possesses. For example, it would be to mankind's advantage to cure the common cold, but I don't think it would be an advantage to have everyone with the same abilities perform acts to perfection. On the surface, this statement sounds elitist, but I don't believe that everyone would act responsibly with this formula. I would not want the entire human species or many people to have access to this potentially life altering chemical. In fact, most people would use it to their advantage and I believe would ultimately destroy our species as we know it today. I envisioned only a select group of people that could be transformed into as close to perfect a human as possible.

With all this being stated, can you just imagine if Mozart, Beethoven, Einstein, Edison, Ford, or anyone that was a great visionary could live forever? How much greater would this planet be today if this fantasy was a reality? The only obstacles stopping this from becoming reality were the current state and the physical reaction to the formula. The formula changes the physical appearance and, most importantly, the mental temperament of the human.

I had so many questions about this formula, ranging from how to recreate it to why the formula physically changes the subject. I would go to the ends of the earth for the answers to all my questions regarding this formula. I had many years to think about this monumental issue before I even went to college. Not a day went by after my parents' death that I didn't think about how incredible it would be if I could have total control over the secrets of this formula so I could contour the formula's secrets to benefit my desires.

I had many discussions with my professors at Harvard about immortal life. Of course, I never spoke of my situation, I only spoke in general terms. Many obviously said that it was an impossibility to be perfect, of which I agreed. I am not perfect. I make mistakes both physically and mentally. Perfection is close to impossible; I had to admit and I accepted this fact. What I sought was being as close to perfect as I possibly could be without any physical or mental deformities. This is what I possess but cannot duplicate. Thinking along these lines, would it not be prudent to have everyone have immortal life or have everyone perfectly healthy? What happens if someone of questionable character were to take the formula? Imagine if some very insane or wicked person were to continue their life. Maybe the world would not be a better place after all with the introduction of the perfected version of Formula L.

So, in my line of thinking, if this formula could ever be reproduced and perfected with no negative side effects, then we must have a selection process of who should take the formula. I don't believe people would want some mass murderer to take the formula just to perfect his killing instincts and live forever. This is not what I would want to spring on the world if I ever get to that point. Maybe my birth father was right in keeping this formula a secret. If it fell into the wrong hands, human beings as we know them, we might be worse off tomorrow if not controlled properly today. So that is why, if this would ever turn into reality, only a few select groups of people would be eligible for this honor to be bestowed upon them, and even that is a utopian way of looking at the situation.

Lewis and I had many conversations about the formula and this very subject. What we agreed on is that what we wanted to discover from our research into the matter was the area of the transformation. We wanted to know what caused the human being to transfer physically and mentally when it encounters the formula. What was the secret to these changes? These secrets are the obvious link from a mutated state to basically perfection, the cure of all cures, and the magical potion that can create an everlasting and healthy life. We had to discover these secrets or at least attempt to try. We were missing something, but the issue was not as simple as it would first seem. The problem was the formula changes as new chemicals are introduced to its world. I learned this fact from my father. It is like the formula had a mind of its own. It would react and change as each newly introduced chemical would be injected into its chemical makeup. There had to be a chemical, or some chemical formula or mixture, that somehow interacts with the adrenaline in the human body to cause the transformation to take place. Lewis and I agreed that we would pool all our time and resources into discovering these secrets.

I remember the first couple of weeks after I returned home from Harvard. I could not help but notice the changes that had developed in my backyard since the death of my parents. I went for many walks and each time I came across something different. I walked past the spot where my mother had killed herself. Not only was the grass still greener, taller, and healthier than any other spot of the lawn, but this area had grown and spread down the hill. Around the tombstones of my parents and grandparents, the grass had this dark and rich color that spread throughout the vicinity. It was very noticeable from my bedroom window, as well as up close and personal. Lewis noticed this anomaly through the years. He took many samples from the soil, as well as the grass itself. He noticed there was a change in the condition of the soil and had it sent off to the local county extension office to someone he knew would keep any information private. All results came back from the numerous tests as inconclusive.

The most obvious change was in the four trees that were planted with Adam's body parts next to the tree roots. Lewis took many samples of this area and said they somewhat resembled the chemical makeup and structure of the plants he took samples of while in the forest in Germany. The four trees had grown tremendously in size and thickness since the trees were planted. It had only been about nine years since his death, and the trees were fully grown and larger in thickness and in height than they should be. The tops of the four trees now bled over and touched each other, creating this thick umbrella that does not permit light to enter its deep green barrier. The number of branches seemed to double the number of the other trees in the area. Lewis told me this was similar to what he saw in Germany where my birth parents lived.

Lewis informed me that part of this formula's secret was from a moss plant that he collected while visiting the forest in Germany. In fact, he showed me the moss planet in his lab years ago. When I

returned from Harvard, the moss plant was still alive and thriving. He
kept the moss in a container under heavy observation. He only kept a
portion of it alive in the lab and did not plant the moss outside since he
did not want to unleash this unknown moss into the estate's backyard.
He had to trim the plant almost weekly and destroyed the trimmings by
fire. Lewis would cut the moss, and when the moss was separated from
the rest of the plant, it died almost instantaneously, which was how he
kept the moss under control in its controlled environment in the
basement. Lewis told me the root of this moss had the shape of a carrot
with a very strong root system. The roots secreted a small amount of
liquid, most of which came from the tip of the root.

During Lewis's trip to Germany, he found that many of the
locals didn't age or seem to have many colds or ailments, if any at all.
His theory, and it seemed to be very accurate, was the root came into
contact with the local water supply in the German forest. Thus, the
chemical that was in this root somehow got into the stream of water that
went down to the local village. The villagers either drank the water or
ate the food that used the water for growing purposes. Maybe that was
one of the reasons the villagers did not seem to age or have many
illnesses. Through further research, he came to find that the villagers
ended up dying eventually, but not until most of them were in their 90s.

I came up with the idea that we needed to test this on an animal
subject to see what happened to them. Lewis thought about doing this
but he was afraid, especially after going through the experiences with
Adam; he did not want to mess with human or animal nature. I believe
he was interested, but he did not want to conduct the experiments on
his own. He also had his small private practice that he went back to
while I was in college, so his time was limited. Of course, when I was
away, I could not conduct any experiments on such matters as it would
have raised questions that I didn't want to answer at this juncture of my
life. I now had the time and energy to see some of these experiments to
the end. Lewis had collected several pints of the liquid that had seeped
from the moss root over the years.

For the first time in my life, after I returned from college Lewis told me, in precise detail, about my birth parents. At first, I was really taken aback with the idea that he had kept this information from me, but I realized he had his reasons. He told me every detail, to his recollection, of their physical appearance. They sounded similar to the way my father, Trevor, looked when he was alive. Lewis told me about the cave that was created for them and his new lab. He described all that he had experienced and saw in exact detail. Lewis told me about the experiments he had created on many of the local animals as well as the Jews that were captured. He told me of some of the results that were quite gruesome in detail. He told me about my brothers that father had killed. He told me of how my mother had saved my life by lying to my father about killing me at birth. He relayed the story of my mother lying me down next to a small river in the hopes of someone finding me. He spoke of what my father said about how there was no cure or correction of the formula that he had found, preventing the physical changes from occurring. That is the price of using Formula L.

I had many thoughts in my head at the time. I was very upset at Lewis and my father, Trevor, for not telling me about Wolfgang from the start. I could have handled the information when I was younger and they should have respected me more because they knew I could handle the truth. Now, over ten years since that last trip to Germany, Lewis was just getting around to telling me what he had found out that night. I was not happy that he had kept this information from me. In fact, down deep, I hated both of them for keeping this a secret. I guess if I put myself in his shoes, I could understand why he made the decisions he made, but I would have handled it differently, much differently. This issue never set well with me and I lost a lot of respect for both Trevor and Lewis. I found it amazing that Lewis never thought once about how this information would have been very useful for me to possess during my studies in college. I came away with a much different attitude toward Lewis after this eye-opening conversation. I always knew they were keeping something from me, but I could never figure out what. From that moment on, I knew I had to take control of my life and this situation. I could not rely on a man that lied to me, especially something as important as this. With everything that we went through, to have him keep this from me was unforgivable, but I also understood that I needed Lewis, so I had to make peace with the situation.

Lewis and I had worked hard for many weeks and we came up with an idea of an experiment just to see the chemical and biological effects of what my bite would do to a live animal. We knew what it did to live humans, but we had not seen up close and personal what it might do to a live animal. Lewis told me how my birth father experimented on live animals. My father even showed him the physical transformations the different animals underwent and documented the chemical changes the animals experienced. Lewis said that Wolfgang would experiment on frogs, cows, squirrels, raccoons, birds, dogs, cats, and many other different types, sizes, and forms of animals. He told Lewis how he documented everything from the experiments, including documenting all chemicals introduced into the subjects and how they reacted to those chemicals. I told Lewis that we needed to conduct these experiments as well, but he was totally against the idea. I don't know why, to be perfectly honest with you. I knew he never in his wildest dreams thought he would be in the position that he was in just ten short years ago. In a short amount of time I ended up selling the idea to him in the name of science and how something like this discovery would put our names in history books forever, not to mention the untold financial reward that would await us if we could ever get the answers to this problem. Lewis was always intrigued with the idea of being famous and reaping the publicity, as well as the financial rewards from a potential discovery.

Over time, I thought about what might happen if we could somehow change the makeup of Formula L so the physical mutations would not take place. What is the secret to why I turned out more normal than my parents did after I bit them? We must uncover that secret. On the surface, it seemed to me that it could not be that difficult, but obviously since Lewis had been working on this for over a decade now and my birth father, whose intelligence is off the charts, had not discovered the secret through all these years of study, it was. Therefore, the answer is not a simple one. Maybe god only knows this secret and maybe it is all for the best. As I have always said, god does not like to be shown up on his stage. It repulses him when his subjects are close to understanding even a little particle of perfection that god wants to hold so near and dear to his bosom. God is greedy in that way. God is very selfish with his knowledge, especially when it deals with perfection, correction of human flaws, or a glimpse into his little private show called heaven. Maybe what I seek is forbidden and I may never get the secrets that I so desire for my loved ones, for my financial benefit, and for the benefit of mankind.

As I have said before, we must be very careful with this formula because if the wrong people get possession of this recipe for perfection, it could be the beginning of the end for mankind. This knowledge of the power of everlasting life must be guarded closely and handled with intelligence and forward, comprehensive thinking. If not, the knowledge of the formula would potentially destroy not only mankind but animal kind as well.

While all this was taking place, I had an experience that I will never forget as long as I exist. Loren was recovering from her heart attack quite well, but it slowed her up physically and somewhat mentally. She could not work the long hours that she once worked so I took over many of her responsibilities. I asked her to retire, but she wanted to continue to work, which was fine with me. I loved Loren and I viewed her like my own mother. I wanted nothing but the best for her. One day Loren wanted to have a serious conversation with me. I can recall it like it was yesterday. I was in my father's library and she appeared at the door. She walked inside, quickly shutting the door behind her. She had a very serious yet nervous look on her aged face. I got up to meet her half way into the room and we clasped our hands together as if they were made as one. Loren said to me, "Garrison, I am getting old and I don't feel as good as I used to when I was younger. My joints ache with arthritis and I haven't had many good days since my heart attack. I have never asked you for anything and I don't even know if I want this to happen, but I am tired of feeling old. I want to feel young and healthy again. What I would like to talk about is the possibility of you making me feel better. Your father shared everything with me when he was alive. We spoke about things that he didn't even speak about with Adelle. One of the things he told me was how alive he felt after you bit him. He never stopped talking about that with me. I knew he was scared and he even told me that he was, but he couldn't stop talking about the way he felt. He told me he never felt so alive and that even the disturbing changes his body was going through didn't take away from how he felt inside. How alive he felt. Would you ever entertain the thought of biting me so I can live forever? To be pain free?"

I remember just standing there shocked, with my mouth wide open. I never would have guessed those words would ever come from Loren's mouth. I quickly said, "No. No, Loren, you don't want that to happen to you. It is a very painful process and one that I cannot put you through. You know you will turn part animal like my father, and like what my mother was going through as well."

Loren said, "I know all this, but would you at least consider the thought?"

I had to say, "No, Loren. I cannot. I cannot allow myself to even think about doing that to you. Now I know Lewis has been working on finding what is in me that makes this transformation possible, and I will attempt to find the secrets to this ability to transform humans, but I cannot in good conscience ever experiment on you. I just cannot do that, Loren." Loren understood, and with tears in her eyes, she left the room. I felt terrible for her, but I could not even let myself think about such an act. I knew at that very moment I had to find the secret to this chemical that had molded my life forever. Now it was a passion of mine, more than ever, to find the secret to this formula, to find its chemical and/or biological makeup so I could somehow alter the formula so the animalistic changes would not occur. I didn't know if this was possible because I didn't even know what it was I was dealing with in the first place.

I felt so sorry for Loren. It must be terrible to have the knowledge that you will grow old, hurt, suffer, and eventually die. From what I am told and led to believe, I will never experience such tragedies in my life. What pains my soul beyond my comfort level is the fact that I will visit these demons all through my lifetime, which potentially is forever. Everyone that I am close to today or will be close to in the future, I will ultimately experience their pain and their eventual death. Until someone takes my life, this is the cross that I must bear. Forever is a long time.

As time went on, Loren grew weaker, angrier, and more upset. She had come to me on many other occasions after her first request about me changing her life by biting her. The last request was quite unpleasant. She basically demanded that I bite her, but after repeated attempts of telling her the horrible side effects, she was still not listening to me. She tried repeatedly to anger me into biting her, and one time she even threw a paper weight in my general direction. I knew what she was trying to do to me. I have worked hard over the years to control my anger and my senses, but she was testing me in hopes that I would fail this time and bite her out of anger. Her attempt was unsuccessful. Lewis talked with her repeatedly, attempting to talk her out of such a wish. This seemed to anger Loren even further and she became even more withdrawn. I could sense the fear in her soul. She was afraid of death so much that the idea of her being turned into part animal did not derail her desire to occupy ownership of what has been duped in the house as 'the blessing.'

CHAPTER 6

Emerge

One sunny, breezy day, I went for a walk in the woods with Lewis. Before we entered the forest area at the back of the house, we walked through the back part of the yard, which was now totally covered with tall, thick, green grass. Each blade of grass had a darker color in the affected lawn. My mother's blood caused the grassy area to grow faster, greener, and thicker, and I dare say the grass was perfect. The area had grown enormously over the last decade. This area was created with the help of whatever was in my mother's blood. As my mother bled to death, her blood poured into the soil, creating this special area of the lawn. The color, moisture content, and thickness was unworldly. Several times over the years, Lewis sent the sample to be tested, and the results that came back were always the same. The samples had the perfect soil content for growing. The grass even stayed green through the winter months. No matter how cold or how much snow was on the ground, the grass always remained that deep, dark green color.

As we entered the forest area that was in the back part of the estate's property, we passed the four large, looming trees that had Adam's remains near the root system. Obviously, the root systems penetrated the bags and encountered the blood that was left over in his body parts. The trees grew huge in girth, tall in height, and had an over-abundance of leaves and limbs. All three of the trees were so overgrown that their limbs and leaves were now touching each other. I could see that other plants around the trees were also growing well and quickly. There was nothing dead around this area until we walked into the forest a little further. That part of the forest was more normal looking with dead limbs and wild plants that looked unhealthy. We were both truly amazed. We knew we were staring at something that was truly magical, something that was so rare that no one had ever seen before.

While we stood there in this special place, Lewis and I talked at great length about the numerous experiments that we wanted to conduct on our own. Lewis was more interested in the plants and how they changed through time with exposure to the formula. I assume it's because of my nature and history of my unique craving desires that I was more interested in the animals and their changes. I desperately wished to see the animal transformation firsthand, but the only way to see this experiment was to capture a living animal. That is not necessarily an easy task.

After numerous conversations, we finally decided to work on both of our interests. Lewis ordered some larger cages for our new experiments. Three of the cages he purchased were five-foot by five-foot cages that he had delivered to the lab. We had these cages installed in one of the bedrooms that we had remodeled strictly for experiments. We ripped up the carpet, laid tile on the floor, and added extra lights in the large room. We set up cameras so we could tape the experiments and the specimen. We had part of the floor broken up and placed a drainage pipe that attached to the sewer line in the other part of the basement floor leading out from the house to the main sewer.

One day I noticed some squirrels running through the forest area looking for food. I could not keep my mind on what Lewis and I were talking about, but after what seemed to be a long conversation, I had to excuse myself and went immediately to our garage. My passion sometimes consumes my soul and I must act on my instincts. I knew my father had many small to large traps that he had placed in the garage when they were not in use. I wanted to set up some traps in the forest, just as my father did when he was alive. I wanted to capture one of these creatures, but I did not want to hurt them by throwing a stone or shooting a bullet at them. When I came back to the overly lush and green area of my estate, I set up a few traps throughout the area. I wanted them to be in as close to their natural condition as possible so I did not want to hurt them in any way. I made sure the traps were working properly, and after a few tense moments of objection from Lewis, we left the area.

The next day we went back into the forest toward the cage and discovered that we had caught an adult squirrel. He was not a happy animal. I sensed his anger mixed with fear. We took the caged squirrel back to the house, placing the cage on Louis's long, large lab table. I put on my leather gloves and opened the trap door. I reached inside to pick up the squirrel, holding the squirrel by the neck area, making sure not to choke him, while my other hand was around the back part of his body. It was difficult getting control of the animal, but I was successful after a few attempts.

The goal of this experiment was to infect the squirrel with the formula that I had in my body. When I held the squirrel, I made sure to increase the adrenaline flowing through my body as I thought about something that made me mad. I prepared myself emotionally for what I was about to do. I waited for the adrenaline to reach a fever pitch as I made myself emotionally upset yet remained in control enough that I would not kill the animal. I lowered my open, saliva-filled mouth onto the back of the squirrel and gently bit down. I made sure not to badly hurt or kill the subject. I savored the fear and the sense of pain the squirrel was feeling during my bite. I inhaled the scent of fear and stress the animal was putting out under its soft coat of fur. I love the way animals sound when my teeth punctures their skin. In this case, I did not bite deeply, but I bit enough to draw some blood. As I stopped biting, I moved the subject away from me to place it back in the cage. The subject was moving around in my hands from side to side, trying to escape. The pain must have been very intense. As with any animal in a great amount of pain, the natural reaction is to run from the place of injury. I had to act swiftly so I quickly placed the subject back into the cage and hurriedly closed the door. Lewis promptly gave the subject some water. I could almost feel the pain the subject was under and I enjoyed the feeling. The sense of power and control was intoxicating, which made me feel alive. I stood there watching as the subject lay there in pain; I could still smell the subject's scent under and on my nose. I licked my lips for another taste of its blood and natural juices. I experienced a fullness of energy and passion that I had not felt since my Adam experience.

For several days, Lewis and I observed the subject. We knew how a human subject was affected after a bite from me. Both subjects, my parents, transformed into part animal with their senses being heighten in ability and keenness. We even knew what happened when an affected human mates with an unaffected human. The subjects create an evil animal with human-like characteristics like my dear brother. What Lewis and I didn't know was how a bite from me would affect an animal. According to Wolfgang, the subjects were grossly transformed into hideous creatures that would slightly resemble the nature of that subject, so we were very interested to see the results of our experiment. Our subject seemed to have been in some pain from my bite, but he was getting more anxious and nervous inside the cage throughout the days. The subject underwent bouts of major discomfort and then suddenly it seemed to not to be experiencing any pain at all. These occurrences happened on and off throughout the day and night, just like they did with Trevor and Adelle. Some of the discomfort was violent. The subject would run around its cage, sometimes slamming itself into the sides of the cage. The pain must have been very intense. The body at times seemed to increase and then decrease in size right before our eyes, as if some air bubble was inside the subject, then without notice it would go away as fast as it would develop.

While we were waiting for the squirrel to transform, Lewis went out and bought a couple of goldfish. When he brought the fish home, he told me he needed a sample of the formula and that he was going to retrieve this from my teeth. I was taken aback and he seemed to be somewhat aggravated when he started to explain to me what he had discovered a while back. Apparently, I have four teeth, two on the top and two on the bottom that are a little longer than the other teeth. Inside each of these teeth I have a small hole that runs the entire length of the tooth. Somehow, when I get angry or excited, the formula will mix with the adrenaline glands then the mixture goes through my system and works its way up to and through my gums. Lewis said this is like a snake and its venom. The mixture of Formula L and the adrenaline in my body is stored in this area of my mouth and waits to be extracted from my teeth during my bite. This is how I can transfer the formula to another while biting them.

I stood there listening to him and I felt quite a bit of anger building up in my system. I didn't understand why he didn't tell me this from the start. Lewis had really kept a lot of things from me and I don't appreciate people keeping secrets from me, especially when those secrets pertain to my life. I know I am young, but I think after everything that Lewis and I had been through I would have at least earned some of his respect. Any information that he had would have been very helpful to me, and it concerned my life and my situation. The longer I had been back from college, the more I discovered just how much information both Trevor and Lewis kept from me. The more I discovered this to be a fact, the more upset I got with Lewis.

When we were in the lab with the goldfish awaiting their gruesome fate, Lewis told me to think about something that would upset me. That was not a tough order considering all the information that my father and one of my closest friends, my family doctor at that, had kept from me all these years. After thinking about this for a few seconds, it didn't take long for my anger to reach a high level. When I told Lewis that I was ready, he extracted the formula from my teeth. The amount was small in quantity, but Lewis said it was the amount he needed. He took the liquid and placed it in a syringe then picked up one of the goldfish and shot a portion of the formula inside it. He repeated the procedure with the other fish. At first, they swam around the bowl rather quickly then they acted more normal. This was now our second experiment on animals.

Over the next couple of days, we noticed some changes in the subjects. The squirrel acted very nervous and jumped around in the cage for hours on end then it would suddenly stop and just lay there motionless. As the hours passed during these days, the squirrel's appearance began to change. The eyes grew larger while the head grew in a narrower shape. The nose developed into a pig-like snout, and the teeth grew so long in length that you could see most of the teeth inside its mouth. The ears nearly tripled in size as they grew long and thin. The torso of the animal grew as the shoulders of the squirrel became more pronounced. The shoulder blades stuck up a good inch from the rest of its back, his tail added two or more inches, and each of the legs grew about an inch. The feet grew to oversized proportions, and the animal had a very eerie, high-pitched sound that it would make from time to time. It also made a distinct tapping sound that was created by moving its lower and upper jaws up and down in a rapid movement.

Meanwhile, the goldfish were going through their own physical changes. At the beginning, both fish were about three inches in length, but their shape changed in less than twenty-four hours. At first, they were very calm, but as they were about to transform they got very nervous and agitated. In less than two days, their transformation was complete. They were mirror images of each other without any physical differences. At the end of the transformation, Lewis examined the fish.

The size of the fish was about seven inches in length, which was more than double their original size. The eyes had grown to a size about five times as large as normal and moved down beneath the mouth of the fish. The mouth grew about twice the previous size, the fin on the top of the body about doubled in growth, and the tail area grew an extra two inches. It grew extremely thick as it made a very pronounced 'U' shaped tail with one fin on the top and one on the bottom. The light fins on the back-middle part of the fish no longer existed. The fins under the fish had also disappeared and were replaced with long arm-like appendages without any fingers. The fish grew large teeth that looked much like a piranha's mouth.

The mutations were stunning at first glance. It was amazing seeing a new species of animal develop from their original physical state right before our eyes. During the conversion of the fish, the alteration would take small respites from the mutation process. When the 'legs' of the fish were developing, you could see them break through the skin of the fish then the transformation would stop. After a break, the process of transformation would begin again, seemingly to provide the subject much needed rest during this makeover. You could see the fins fall off and even physically witness the eyes move down the sides of the fish. Because of the many transformations of the two fish, the water became very dirty and had to be changed multiple times during this process.

We continued to observe the two newly-created species. The most obvious conclusions we noted were that the animals became more violent, active, and aggressive than they were in their previous physical state. We drew blood from the squirrel and analyzed the sample. The blood type had changed from its previous state, as expected. We then compared the sample from the squirrel to the samples from my parents and Adam. It seemed the animal's blood, at least in the case of the squirrel, had a somewhat different reaction to the formula as compared to the human subjects. The samples we drew from the fish were similar to what we found in the squirrel. This was in concert with my birth father's notes from decades ago saying animals had a different type of reaction to Formula L than humans had. The theory was bantered around that in some cases an animal's blood is warmer than a human's. The heat from the blood reacts positively with the formula, thus jump-starting the mutation. When the blood is cooler than normal, the formula does not work or is relatively non-effective when it comes to any evidence of mutation. Now to further complicate the issue, this is not necessarily true when it comes to plant life. As evidenced by the grass and trees in the backyard of the estate, the cold-infected blood does influence plants such as grass, trees, and other vegetation.

As the transformations of the specimens were complete, we wanted to move on to the next stage of our experiment. I ventured into the woods again to find another squirrel and Lewis went to the store to buy another goldfish. He kept the newly purchased goldfish in a separate fish bowl. Our thought process was simple; we wanted to see what happened when an infected animal bites a non-infected animal. We knew how the formula reacted with a subject when it came out of my teeth, from the start of the bite to the end of the transformation. This process we label as the 'Stage One' effect. The next question or area we wanted to test was if the formula would react differently if the mutant would be the carrier of the formula. Hence, this part of the experiment was labeled as the 'Stage Two' effect. I set a trap just as I did before, and the next day I captured another squirrel. As soon as I brought the squirrel into the basement, the mutant squirrel quickly became annoyed, jumping around and hitting his large, grotesque head on the bars of his cage.

Lewis put the mutated squirrel that we had named Timmy, into the newly built five-foot by five-foot cell. Lewis had this long pole with a rope with a loop at the end, like dogcatchers use when they are catching stray dogs from around the city. Lewis got the loop around Timmy's head and held him from outside of the cage. I had trouble getting the non-affected squirrel out of his cage. He was scared and jumping around, trying to escape. With lots of effort, I finally got the squirrel out of the cage with my gloved hands. Lewis helped me as best he could with Timmy's cage door. I quickly threw the squirrel to the back end of the cell and slammed the cage door. Lewis then released Timmy from the loop. The squirrel I had just captured was very frightened and ran all around the cage, attempting to get away from Timmy. Timmy just stood there and in one straight shot ran as fast as any squirrel I have ever seen, grabbing the new squirrel by the neck and biting him deeply in a matter of seconds. Lewis then took the pole and whacked Timmy on the head. Timmy reacted to the hit by growling at Lewis. Timmy's reaction time was off the charts, so I was surprised that Lewis got the chance to hit him. Meanwhile, I took advantage of this distraction and, with another pole, I quickly hit Timmy's head as hard as I could, giving Lewis time to get the loop around Timmy's neck. We were afraid of killing him, but I knew we could always start over with another squirrel if we needed to. My attention then shifted to the bitten squirrel. He was hurting, but he was okay. Lewis maneuvered his pole through the bars and gradually drug Timmy out of the cage. We then put Timmy in the smaller cage, being very careful not to let the bitten squirrel out of the larger cage. I jokingly called the bitten squirrel 'Adam' and the name eventually stuck. Adam seemed to be very hurt so I placed a small bowl filled with water inside the cage as Timmy was beginning to awaken from the blow to his head. He got up on all fours and was very stunned at first, but after he got control of himself he became even angrier.

Lewis took notes about what had occurred, and we studied Adam throughout the night. Since I do not require but a few hours of sleep at night, I took the night shift and watched Adam closely. We videotaped Adam from all four corners of the room. We even had a camera on the floor near the cage. We wanted to tape everything for documentary purposes. I recorded any signs of physical or behavioral changes into the computer. I also took numerous written and oral notes. Our theory was that if our infected squirrel, Timmy, would bite a normal squirrel, the change would result in greater amounts of transformation in the newly infected subject than with the first squirrel, Timmy. Our basis for this reasoning was simply that the formula had this inherit change in its structure, thus will cause a different type of mutation as it is exposed to other forms of cells and/or chemicals. How severe of a change would take place was unknown. We figured the transformation would be more severe in Adam's case than in Timmy's.

What we wanted more than anything was to have complete control over this experiment and not have any mistakes. We could never allow these subjects to escape their cages. That would be devastating for us because we did not want this mutation to spread beyond our caged experiments. We could not afford for either of these animals to get loose from the contained area. If one of our experimental subjects would happen to get loose and escape into the forest, it would spell disaster for us and potentially change animal life as we know it forever. If a mutated animal would bite another animal, then the process would accelerate to a level where, over time, the transformations would get out of control. The subjects would become wilder than the last subjects and more uncontrollable. They would be more mutated and probably more dangerous. That is why we had to run this experiment without any mistakes.

In the middle of the first night of the experiment, I was sitting in the room with little Adam and suddenly he started to whimper. I walked over to the cage as Adam vomited on the cage floor. I saw him starting to shake and move around on the floor as if he was in pain. I thought he was going to die from the bite because it looked seriously infected. The open bite was red, swollen and puss was forming in the deepest part of the bite. Lewis and I thought afterward that we should have had a more controlled setting for the bite where we could have controlled the amount of force Timmy used. But hindsight is always 20/20, I guess. Throughout the night, Adam crawled around on the floor of the cage in severe pain. He cried out in little squeals and moans then just before morning, something strange happened to his body. Adam started shaking hard then would stop, then the shaking would start up again.

Later in the night, Lewis entered the room after he awoke from his sleep. Suddenly Adam, while on the floor, stretched out his body as far as it would go then his body shook and jerked violently. As we looked closely, we could see the torso grow little by little. This was one of the most fascinating events I had ever witnessed in my life. After about an hour of this, my eyes were getting tired and to be honest with you, I was getting a little bored with the show since I had been observing this animal for over seven hours. Lewis told me to go upstairs and get some breakfast and maybe some sleep, he would take over and the videotape would capture everything so I would not miss the transformation. I just knew I could not leave the re-birth of a new species that was happening right before my very eyes. I never saw anything more amazing in my life.

I told Lewis that I wanted to stay to the end of the mutation. Several hours went by and more activity happened inside the cage. The growth of the body was still taking place, but the rate of mutated growth was not as dramatic as it was when it started. Through the naked eye you could not see the growth, per se, but after a few minutes or so the length of the animal was noticeable. The torso of the squirrel appeared to have grown about three inches in length. Adam just laid there motionless for a while in a small puddle of his own blood. As the body grew in length, some of the squirrel's fur fell out and ended up mixing with the blood on the floor of the cage. Suddenly, the squirrel started to rub and hold his face with his front paws, and without warning, a small amount of blood came out of his ears and nose. After more violent shaking, I could see the legs and feet of the squirrel change in size and shape. It took about five painful minutes as I watched the feet of the squirrel change physically. First, the extremely swollen feet got larger. As the foot got to a certain size, the squirrel abruptly moved its legs around very quickly, like something was burning them. After a few minutes of this, one by one, the feet would burst like a small bubble, and blood gushed out of each foot like a small, busted water balloon would react to being punctured.

The squirrel agonizingly moved around on the floor. It was hard to see with the naked eye, but in a matter of minutes, three small finger-like appendages slowly grew out of the bottom of each foot at different time intervals. After several additional minutes, the appendages were over an inch and a half long, three on each foot. The original five fingers of the squirrel were still attached to the top of the foot above these newly formed growths. They seemed to just lay limp as if they were paralyzed or something to that effect.

My attention then turned to the legs as they grew about two inches in length. All four of the legs were bloody and looked swollen, with thick, bulging muscles. New skin seemed to develop under the old skin, causing the old skin and fur to fall off. As it shed off the legs, the previous lifeless fingers of the squirrel fell off with the skin. We then noticed the head changing. Right before my eyes I saw its head shake like a nervous cat, the skin around the expanding skull stretching so tight that it looked like the skin was going to split in all directions at any moment. Like the legs, the fur peeled right off the head while the swollen, pinkish-colored skin developed underneath. Large blue veins popped out randomly around its head, and the eyes grew at an astonishing rate, more than quadrupling in size. A large, pronounced bone developed between the two eyes, making the eyes move rather significantly downward on the side of the head. We thought a horn might develop, but instead it was just a large bump that formed. The ears more than doubled in size and became pointier than what you would normally see on a squirrel. The nose grew out about an inch, resembling a small dog-like nose and nostrils. The teeth began to fall out and at one point I thought the squirrel would end up choking on the extracted teeth. In what seemed to be only a few minutes, new teeth formed and they were much larger than the previous set. The front two teeth were extremely long and very sharp looking, while the other teeth were wider.

Lewis noticed the back part of the animal while I was focused on the head area. The hindquarters of the squirrel grew very large both in width and girth. The leg bone of the squirrel was very prominent as the bone stuck up from the rest of the body about three quarters of an inch over the spine. The leg resembled the back leg of a grasshopper. The tail, at this point, had lost all its fur and grew about six inches in length. It was also about three times as thick as its previous state.

All these changes occurred in about thirty to forty minutes, and through the blood, teeth and fur, the new squirrel emerged from its transformed place on the floor as it got up slowly and walked around as if it were trying on new shoes to see if they fit. The squirrel was noticeably shocked and you could clearly see it was trying out its new body. At first Adam seemed to be very shaky, but after a few steps he regained his sense of balance. He looked around the cage as if he was studying his environment and looking for an escape route. His large, glossy eyes caught me staring at him and without any notice, he suddenly leapt towards me and grabbed the metal bars with his long, finger-like toes. His long tail wrapped around one of the bars on the top of the cage as he looked at me with a gleaming, angry stare. Then a long-sustained growl developed as his head pressed against the bars of the cage. A long, snake-like tongue lashed out in my direction as he hung there watching and studying me. I stood there in astonishment, admiring this most incredible new species known to this world. It was an absolute honor to witness what had just transformed before us; it was quite impressive, to say the least.

Lewis and I were amazed at what we had just witnessed. We were like small children in a candy store. Lewis, as best he could, did multiple tests on the squirrels. He tested their hearing, eyesight, and reflexes, amongst a whole host of tests. Of course, these tests were amateur at best, but he and I tried our very best to document any results that we found. What he did find out about the squirrel was that the reflexes were even faster and keener in the Stage 2 state of the formula as compared to the Stage 1 state. We then let the Stage 1 squirrel, Timmy, loose in the cage with the Stage 2 squirrel, Adam. Lewis had to restrain Adam while he was in the cage for me to let Timmy inside. Timmy didn't want to go inside at first and seemed to be very frightened of Adam. As I closed the door to the cage, Lewis released Adam who immediately went after Timmy, almost killing him instantly. He jumped high in the air like a bullet out of a gun and caught Timmy as he was trying to escape this lunge. As Adam came down, his teeth were already in Timmy's neck. Adam's tail uniquely wrapped itself around Timmy's back leg and seemed to squeeze the leg rather hard. After a few seconds, Timmy expired. As Timmy's body laid in Adam's grasp, Adam began to quickly feast on the dead body of Timmy. We allowed him to eat the carcass, which he ate from the neck down to the hind legs. Most of the flesh was eaten to the bone. Adam even licked the warm blood from the bone as well as from the floor.

We had seen a few transformations happen right before our very eyes and we wanted to see more. Therefore we knew, at least from the testing of the squirrels, that a Stage 2 infected squirrel is more dominant than a Stage 1 squirrel. This hypothesis was what we expected, but we had to test to prove the theory. Lewis was excited and wanted to run the same test on the goldfish. The problem was to not allow the infected goldfish to kill the non-infected one. The infected goldfish was ferocious looking with its long, razor-like teeth. There was no doubt the infected fish would kill anything that would be placed in the bowl with him. Lewis retrieved one long, leather glove and I offered my hand, literally, in assistance. I placed the glove over my right hand and forearm. The glove was one of those types of gloves that fishermen wear on a crab or shrimp boat. I went over to the large tank where the mutated fish was madly swimming around. I had a devil of a time trying to corral the fish with my one hand but with Lewis's help, I got my hand around the fish then gently moved my thumb and forefinger to the sides of its mouth. Lewis got a small net and captured the new fish and made sure the fish would not escape. I removed the infected fish and brought it to the non-infected one, letting the mutated fish bite into the non-mutated one. After a few seconds or so I pressed rather hard on the sides of the head of the fish. It quickly released its grip on the non-affected fish then we put our fish back into their respective bowls. The newly bit fish that we named Henry, was noticeably in pain, swimming around its small, sheltered world as if he was crazy.

We wanted to see if the mutation would be different from the formula from my mouth versus the mutated formula from the transformed fish. We figured the mutation would be different as it was with the squirrels; how different was what we wanted to discover. After several hours, the mutation started on Henry. The change was very similar to what had happened with the first goldfish. After three or so hours of violent shaking, movement and convulsions, Henry changed quite differently than the first goldfish in the Stage 1 state. The originally infected goldfish had lost its fins and developed what looked like arm-like appendages. The goldfish in the Stage 2 state's transformation was more severe than what the Stage 1 subject experienced. The appendages below the Stage 2 fish developed like the previous one, but with this subject three fingers, about half an inch in size, were formed. Much to our surprise, even fingernails developed on the fingers.

The top fin was replaced by a long and rather thick, rubbery, curved horn that was snake-like in movement. At the end of the horn was a very sharp point that made one think the horn would be used as a weapon. The fins in the back, just like the original subject, lost its feathery fins and were replaced with a tail. The tail was very thick and had a hard bone-like texture, which was black in color with thick spikes randomly placed along the bone-like tail addition. The end of its tail had this U-type formation. At the end of each point of the U-shaped tail were two spikes on each side. This new addition was strong and versatile enough that the fish could use the appendage as a weapon.

The eyes, instead of growing larger, grew in an elongated, oval shape and the pupils resembled a cat's. The fish developed an eyelid that could close and protect the eye, like a shark. The mouth was larger than the original subject as well, sporting larger and sharper teeth. The most fascinating feature that developed in this new species was a very thin but long tongue. We discovered the tongue by accident when we examined the fish. We were very close to the fish bowl when suddenly the fish looked at us and quickly moved to point his head in Lewis's direction. This three or so inch newly-formed tongue that looked like an extremely thin pencil, darted out as fast as it was retracted, comparable to a snake but much quicker. The length of the fish increased about two inches longer than the original mutated fish, and the girth increased about an inch in circumference. The newly formed species was more aggressive, quicker, more sensitive to sound and movement, and much stronger than the previous species.

What we learned with both the squirrel and the fish going from the Stage 1 effect to the Stage 2 effect is obviously the more mutation, the more aggressive behavior, a larger body was developed, and it was more combative. It seemed the senses of both Stage 2 specimens were far more developed from their original, natural form of that animal. The transformation was off the charts in both physical appearance and natural instincts. The subjects were stronger, keener, and just a better and more aggressive species. If there were many of these species out in the wild, it was our conclusion they would eventually eliminate the weaker group of their original variety. What we also learned was that the chemicals the animals had in their systems react differently with the formula than with humans. It seemed the animals either tended to grow horns or the appendages to astonishing lengths.

My father added four to six inches to his height, and my mother, although she ended her life before the process was complete, grew several inches as well. There were drastic physical changes to my parents, but nothing compared to what our animal subjects had gone through. We needed to study why the formula reacted differently in humans than in animals. In addition, some animals seemed to react and change more than other animals. If we could find the secret to that phenomenon, then we could get closer to the answers we desired.

Another area that Lewis and I had wanted to explore was the speed of the reaction my mother had compared to my father. When I bit my father, the total process took about three months, but we had to wonder if the process stopped at that time. What if he had been 'allowed' to live longer? Would the process have changed him more? According to Lewis, when he went to Germany and saw my original birth parents that had been changed for seventy-five to one hundred years, they did not look much different than Trevor. However, I often wonder about this potential issue: my birth parents had the formula injected into them from a needle, whereas Trevor was bitten by me. Is there a difference between the two methods or are they the same? Will the reaction to these methods produce the same results?

It was Lewis's opinion that my mother, who was bitten by Adam, would undergo a more dramatic change than my father's altered state. This cannot be absolutely proven, but according to him and through his studies, this could be a very real possibility considering what happened to the subjects in the Stage 2 phase. When my parents were bit, we did not have this knowledge. It seemed that the formula does not change while in the system of the first host. Therefore, the formula that I have flowing through me can be passed along to someone else, and the physical and mental changes will develop, but when you start changing the host is when the formula has a more violent reaction. This was proven when Adam bit my mother and, of course, through our experiments with the fish and squirrels. My father was infected by me and he mated with my mother who was not infected. They produced a child, Adam. Adam's physical change was far more advanced than my father's change. Somehow the chemical or the cell structures of my parents changed those structures and produced a monster, like my brother. This is even more dangerous than what appeared at first glance.

Obviously, something is happening to the DNA in these subjects and I believe that is the secret to developing a controlled Formula L that we could use on a mass number of the population. But as of now, we have many problems and issues with the formula. For instance, if you had a population of one hundred people and all were infected at the same time, either by injection, pill, or bite with the formula, then the population, after several months, could co-exist and live, albeit a totally new way of life, together rather peacefully. But this is only based on theory. In reality, you would have infected subjects with non-infected subjects. If they happen to produce children, then a whole host of new problems would stem from that action. As you can imagine, we could never take this formula as we know it to the open market. It must be developed to a stage were the mutation would either not take place or not be as severe as we had seen. As of now, we still had the issue of non-affected people mating with affected people, thus causing a monster to be born.

These are the problems with marketing this product, if we ever got to that level. Lewis, and especially I, owe it to the human race to tread very carefully regarding this issue. We need to conduct a multitude of tests to first see how we can control this mutation process, if not completely eliminate the physical mutation. Like my birth father, we knew we had to perform many experiments not only on animals, but humans as well, to at least see what we were dealing with on a small scale. My purpose for these experiments is not to hurt human existence, but to help human existence. My goal is to help humans be close to perfect and healthy, beyond human comprehension. I am not interested in destroying man.

We continued our experiments for weeks on end. We wanted to see the different effects on numerous subjects and to test the reaction speed of these subjects. One of our subjects was a turtle that we found in the woods. We brought the subject to the lab and Lewis injected the turtle, this time with the formula from my gums. The turtle took a few days to fully mutate. As in the prior subjects, the turtle experienced great discomfort in the beginning of the process. The turtle would move around in circles, then disappear inside its shell for a few minutes, then come out and move around faster than it normally would. After a few hours the turtle would shake, then relax, then shake some more before it laid itself out on the floor with all its extremities stretched out as far as they would go. You knew the turtle was experiencing extreme pain. Before long, the turtle started to move as if someone was cutting one of its arms or legs off. The head moved from side to side in reaction to the obvious pain the creature was feeling.

Then right before our eyes the turtle started to grow. As it grew, the turtle started to rock back and forth and the shell began to split down the middle, from its head to its tail. About four hours passed and the two halves of the shell completely fell off. The soft skin of the unshelled turtle started to develop this hard leather-like texture that looked similar to the way a brain looks; deep crevasses and curved lines running haphazardly over the surface where the shell was once located. The legs grew to more than three times their previous length. The head grew in mass as well, and in the same proportional size as the legs. The nose and mouth grew about two inches outward from the rest of the head, resembling a small newborn dog-shaped nose and mouth. Just when we thought the mutation process on the head was complete, a large horn developed on the very top of the turtle's head. The turtle was in tremendous pain and stress as the horn developed. It seemed to press its head firmly to the ground, all the while its eyes were shut and its mouth slightly open. We heard a faint popping sound when the horn finally developed to such a state that it broke through the skeletal head of the turtle. The horn grew rapidly then stopped when the horn reached the height of about an inch and a half. Then, to our continued surprise, we saw small, thick, black dots appear all over the back of the turtle. In about a minute the black spots became thick and very stiff, like hairs that stuck out of the back, about an inch or so in length. The hairs, if you would give them that name, looked like spikes and they moved constantly in all directions. We assumed this was similar to the antenna on a roach or an ant. The tail grew very long and thick, to about seven inches in length. With its newly formed legs, head, tail and body, the turtle got up from the floor. He walked around the cage testing out his newly created body. The animal was about half the speed of a normal sized dog. It was fascinating seeing this species manifest itself into a species that was unrecognizable to its natural state of being.

The next day, Lewis showed me his notes from his trip to Germany. My birth father, Wolfgang, experimented on turtles, but according to Lewis's recollection and notes, Wolfgang's turtle subjects did not take on this drastic of a mutation. Wolfgang used the formula without a host. The formula he used was developed in a container and was never in a host. Of course, the formula we used came from my body, thus I am the host. We thought at the time that my body temperature had something to do with changing the chemical structure of the formula. We wanted to do more testing and compare the results we achieved with Lewis's notes and what he observed and took from my father's experiments.

We continued our experiments on different animals. One day, we bought an average sized dog from the local pound. He measured, from his head to the beginning of his tail, about twenty inches. He was of average weight and his fur was short. The dog was a mixture of many different breeds, but it appeared that a hound breed was mostly present. We experimented on this animal like the others. Lewis administered the shot into the dog. The shot, like on the other subjects, was used instead of using my mouth to bite into the subject for reasons previously stated. We did not want to injure the animal or cause it more stress by dealing with an open wound. We did take great caution in making sure the formula maintained the same temperature when administered to the subject as it was when it was first extracted from my gums. After a few days, the mutation was complete on the mutt. The transformation caused the dog to have longer than normal ears, tail, and legs; in fact, those parts of the dog basically doubled in size. The head grew about three times its size, but the nose area took on an almost completely different look. Instead of the snout growing out longer, it grew in a banana shape with the nose pointing up higher than the head of the dog. The hair fell out and there was only pink skin showing on the oddly-shaped nose. The neck area grew to twice its original length. In fact, the dog looked like a miniature giraffe. The body hair grew out to about an inch longer, which was a mystery to us because in the other specimens we tested, their hair fell off.

After the mutt's transformation, we started to experiment with some purebred dogs. We ended up buying a Pomeranian and a Dachshund. Again, both were injected with the formula and, as expected, the characteristics of that breed's former state were either enhanced or exaggerated to its current state with some rather odd differences. Both breeds' heads grew larger, and the legs on the Dachshund were still short but longer than the former state, growing thicker and stronger. The body grew longer and moved around more in a snake-like fashion. Its hair fell out and the skin developed a leather-like texture. The Pomeranian's hair, on the other hand, got longer and thicker. The tail also grew longer and formed into a corkscrew shape. The neck was extended about six additional inches and was extremely thick in girth, which was fortunate for the dog because the head turned out to look like a small shaped pumpkin. The ears grew further apart and were very long, but also stout and stiff.

For about three months we experimented with many different smaller animals, and roaches were very interesting. The roach subject grew more legs, an extra pair of antenna, and a neck was formed. The head on the end of this visibly long neck was shaped like a three-leaf clover. The head had three very pronounced lumps, with the top lump located on the top of the head. The other two lumps had an eye located in the middle. The lumps were on both sides of the head, just underneath the top lump. The top lump was higher than the eyes and this area is where the mouth and nose were located. The mouth was very large and had small yet very sharp teeth – and many of them. On the top of this lump, two long, sharp, claw-like appendages were also formed.

We took extra special care in making sure that none of the animals would escape throughout all stages of the experiments. An escape by any one of these mutants would be disastrous for everyone and everything involved in our little process called the world. Lewis and I were totally in agreement with my father, Wolfgang, in not allowing this formula to spread throughout any – and I mean any – part of this world, because in no time, the transformed species would take over the world. This could never happen unless it was somehow controlled or, better yet, developed to where the physical as well as the mental mutation would not be so severe. The animalistic aggressiveness must be controlled in order to mass market this potential life-altering product.

When we first started these experiments, we knew we had to dispose of these newly formed creatures. The most popular way of disposal we had was to burn the specimen. We created a small pit near the back of the property, close to the forest line. Late at night we would take the caged animal back to the fire. Lewis and I had his long pole that we used to help carry the cage to the fire. Lewis would get on one end of the pole, I on the other. We would slip the pole through the handle located on top of the cage or we would slip the pole through the top part of the cage. Sometimes we would have more than one animal in the cage at the same time, and would burn the animals while they were inside the cage.

As part of our experiments, we would purposely place two different mutated animals in the same cage. When we did this, it made for some very interesting fights. At first, we wanted to see how the animals would react to each other, but we did not want to make a huge mess with this final part of the experiment, so we decided to have the differently formed animals fight each other before we burned them. From our limited study on this part of the experiment, the size of the mutated animal did not really determine who was the more dominate animal. Each animal had their own brand of fighting techniques and characteristics.

CHAPTER 7

Relevance

I always allotted time for my music. I love all forms and styles of music, but of course I prefer the musical style and structure of Mozart. I continued my life outside of my role of playing scientist with Lewis. I had a multitude of offers as a guest performer at many orchestras in America and throughout Europe. Many orchestral establishments are constantly after prodigies because they draw well at the ticket office. I most often played at the Louisville Orchestra as the guest violinist but had appearances as a pianist as well.

I will never forget one night when I was making my entrance to the podium to play a rather short Mozart Serenade. As I walked toward the podium, as I have always done in the past, I cast my eyes out over the audience. I have so many friends and business associates that I always remember to acknowledge their presence when I am on stage by a nod or a glance.

I had been performing for many years now and always felt comfortable and confident when it came to performing a piece of music in front of an audience. So obviously, I rarely worried about my performance, which is not a good thing, I might add. Remember, when my adrenaline interacts with the formula, that makes projects or performances easier for me. Most of my life, when I've needed to perform on a high level, whether it be in school, in a concert hall, or playing a sport, I had to get my adrenaline flowing to better my performance. Sometimes when I faced the audience, that tends to get the blood flowing a little faster, making my performances better. This particular night I was calm and relaxed. Somehow, I needed to change my mood to better my performance.

As I walked across the stage floor, my eyes quickly glanced over the crowd. Just as I was about ready to take my eyes off the crowd, I noticed someone in the audience that I hadn't seen in a long time. This person's beauty was unlike any I had seen in my life. Years ago, I had seen this beauty in attendance and wanted to introduce myself to her, but I never got the opportunity. After the concert was over, I went onstage to see if she was still in the audience, but she had left before I could say hello. Since the first time I saw her, this perfect-looking creature had captivated me. I made a habit to, just before the beginning of every concert, cast my eyes over the audience to see if this beautiful woman was in attendance. Since the first day my eyes had the pleasure of seeing such a beauty, I had always been in search of this most beautiful human during every concert I attended.

This special night, as I continued to walk toward the conductor, I thought I finally saw this woman for the first time in over a decade. I kept my eyes on this young creation that was looking directly at me with this incredible smile and star-studded eyes that seemed to dance in her head. She was beautiful, a total vision of perfection at its finest. I stopped near the conductor and could not take my eyes off this wonderful, perfect creature. Then I was sure it was her. Faces and bodies change over time, but a human's eyes never change. Our eyes are the windows to our souls and I never forgot those eyes that had pleasantly haunted me most of my young life. She was very unsettled and embarrassed, looking away as she batted her long eyelashes, very uncomfortable with my stare. The people around this lovely vision noticed the attention I was giving her. She looked up a time or two, but each time she noticed my continued gaze. I knew I was making her uncomfortable so I slowly lowered my gaze after I winked at her. I refocused and directed all my attention on the conductor. I know many people around her were whispering and moving around after our eye exchange. I could hear what they were saying although it was very difficult to differentiate between ten to twenty people talking and whispering to one another at once. Many people glanced up to that vision of perfection and wondered aloud if she and I knew each other. I then felt bad for her and the position that I put her in because she was obviously very nervous and shy.

The auditorium began to settle down and the orchestra got into position to begin the work. As the music began to flow out of the many manmade instruments, you could feel the power they made as the notes passed. I wanted to impress this lovely vision so I used the power the orchestra members were creating to get my adrenaline flowing fast and strong. I wanted to play and play well for this lovely, estranged creature from the night. I could do nothing but think of the lovely vision that graced my eyes, my heart and all my senses. What power she had over my being and, unbeknownst to her, she was slowly and quietly stealing my heart from my soul.

I played about as well as I could play. My senses were on fire and on a high that I had only felt once in my life. When I finished playing, I exited the stage then returned for the standing ovation. I made sure not to stare at her again because I did not want to make her feel more uncomfortable. My performance was the last piece played before intermission. While offstage, I put my violin in its case and told Carolyn, who was always backstage with me, to look after my instrument until I came back. Unlike most performers, I was about to do something that was rare and something that I had never done before. I was going to go into the audience and find the creature that had captivated me so unlike any other creature had.

I made my way out onto the stage and looked where she had been sitting, but she was not in her seat. I went backstage and down a hallway then finally made my way out to the lobby. I knew this was going to cause a small disturbance, but I worked my way around the lobby. I saw nothing but people reaching out toward me to shake my hand. I knew these people were going to tell me how honored they were having me in their presence and meeting everyone. The crowd gathered around me so quickly that it impeded my search for the lady. I did not want to be rude to my fans so I acknowledged everyone but told anyone that cared to listen to me that I was looking for someone special. I was not familiar with being in such a large, crowded room. The noise level was very disturbing to me and I was not comfortable with my surroundings. I wished everyone would have gotten out of my way. Their voices were so loud and there were so many of them that they were overloading my senses. My ears hurt from all the noise; the sound of their voices, their arms moving around, and their feet shuffling across the carpet of the lobby.

I was so focused on finding this special creature of the night that I felt my blood pulsing through every inch of my body. My mind and senses were on total overload and it became hard for me to concentrate. This experience became increasingly unsettling for me because I could not find her. I continued walking through the maze of human bodies in search of that beautiful vixen that had possessed my thoughts. My eyes rapidly moved across the lobby, but all I saw were average sub humans, not the one that I was the most interested in seeing. I decided I would make my way down to where she was sitting and introduce myself just before the second half started.

I came across a couple of the board members from the Louisville Orchestra and stopped to say hello. A feeling came over me, covering my body like a warm shower on a cold winter night. I sensed someone staring at me, but I could not figure out from what direction. Of course, there were many eyes staring at me and stealing glances my way, but this feeling seemed different. The pair of eyes that were bathing me in their warm, longing sensation was different from the mere mortals that crowded the room. While I was listening to the conversation with some of the board members, I quickly glanced up, moving my eyes to the right rather slowly. About seventy feet away, I noticed this beautiful vision of perfection looking at me. I don't know what was more intoxicating, her eyes or her flawless doll-like face, but as a unit they took on the aura of Venus, the Goddess of Love. Her eyes were large, bright, and full of life. These were the same eyes that I remembered seeing over a decade ago. She had a look of unmistakable beauty, but a hint of haunting devilment. Her face seemed to float on air as if nothing around it existed, as if only her face was highlighted in my sight.

As our eyes met, I quickly but calmly nodded my head toward her and smiled as gracefully as I could. She returned my gesture with a slight smile. Her facial expression did not change, as if she knew she had my attention. She knew she was now in control. This is an art that most women learn from a very young age. She was using the power that nature gave her to keep my interest by using those hauntingly intoxicating eyes of hers. They were alert and sparkled as she continued to cast her spell upon my heart. There was an air of confidence about her that made me aware that she commanded respect. Her lips were perfectly shaped. They were slightly opened, as she seemed to inhale through them during our eye contact. After a few playful moments, I could sense that she was getting nervous and anxious with our non-verbal greeting so I excused myself from the conversation with the board members. I began to walk toward her, but noticed some other people coming toward me, asking for an autograph, and another orchestra board member also stepped toward me. I ignored these people as I maintained my eye contact with this gorgeous and mysterious creature of the night.

After what seemed to be an eternity, I stepped in front of this lovely being and extended my hand. She batted her large, puppy dog eyes at me as she looked down at my hand. She raised her eyes toward mine and touched my hand. Her silky, gentle grasp sent a feeling throughout my body that I had never experienced in my life. I could not believe this was the same vixen that I had noticed over a decade ago. This was that living being that I so desperately wanted to meet after my performance years ago. Now she stood before me and I was holding her onto her hand.

I took advantage of this meeting as I began to take in all her essence that made her so attractive to me. Her eyes were large and very blue, so blue that you noticed their color a long distance away. Her hair was thick, long and blonde. Her lips were full and very pouty. Her skin was flawless, absent of any blemishes. She was wearing a nice but very inexpensive white, flowery blouse with wide straps that went up on her wide and rather toned shoulders. She wore a small but very refined skirt with matching shoes that seemed to not fit well. She was holding the night's program in her left arm up next to her breasts that were overly large compared to the rest of her shape.

This creature stood extremely straight and tall, yet seemed anxious about her surroundings, while at the same time appeared confident of herself. Her height had to be in excess of five feet ten inches. I stand at six feet four inches so I was pleased to see more eye to eye with a woman instead of having to bend down all the time in order to speak, as I have to do with most others. Her hair was pulled up on both sides of her perfectly round head as the rest of her hair fell freely in the back and was ever so close to touching the back of her neck. The front of her hair was in a simple but elegant straight cut. She was the type of woman that didn't require any makeup to be attractive, but the little makeup that she had on made her look like she belonged at this form of entertainment. I noticed her long arms and legs. They were desirable, well-tanned and had no intrusive marks. She was flawless and as perfect as any human I had ever seen in my lifetime. I begin to speak while I still held her hand firmly, but comfortably.

I said, "My name is Garrison Seawick."

The vision broke out in all smiles, which made her eyes light up like a three-year-old child that had woken up early on Christmas morning. Her eyes fell to my chest then slowly rose to greet mine. She laughed and looked to her right and then back to my eyes once more.

She said in the most delectable, soothing voice, "Hi. My name is Marci Singleton."

"Marci. That is a beautiful name. Thank you for gracing my eyes with your beauty." I was so captivated with this woman, but I could not understand what made me so drawn to her.

I said to her, "I have seen you before, a long time ago, right?"

Marci seemed to be a little bewildered, "I am sure we have never met, Mr. Seawick."

"Please, call me Garrison. My name is Garrison to you." I smiled and told her, "I remember you sitting in the audience many, many years ago. You have eyes that are so intoxicating, and on that night, you single-handedly made me stumble out of the gate, so to speak. I remember that I had to compose myself and get my concentration back on track. It had to be a good ten years ago, so I am sure you don't remember, but your attractiveness was something that I have not forgotten throughout these years. A man does not forget such beauty. I am so delighted to be standing here in front of the person that I considered, and still do, the loveliest vision I have ever seen."

Marci stared at me for a while as this came to a great surprise to her. She finally spoke after an awkward moment, "Really? You remember that far back? I am surprised you even saw me that night," she said rather excitedly.

I said with a laugh, "I remember everything and forget nothing."

Marci return my laugh with one of her own. "Oh I know. I have followed your great career; not only your performances, but your academic work as well. You have to be one of the most gifted men in the world."

The lights in the lobby blinked off and on, indicating intermission was ending and the second half of the performance was about to begin. Our concentration was interrupted, but we did not want our conversation to end. I spoke up saying, "Would you like to come with me to the balcony? My family has had seats there for years and if you would like, after the performance you could meet some of the members of the orchestra."

Marci was totally taken by surprise by my invitation and wanted to go with me, but I sensed she was frighten and somewhat confused by my invitation. I said, "Please come with me. Or do you have someone waiting for you?"

Marci quickly said, "No… oh no, no, I'm alone. Well, I guess I will take you up on your offer. Why not? I would love to come with you."

I led Marci to the private balcony where I introduced her to
Loren, Carolyn, and Lewis. They were all quite surprised that I had
brought a lady to the balcony, something I had never done before. Lewis
offered his chair to Marci while he stood in the back of the balcony area.
To this day, I remember the turn and nod of this head in surprise and
approval of my finding, although I sensed a rather uneasiness that Lewis
attempted to cover up.

The second half of the performance began as Marci sat to my
right. I could smell her perfume, her hairspray, and her own personal
scent. I could hear her breathe, the air passing in and out of her nose and
mouth. Her breathing was erratic and I could sense that she was
uncomfortable, so afraid she would make a mistake. I enjoyed the way
she moved the chair, how she crossed her legs at the ankles, and how
she rested her hands on her lap.

I sensed that she was enjoying the music, which featured a
soprano singing a few beautiful arias. I felt Marci tense up when the
singer hit certain notes. I could tell she loved the operatic venue, which
I found highly desirable. When the performer finished her piece, I leant
over to Marci and asked if she would like to meet the singer that had just
performed. She said she would love to if it would not be a bother.

When the second half concluded, we exited our balcony and
went backstage. The area was noisy and crowded with lots of
movement. There I caught the attention of the opera singer, Connie
Dukac. She was your typical operatic singer; a large lady, nice enough
but seemed a little haughty and pampered. I introduced her to the shy
woman who many saw to be unsuitable as my date. Connie did not like
meeting her fans backstage and she was annoyed when I introduced
them. After a few moments, Connie began to speak in a friendlier tone
after becoming comfortable in Marci's presence.

Marci said, "Mrs. Dukac, you sang beautifully. I only wish I had
an eighth of your talent."

Connie said, "Do you sing, my young lady?"

"Yes I do, but nothing on your level. I am a music student at the University of Louisville. I study the violin, but I also take some singing classes."

"Oh, so you are a music student, are you? Did you enjoy Mr. Seawick's performance tonight?"

"Oh yes, ma'am. I have followed his career for many years now. I've seen him perform before, but many years ago in this very place. His playing style is my inspiration. He plays with so much passion and elegance. I just marvel at his command and mastery of the instrument." Marci quickly stopped talking as she became embarrassed, believing she had made a fool of herself in front of me and Connie.

I, on the other hand, was flattered by her compliments on my abilities. I said, "That was a very nice compliment and I am honored."

Marci said very sheepishly, "You and Mozart's music go so very well together."

"Thank you so much for the kind words. I would love to hear you play some day."

Marci moved around slightly and was uncomfortably shy and said quickly, "Oh no, you don't want to hear my playing. I pale in comparison to your skills, especially with your supreme command of Mozart's music."

I responded, "Throughout my life I have listened and played the music of Mozart. He is my favorite composer. Many times, I have wondered if god killed Mozart because he was jealous of his creation. I believe god has done this sort of practice on a regular basis since the beginning of creation. Regularly, I contemplated the fact that Mozart was such a genius in every genre of music. He blessed us all by allowing us to experience what was going on inside his head when he composed his music. He graced us by letting the average person peer into his perfect musical mind. He went to places that no composer has ever gone. He touches the soul of every human. He can stroke all our senses just as I can tap into all of mine at a moment's notice. Maybe that is why I love his music so much. I can relate to him like no one else that I have studied. He was as perfect as anyone that I have ever known, either in person or by reputation, when it comes to music. In many of his works, he had absolute control over his musical perfection and it shocked the world."

"When Mozart dove into his world of perfection, he was not only locked solely into his composing talents, but his talents for playing a musical instrument was also affected. His mastery over the violin and piano is something special to behold."

"What I find so amazing is the earthiness of his music. He reaches out and informs the dull witted as much as he understands and connects with the intellectual. Therefore, my questions to god are as follows: Why did god end his life at such a young age, and why did he make his life so hard? Is it because he was jealous of what his own creation had manifested into during his lifetime? Is that the reason he 'allowed' him to die so soon?"

Marci said confidently, "I don't believe there is a god. God only exists for the weak minded. The belief in a god is for people whose confidence has abandon them. God is only a fictional character that man has created as a form of an unseen security blanket, so in reality, he never truly existed."

Connie was processing all these playful exchanges and finally she spoke, "I think you two make for a fine couple. How long have you guys been dating?"

I smiled, while Marci was at a loss for words. Finally, she spoke and said anxiously, "Oh, we are not dating. We just met tonight. Mr. Seawick asked me to join him and then come back here to see the backstage."

She said with a small laugh, "We are not dating." I just looked at her. As Marci looked up at me hesitantly, she caught my eye then looked back down at her dress. Suddenly I sensed that reality had set in for her. She felt that she was out of place and did not belong with this class of people. Her dress was cheap and she did not possess the money or the prestige of the people in the room. I sensed her feelings of being uncomfortable and lonely.

I had to speak up, "Maybe one day we will go on a date. I would like that very much. In fact, I insist, if this would be okay with you, Ms. Singleton?" Marci was a little stunned and didn't know what to say.

Connie said with a smile, "I think she would love to go out on a date with you, Mr. Seawick." She stepped forward and placed her hand on Marci's arm and said to her, "My dear, never hesitate on something you want. Remember, honey, nothing ventured, nothing gained," Connie said with a hearty laugh.

Marci smiled and then looked rather confidently at me and said, "Okay, if you are asking, I will go out with you."

I smiled, quickly batted my eyes, looked up, laughed, and said, "Of course I am asking you out. I have wanted to go out with you for a long time. You have captivated me with your beauty since that night over ten years ago. I know we were only nine or so, but I was interested in you back then. Never have I seen such a beautiful vision in my life. You, my lady, are just perfect in every way." Marci's eyes dropped as she smiled and then she looked up. I said, "You have so much in common with Mozart's music. You are perfect in every way."

Marci said, "I am not perfect. I strive to be, but I keep making mistakes. I hate that about myself. I don't know why I keep making mistakes, especially the repetitive errors that I keep making. I try to sing, but I am not very good at it yet. I practice every day, but my first love is the violin and I so desperately want to perform onstage someday. That is my dream. Oh, to sing in an opera, now that is my greatest dream. What I wouldn't give to have the talent to perform in an opera, a Mozart opera. I love Mozart's operas because they are filled with so much passion and desire, and I just love it."

I quickly smiled, knowing this meeting was just too good to be true. I noticed a few of the musicians from the orchestra were standing around listening to our conversation. I looked at Connie and gave her a wink then looked at Marci and said, "Oh my dear, opera is one of the most beautiful jewels that life has to offer the human race. Without opera there is no passion, no love, no understanding of the vast repertoire of what is known as the human emotion. Emotion is love and love is passion. Without emotion and passion, love cannot exist. Passion is the desire to capture the essence of what makes you complete. Emotion is the effort that you put toward that desire of what makes you whole. Passion is the thought. Emotion is the action. Without one another, the two exist only as theory. If you combine the two, love is formed and will nurture through time. To me, opera, as well as the violin, touches the very essence of human desire for love. They stir the passion and desire in one's heart and soul. They exhume the emotion from within, only with the sole purpose of attempting to understand what is present in the heart and soul."

"Operatic singing and violin playing are vehicles that allow us to navigate through our souls to discover the truth, and to find our purpose of being. They provide us an understanding of life in general, and the many roles it offers. It teaches us the values of basic human existence. Without passion and emotion in life, it will lead to an existence of incompleteness."

"Opera gives us a blueprint for life. Some of the most complex and compiling questions are asked in opera. A well-tuned and interested ear will hear the answers to those questions. The answers are not only spoken, but also demonstrated by acting out emotions. The answers are buried deep within our soul. Opera is one of the few instruments that we have in this world that we can use to uncover those answers."

Marci and Connie stood in silence, both understanding what I was saying. Marci broke the silence by saying, "In my opinion, Mozart understood the many levels of human emotion better than any composer. Would you guys agree with that?"

Connie answered with, "I have sung many works by many composers, and Mozart is definitely one of the best and the most entertaining to sing, as well as to act. His operas tend to have so many themes running through the numerous plots, but other composers certainly follow this outline."

I noticed more members of the orchestra and some board members were gathering around as our conversation intensified. Many of them encouraged us to continue our dissertation about opera and

Mozart. Throughout my youth I had always admired the music of Mozart, but I rarely found someone that shared my passion for the composer's music. I could sense that Marci had this passion, but I wanted to test my newly found friend to see just how deep her passion ran for the greatest music maker of them all.

I continued with my opinions, "One genre of Mozart's music that I love is opera. In my opinion, opera is the essence of human life. It encompasses all the human emotion that life offers. Opera allows and permits you to experience all human emotions. Mozart can say more in one minute than any other composer can say in an hour. Mozart is straight and to the point. He is not boring or dry. Mozart can make the most mundane action be the most exciting. Mozart's music is bouncy and fun loving. The music can be understood and enjoyed by the common listener or by a well-trained ear. Sometimes my heart stops while I listen through certain parts of his works, and this is no more demonstrated than through his operas."

"Opera, to me, is the true sign of a composer's genius. Opera mixes the symphony, the theater, and the singing talents all together to make the grandest part of all musical genres. It takes a very disciplined and well-educated person to understand opera. Opera reaches down into a person's soul and plays with your spirit like a child would play with a new toy. Opera cleans and purifies the soul. In my opinion, when it is listened to properly, it brings us closest to god's perfect little world that he apparently created and has waiting for some of us in the distant future. Opera gives us a glimpse into what it would be like in this little perfect, yet unseen world. This gift only happens when opera is sung with passion and conviction."

"In general, Mozart operas all seem to deal with the love, lust, passion, glory and confusion which is present in all our lives. I believe, through Mozart's operas, there is an underlining theme that is present. That theme represents his emotional state when he created that particular piece of music. Mozart gives up his soul and passion in his work. I believe Mozart was always looking for the perfect love, as well as the perfect sound. He wanted to be perfect and he had to demonstrate his idea of perfection to the world. He wanted to be great, but society would never let him achieve the status of greatness he so desired. The world did not understand Mozart; of course, there is a good chance he did not understand himself."

"If there was a god, he almost created a perfect creature when it came to his musical talents. I believe Mozart knew how much he was touched by his version of god. It had to frighten him until his last day. Seemingly, on the surface this would be too much for any one man to endure through his lifetime. Mozart was a man that was probably confused by his genius as most geniuses are troubled by their gifts from the imaginary divinity."

Marci awkwardly interjected, "I love opera, but it scares me. I feel that I am better with my hands than with my voice. I have loved the violin since I can remember, so I only focused on that instrument. I am just not capable of understanding all the nuances that classical music has to offer, especially opera."

I said, "Never underestimate yourself, my dear. It is amazing what can happen if you love something enough and you focus all your efforts on learning a subject that you want to devote your time to." Marci smiled at me and listened intently as I continued my talk. "In Mozart's operas, there are many themes presented and they all have the basic theme of love flowing throughout his music. Mozart's voice always speaks through his musical notes and, of course, is carried by way of the person singing and acting on the stage. Opera is difficult to follow and comprehend. To understand opera, you are forced to listen to the music. You must listen to the words and watch the acting. In Mozart, as in most operas, the facial and body gestures of the characters are just as important as the music and words themselves. Opera mimics life in general, and that is why very passionate people love opera. Passionate human beings study their surroundings and the people that occupy their environment, just like an animal would conduct its life either in a forest, a jungle, or a desert. They study the movements, the habits, and the history of their prey. It knows when to attack and when to hold back."

"As I said before, there are many themes in a Mozart opera. Love is the basic theme, not only in Mozart, but in basically all operas. Love is a part of life in so many ways; love of another person, love of a certain way of life or love of material items. In Mozart operas, he is enamored with confusion and loves the complicated twists of the plots, just like what life offers each of us. He bombards you with so many different situations in the beginning of his operas that is takes a well-educated human to understand what is being presented. For example, every character in his operas is there for a purpose. In every one, there are characters that are the personification of love, hate, mistrust, happy, sad, good, evil, or mischievous. All these characteristics are a part of Mozart himself and, of course, part of the spectators as well. Mozart operas are about people and everyday problems that people face."

"On the other hand, if you could just listen to the orchestra and not the words to his operas, you have some of the most melodious sounds the world has ever heard. Mozart opera is very complex in nature, but simple to understand by ear. It touches your heart and wraps your soul in a warm blanket. The true Mozart comes out in his operas and his piano concertos. These genres bring out the best of what Mozart had in his mind. When you listen to Mozart you see, feel, and experience the composer's ideas and thoughts without many restrictions. Opera is freedom of expression. It is one field where Mozart outdid himself. The orchestration, the arias, and the storylines make Mozart opera timeless. The music and the melodies will never die. Passion is what drives the soul and through a Mozart opera, he has the listener on full open throttle. Opera is the essence of human life. It encompasses all the human emotion that life has to offer. It allows and permits you to experience love, hate, laughter, weeping, and happiness, as well as sadness. Mozart is not boring or dry. He can make the most mundane action be the most exciting."

When I finished talking, a small crowd of thirty or so people all clapped in unison. Meanwhile, Marci was star-struck as small tears formed in her sky-blue eyes. I felt the passion flowing throughout her body. I smelt her scent, I heard her heavy breathing, and I saw the lust for passion that she had in her eyes. The eyes of Marci were an open window to her soul, and I loved everything I saw while peering through this porthole to her essences. I saw with my own eyes, a glimpse of what makes up this creature's great fervor and passion for life. At the moment, I knew and sensed that she was different from any human I had yet to encounter in my young life.

That night Marci and I exchanged phone numbers. Into our conversation, I discovered that Marci was an orphan. She was never adopted but was in and out of many foster homes throughout her life. She was dirt poor, thus had nothing to her name. She worked at a small store that rented out musical instruments. Before we left, I sensed that she did not want this night to end. I worked so hard to make her interested in me and I believe I accomplished what I wanted. Marci had followed my musical and academic careers for over a decade now. She told me that her goal was to play for the Louisville Orchestra or some organized orchestra as a player in the violin section. I told her that I wanted to hear her play and that if she wanted me to, I could give her some pointers. She seemed to be very excited at that possibility.

A few days went by before Marci and I went on our first official date. We ate at a local restaurant, nothing fancy, but nothing cheap either. She told me more about her life, how she was literally left at the doorstep of the adoption facility when she was first born. She had no clue as to the whereabouts of her birth parents, which is something I could relate to. My heart poured out with sympathy for her of which she did not want. Marci was a strong woman and did not want anyone to feel sorry for her. She wanted to make it on her own. I sensed a lot of anger in her heart from so many years of not being wanted by willing parents.

Marci was beautiful, smart and a good person. For many years she thought something was wrong with her or felt that she either did or said something wrong that prevented a family from taking her into their home and loving her. My heart just broke in half after hearing her sad story. I felt a unique connection with her, something that I had never had with anyone in my life, apart from my mother. I never fell in love with anyone outside of my mother. The people that I live with are my family now and I love them, but not like I loved my mother. Marci was as close as anyone has been to my heart since my mother passed away.

Meanwhile, Lewis was not happy that I found Marci; in fact, he did not want me to even date her. Lewis had always been concerned for the family, especially me. He was always the big brother to me, consistently, without fail, overlooking my actions. That is what he had been to me, at least in his eyes – a paid overseer for a client that had strange and unusual problems, both physically and mentally. Oh, Lewis ended up caring about me, but only as an interesting experiment, not as a friend. He is more in love with my condition and has viewed me as a specimen rather than as someone he truly cared about.

Lewis told me before my first date with Marci that he knew this day would come, when I would be going out on a date. This always worried him because if I would ever mate with a woman, I would create another beast like Adam. I never had the heart to tell Lewis, but unbeknownst to him and even Carolyn, I dated while I was at Harvard, but nothing serious ever came from those women. I am sure Carolyn suspected that I did, but she never led on that she knew. I am sure Lewis knew I would eventually end up meeting someone. Therefore, I am sure he was prepared for the occurrence to eventually happen. He knew that ultimately there would come a time when he could not totally control me. This was one of his utmost nightmares.

I had always wanted to meet someone, but considering my condition and my way of life with all the unexplained issues, I had never fully entertained the idea. Lewis wanted me to be careful and not fall in love or, worse yet, 'father' a child. My condition would be very hard to explain and, of course, it would possibly jeopardize our experiments and my way of life. No one would approve of my lifestyle, so finding someone would be almost impossible.

During this moment in my life, I had to accept that this was going to be my lot in life. In addition to this sad but true tale, since I am going to life forever, I will outlive any of my lovers and friends. However, I had always longed to love someone and to have someone love me, outside of the people that I grew up with. I think Lewis understood my situation, so even though it was against his better judgment, he did not try and stop me from going out on dates with Marci. He knew he couldn't control my dating life. He knew if I wanted to do something, I would end up doing it whether I had his approval or not.

I do respect Lewis and I would not want to totally jeopardize our affiliation. Our association is special and very important, not only to the both of us, but to our experiments and the studies we have been conducting. We had spoken about this a few years ago before I met Marci. The subject was brought up again just after Marci and I met. Lewis understood my desire to have a companion to date and share thoughts with besides the family. We talked at length about the potential dangers that this relationship, if allowed to blossom, could possess.

Marci and I dated for a few weeks. I didn't take her to the best restaurants in the city, but instead took her to inexpensive places. In fact, on all our dates I used Lewis's car, an old Ford SUV, to pick her up. I told Marci that my car was in the shop. Truth be told, I didn't want Marci to fall in love with my money. I don't think she was interested in my money from the start, but I didn't want to flash too much of it in her face at the beginning of our relationship. I knew she had to know I came from money and that I lived well from all the newspaper articles that were written about me in the past. If she truly followed my career over the years, she would have had to know that I was not poor.

While I was in college, I had many women that wanted me just for my money, my fame or both. Marci seemed different and I wanted her to like me for me, not for some image that she dreamt up in her head or to worship me as if I was some false prophet. While on our dates, we watched a few movies, some plays and went out to eat at various restaurants. We even went bowling one night, which I had to be careful not to bowl well since she knew I had never bowled before. The sport was quite easy and I believe I could have bowled a perfect game if given enough practice, but that is pretty much the story of my life.

One night I told her that I wanted to hear her play the violin and I would not accept no for an answer. I had been after her to perform for me since our first date. I understood that she was just a student and her playing skills would pale in comparison to mine, but I didn't care. I wanted to hear what was in her heart and what was on her mind. I could tell a lot by the way someone holds the violin, how they stroke the strings, and their tension and vitality by how the instrument is used.

Playing a musical composition with an instrument is like having sex with someone you lust after; the more difficult the piece, the more of your attention is required. If you are successful in playing the difficult piece of work, usually that experience is heightened to a level of bliss, thus making the experience even more special. If you master an easy piece of work, the pleasure is usually not so great. The sense of accomplishment is the main ingredient to being totally fulfilled when you complete a difficult piece of music. Sex is no different. Any person or animal could have sex with a normal or average mate. To mate with the best animal in a pack or to mate with the best-looking woman in the room is a challenge for any man. The same could be said for the woman as well with her potential sexual encounters. The thrust of the issue is the more attractive the mate, the better the sex, at least in my theory.

One night I finally invited Marci over to the estate. To my knowledge, Marci didn't know where I lived. I am sure she had envisioned a big house, but I sensed that she was not expecting the grandeur of my home. Marci drove her small, very old and loud car to the gates of the estate. I was on the loudspeaker and told her to come in after the gates opened. She was very nervous and said, "Wow, Garrison, what a spread. Locked gates and all... really?" I opened the gates and was thinking about what was going through that beautiful head of hers. I felt a little embarrassed because I know she didn't come from money, being an orphan. She had to know I was a multi-billionaire if she read the newspaper or followed my many careers, but sometimes seeing is believing. I stepped out of the house and stood in front of the massive door that was the entrance to my home.

My mind raced and for some reason I was nervous, which was good because that caused my senses to be lifted to a level where I felt like I was in total control of the situation. I had many thoughts bouncing around in my head while I waited for the car to approach. I wondered if this was how my adoptive father felt when he took my mother on her first tour of the estate. Is history repeating itself? Am I making a big mistake by letting this most beautiful creature into my life?

I felt selfish and hollow inside. I would never want to hurt or cause any discomfort to this lady in any way, but of course, I was trapped and could not tell her the truth. She would never have accepted it or believed it, for that matter. How do you explain to the one you love that you will live forever and she will live a normal life and will die long before you? How do you explain that to someone? How do I explain my eating habits or my future plans for experimentation on animals and their grotesque metaphoric changes? How selfish am I to be leading this woman on? I then thought maybe I could make it worth her while. Maybe I would shower her with gifts. Maybe that would help ease any pain that I might cause her in the future. I felt as low as I had ever felt in my life, but the desire that I had for her forced me to continue down my shady path of deception.

Marci stepped out of the car with her mouth open saying, "Oh, my god, oh, my god! What a big home. Is this a hotel? Is this for real, Garrison? I mean, I knew you were not poor, but I didn't know you were so… you know… rich."

I laughed and walked down the steps to meet her. As I walked, I stared into her eyes without say a word. She stopped and allowed me to walk toward her, her eyes never losing contact with mine. I kept my pace and before we knew it our bodies touched as I put one hand on her shoulder while my other hand ran up the middle of her back. I gently but firmly pulled her toward my lips and kissed her. My tongue went deep inside her mouth and she tasted very nice. Then my animal-like senses took control. I tasted what had been in her mouth that day; what she had to drink, what she ate, the toothpaste that she used, and even the mouthwash she used. I smelt her scent and felt her heart racing inside her chest. I could almost read her thoughts during our kiss.

At first Marci was surprised by the kiss, but when she collected herself, she didn't want to stop, and her kiss was very responsive to mine. I gently backed away as I could feel my lips being removed from hers. I felt the warm sun on my face as the wind blew across my wet lips. I released my hold on the most interesting and desirable creature I had ever seen in my life. She stood there a little shocked, but that smile, oh that smile that she had on her face! The right corner of my mouth turned up slightly more than the left as she smiled, and her eyes literally looked as if they were glowing inside of the lustful-looking face of hers. I then said, "Please, let me get your violin case and I will show you around the grounds, if you would like."

Marci was confused at first, "Oh, that's okay. I can carry my own case, but thanks."

I opened the front door and let this vision walk in. Little did I know at the time that from this moment forward, my life would never be the same. I showed her around the first level of the house. She was very surprised at the initial size of the place, especially the kitchen and great room. We went downstairs, but instead of taking the door on the right of the landing, we took the left. I showed her the many bedrooms, family room, game room and rather large movie theater. I told her that on the other side of the house, in the basement, was Lewis's headquarters, which contained his laboratory, kitchen, bedroom, and family room. I told her it was like a small house in his area of the basement. Marci knew that Lewis, Loren, and Carolyn all lived with me and she knew some of the reasons why they did. She seemed to be rather touched by the reasons why I had allowed them to stay with me through the years.

I wanted Marci to see the upstairs. I wanted her to go up the stairs ahead of me. I walked several steps behind her when we made our assent. I watched her every step as her perky ass moved with the rhythm of her steps. Her tight-fitting jeans were making a rubbing sound with every step. I could smell her essence as she quickly moved up the steps like a doe running haphazardly through a forest. She didn't have a clue about the thoughts that were going through my perverted head. As we got to the second floor, I showed her the vast number of large rooms. I then showed her my adoptive father's office, which was now mine.

Marci loved the dark, wooden walls and ceiling of the room. She stood close to the spot where I enjoyed my meal of Snowy many years ago. I looked down at the very spot. A smile came over my face, knowing the history of what I did, and I wondered how that would be received by Marci if the story were to ever be told. Of course, she would run for the hills and I would never see her again. She must never find out the truth about me. This could never be a possibility because I really liked this young lady and I would always want her to be in my life. Now the trick was to have her fall for me. I knew there was an attraction to me on her part, and I believed that feeling was very strong. Where we went from there was up to us and I hoped I would not ruin the relationship that we had already established over the last few weeks.

We made our way down to the great room and Marci released her violin from its case. I did the same with mine. I knew she needed some sheet music so I had some from years ago that I dug out of boxes stored in the basement. I sat at the piano and she stood near me. We both knew the music might not be played at its best since we were not familiar with the piece. We also did not have any page turners at our disposal. When we started playing, Marci and I began to play a very nice violin sonata by Mozart. I knew she was nervous, but I assured her that she did not have to feel uncomfortable with me. I told her I would not judge her harshly. Marci wanted me to give her some pointers and after listening to her playing, I was rather surprised at her skill level. After we played the first movement, we stopped. Marci was just beside herself at my ability on the piano. I gave her some pointers on my violin and attempted to show her the mistakes she made during the piece by showing her the way those parts should have sounded. To her astonishment, I remembered every note she played. This alone amazed her to no end. There were parts she missed that even she didn't remember playing. I made sure not to be overly critical, but Marci was the type of person that wanted to learn and was not easily offended. Of course, there was not much I could teach her. Most of the missed notes on her part where just that, missed notes. It is nothing that a lot of practice wouldn't cure. She wanted me to play the violin piece along with her for the second movement and I did. As we started the second movement, she had some trouble staying in tune and in rhythm with me, but she caught on quickly. We played a few pieces and I showed her some 'moves' that I found interesting; she was much appreciative.

As the weeks went by, Marci's playing style and ability improved greatly. Part of the problem, which was a good problem to have, was that she had so much passion when she played that this tendency would distract her from concentrating on the work at hand. What she needed was someone to help her channel this passion into her playing. I tried to teach her how to control, and the next moment how to release, that passion. Each note, each bar, each measure had its own distinct personality and I taught her how to read those personalities. She had to trust her skillset and let her emotions take over the instrument. I had to keep reminding myself that maybe this was too much for her. For me, this came naturally. Maybe I expected too much from humanity to perform on a level that is still several levels beneath me. All through my life I had been around people that were not as developed as me so it was hard for me to gauge a person's skill level or what my level of expectations should be.

Marci and I dated for several months and our relationship got stronger with each passing week. I knew that she loved me from the start. She had been obsessed with me years ago with the kind of obsession a person would have with a rock star. She never let me forget how impressed she was with my mastery of the violin and how my piano playing totally shocked her to new levels. To her and many others, no one person should have this much mastery over any one instrument, much less two instruments. She was impressed with my academic career as well as my musical talents. Marci loved intelligent and talented men, and in her eyes, I was the best in both of those prerequisites for her attention.

During our courtship, I played once at the Louisville Orchestra and she was in our balcony seating area. I could tell that she was more nervous for me than I was at the time of the performance. I really wanted this relationship to work out, but I knew that she could never find out the true secrets of my world. She wouldn't understand or approve, but then again, who would?

I wanted to help Marci financially, but I didn't want her to think that she owed me in anyway. There were times where we would be on a date and I would buy her a thing or two, usually clothes to wear to the orchestra. Marci loved the gifts that I bought her, but she would not accept them right away because she felt as if she was stealing them from me. She was not used to having someone give her anything, and at times it was uncomfortable for her. I never wanted her to think she was some charity case, so I had to be careful how and what I gave to her. I did offer a seat in our balcony anytime she wanted because she truly had appreciation for the orchestra.

We talked about our relationship regularly, and she would never shy away from the subject; in fact, she was always excited to talk about us. Over several months of studying her, I could sense that she didn't have interest in me just for my money or what I could buy her. One of the many advantages that Formula L has given me is a keen sense to read people and their emotions. Marci didn't care about money. Of course, when we talked about the subject, we agreed that having money makes life easier than not having it, if money is used correctly.

CHAPTER 8

Logistics

While Marci and I continued our relationship, Loren aged rather quickly. She was constantly tired and complained of not feeling well. Loren ended up going to the doctor and after a few tests, she was ultimately diagnosed with lung cancer. The cancer was very aggressive and this surprise came out of nowhere for all of us. I was very depressed to hear the news when she came to me in my library one night. She was very shaken and worried, but being the strong woman that she was, she showed lots of courage when she told me. I remember crying very hard and she had to console me. It seems sad to me that usually the people who are sick are the ones caring for and consoling the people that are not sick. The true lot in everyone's life is not what you can control or change, it is what you cannot control or change. We are so vulnerable to everything life throws at us, it is truly amazing. Humans are so fragile, so delicate, and so weak. A common cold can bring someone down to a point to where they cannot function at a normal level. It must be hard having to accept death at any age and having to come face-to-face with the emperor of death, the dealmaker of all dealmakers.

Loren was not ready to die and she again pleaded with me to infect her with the formula. I just couldn't do that to her. Oh, what a decision that was at the time. This was a woman that I loved nearly as much as I loved my own mother. In fact, I spent more time with her than I did with my mother. She taught me our business, I trusted her with all my family's money, and through her leadership, the family businesses flourished beyond comprehension. I owed Loren everything, but I just could not infect her as I did my father. I saw what could happen. Things can get out of control rather quickly. Loren begged me to let her into my world. She didn't care about her physical appearance; she just did not want to die.

These are the types of decisions that a young man should not be forced to make. This was one of those times that I cursed god, if he existed. How can any truly loving and caring god put a simple being like me under such a strain? The guilt that I felt was extremely heavy and even to this day, I feel that I disappointed my friend, my leader, and my teacher. Loren made it easier for me by saying in the very late stages just before her death that she was sorry she had put me through hell. She said she was sorry that she tried to force her desires on me by asking me to do something she knew was wrong and that I couldn't follow through with.

Loren lived, if you could call it that, for about six months after her diagnosis. The last week was the worst. She was in the hospital but wanted to come home to die. I was honored that she thought of the estate as her home. It was understood that she and the others were always welcome to stay until their deaths, but to hear one of my friends call Seawick Estates home was extremely special to me.

Marci was there by my side the whole time. Loren's cancer experience brought Marci and me closer. For some strange reason, Loren kept saying that it was her final calling to push us closer to one another. Loren never had any worries about Marci and me, she just wanted me to be happy, and she knew Marci made me happy.

In so many ways, Loren was an extension of my mother. I loved them both so much and I curse the very days when god took them both from me. I will never forgive its control over this horrible phenomenon called life. Well... god got his way again. After he took both of my parents in a horrible fashion, he too took my second mother in the same cruel way. He took her life on a rainy Friday morning, and I was there to witness the thefts. I didn't sleep for three days after the event.

Loren was in great pain and the drugs the doctors gave her only helped to a certain degree. I was so tempted to ease her pain and suffering, but I just couldn't. I could not have her going through life as part animal and part human. I just could not bring myself to commit this act. It was a minor miracle that Marci never got wind of what we were talking about through this process. On top of Loren's pending death, I felt so guilty keeping my secret from Marci.

Lewis was my spine. He helped me so much through this decision-making process. In fact, of all the people I thought would object the strongest, he stayed out of the decision. I guess he trusted I would make the correct decision at this point in my life. I will never forget the latitude Lewis gave me regarding this situation.

On Loren's deathbed, her final words to me were, "Garrison, I love you and I hope you find what you are looking for in life. Please don't let this control or dominate you. You control and dominate it, whatever it is. I just hope that God forgives you and Lewis, but the truth must be found. If you could ever find the secret to everlasting life, Garrison, do you know what that would mean to this world? But like you have said from day one, it must be controlled because it can be a very dangerous weapon if not used properly. I love you, my Garrison. I wish you nothing but happiness for the rest of your life, which is going to be a very, very long time. Just please don't forget me and always remember that everything I did, I did for you." With that, Loren closed her eyes, turned her head away from me, and while I held her hand tightly, she expired.

I sat there on her deathbed, looking at the corpse in front of me. The only person that I truly loved just died before me. I loved her with all my heart and could not stop thinking about the concept of love as I watched her take her last breath.

At that moment, I perceived love as something that one must act out in demonstration only, not to hide behind the veil of secrecy like god practices. Our shy leader expects everyone to love and worship him just because some people in life told us that is the right and proper thing to do. See, I believe one must act out their love instead of just speaking about the love they possess for someone or something. Loren, unlike god, proved her love for me.

A person needs to prove their love for an object or person, they should not take that item or person for granted. Love must be felt, but to feel love, you must see or experience what you want to love. Love must find its way to the individual with a little help from the person that love is trying to affect. In other words, loving and being loved works both ways. To love something that does not love you back is just an obsession, not true love.

I also believe that if you are looking for love, you will never find true, pure love. It will be a falsified love instead of true, unadulterated love. Love must be experienced and created from the start, and based on mutual respect and adoration for one another.

This concept of god is truly absurd. How can you create a relationship with something that only places obstacles in front of your path to him? It is like he creates this maze for his own twisted enjoyment. You are required to meander through just to get to meet him so he can decide whether you are worthy of his glory. On the surface, I sometimes speculate if he knows what a pompous asshole he seems to be.

A couple of days later I had the funeral at the grounds and again, I had to bury another one that I loved so much on the grounds I own. I laid her body to rest near my parents and grandparents, making seven individuals that were laid to rest on my property. Many of the managers and business people came to the estate for the burial. I spoke at the funeral services with Marci at my side. She never left me during this most horrible time. Again, that is something I will never forget.

My eulogy during the burial ceremony was simple, but strong. Everyone in attendance had their eyes on me as I walked toward the pulpit in the nearby Catholic Church that Loren had attended. I said to my audience, "Death has many faces such as emptiness, coldness, fearfulness, and darkness. Death is a kingdom that we all are destined to visit and experience in our lives. Death, to many people, has such a finality to it. To me, death is the end of a current existence and hopefully it can be or is the beginning of another existence. At least we hope there is another existence after death. If this is not the case, then the despair is even greater than at first thought. But if one would view death in a different light, then death can reawaken an area in one's heart."

"Death can make love stronger; it can create or complete a bond between people that have passed and the ones that are momentarily left behind. Death, by itself, is black and cold, but the effects and after-effects of death is what you make of it. Death is what we strive for ultimately in life, is it not? If not, then we have not come to peace with this god or ourselves. Many people view death as a release from this world, while at the same time having an open invitation to a better world after death. True death is experienced by beings that escape its grasp. True death is the total release from the old world and acceptance into a new and better world."

"Death can be viewed as a positive event for many because death brings a person closer to their maker... their god, which for many is their main goal in life. They want to find their god's love. Many believe that one can find true, pure love in death. Many seek the pure love from their god. We all must die; in fact, some of us live to die. Some people want to spend eternity with this deity and be at peace forever. Many people that are not at peace with god will not share in his glory, thus they will suffer in the afterlife. Many people prepare daily for their death. At least in theory, the older we get, the closer we come to death. Through life experiences, we are constantly preparing for our own death every day. Death affects both the living and the dead.

The easy part is when you die; the hard part is dealing with a death. In my opinion, death for the person who is dying is not really death. Oh, you die and your body decays in a box in the cold ground, but if you have lived a good and honest life in the eyes of your god, then death is just the beginning. What is truly the tragedy about death is the people left behind. I should know this more than most people. When someone dies, that death affects so many people that surround the newly departed. The secret to dealing with the death of someone special in your life is to prepare for your own death. Learn from the dead. Do not be afraid, just be prepared."

"Loren was my friend. She was very special to me. She was always in my world. I fear I will experience far too many days like today throughout my life. I say goodbye to you, my friend, because I don't know if I will ever see you again. Such is my lot in life. The price I must pay for my own personal blessings. Can you imagine if you were to live forever while others around you would eventually die? It is a cold and sober feeling. That is what I am experiencing right this very moment. Goodbye, Loren. I love you." When I said those words, I thought maybe I had said too much, but I had a nice recovery at the end of the eulogy.

After the services, we placed Loren's body in the ground near my parents on the hill that faces the deep valley of trees. Again, I stood by the gravesite and watched the dirt being poured into the hole. Marci was there beside me, wrapping her arm around mine and holding my cold hand. Not one word was shared between us, but many thoughts were exchanged in my mind. Knowing that I would never see Loren again made me sad, but also very angry. Angry with god for putting me into this position, a position that I did not ask for, that I must carry around the memories of the deaths of my loved ones for eternity.

The anger and guilt was pouring into my soul, stronger and deeper by the minute, as each shovel full of dirt hit the inside of the dirt trap. Did I make the right decision by not giving Loren what she asked for? I could have saved her. She could have lived forever and pain free, as well. I chose not to give her that gift and it was a choice that I regretted making. What made all this worse was that I couldn't share this with the one person I loved the most in my life, my dear Marci. I was lying to her as well, which made my pain even deeper.

All my senses were on high alert as I inhaled the scent from the moist dirt that was being disturbed by the two men covering Loren's tomb. I saw many worms and various bugs moving around in the loosened soil as each shovel filled with dirt was being slung onto the vault. I heard and felt the wind as it passed through the trees and made its way to my being. I heard the guests as they left the site. Some talked about getting something to eat, some talked about finding their car, and some talked about getting back to their jobs. I stood there thinking about this situation. The more I thought about it, the more upset I became. Do people even care about losing someone in their lives? Do they even care about what others are going through when the death of a loved one happens in someone's life? The more I thought about these questions, the angrier I became.

My mind raced as fast as it could to contemplate and process the information streaming through my mind. My thoughts turned to my favorite subject, life after death. I heard from some of my guests that Loren was in a better place. *Better place, really?* I thought. Are these humans that confident that a heaven does exist or that they will be invited into this unseen place called heaven? So many thoughts entered my mind I could hardly think straight. My thoughts quickly turned to Marci. I thought about our relationship and the fact that one day she would grow old and develop a disease and die. Meanwhile, I would still be alive, living my life, alone forever, and at that moment I knew I had to do something about my situation. If I wanted to ease my pain and prolong my stay on this earth with my Marci, I had to somehow find the secrets behind this formula.

After the burial of my special and close friend, I was busy with the financial end of the businesses. I had less time to spend on the experiments like I wanted. For many months, I devoted all my time to running the business, and in my little spare time, getting to know my Marci better. She was very understanding of me and my situation through this whole process, and she even helped me when she could. I felt bad that I couldn't spend the time I wanted with her, but I knew that I could not ignore my companies. If that happened, I would have nothing. I met with all the managers and CEOs that were part of my holding company. I told everyone involved that I was not interested in changing the direction of the company, and to continue with business as usual. I sensed that many of my trusted CEOs were gradually gaining more respect for me, but at the end of the day, I honestly didn't care what others thought; I am more interested in getting the results that I want achieved.

Speaking of Marci, I was careful not to over shower her with gifts. I wanted her to love me for me and not for what I could give her. But there were times that I spoiled her, and sometimes during those moments she let me indulge her. For starters, I bought her an entire new wardrobe. I took her shopping and we visited many stores in town. She didn't want the most expensive items in the stores, but her tastes were not cheap. She was very cost-conscience and many times she left an item on the rack or shelf because it was too expensive. Usually I would end up purchasing the item for her and the clothes would find their way into her closet. She would get so mad at me when I did that sort of thing. I also bought her a new sports car, which she about killed me when I gave it her. She didn't talk to me for a few days, but after many hours of convincing her that it was something I wanted to do for her, she finally accepted the gift.

As the months went by, I taught her more about the violin. She had improved greatly, but she was not at the level that she desired. Marci was a perfectionist and she wanted to be the best, play the best, and be able to perform at the highest level possible. That is why she liked and admired me so much; because I could achieve those levels that she lusted for, or at least that is what she told me from our numerous conversations.

As time went by, I got my financial affairs more in order, and Lewis and I continued with our experiments. This time around, Lewis used the formula that we excreted from my teeth and gums on small bugs. We first experimented on wolf spiders. Their transformation was special to witness. They tripled in size and grew huge pinching claws that extended from their head. The claws grew about three-fourths of an inch in size. The spider grew wings, while the legs almost tripled in length. The spider couldn't fly and, for that matter, barely had control of its newly formed wings. We tested other species of spiders and got different results, but the main areas of mutation were basically the same as the wolf spider. Again, more proof that each species reacts differently when exposed to the formula. The chemical or biological makeup is different in most animals, and Formula L changes the host accordingly to their cell makeup.

One day we trapped a fully grown Cardinal bird in one of the traps that I set for my meals. I took the bird back to the lab and injected the animal with the formula. After a couple of days, the bird turned into what looked like a small, mutated dinosaur. The bird lost all its feathers while the legs grew longer and thicker. The wings withered away from the body, and just after they fell off, small arm-like appendages grew. We could notice the growth with the naked eye. When the arms stopped their growth, they transformed and got thicker. After a few hours, the end of the appendages started to change and a new growth developed. Where the new growth developed, an elbow manifested itself between what was the addition and the newly developed forearm. Two small fingers developed on the end of the new arms. The beak turned into a large mouth full of teeth, and the head grew, but mostly got wider which caused the eyes to further separate from one another. The neck grew longer, and a thin mouse-like tail developed. As the feathers fell off the bird's torso, a scaly, leathery skin was its replacement.

We tested worms, crickets, grasshoppers, butterflies, and flies. The fly and the butterfly had the most mutated forms. Both specimens lost their wings and added additional legs. The butterfly turned back to its worm form but grew teeth. It had two large arm-like appendages on each side of its body and it would use these arms to push its head area up from the ground. At the very end of the worm, an inch and a half long black horn-like crustacean came out of the body. It would ooze this watered-down, white liquid from where the horn came out of the body. After a few months of these experiments, I told Lewis that all we were doing was basically seeing how the different types of animals would change. We ran many tests to see if we could find any clues about how the cell structures changed or how the different chemicals would react to the other chemicals. We were getting nowhere. Whatever we were dealing with was beyond our comprehension and understanding.

We normally kept the specimen alive for just a few weeks and then disposed of them, usually by fire while they were inside of a locked cage. We had this area near the forest that looked like a campfire site where we burnt the animals. Again, we had to be very careful not to allow the blood of the mutant to ever encounter another animal, bug, or any living animal. We always kept very close tabs on the specimen while they were alive because we did not want them to get lose and bite other animals or humans. That would be disastrous and would cause a terrible chain reaction in the animal and human kingdoms. One of the oddities of this formula that we discovered by accident, was once the infected blood was out of the human or animal host for a short period of time, the cell structure of Formula L lost its identity. Thus, the infected blood turned back to the original structure. We concluded that oxygen, as well as the lack of adrenaline and warmth from the body, caused the structure of the formula to change.

One day I was with Lewis as he was destroying one of our creations. Lewis told me that Wolfgang, my original birth father, had a few gallons of this formula on hand, but he kept it in a container where no oxygen got to the formula for it to be broken down. What caused us great concern for a while was what if Adam's body and blood seeped out of the plastic bags or the plastic bags decayed and the blood was mixed with the earth's soil? What would happen, and we knew there was a one hundred percent chance that it would happen, if a worm or some bug got into the blood. Then they would mutate and we would have no chance to control that widespread infection. We tested the soil hundreds of times and came up with no mutations. This confused us to no end. It was one of the reasons why we stopped mutating bugs and animals in our experiments for a long time.

The answer as to why the blood did not affect the worms or bugs in the ground was right under our noses. It was the temperature change. The formula apparently does not work under cold or semi-cool conditions. The host must be warm for the formula to take effect in the infected host. When Adam died and we buried him in the hole in the backyard, as his body temperature decreased, that temperature change affected the formula so the bugs and animals in the earth's soil were not affected as they came into contact with the formula.

Now what was strange was that the plants, like the trees, shrubs, and grass, just to name a few, were, on the other hand, infected. Over time, we took samples from these trees, shrubs, and grass, and tested them to see what the effect would be when bugs or animals would eat from these plants. We found nothing except the possibility that the animals and/or bugs that did eat the infected plants might live a longer life than they normally would. At least in theory, that is what Wolfgang told Lewis would happen, according to his findings. According to Lewis, while he was on his Germany trip, the village near the forest where my parents lived was older and healthier than normal. They didn't seem to get sick or not as often as an average human. It would seem that the plants and bugs had this same trait.

As anyone could imagine, we had some very tense moments. We thought we screwed up and had potentially released the formula on the world, and it happened in my own back yard. But to our pleasant surprise, or should I say to our delight, we kept the formula at bay. Lewis and I spoke about this for hours on end, about how lucky we were. We were dealing with something that doesn't make any sense, and if we screwed anything up, we could change nature with just one little bug or fly. The responsibility that we shared was incredible, and it made us both very uncomfortable. You think at the time that you have processed all the information and you make all the necessary precautions so you don't make any major errors or mistakes, then, after so long of a time, you discover that you missed something and your heart tends to sink after that awakening. We were very fortunate that we did not screw up as much as we could have.

After all these experiments, we were not getting anywhere. We were not getting the solution to this mystery. I was beyond frustrated. Furthermore, Lewis was slowly informing me about my birthparents and some of the experiments that my father did many years ago.

I was thinking about my birth parents like no other time in my life. With of my adoptive parents dead, I felt a sense of loneliness that was getting stronger over time. I felt empty and not complete inside, but mostly I felt that they knew something that we didn't regarding Formula L. I was to a point where I wanted to see them, but not because I missed them or was interested in seeing them, I had to see what they knew and what we were missing. The only way we could cut to the chase for knowledge and the answers to the secrets of the formula was to talk to the source of its creator.

When I approached Lewis with this idea, he about had a heart attack. He told me to forget about the idea and that they were very bad people. He told me that if we went deep enough in that forest to visit them, they would probably kill us on the spot. I had to admit, at the time I was very concerned and took what Lewis was telling me to heart. He had been there and experienced them, and it was painfully obvious that he was scared, even years after the incident occurred. On the other hand, if I could at least try to speak with my parents about the formula, they might be inclined to speak with me. From what I could gather from Lewis, they didn't seem to be upset that I was still alive, but more interested that I survived. Perhaps Lewis was just being too over-protective of me and moreover, of himself.

As the weeks dragged by, I became obsessed with the idea of meeting my parents in Germany. I remember the day Lewis and I had a conversation about my father and some other issues that I brought up in our talk. I said, "Lewis, I need to speak with you. I know you are against me finding my parents, but I feel if I could at least speak to them, I could learn more about the formula. I just need to pass along some ideas that my father could assist me with and see if I am missing anything."

Lewis said angrily, "Garrison, I promised your father that I would never come back nor tell anyone about their existence. I was fortunate that your father allowed me to leave. I break out in a cold sweat many nights after waking up from my sleep. I am scared of what he might do to me if he found out that I even told you about their existence. If you, and especially if I, went to that forest, they would kill me right there. And as for you going, they might talk with you for a while, but they would eventually kill you. They are evil and nasty people. Wolfgang doesn't care about money anymore. He has been living in the forest for over a hundred years now. For God's sake, wake up, Garrison! Can't you see that he is an evil man? He killed three of your brothers and was going to kill you, if not for your mother. He has killed thousands of people, thousands of animals; mutilated them, changed them, made them suffer, and enjoyed doing it, man."

I then spoke up quickly, "Just like we are doing today?"

Lewis said, "No! It's different, damn it!"

"No! No, it is not. You and I are the same as my father. We just want the truth so we can use it to our advantage. The formula was going to make my father immortal in so many ways, and the financial possibilities were endless and he knew it, even during the World War II era. You and I administrated these experiments on those animals to seek the truth, to see if we could find any information on what makes the formula change animals into another species, altogether different from their original state of being. During those experiments I could sense, I could feel your astonishment along with mine, that we were doing something that made us feel like we were playing god. We were creating something new, something different, something better, and that search, the lust for that knowledge is what gave you and I a purpose and you loved that feeling didn't you, Lewis?"

Lewis stood there and said nothing so I shouted, "Didn't you, Lewis?"

Lewis had to respond to my question. "Look, you will die if you go to that forest. They will kill you. They certainly will kill me, especially after I promised them that I would never come back."

I shook my head in understanding, "I understand your predicament, but that is your business, not mine."

Lewis, getting increasingly angry said, "Jesus christ, Garrison, I am just telling you this for your own good. I don't want to see you dead."

"Fine! We will do it your way for now, but we must find the answers, and fast. I want to find the correct makeup of the formula so the mutation will not be so hideous after the transformation."

Lewis said, "Okay, I understand your passion, trust me I do. But why the hurry? Why the rush? You have multiple life spans to find the answers. Why are you in so much of a hurry?"

"I owe it to them, the humans on this planet, to beat god at his own little twisted ass game that he has been playing since the beginning of time."

Lewis said in a smart-alecky tone, "Oh really! You are doing all this just to help us lowly humans so you can save us from that awful being called God? That God that you speak so ill of has been pretty good to you, son…"

As I heard those words flow out of his mouth, a rush of anger ran up my spine. I lashed out and grabbed Lewis by the throat and pushed him back up against a wall. I put my face just inches from Lewis's face. I opened my mouth and growled rather harshly, "Don't you belittle me or my opinions on that god that you support ever again, because this is my world, my life, my game that you are playing, you son of a bitch. You can play that subservient, ideological bullshit to some mythical being that no one has spoken with or seen to someone else, but please spare me that crap. I have experienced and encountered more emotional suffering than you have during your sorry-ass existence. I have lost a lot and I have memories that will haunt me for the rest of my life. We do things on my terms, we do things my way. Understand?"

Lewis was visibly shaken and surprised by my emotional outburst, which was uncommon for me. He shouted, "Let me go!" I released my grasp from Lewis and at that moment, I knew I had gone too far. Lewis continued, "Look, I am fucking sick of this shit. First it was your father's threats, then I had that fucking brother of yours to deal with, and then your mother's highly distorted emotional states. I had to meet your parents in fucking Germany, and they ended up being monsters out of some god damn circus freak show. I am sick of being shit on by this family. I never asked for this, you self-serving, spoiled son-of-a-fucking-bitch. How dare you threaten me like that! Don't you ever do that to me again, do you understand? You have to control your emotions, Garrison, or you will cause even more pain and suffering in your life!"

I retreated angrily and said, "Fine! I understand! I should not have attacked you, Lewis. I do love you. You have been my friend and I am deeply sorry for my outburst."

Lewis tried to compose himself, all the while thinking that he got lucky this time that I did not take a bite out of him. He never saw me show this type of aggression toward anyone except for my brother, Adam. Even with that issue, I always remained calm, cool, and collected.

Lewis begrudgingly said, "Okay, Garrison. What is going on? Something is bothering you. What is it? Just talk to me."

I sat down in a chair. I said in a low, humbled voice, "I am in love, Lewis. I am in love with Marci, and the thought of me outliving her is just too unbearable for me to contemplate. What am I going to do? How can I keep all this a secret? I will never die. According to you, I will not age beyond a certain point. As she would age, my looks and physical being will remain young. How would I ever explain that to her? How could I explain all this, all our experiments? Would she accept my secret? Would she keep my secret?"

Lewis grew increasingly nervous by my comments. He said anxiously, "Garrison, you cannot tell Marci about any of this, you know that, right? I mean, please tell me you know that."

I shook my head while staring at him. "Lewis, I love her, but I don't know what to do."

Lewis said after a deep sigh, "Garrison... if you tell her everything, you will lose her."

I quickly replied, "If I don't tell her, I will lose her. I cannot keep this a secret from her much longer."

This comment made Lewis even more nervous. He had dreaded this day for years. He knew he couldn't control me and he knew that I, one day, would find a girlfriend. He didn't know how to control this, but thankfully for Lewis, he knew I was aware of the consequences and was of sound mind about this issue. Lewis said, "I understand, Garrison, but you have some time. We must be careful not to trust just anyone, although I am sure we cannot trust Marci. I know you don't want to get too deep and then spring this on her."

I nodded in approval. I stood up and smiled at Lewis and said, "Well again, I am sorry, Lewis, for being angry with you. I will not tell her anytime soon, but I think we agree that sometime we are going to have to let her in on everything."

Lewis, although he did not concur with my feelings said, "I agree, Garrison." I could sense that he was lying to me. I could always sense people who lie.

A few months passed and Marci did very well with her studies on the violin. She had improved greatly and her grades were proof of her hard work. She was grateful for my services. I tried to help with her other studies, but I had to be careful not to get impatient with her. Marci would get discouraged whenever she was around me because her intellect and her musical talents were not to my level, which frustrated her to no end. Marci was never jealous of me, but she was envious of my talents and how easily my talents came to me. I could only imagine how she felt, so I attempted to downplay my gifts. This did not sit well with her, and she was always stern with me and never wanted me to hide my skills from her or anyone. Marci always knew when I was hiding my talents from her. She knew me better than anyone ever had. She marveled at my abilities, such as my ability to go on only two to three hours of sleep each night, my knowledge of chemistry, biology and, of course, my skills on the violin and piano.

When my Marci said she would give anything to be like me intellectually, I felt as if a piece of my heart was amputated from my body. I wished I could tell her that I could make her dreams into a reality with just one bite, but I could never do that to my love. Marci and her desire for perfection gave me additional incentive to perfect Formula L. I had to find its secrets so I could somehow change the chemical structure of the formula so the mutation would not cause physical changes to the infected host. Then I could live out eternity with the one that I loved the most. I could not imagine what it would feel like for both of us to be perfect in every way, living every day as perfect beings forever. Oh, what we could conquer if this dream would become reality, not to mention what I could do with the one that I love, with Marci in my life.

One day I suggested to Lewis that we needed to start changing the chemical makeup of the formula during our experiments. I based my theory on several assumptions. If we could change a certain type of species, like a rabbit, and that subject's change is constant like in our past experiments, and if we manipulated the formula somehow, then maybe we could discover the right amount of change needed for the mutation not to be so drastic.

For several weeks we worked on this issue, but like Lewis told me from the information he got from Wolfgang, he attempted this, but his subjects would either grow too fast or the mutations were too extreme. He told me that because of the extreme and rapid growth of the tissues, the tissues would rip and tear because the bone would grow faster than the muscles.

Lewis told me of the thousands of experiments that my father did on Jews during World War II and how many died from the accelerated growth caused by the formula. Wolfgang's years of work resulted in the final product that was in my body, but there would always be a physical change with Formula L. Per Wolfgang, the physical mutation that would occur to the host of this formula was the best he could hope for. In other words, this was the best he could do. He tried the newest and most advanced formula that he created on himself and his wife, both of whom suffered severe physical mutation.

Lewis informed me that when my mother gave birth to me and my brothers, what was so shocking to Wolfgang was how we turned out to be a physically normal human. He couldn't understand how that had happened since he and his mate were so grossly mutated. He spent many decades trying to solve this piece of the puzzle, although he never reached a solid conclusion as to why that was the fact. He had many theories but did not have actual scientific facts for a base to any of those theories.

I couldn't accept this to be the end fact. Now, more than ever, I wanted to make the mutation of the formula not cause any physical changes in the host. I wanted my Marci to be in my life for as long as I lived, which would be forever. Also, if the formula was perfect, we could market it, and my company would be the wealthiest and most successful company of all time. The richest, beyond anything anyone has seen. Not to mention, I would be able to play god, which was something that really intrigued me.

Can you imagine having the power to give someone everlasting life, a life that is better, both physically and mentally? Not even god can create this potential mass development of the perfect race of human beings. It could possibly even be used on animals as well. Maybe this formula would make a cow bigger, stronger, and therefore taste better than its predecessor. It would be able to provide more meat so it would feed more people. A hen might be able to produce more eggs, fish would be larger, all livestock would be larger and even horses would be stronger, thus would work harder and longer. We had the opportunity to make the world a better place, or at least change some of its inhabitants' world for the better.

I struggled with the idea of continuing these meaningless experiments on animals. These experiments were getting me no closer to the answers. I thought long and hard about the notion of experimenting on humans. When I approached the subject to Lewis, he was very upset with me for even thinking about using humans as subjects. I remember that day well. I said to him, "Lewis, we could better gauge how to change the formula using humans as test subjects. At least they could talk or better communicate than an animal."

Lewis said, "Garrison! I just cannot believe you would even think of such a thing, much less say it. I mean your father, Wolfgang, he did thousands of experiments on humans and it basically got him nowhere."

"Lewis, that is not true and you know it. My father invented the formula because of his experiments on human subjects. They could better communicate what they were feeling and what they were thinking during the transformation process."

Lewis was at a loss for words. "Garrison, you cannot go out and start testing on humans. What the fuck are you thinking? I mean, who are going to be your subjects? Marci, me, Loren?!"

"No! Not on my Marci. Not until the formula is completely perfected. Marci will never be harmed by me, you, or anyone that I love, for that matter. What I fear is we keep wasting our time on animals and we should be focusing on humans. The cell structure and chemical structure all have to be different between the two subject matters."

Lewis quickly grew more concerned and nervous over the comments I had made. He didn't want to be part of murder, on top of everything else that was planned for him. He said, "Garrison, this is not the path that you want to take. Your father went down this path and after thousands of deaths by his hands, he sits at the mercy of God..."

I quickly interrupted, "Let's leave god out of this. He is the one that screwed up everything from the start. I am not like my father. All I want are answers to the secret that the formula holds. I must start testing on humans, not animals. As for now, I don't want to prolong an animal's life, just humans. From what you tell me, my father is evil, but I am doing this in the name of science."

Lewis said, "In the name of science? You are doing this to see the mutation of some poor, innocent man just to get your jollies."

I quickly said, "No! No! That is not true. I want this formula to be perfect so my Marci can live with me forever, and a side benefit would be to help people in general."

Lewis shook his head, "Marci, Marci, you are so obsessed with Marci. How about the human race and making them better? Marci is going to destroy you someday."

These words angered me, so I shouted back, "Shut up! Just because you are old and lonely doesn't mean I must turn out like you. I love Marci. I am a man and I have my wants and desires. Remember this, dear Lewis, I will outlive everyone. I have to live on this planet longer than you can ever imagine so don't tell me what is wrong with my girlfriend or my feelings toward her." Nothing more needed to be said as we parted ways for the night.

During this part of my life, Lewis was growing more uncomfortable with me. My eating habits changed to a point that I was eating more live animals by the day. I preferred that type of cuisine over the more traditional human meals. Lewis had to learn to be more understanding of my diet. He became more accepting over time, but I sensed that it bothered him greatly. I usually ate my meals in the forest area, out of Lewis's sight. I always made sure no one was around to witness my feasts. Because of my excellent hearing, I could hear if anyone was walking around.

As time went by, I started to enjoy the delicacies more. I had deer, rabbit, squirrel, and raccoon. I had some of these creatures shipped from local animal shelters onto my property. Many of these animals were caught by people who would drop them off at the local shelter. Many animals would either be taken to a nearby forest to be released in the wild or they would just be euthanized. I would pay the owner of the establishment a generous sum of money before they would kill them. I bought the animals from these places and instructed them to release the animals onto my property. I had food stations placed all over my wooded property in hopes that they would stay on my land.

My killing methods stayed unchanged throughout the years. I caught them by either using traps or by throwing a rock at them, which was the preferred killing method. I always wanted the prey to be alive because I loved the scent that the animal gave off when it was afraid. I usually started to bite at the top of the spine, especially in the smaller animals like rabbits, squirrels, and raccoons, then rip the spine away from the body of the animal. I would peel the tendons and muscles from the meat portion of the carcass.

I started being more careful not to waste the blood of the animal. I would take a large cup or mixing bowl with me on my hunts.

After a kill, I would let the body bleed out as much as possible. I loved the natural heat of the animal's blood. I didn't like heating up the body because it would tend to cook the meat, which I didn't find appetizing. It was weird, but I didn't like blood by itself, although I do enjoy dipping a piece of muscle into the warm blood. Sometimes I would warm up the blood by fire, but I didn't like when the blood would clot, so I would stir the blood to avoid clotting. Over the years, I would take some of the animal blood and gently warm it up in a large beaker in Lewis's lab. He hated it when I did that, but the taste was not that bad and after a few tastings, the blood became more palatable to me. The fat on an animal was disgusting and I always avoided that portion of the animal. The meat of the animal was okay, but for me it was like a normal child forced to eat his vegetables. Sometimes it was good and sometimes you could hardly get it down. It really depended on my hunger, but what I preferred most was the tough muscles of an animal.

CHAPTER 9

Accumulate

*L*ewis and I devoted many months researching the cell structure for all the animals we had experimented on over the past year. We developed a complex conclusion that the cell structure of Formula L changes each of the diverse species of animal differently. For example, the turtle changed into a certain type of creature that would look dissimilar to what the rabbit or a squirrel transformed to. Each animal had their own special form or mutation. It was our conclusion that whatever main traits an animal would have, those traits would be more affected. Therefore, the essential point is the formula enhances the traits of the host. The formula would cause the ears on a rabbit to change differently than the ears on a turtle. Some of these changes would turn out to be an extreme surprise to us.

The horns that developed on many of our specimen astounded us. We didn't have a clue as to where some of these extra appendages came from. We thought that maybe the cell structure of these animals had hidden or recessed genes from millions of years previous, that maybe at one time they had these horns, wings, or large teeth. Some think that birds are a descendant from dinosaurs. This was evident with our experiment with a red bird. The bird turned into a small creature that resembled a dinosaur.

Obviously, the DNA structure had to be the cause or the basis for these deformities. I hesitated to use the word deformities because the formula changed the previous animal into a whole new species. In essence, the 'deformities' were a brand new and better species that we had created. Lewis disagreed with me on some issues. The physical appearance and the animal's behavior changed into a creature that would not be recognized to be related to the former state of being, but that was strictly semantics with me. I didn't care what Lewis's thoughts were on the issue or what he called them.

Some of these creatures looked, sounded, acted, and had different cell structures than in their previous state. I believed the hidden DNA somehow was stored and passed down from generation to generation of certain species. When the formula activated the original DNA, it somehow awakened these strands. These animals' DNA structure caused a certain eccentricity to develop that was not there before. At least, that was my theory.

Lewis and I were just shooting in the dark for explanations. If this theory had even an ounce of truth to it, I wondered if there was a new set of rules for us humans. From the four people that have transformed, that we know of, all grew taller, their arms and legs grew longer, and their heads grew and took on a wolf-like shape. This type of change didn't seem to fit what was in our human DNA structure through thousands and thousands of years of evolution. We knew the DNA structure of humans was different from animals, but what made the humans change the way they did?

Through more of our research, we found that as the formula passes through an unaffected host, thus infecting the host, a change, both physically and behaviorally, takes about three months to complete its full transformation. If that affected host would transfer the formula to another unaffected host, the change was more intense, violent and the length of time of the complete transformation was shorter than three months. The reason for the change between the Stage 1 effect and the Stage 2 effect was the change in the cell structure of the formula and the host. From my years of studying at Harvard, all cell mutations are a continuing process. Formula L is certainly not immune to a change.

We thought if the formula's cell structure changed by different hosts and could be changed by transferring from one host to another, then obviously its cell and DNA structure could be changed to accommodate any transformation that its creator would choose. At least, that was the theory, but to get the right form of cell structure seemed to be close to impossible. There were so many variables, but one thing was clear, the cell structure of each species was relatively the same, with the exception of male and female cell structures. The physical changes in female hosts were noticeably different from that of the male hosts.

Lewis said that after his visit with my parents, from his recollection and the notes he had taken, my father's mutation was different from my mother's. He learned from my father's studies a simple yet complex theory; the changes that took place in the same species of animals, including human beings, transformed to the same basic appearance, but with slightly different details. The change enhanced only the traits of the host. If the host had large ears, then during and after the transformation, the host's ears would be large as well.

As for defective cells in the body, like cancer cells or a defective cell that would cause heart problems, arthritis, or any other disease, the formula would 'correct' the cell structure in the host. One of the primary secrets of the formula was that somehow the formula stops the aging and disease processes. According to Lewis's conversation with my father, he had not aged since he took the formula over a century ago. I spoke with Lewis about these issues and we went over all our data and notes hundreds of times but could not figure out the reason behind that trait. Maybe we will never find the answer to what causes these changes or how to manipulate those changes to the benefit of the host's physical appearance. Why does the formula change the host physically? Our only discovery was that for the formula to work properly, it needs to travel in warm blood. The warmth of the body is what triggers the formula's full mutation process. It reacts with the DNA and cell structures of the body, causing the transformation to be so dramatic.

I also believed that adrenaline reacts with the formula. With the warmth of the blood and adrenaline being mixed in, this is the basis of the change in the affected animal. In my personal experience with the formula, when my adrenaline glands work overtime or when I get excited, nervous, or anxious in any way, I can feel my senses become more alive and keener than before.

We tested the adrenaline in both animals and humans with the attempt to understand why the host reacts the way it does with the formula. After numerous tests, we didn't discover any additional or useful information. The formula acted like an alien substance from another world. Of course, we don't know if other places on earth have this formula or its chemical makeup.

Wolfgang had to be extremely intelligent to somehow figure out the formula's makeup. The main ingredient in the formula is from a moss plant that Lewis found in the forest of Germany. It had a large, white root in the shape of a carrot, and that plant held one of the many secrets to the formula. Lewis had done a lot of research on the history of this plant, but as of this date, came up with nothing. He sent descriptions to people he knew who had knowledge of all rare plant species. They all came back with the same response; they had not seen anything like it before in their lives. Nothing was documented in books or the internet about this type of plant. Lewis still had that plant from Germany and it continued to grow in his lab. He was afraid to plant this anomaly out in the woods or on the grounds because he didn't understand what kind of damage it might potentially cause.

Lewis and I reviewed and discussed his notes taken when he interviewed my father. Wolfgang told him everything that he went through during his mutation. We also considered his notes from my adoptive parents' changes, as well as the birth of the creature that was my brother. Lewis took meticulous notes on all of them, especially Trevor, and documented their entire transformation process. We focused and studied Trevor's bloodwork, we listen to the recordings he took, and we studied his physical change. There were gaps in time of the recordings from the start to the end, but there was enough data to sift through. It was weird seeing my father on tape, seeing him transform through the different stages of the mutation process.

Down deep in my heart I loved my father, but he showed little emotion toward me. He was a cold man with an even colder heart. He did love my mother, but I knew he never wanted me. Maybe it was because I was adopted and he wanted a son biologically. Oh well, I had been over the feeling of not being wanted a long time ago. What was more difficult for me was watching my mother. I remember that she was very scared through each stage of the mutation process. I cannot imagine what a person would be thinking while going through that kind of drastic change. I don't know what was worse, not having a clue what was happening to you or going through the changes and knowing what the outcome would be.

According to Lewis, the information Wolfgang told him about his and Zelda's change was similar to the change in Trevor. We knew the kind of change that would take place in the infected host from either a bite or an injection of the formula. From what Lewis told me, I could infect someone by biting them, injecting the formula with my teeth. The formula would flow through the inside of my teeth, much like a syringe. The mutation process would only happen if the temperature of the blood was constant.

What really puzzled me was that my birth father didn't experiment on procreation of the subjects. We knew from one sample, my brother, that when an infected host mates with an uninfected host, the results would be a more deformed version of the mutation. The offspring would be more animal than human while still retaining many of the human traits. This is the stage of Formula L that Lewis and I have aggressively studied over the past few years.

I feel like I need to recap the different stages which are extremely confusing to average intelligence. Stage 1 is when the formula is first introduced to the host by a bite, an injection or by an ingested form. Stage 2 is when the formula is transferred from the first host to the second host or when an infected specimen bites the non-infected specimen. Somehow the 'changes' that occur are more violent and aggressive because the cell structure of the DNA changes from the first stage to the second stage. Stage 3 is when the second infected host transfers the formula to the third host. In theory, this level is where an infected host, bitten by the Stage 2, would bite an uninfected host. The possibilities are endless from there. In each stage, the mutation becomes more aggressive. As for as the change, each host is different, either physically or mentally.

What I wanted to see was if the traits of an animal, like a rabbit, could be transferred to another animal host. If an infected rabbit would bite a horse, would the horse mutate with some of the rabbit's traits? In theory, it would seem to be possible, if not probable. On the other hand, if two hosts are infected with the formula, apparently the offspring would turn out like me… perfect or as perfect as a human could be. I have no physical oddities associated with my body. No excess hair growth or any physical animalistic appearances.

I have traits different from the normal human. The most dramatic difference is my appetite and unworldly intelligence. I have advanced hand and eye coordination that allows me to play a musical instrument at the highest level. Other traits I possess include my lust for eating live animals. My senses are elevated to levels that no human can fathom, and my growth rate was extreme in my youth. Most importantly though, from Lewis's understanding from Wolfgang, is that I will never die nor age beyond a certain point. I did not know what age that would be, but I believed it would not be too far into my life.

After more extensive reviews of Lewis's notes, especially the notes from his Germany trip, it appeared that my birth father experimented on many animals and humans that at first were not infected with Formula L. What he didn't test were three issues. The first issue is what happens if the human mutant in a Stage 1 level of the formula, like my father, Wolfgang, would bite a non-infected human. This had never been tested to our knowledge. Wolfgang, at least from what we understood, never bit an animal or a human. He always injected the formula into the hosts via syringe.

I was growing tired of toying with animals, especially small animals with no intellect whatsoever. The tests that Lewis and I were conducting were basically the same tests that my birth father had conducted years ago. Our experiments were not getting us anywhere. I had the unique experience of witnessing firsthand the different forms of transformation that took place in my own family. I personally witnessed the transformations of both of my parents, as well as my brother's development from being a freak at birth. I wanted to explore practical ventures dealing with the effects of the formula on humans, not just animals. I have had so much personal experience with humans in my life and that was my main focus dealing with Formula L.

There were many different levels that I wanted to explore. The area that interested me the most was what would happen if a non-infected human was impregnated by an infected human and produced a child. What if that child bites another human? The child would be in an advanced stage of the formula, like my brother, Adam.

In our situation, my birth father started the process. He injected himself and my birth mother with the formula which was the Stage 1 level of the formula. They produced me, Stage 2 level. I then bit my adoptive father, and he entered the Stage 3 level of the formula. When he mated with my adoptive mother, Adele, they produced Adam. My adoptive mother was Stage 4, so Adam was in the Stage 5 level of the formula. In this situation, my mother cut her life short, but according to Lewis's documentation, the change was faster and more aggressive than Trevor's mutation when I bit him. Her physical change would be different than my father's change, but since her life was cut short by her suicide, we didn't have the luxury of knowing what would have happened.

The second area that interested me was what would happen if an infected animal would bite a non-infected human. This was never tested by my birth father. The third issue or issues would be ongoing problems that would have no ending. What happens if an infected animal would bite a non-infected animal? This process would continue until infinity, and each stage, in theory, would create a different set or form of mutation, although we don't know this to be the absolute truth. There is so much we don't understand about this formula and how it reacts to the many potential hosts. Trying to pin down the answers to these questions was more difficult than trying to find a needle in the Atlantic Ocean.

So many questions have gone unanswered and it seems there is a high probability those questions will stay unanswered. Someway I had to tinker with the DNA structure of the formula. Then again, what if all I needed was to adjust the cell structure of the formula? There were so many possibilities that seemed endless to me, and I was getting the feeling that I would never get to the secret of how to adjust the formula so the physical appearance of the mutation would not be as aggressive as in its current state.

I knew down deep in my soul that if there was any possibility of me finding the answers to the perfect life, I had to experiment on humans. I needed to find out what happened if a mutated animal would bite a human that is not infected. I would imagine the mutation would be more extreme than a Stage 1 mutant's bite, but then again, we don't know. How can you explain my original birth parents, who are both mutants yet had a rather normal child like me? This type of experiment had not taken place, at least according to Lewis in his conversations with my biological father. If we could run with this experiment, gather as much data as possible, and then compare it to what we already had, I would think we would get a better understanding of the formula.

Would there be any differences in the mutation process if the formula from an animal was transferred to a human? If we could study that case or cases we might stumble on something that would give us the clues needed to unlock the formula's mysteries. I knew that if I was going to start experimenting on humans, I had to be extremely careful. The biggest problem I saw was that I didn't want to be placed in jail for murder, so I had to be careful which subjects I chose. My next issue was who the subjects were that I was going to capture for these experiments. I pondered this problem for a few days and the only answer I came up with was the homeless people in the inner city. They could be the answer because there was a good chance no one would start looking for them when they came up missing. If I could coax one or two into my car without anyone seeing, no one would know what happened to them. They would be gone forever and no one would be the wiser. In theory, this seemed to be the perfect plan of action.

I approached the idea of capturing some homeless people to Lewis and, not surprisingly, he was aggravated, annoyed and lost control of his emotions. He yelled at me for what seemed to be hours on end and begged me not to do such a terrible and unholy thing. Unholy! He used that word with me. I never understood why people felt compelled to be the secretary to god, to call out everything they think is wrong in their eyes to people that are trying to do good for the world or even just for themselves.

Lewis was the kind of guy that if you didn't know him, you would think he would be the least interesting person in the room, but the opposite was true. I loved Lewis and he was always there for me and my family. He was a wonderful support for us all, but his problem was that while he was aggressive with this thinking, he was not with his actions. Even with all his faults, I always gave Lewis the benefit of the doubt.

For days on end, we had some very interesting discussions about my idea of human experimentation. Lewis threatened to leave my life and venture out on his own. I thought I could wait until he died and then start my experiments, but there were two problems with this line of thinking. One, I am impatient and would like to at least attempt to find the secret to a better life so I could get richer and better mankind. The other reason is Marci. She would age and grow old through time. If I was going to marry her, there would be some point in my life where she would keep aging and I would remain a certain age, whatever age that would be; she would continue to age and I would not. I think that would be hard for me to explain to her. Also, I knew if we were in a relationship, I couldn't continue to keep my secret life from her.

A few days went by and I used most of that time thinking about what type of measures I needed to take regarding my experimentations on humans. Lewis would not leave me alone during my time of contemplation, so I just told him that I had discounted the idea to shut him up. I believe I was very convincing because I sensed that he thought I was sincere with my words.

Meanwhile, I thought about what kind of condition or state I wanted the subjects to be in before the experiments began. I didn't want someone too young or in too good of condition. Those types of homeless people might still have relatives that are either in contact with them or cared about them. They would be too risky for me to pick up off the streets. The older homeless people are the ones that I thought I should go after, but they had to be in relatively average health.

I needed to find one that was a loner or one that was unpopular. Those types would not be missed amongst the homeless creatures. Another area that I needed to be concerned about was their willingness to come with me quietly and to get into my car without any trouble. I worried about my safety and if I could trust them once they were in my car for transport back to my lab. I figured that some way, I was going to have to drug them to get them into my car. Some way, I had to work this out by myself. No one I knew would help me on my endeavor. I figured if I could get someone that is very drunk, that would be my best bet. I also wanted to make sure I picked up two homeless people, not just one. Another prerequisite was that I wanted to make sure I had both a female and a male subject. The reason is obvious; I was going to have them infected with the formula, then given the opportunity, I wanted the option of having them procreate down the road.

The first step was to create housing for the subjects. This would call for restructuring the lab and building cage-like structures like Adam's room in the basement. I also needed to plan other amenities like toilets, showers, and any monitoring devices that I needed to observe the subjects during their transformations.

I was prepared to use the cameras located in Adam's old bedroom to monitor the subject's actions and reactions to the formula. Lewis had a very nice set up that he used during the time Adam was alive. I had extra supplies ordered that I kept out of Lewis's sight for this very extensive experiment that I had planned. The goal or reason behind this experiment was very complex and I am sure in many people's view, very unnatural and unholy.

I wanted to see what kind of affect the transformation would cause on the human subjects. What I was most interested in was the cell and the DNA structure of the humans and how the cell and DNA structures reacted to the newly introduced formula. I wanted to see what kind of changes would occur and how I could manipulate the change in those two areas. Of course, I knew I probably would never get to the answers, but I had to try. If I could somehow change the formula, just a little tweak here or there, then maybe there would be a possibility that I could lessen the physical transformation without jeopardizing the positives of what the formula offers to the infected subject. I was prepared to take countless notes and blood samples, and do numerous tests on the subject during this process. The question was, should I infect both subjects or just one of the subjects? After careful contemplation, I arrived at the conclusion that I would need to separate the two subjects and probably use chains on both.

Meanwhile, Lewis went out of his mind when I told him about the new project I was orchestrating, but I told him I wanted to have the option of two separate cells for potentially larger subjects. I left the future human experiments out of the conversation. Of course, Lewis knew what I was doing, and he and I had very intense arguments over this. Lewis again threatened to leave, and I told him that would not be wise on his part because he would regret that move. Three forces drove Lewis; one was money, two was a quest for knowledge and discovery, and three was fear. Sometimes I had to use the third to express my views to him.

After a massive amount of planning, I had to do extensive remodeling to Adam's old bedroom. I hired a local construction company to do the work and told them I was working with a veterinarian that worked with large animals. I told them I wanted the cells to be extra strong so there would be no chance of escape. They seemed confused by the idea, but I offered them more money, and they quickly understood and were prepared to start the job. I had the walls of the bedroom torn down so the cell could be viewed from Lewis's lab. In place of the walls, I had large steel bars installed from floor to ceiling. I made sure the entire length of the ceiling in this caged area was barred as well. I had an extra bathroom on the right side of the bedroom entrance installed. They installed an extra set of pulleys inside each of the two cells, on a large brick wall on the left side of Adam's old room and on the left side of the new cell. I had this area set up this way so two subjects could use separate bathrooms, as well as separate living quarters. I also had a cell wall with a heavy metal door built in the middle of the cage so I could separate the two subjects, at will.

In addition to all this planning, I had a human cremation machine purchased and placed near Lewis's lab. I had a separate generator that operated the cremation machine and spared no expense in getting the best one on the market. We had to rework Lewis's living quarters, but for the most part the machine fit into the area quite nicely. What I didn't want to do was have to worry about disposing of the human or animal parts and risk infecting other animals in the sewer system or in the wild. Lewis tried to leave the house many times, but I knew he would never follow through. I knew he was afraid to make any such move, fearing what I might do to him. To be perfectly honest, I would never have harmed Lewis, but he had doubts and that was all I needed for the time being. He knew I had the power and money to do whatever I wanted when it came to my house, of which he was one of its guests.

After the construction of the cells, the lab area had a completely new look. I could sense the fear in Lewis's soul, but also noticed a sense of excitement in his old bones. I told Lewis that I would not experiment on humans and was very convincing in my presentation to him. He reluctantly believed me for the time being. I just needed him to stop his constant nagging. I knew deep in his soul that he didn't completely believe me when I told him that I was not going to use humans as subjects. In a twisted way, I made him feel somewhat better just hearing me say it. Lewis was always a man that lived in denial and he did this to make himself feel better about any situation he got himself into. Deep down, Lewis lusted for wealth, but mostly he wanted recognition. He wanted to be written about in history books. He wanted fame more than anything. I knew this and I used this knowledge to my advantage while reconstructing the lab area.

After the construction was complete, the issue now was where to find human subjects for my experiments. I didn't have a clue where to even look so I needed some help. I called a few of the local charities and got some information about where most of the homeless people hung out at night. One charitable service was more helpful than the rest. I ended up speaking with a lady named Jill who told me where most of the people hung out during the day and at night. I pretended I was looking for a friend I had lost contact with a while back. She was very sympathetic to my story. I mapped out the area on the Internet before I started out on my quest. There were many streets where these inhabitants wandered. The most popular areas were a mixture between high traffic areas that led out of downtown, and the not-so-traveled areas of downtown. I thought the less traveled areas would be my best bet for not being caught.

The first night when I went out to search for my subjects, I was very nervous. I told myself that I was going to just make a run to the downtown area to check out some of the areas where the homeless hung around. I waited until it was very late at night, and since I only sleep two to three hours a night, I took advantage of this abnormality. All my life I had made use of this time because everyone else was asleep and I had no interruptions.

I didn't know exactly where to go in the downtown area, so I rode around, looking for the right type of place and subjects. I had my syringes filled with tranquilizers, along with ropes and towels. I also had a couple bottles of whiskey for bait. I wasn't used to driving in the downtown area of the city so I drove around from street to street, paying very close attention so as not to hit the parked cars lined up on some of the streets. I saw some interesting prospects that night, but I ended up driving back home without a prize for my troubles because I couldn't find anyone alone for an attempted capture. When I did find an interesting prospect, something in my mind would stop me. I was afraid because I didn't want to rush anything for fear of being caught. I also didn't want to put myself into a bad situation that might end up causing me to be arrested by the police or assaulted by these creatures. This continued over the next couple of nights.

The fourth night I got up enough nerve to exit my car and walk around the area. Not two minutes into my walk, one of the street people yelled an obscenity at me. I said nothing and tried not to make eye contact because I wanted to be noticed as little as possible. A few seconds later some of the others looked at me angrily. I was now beyond scared, I was growing pissed and upset. I knew this night was not going to be the night of any great significance for me so I went back to my car and drove home. During my long drive home, I grew increasingly angry. I didn't like to be afraid, and certainly not from these kinds of humans. In fact, I didn't view them as humans any longer, I viewed them as specimen. They provided nothing positive to this world, from my point of view.

The next night I was better prepared. I wore some of my older clothes and made sure my shirt and pants were black. I rubbed some dirt on the sleeves, pants, hands, and face to make myself look part of the area. I ventured out to the same area as the night before where I had my unpleasant encounter, but I parked my car a block over. I got out of the car and walked around with a few syringes in my pocket. I walked the same few blocks as I had walked the night before. Sometimes I would stop and stand on the corner of the street and try to blend in as much as possible. I was taking inventory of my entire environment.

My senses were on a high-level alert, so I knew what was going on around me every second. As I stood there, my eye gazed upon a man who looked like a promising prospect. His age was hard to determine, but at the time he looked to be in his 40s. He seemed to me to be a man that had been living on the streets for a while because of the way his clothes looked and how dirty his hands and face were. I stalked him for a while, watching him closely. He would walk a few steps, stop, then sit down. He would look to his left, then to his right, and then he would look up, then down to the ground. He was not looking for anything but seemed to be bored and wanted to find something to keep his mind occupied. He got up from his seated position and finally walked about a block down the street. I looked around and no one was watching me so I followed him from a safe distance. I walked as softly as I could behind him. For some strange reason, I was not paying attention to where I was stepping as my foot accidentally hit a rock lying on the sidewalk. The rock went flying across the pavement and went right past my prey. The man quickly turned around and yelled at me to stay away from him. I was afraid he might draw attention to himself so I told him I was sorry. I wanted to maintain contact with him, so I tried to befriend him. I told him that I had some liquor in my car but wouldn't be drinking it because I didn't like what I had. I told him that a friend gave me the bottle as a present and that it was his if he wanted it. The man just looked at me for what seemed to be minutes, but in reality was just a few seconds. He mumbled something that I couldn't understand, but not to push the point I said, "If you're interested then please follow me."

I turned my back to the man and began to walk away, which made my spine tingle, fearing what he might do to me. I figured that my fast reflexes would work to my advantage. I could hear his footsteps if he was going to come at me in an aggressive manner, but I didn't want this situation to escalate to that level. I walked rather slowly and could hear that he was following me. I estimated that he was about ten feet behind me and that distance remained constant through our walk. After what seemed to be hours, I finally reached my car. Out of the corner of my eye, I noticed my homeless guy had stopped and was standing on the other side of the street. I pushed my luck a little and told him to come over to the car. I told him the bottle was in the trunk but thought it had rolled toward the back of the trunk. I said I had a bad back and that he had to retrieve the bottle for me. The guy looked at me rather oddly, but he slowly came over to the car. He kept his eye on me the whole time during his short walk. I acted like I was busy looking for my keys in my pocket as I walked toward the back of the car. I opened the trunk, pointed, and said, "See… there it is."

The specimen's walk sped up greatly as he came closer to my car. He stopped as he neared the front of my vehicle, and kept looking toward the back of the car as if something was going to bite him. As he stood there, he kept looking at me with a very concerned looked on his dirty, wrinkled face, then he began to walk to the back of the car. During this time, I put the syringe in my right hand, and as the man got closer I leaned toward him as if to point out where the bottle was, then as quickly as I could, I jammed the syringe into his upper middle left shoulder. I plunged the syringe into him as hard as I could because I wanted to make sure the needle went through the clothing. As I jammed the needle into his body, I quickly moved toward him and used the force of my body to pin him against the open trunk of my car. With my free arm, I held him down as I injected the specimen with the tranquilizer. He made a dreadful sound, and with all his might he rose up and pushed me off his back while he swung his right arm around, hitting me in my chest. As quickly as I could, I rushed toward him and pushed him backward into the trunk of the car. His head hit the back part of the trunk lid, and he seemed to have already started feeling drowsy from the tranquilizer. He moaned and grabbed the back of his head. I stopped, looked around and I didn't see anyone around, so I quickly forced his legs and feet inside and closed the trunk. I heard his hands and feet knocking on the insides of the trunk, then suddenly the noises ceased. He was out cold. I knew I had enough tranquilizing medicine in the syringe to keep him sedated for a solid twelve or so hours.

I was feeling rather excited that I had pulled off this challenge, which created confidence for me to look for another subject. I wanted to find a female, one that was young enough to bear children. In the back of my mind I wondered if the formula would allow any female at any age to be able to bear children. This has been shown to be the case by my birth mother who was rather old to have children; it was after she was infected that she had her four offspring. I didn't want to push my luck and end up getting an older lady that could not get pregnant. So now my search was for a younger woman.

I was feeling brave after the successful capture of the male specimen, so I walked along the edges of the main area where many of the bums hung around. I didn't want to cause a scene, but I needed to research the multitude of potential specimen that might be what I was looking for. I walked over to one man and asked him if he had seen a lady that goes by the name of 'Mary' which I told him was my aunt. He groaned at me and pushed me away. I repeated this exercise a couple of times to other homeless people to give off the impression that I was looking for my lost aunt.

I continued my walk down the road and came across this older lady pushing a shopping cart. I followed her from a good distance away and waited until she was in a place without many other people. She was older than I wanted, but at the last second, I thought that if I picked up a younger woman there would be a greater chance that someone would be looking for her. I needed to find someone that had been on the streets for a long time and had been forgotten by her loved ones.

I quickly decided that she would be the one. I approached the woman and told her that I was here to help her and all she needed was to come with me. She bluntly refused my offering. I told her that I had some warm blankets and hot food. She still refused my offering. I told her that I also had booze for her and all she needed to do was to follow me. I left her and walked slowly away. She didn't follow me so I knew I had struck out with her. I am used to getting what I hunt, but this was new territory for me. I gave up on this individual hunt because I did not want to create more suspicion. I had one specimen for the night and I didn't want to push my luck.

As I made my way back to the car, I noticed a woman sitting in a dark alley between two abandoned buildings. I approached her and introduced myself under a fictitious name. She was another older woman, or so it seemed to me at the time. It was dark and the lighting was not good. She was rude and feisty, as most of them are, and I told her that I needed to speak with her. She was similar in age to the previous woman that had no interest in coming with me to my car. She was dirty and seemed to be one of the veterans of the street. I had the syringe in my pocket, which I quickly put in my hand. I was ready to use the syringe at a moment's notice.

I bent down toward her and as quickly as I could, forced the needle into her upper arm. I quickly placed my left hand over her mouth to muffle any sound that she was might make. She was quickly out and fell over on the hard and dirty cement ground of the alley. I reached down and attempted to pick her up. She was heavy, but I didn't have far to walk to my car. I then noticed there were two other bums sitting in the alley. At the time, I didn't know how much they saw or what they were going to do, and I was worried they would either come after me or start yelling and causing a scene. I quickly told the bums that I knew this woman, she needed help, and I was going to take her to the hospital. As I was walking to my car, the lady I had attempted to capture came walking behind me. She looked at me with these crazed and glossy eyes. She was noticeably confused as to what was happening around her. I quickly told her the same story as I told the two bums in the alley. From what I sensed from them, they knew her and I thought I was going to be caught. I was prepared to just leave the body and quickly get into my car and get away, but I sensed they thought I was trying to help her. I told the lady to wait there on the street. I again told her that she had collapsed and I was afraid for her life. It looked as if the lady understood what I was saying and seemed to be very concerned. I opened the side door of my car and placed the drugged lady's body inside. As I closed the door of the car, I told the lady that was standing on the side of the street that I would take her to the local hospital and she would be fine. Meanwhile, the two other bums went on about their business.

I quickly got into my car then closed and locked the door. I looked around to see if others were around. To my pleasant surprise, no one was around except the three bums. I started up the car and got out of the area and headed home. My heart was beating so fast and I could feel the adrenaline just rushing through my body at a rate that I hadn't felt in years. I felt so alive. All my senses were on high alert. I could hear the heartbeat of the woman sleeping in the passenger seat. She reeked of whiskey, body odor and shit. As I drove through the streets, I could even hear some of the bums on the street talking. I sensed everything around me and my mind was on a sensory overload.

I hated the fact that bums were in my car. The woman's smell was disgusting and no telling what the bum in the truck smelled like, but I kept thinking this was all in the name of science. I got home and picked up the disgustingly dirty specimen. I thought to myself that I should have picked up a cleaner person. She was not that heavy, so I didn't have much trouble getting her to the basement cell area. I put her in the left cell and placed the restraint around her neck. The restraint was attached to the chain that was part of the pulley on the wall. I then closed and locked the cell. I looked at the lady while she lay sleeping on the cot and felt very proud of my accomplishment. I did feel a little worried that someone might come looking for these bums, but I felt confident that would not be the case.

I went outside and opened the trunk of my car. I had some trouble getting the male out. I had to pull his feet out first and then I pulled him up by his arms. I placed him over my shoulders and carried the son of a bitch back to the basement. He was heavy and smelled worse than the female bum. As I got to the basement entrance on the side of the house I had to rest again. My heart was beating wildly and my head was racing at a fever pitch. As I caught my breath, I opened the door to the basement and carried the specimen inside. I placed him in the right side of the cell area on a cot, just as I did with the female. I placed the restraint around his neck as he was still out.

I allowed them to have enough chain to move around freely in the cell. I thought about giving them a sponge bath or somehow attempting to clean them both up, but I was very tired from my workout. I thought to myself that I would worry about cleaning them up later; for the time being I needed to deal with the reality of the situation and, of course, deal with Lewis and what he would say when he found them in the cells. I kept a few lights on in the basement and walked upstairs. Lewis's living quarters were in the basement on the other side of the lab area. I was a little surprised that I didn't wake him from his sleep when I was moving the bums into their new home.

It was about four in the morning and everyone in the house was still asleep. I got my shower and retired to the great room. I fixed myself some bourbon on the rocks and relaxed. I had a feeling that in a few hours or so I was going to have a rather interesting discussion with Lewis and Carolyn. What was concerning me the most was my Marci and how I was going to keep all this from her. Knowing what I know of Lewis, he would probably go running to her and tell her about the specimens. On the other hand, I doubted he would because I could turn him into the police with all the evidence that I had on him as well. Lewis had worked closely with me and my father throughout the years. He had no choice. He was drawn so deeply into my family's problems and issues that he couldn't tell anyone without implicating himself. He also wanted fame and fortune, and as much as he hated the thought of killing humans or even animals, he knew I was his best chance at the lofty heights that he envisioned for himself.

As I rested I played a Mozart serenade in my head, and after a few moments I drifted off to sleep for about an hour. When I awoke, I went into the kitchen and fixed myself something to eat. As the morning continued, I decided to play a little Mozart on my violin. My senses were on a high level that morning because I was ready for the encounter with Lewis. Through my playing, I heard Lewis in the basement. Normally a person couldn't hear what was happening in the basement when you're on the first-floor level since the floors were almost as thick as concrete. With my exceptional hearing, I heard him scream and then heard footsteps as he ran up the stairs. I continued my playing, enjoying every moment of the Mozart piece, as well as the Lewis entertainment. Lewis was screaming for me, and when he turned the corner he saw me. He came running toward me, but I continued to play. I even put more pressure on the bow so the sound would be louder to drown out the noise, but of course, it didn't work. As Lewis got about six feet from me, I stopped abruptly, looked at him and smiled. Before I could get anything out of my mouth, Lewis was yelling at me saying, "I told you not to do it. You promised me that you would not do it and I was so fucking stupid to believe you. I believed you… I trusted you. Then you go and do something like this, you crazy, sick, demented fuck."

At this moment, Carolyn came rushing into the room saying, "What is going on here, guys?"

Lewis said, as he looked at Carolyn, "Your prized student here just captured two homeless people and placed them in the basement in Adam's old room. He has them chained up by the neck like animals."

Carolyn was shocked and in total disbelief. I walked over to my violin case and laid my violin down softly. I turned to Lewis and said, "Calm down, Lewis. I take full responsibility for my actions. Oh, and you didn't object to the neck chains on my brother, so it's not like you haven't done something like this before in your life."

Lewis was pacing back and forth, with no idea as to what to say or do next. I sensed his fear, his anger, and some hatred for me. Lewis said, "Garrison, these are human beings. They are not some created unholy animal."

I said, "Lewis, you know that we have to experiment on a live, human subject or two to see what we are dealing with here and to attempt to get some answers."

Carolyn quickly spoke up and said, "You are not going to experiment on humans are you, Garrison?"

I said, "Of course I am, Carolyn, and you and Lewis are going to help me. I can make you richer than you could even imagine, and just think how much fame you guys will have in all the history books if we can find the secret to life or the secret to being as good as god when it comes to creation."

Carolyn said, "I think you just lost your mind. What are you talking about, Garrison?" She turned to Lewis asking, "What is he talking about, Lewis?"

Lewis stood there looking guilty as sin. He was forced to tell Carolyn everything. He told her about the many secrets that were hidden from her since the very start. He told her more in-depth of what happened on his trip to Germany, about my original birth parents, what he witnessed while he was with my parents, and he told her about our experiments on animals. Carolyn was very upset, and at first, I thought she was going to run out of the house, maybe even to the authorities, but to my surprise she stayed. I know she was in shock and part of her didn't believe a word Lewis was telling her. She was calmer than what I thought she would be during his confession.

I knew Carolyn loved me with all her heart and would do nothing to hurt me. She might not understand some of the things I do, but overall, I knew she was a very forgiving woman. I used this to my advantage. I spoke to Carolyn and said, "I know this disgusts you and I don't blame you for feeling that way, but I need to find the answers, Carolyn, and working on some cockroach or rabbit is not going to enhance what we need to do to make this formula work as intended." Carolyn nodded as she seemed to understand what I was saying but didn't want to totally comprehend my message. I sensed something about Carolyn, like she had something buried inside of her. I knew she loved me like a mother, but she seemed far too understanding about the situation she was presented with, and I felt that something was not quite right.

I looked at Lewis and said with a straight and serious face, "I know I lied to you, Lewis, but what is done is done. They will awaken sometime this afternoon and I am going to need your help. Are you with me or against me?"

Lewis said, "Damn it, Garrison. Why didn't you just wait? How in the hell did you get them here? Did you have help?"

I said, "No, Lewis. I had no one to help me because I knew you would not be behind me. Like every other time in my life, I had to go alone. I had to walk down the path of the unknown, much like you have had to do over the past ten to fifteen years. Did you have anyone with you when you walked your own path in Germany, Lewis? No, you did not. You went alone, by yourself, with no help from anyone. Look, I need to run some experiments on these specimens. They are going to die on the streets, and you know it as well as I do. There is no hope for these inhabitants and there is no helping them. Although if I can experiment today, maybe I could help natives like these down the road. However, I cannot help humans by experimenting on bugs and little furry animals. I cannot read their minds, I cannot feel what they are feeling, and I cannot understand what they are going through when the process starts. At least with these subjects we have a fighting chance to be able to communicate with them."

"Look, I saw my parents change into something awful, something terrible, something that no one could or would ever imagine. Yes, I know you were there, but they were not your parents. What were you doing with your parents at age nine, huh, Lewis? You know what I was doing at age nine? Do you? I was eating a fucking animal's muscles. I learned to rip the tendons from their live, warm bodies, lap the blood up from those very tendons, and I consumed every inch of the tissue. Then I taught my father to do the same. I saw my brother, who was part animal. I then saw him kill my father. I saw my mother take a knife to her neck. I think sometimes people forget the many issues that I have had to deal with in my life."

Lewis stood there, and as he bowed his head he spoke, "You are right, Garrison. You are right. You are one hundred percent correct. I do forget how difficult you have had it over your life. Sometimes I forget. I just take it for granted that you can handle the pressure of what has happened to you during your life. You have not had much of a father-figure in your life."

"Lewis, I consider you, during this point in my life, to be more of a father than Trevor ever was. I love you and I want you to help me attempt to recreate and correct the formula." Lewis was torn between knowing what was right and what he wanted deep in his soul. He was more like me than he wanted to admit. He was absolutely against me capturing these subjects, but he knew I was right and he knew he was not getting anywhere just watching a captured animal mutate in a few days. Lewis knew I was getting to him, and although he didn't want to admit it, he wanted to perfect this formula almost as much as I did.

After more discussions about this subject, it seemed that all three were on the same page, although I knew Carolyn was not comfortable with the situation. I asked Carolyn to take care of the estate, which she agreed to, and I told her that everything would be fine.

I assured her that she was safe and that no mutated animal or human would ever harm her. She was feeling better and calmer about the issue.

Carolyn loved the estate and loved living on the grounds. It was home to her and throughout the years she came to view me as her adopted son. We had many at-length talks when we lived together while I was at Harvard. She was just having trouble getting past the idea that I was a different person than she could ever imagine. She needed to get her head around the truth and was struggling with it, as anyone would under the circumstances.

Lewis didn't like the idea either, but the scientist in him was winning him over to my point of view. His curiosity got the better of him, and his drive for his personal pursuit of fame and fortune was just too over whelming for him to resist. He knew I held his future in my hands. He knew I could make him famous and rich beyond his wildest dreams. He also knew he couldn't discover the secrets to the formula by himself. He needed help, and I knew this to be true. I used this information to convince him that we needed to run these experiments on humans, not just animals.

I went into the kitchen and made my coffee. Lewis and Carolyn talked to each other for a long time then Lewis finally walked up to me and said, "I am not for this, but in the interest of science, let's see what we have downstairs." After I took the last few sips of coffee, we walked downstairs to check on our specimens. I could sense that Lewis was nervous, but at the same time he seemed to be rather eager to see what I had captured for the two of us.

When we entered his lab, he was rather shocked when he saw the two. They hadn't moved from where I left them a few hours ago. As we waited for the bums to wake up, I explained what we ought to do and the steps that I thought would be appropriate. I attempted to outline the experiment orally. The way I figured this experiment, there was no sense in feeding them the formula straight because we already knew what would happen to them, thanks to my parents. What we needed to find out was what kind of changes the human body would go through when a mutant animal bites a human. Since this theory had never been tested or documented to our knowledge, we needed to run this experiment first.

As Lewis sat there listening, I knew I was upsetting him. He had a constant battle inside his soul, not only over the new issues that had developed, but ever since he was introduced to me and my problem at the start. He was in a constant struggle between what he thought was right and what he knew he wanted to discover regarding the formula. After careful thought, he reluctantly agreed with my ideas on the experiments we would conduct on these two subjects. He felt extremely uncomfortable in mutilating a human and putting them through incredible pain, but as I explained to him, I could see no other way around it. We talked about all the possibilities that existed, how we were going to administer the formula, and from what animal. We even talked about how we were going to dispose of the bodies when the experiments were over.

The problem was getting the animal to bite the humans. I wanted a bite from an animal, not drawing blood from the animal and injecting the formula into the human subject. I wanted to annoy the animal and get it so mad the adrenaline would be flowing strong with the formula just before the attack. I didn't want to affect the temperature of the formula in any way artificially. I knew various changes in the temperature affected the formula, thus affected its reaction to the subject being exposed to it. I was also concerned about what kind of animal I should use to bite the human subjects. After going through all our notes taken on the numerous animal subjects that have mutated, we found the least amount of change from the structure of the blood from squirrels, deer, and rabbits. The insects changed the formula more than these animals, which caused another problem for us down the road. If insects changed the formula the most, then what would happen if the insect bit a human? As you can see, there are so many problems associated with these experiments. We wanted to make sure we chose correctly and made sure to think of every possibility within our intellect.

Lewis had no written notes or mental recollection about why the formula mutates differently from some animals to others. He did see the same results that my birth father had when he discovered him during his trip to Germany. Again, the different cell structures affect the formula in different ways. The formula enhances the good and the bad, and the normal or abnormal traits of the subject it has under its control. What I wanted to see was what kind of changes would take place when an infected animal bit a non-infected human, compared to the changes that my adoptive father and mother went through. It was already documented that Adele changed faster than my father, and the reason is because Adam bit my mother. His cell structure was different from mine because his father had the formula in his body, but my mother did not. Adele's DNA basically screwed up the formula and mutated the original structure.

I turned out normal because my biological parents had a pure form of the formula flowing through their blood. Thus, the DNA was changed, but the formula itself, with no other outside influences, changed the structure of the original formula.

I also worried about the type of chemicals flowing through the bum's system, and would a high level of alcohol or drugs in their blood affect the formula's chemical structure?

Lewis and I thought it would be in everyone's best interest to let the subjects 'dry out' and hopefully they were not too removed from the normal state of an average functioning human when they sobered up. The only problem I had with this was how long would it take for them to dry out. I didn't want to make any mistakes on this experiment, so I had to make sure that I was patient and thinking with a clear mind.

While Lewis and I were discussing these options, we heard one of the subjects waking up. It was the male subject. With a slurred, drunk voice, he was yelling and demanded to know where he was, why he was behind bars, and why he had a collar around his neck. We hurried over to the cell area and I spoke, "Good morning. My name is Garrison Winthrop and this is Lewis. We will be taking care of you for the next few weeks."

The bum said in his slurred voice, "What the hell is this, why am I in jail?" He looked around at his surroundings and asked, "Why is there a lab in this jail?"

I said, "Do not worry, no harm will come to you. We are here to help you. We want to make you better."

The bum said, "I don't need any help."

I quickly interrupted him by saying, "Quiet! You need to learn to listen and stop talking. You are going to detox, and that means no drugs or alcohol shall enter your system. If you do not listen or accept these terms, we will force those terms on you. You are an embarrassment to yourself, to your family and to mankind. You are the lowest form of parasite known to man."

Lewis took his hand and gently bumped my arm as if to say I had gone too far. The bum was very upset, "Who in the fuck do you think you are talking to me like that?" Just then I walked over to the pulley and hit the automatic button that pulled the chain in toward the wall. This frightened the bum as he was attempting to get out of the strap around his neck. He was yelling and cussing as the chain moved him closer to the wall. He didn't understand what was happening to him. The chain continued to disappear into the wall until it had about six inches of space between the wall and where the chain was attached to the leather collar. The subject attempted to do anything he could to free himself from the chain; kicking the wall, and jerking and pulling on the chain.

I unlocked the cell door that connected the two separate cells. I had this area, between the two cells, installed just in case the cage door would either not lock or the cell's occupant somehow unlocked the cell door. If that happened, at least we would have another cell door as a safety precaution.

I opened the cell that the subject was in and walked inside. I walked toward him, got into his face and said, "Look. You shut the fuck up and do what we say. The less you say for now, the better off you will be. So, I suggest you dry out, and get your little convulsions over as soon as possible because I don't like to be kept waiting. The faster you dry out, the sooner I can begin your rehabilitation. Yes, you will be rehabilitated whether you like it or not. Do we understand each other?"

The subject spit in my face and yelled, "Fuck you. Release me now. You have no right to lock me up in this jail."

I made a fist and punched him across the face as hard as I could. I then hit him in the stomach as I said, "No... fuck you." I turned, walked out, and locked both cell doors. I then turned to the bum who was coughing hard and said, "Oh, and by the way, you are not in jail. You are a guest in my house, so I would suggest you act like a guest."

As I walked away from the cell I heard the other homeless subject waking up from her drugged nap. I walked over to her and put my finger to my mouth and I said, "Good morning, young lady. I know you are scared, but rest assured that I will not harm you if you remain calm. I picked you up from the streets and placed you here in my house. It is my mission to get you drug and alcohol free. I don't care what you want or what you think about this situation. You will do what I say and when I say it. You are a guest in my home and I would appreciate you respecting my wishes. My name is Garrison Winthrop and this is my good friend and assistant, Lewis. We are going to help you and this gentleman over in the other cell. I placed you in a restraint that is around your neck. It is for our safety, as well as for yours. Do I make myself perfectly clear?"

The woman looked at me and then down at the floor, just as she had done multiple times during my speech. She didn't utter a word. She just moaned and grunted a few times. I attempted to get her to speak, but she didn't respond. She seemed to be rather docile for the time being and didn't seem to be with it mentally, so I left her by herself.

Lewis and I began to plan what we needed to do while the subjects dried out. We found out that the man's name was Johnny, but we failed to get the woman to tell us her name. We ended up calling her Mary. We allowed Johnny and Mary to dry out, which took a long time; over a couple of weeks. Lewis drew their blood every day to check the alcohol and drug level left in their system. Both had some wild days and nights in their detoxification, but after some time we got them to a level where we felt comfortable introducing the formula to them. It seemed that Johnny reacted more violently to the detoxification than Mary. He would shake, hallucinate, and have cold chills that came and went throughout the day. At times, I didn't think they would survive the detoxification process, especially Johnny, but after a week or so they seemed to improve greatly.

CHAPTER 10

Sincere

During this exciting time of my life, Marci continued with her college studies and exceled with the violin lessons I provided to her. To her, the progress she was making in her education and violin training was not to her liking. Marci was the type of person that placed extremely high standards on herself. I didn't want to push her too far because I knew I was extremely advanced. Although Marci was an intelligent woman, she could only retain or perform to a certain level. Her skillset on the violin, like most people, unfortunately had a ceiling, and some people's ceilings are higher than others. Her ceiling was very high, but not on virtuoso level. I told her of this fact in a constructive way and she understood, but it angered her to a point that she practiced even harder to prove to me that she could reach the level of virtuosity needed to be a performing concert violinist.

Marci was an intuitive person. She was excellent at reading people and could guess what others were thinking with a high degree of precision. Over the past few weeks, especially over the last few days, she could sense the tension building in the house. Marci would come over to the house nearly every other day. We were a couple now, for all intents and purposes. We enjoyed our time together, but she was sensing something was wrong during the days I had the homeless people locked up. She constantly asked me what was wrong with everyone. She knew something was going on in the house but couldn't put her finger on what was causing the tension. The stress level between Lewis and I was very high.

Ever since Carolyn knew about the homeless specimens occupying the basement, she had been noticeably upset. She had changed completely since the meeting we had with her. Her demeanor and attitude severely changed toward me and Lewis. She was afraid and confused about the situation.

Carolyn was not a religious person, per se, but she knew the difference between what she thought was right and what was wrong. She was always short-sighted when it came to religion and doing the right thing. To her, what we were doing was unholy and it wasn't right to treat human beings like caged animals. I loved Carolyn and I respected her opinion. We had spent so much time together in the past that I had learned to appreciate her views on issues. I understood where she was coming from, but I also understood that throughout her life she seldom took risks or accepted challenges. The most pleasant fact about Carolyn was that she gave her opinion, but she didn't pass judgment to a point where it changed her views toward an individual. She loved and supported me, and I always used this to my advantage when I dealt with her. She was a sweet woman and she needed me to be in her life, so she tended to overlook certain details that she might not agree with.

All the tension that existed in the house influenced Marci as well. With all the stress and the strain Marci was feeling in the house, she continued asking what was wrong with everyone. I sensed that she knew I was keeping something from her and I knew it hurt. I didn't want anything, especially the truth, to come between and disturb our relationship. Marci knew something was going on because of the way Carolyn acted. This was the tipping point for my Marci because when Carolyn got upset, she knew something big was happening in our lives. Even Marci knew that Carolyn was not one to get upset over just anything. Marci wanted to know what was going on and she deserved to know. I felt that the longer I waited to tell Marci, the harder it would be for me to hang onto our relationship. Losing Marci was not an option for me to even consider.

About a week after I captured the bums, I informed Lewis that I needed to tell Marci all about me. I wanted to tell her everything, including my family's history. Of course, he was upset with me again. I told Lewis that I was tired of having to lie to Marci every time we were together. She was too smart not to notice that I was lying to her, and I was afraid that I was going to lose her. Lewis always looked out for me, but it was more as a manager, not as a friend or a father-figure. He was more like a businessman and the deeper our relationship got through the years, the more I noticed that he ran our relationship as a business.

Lewis's fear was that Marci was going to run off and 'tell the world' about me and our experiments. I understood Lewis's concern, but losing Marci was not an option to me and I was willing to take the chance.

I strongly felt that even if Marci were going to tell the world or the authorities about my situation, no one would believe her. It was my good name and reputation that was up against someone that had no credence or respect from my social world. I could always use the hurt ex-girlfriend as a reason for her outrageous attempts to get back at me, but I sensed Marci wouldn't do that to me or my family. I could sense that she loved me, but also cared for both Lewis and Carolyn.

One day I approached Carolyn with my desire to tell Marci about our family history. Carolyn was totally against me telling her anything. She loved Marci and wanted her safe and thought I would end up hurting Marci in the future. This was a powerful assertion coming from Carolyn, because normally she was always soft spoken and not as opinionated as others in the house. But as I have stated before, Carolyn knew that she was in over her head and that no matter what she said, I was going to do what I wanted. Carolyn wasn't happy that I was going to tell Marci yet knew it was a foregone conclusion. Carolyn had changed over the past few days and grew more suspicious of me by the day.

Of course, I had no intention whatsoever in hurting my love. Marci is the crown jewel of my life and I would do nothing that would cause harm to befall her. Down deep, I believe Carolyn knew this, but she had witnessed what had happened to my mother, my father and to Adam. Then she found out about the homeless in our basement, making her more nervous than ever before. Her fear was understandable from my point of view.

After some agonizing days of deep and well-planned thoughts on this issue, I told Lewis and Carolyn that I was going to tell Marci the next time I saw her. Neither were happy, but they knew I would eventually tell my love. Carolyn knew from the start that I was going to tell Marci everything. Carolyn was very fond of Marci and felt that it was her place to protect her. They had bonded the first time they met.

The last time Carolyn saw Marci, I could sense that she wanted to protect my love from me, which I had anticipated, but nonetheless it made me angry. I knew the next time Carolyn saw Marci, she was going to back her into a corner and tell her to leave me before I could tell her the truth. I knew it, and I could sense it.

A few days went by and everyone knew that Marci was coming over to the house. We were going to play the violin together and I was going to show her some other bow techniques. I could sense Carolyn was more nervous than usual, and she wouldn't look at me all morning. I knew that today was going to be the day Carolyn was going to say something to my love.

I waited upstairs until I heard Marci's car pull up the driveway. I watched from one of the bedroom windows as she got out of the car. I was nervous because the vision I saw getting out of the car was the person in this world that I loved the most. I could not ever lose her. She was my world and reason for living. My heart ached for her like no other. I was in love and had been for a while. I was obsessed with her and I could not let anyone come between us. As I stood by the window, I watched her get her violin and bow out of the trunk. When she started to walk up to the front door, I went to the top of the stairwell. I made sure that I was not seen. Carolyn half ran to the door, then opened it and let my lady inside.

Carolyn whispered to Marci, "I need to talk to you."

In a bewildered state, Marci asked, "What's wrong?"

They moved to the great room. I hurried down the steps, being careful not to be heard or seen. Carolyn said in a nervously deep, whispery voice, "You need to leave him. It is not safe here. He is not safe to be with."

At this time my ire was up and I couldn't believe she was telling this to the face of the one that I loved. Marci said, "What! What are you taking about? Are you talking about Garrison? What happen?"

Carolyn said, "I love Garrison very much, but I don't want to see you hurt. He is dangerous, and what he is planning on doing is just... well, it's a terrible thing."

Marci said, "What are you talking about? What terrible thing are you talking about?"

Carolyn said, "Just leave and don't look back. Don't ask any questions. Just go while you have the chance."

Marci said, "Carolyn, you are freaking me out. What is going on here?"

As I stood there hearing this, I was feeling extreme anger. I was filled with fear that I could potentially lose Marci, and had to stop this from happening. I just could not take this anymore so I hurried down the steps and entered the room. I made sure my step was a heavy one when I made my entrance. As I bullied my way inside the room, the two ladies quickly stopped talking and looked at me with a surprised look. I noticed Marci's face turned from surprise to concern as soon as she noticed it was me in the room. My heart sank at that moment because for the first time, I felt there was a chance that she might leave me if I didn't play out this situation correctly. It was my turn to perform. Now was the time to tell my love everything.

My eyes left Marci, and as I glanced over to Carolyn our eyes met. I knew that in her heart she thought she was doing the correct thing by trying to protect my Marci. I even felt some pride in Carolyn's loyalty toward her, but at the same time I felt great betrayal. After everything we had been through, she was picking the safety of a stranger over my happiness.

As I looked at Carolyn I smiled and said, "So, what is going on in here? Why are you asking my girlfriend to leave me, Carolyn?" Carolyn was nervous and her hands began to shake. She quickly looked away. I said rather bluntly, "Carolyn, I love you, but I don't understand why you would do such a thing to me and my relationship with Marci." As Carolyn stood there, speechless, I continued, "Carolyn. Why? What is wrong?" Carolyn's glossed over and scared eyes rose to look toward me. She tried to focus on the next object that her eyes saw, making sure not to look at me or Marci.

She then spoke, "Garrison, you know what is wrong. I am just trying to protect her from... you know."

I said, "From me? Am I really that terrible of a person that you feel you have to go behind my back and tell the only true love of my life that it would be wise to leave me?" Just as I spoke those words, Marci looked at me with a heavy stare, and a smile developed on her beautiful face. She was lost in the moment. She didn't have a care in the world for one short moment. I sensed her heart rate increase and her state of happiness increased greatly.

Marci looked at me and said, "Garrison. Do you love me? I mean, really love me? Am I really the love of your life?"

Carolyn quickly looked at Marci and said, "Honey, don't..."

I interrupted and said, "Yes, Marci. I love you and you are the love of my life. However, you have a decision to make, my dear, because I need to tell you a few things about me and my world. All I ask of you is to hear me out, and after I am finished to please understand my position, then make your decision on whether you want to stay with me or go. It will be your decision and I will respect your wishes either way."

Marci said, "Sure, Garrison, I will listen to you. What is going on here... I am so confused right now."

We made our way to the couch in the great room. I gently extended my arm as I pointed toward the couch for my love to rest her lovely body on. As Marci moved toward the couch, I quickly caught her scent. I could smell the body wash she used that morning, I could smell the breakfast lingering on her clothes and breath. As she glided across the floor, she sat her lovely figure down on the most fortunate couch in the world. I then made my way to sit next to her, making sure I gave her enough space to make her feel as comfortable as possible.

Meanwhile, Carolyn sat in a chair away from us. Her heavy steps and cheap perfume disturbed my sensory pleasure of enjoying my Marci's movements and scent. She sat down in her chair as if she was controlled by destiny, knowing full well that this moment was going to display itself in front of her. I quickly gathered my thoughts as I gazed into my Marci's eyes, and I began to speak.

"Marci, I have a lot to tell you. Some of what I am about to say will shock you. Some of it you will not believe. At the risk of losing you, I regret that I need to tell you the facts and the truth about me personally, as well as my family's history. I regret not telling you sooner because I didn't want to scare you off and lose you forever. I also regret not telling you my secrets from the beginning of our relationship, but what I am about to tell you one cannot just volunteer this type of information at the beginning of a relationship. First, I have told you my family history and how we have a rather large sum of financial resources. I told you that I am adopted and that my parents died at a very young age. What I have not told you will be very disturbing, but first I want to tell you how I feel about you and our relationship."

"When I awaken in the morning, my conscious thoughts are dominated by you and your existence. My world is much better because you are part of my life. I go through the days experiencing both the happiness and sadness that life offers. My soul sometimes cries or laughs, and at times it is balanced between those two emotional states. I have lived for only a short time, but I have sensed an emptiness that has existed in my soul. I was lonely and sad, but that moment when my eyes were first blessed when I saw you, I knew from that moment on what I was missing. Since then, I have looked for that missing piece that links my old world to a new and better world. The strange thing is, at that moment I didn't know what I needed in my world. It took years for me to discover what I was missing, what I needed, what I longed for. What I desperately craved then, and most certainly crave now, is you. You have somehow captivated my heart long before my mind could even process what my heart already understood. You have always been what I sought after, what I needed. For you, my love, make me complete."

"Forever, that is a long time, a very long time to be alone. I cannot live my life without you in it. This love that has been created from not only my imagination, but from our brief encounters throughout time, is as much of a passion as any feeling I have ever had in my short life. A love that, for me, is pure and untarnished."

"In my dream world, we smile and laugh together, all for one reason – not to be alone and unloved. For when I am with you, I am at peace mentally and physically. I am only truly happy when I am with you. When we are apart, my heart and soul aches. When you are with me, I feel healthy and complete. Throughout my days, when I am thinking of you, it is like thinking of perfection, a perfection that makes god envious of his creation. He is upset that his creation developed through the years and has made itself better than even he could have imagined. For in my thoughts and in my heart, I have found the most special love, for my perfect mate. This perfect love is only shared with you."

"When I am not with you during the day, my mind forces me to fantasize about you. My mind is in my own private, lonely world, punishing me every minute of my life by reminding me of your beauty. I go throughout the day experiencing both happiness and sadness. I sometimes cry, sometimes laugh, and sometimes I am balanced between those two emotions. When I close my eyes, I see you and you are in love with me. For only on those special moments throughout my day when I think of you and only you, that is when I am truly happy. For our pure love is happiness, a happiness we share together only in our hearts. When I open my eyes, your vision vanishes before me, but the love I have for you stays within my faithful and timeless heart. My love for you remains pure and untarnished."

"I believe we must experience art, music, nature and all that life has to offer to gain insight to our love for others. We constantly build on all the experiences we go through in life to find love and understand its many meanings. Through our time together, I have witnessed your passion for the violin, for knowledge and for opera. You, my love, have demonstrated this in my presence. We have shared so much in such a short time together."

Marci was stunned and began to cry. She was very happy that I had expressed my love for her because she had always felt the same for me. She said, "Oh, Garrison, I love you too. I love you so much. When I saw you on stage with the Louisville Orchestra, I fell in love with you and have been in love with you since that day. I have followed your career and your life in exact detail. In the beginning, it was like puppy love. I had a major crush on you, but then it soon developed into something more powerful. I admired your playing skills and your intelligence, and I have fantasized being with you since day one."

I sat there and smiled as I looked from her beautiful blue eyes to the floor that her feet rested upon. I hated the upcoming moment of what I was about to say, but I needed to say it or I would lose my Marci forever. I needed to be honest with her and it was time for no more covering the facts with lies or mistruths.

I said to Marci, "So now I need to tell you a darker side of my life. From a very young age, I knew I was different. So different, in fact, that I had to be taken out of regular schools. I could understand and comprehend better than others, so much so that my intellect was tested at an off-the-charts genius level. I picked up the violin at a young age, and in less than a year I was playing it perfectly. I have uncanny hand and eye coordination. With little practice, I could perfect a golf swing, throwing a rock at a target, shooting a gun, and playing the piano; you name it, I could perfect it without much trouble at all."

"Throughout my life I noticed that I saw, smelled, and heard things that others could not. My senses were so keen that I was completely aware of my entire surroundings. I couldn't understand why others didn't possess the same level of experiences I was experiencing. I came to find out through Lewis's research that I have this formula, for the lack of a better word, trapped inside my blood. This formula is about as rare of a commodity as you could find in this world. Because of this formula and the way it reacts with my system, it allows me to experience events and be able to demonstrate actions that very few have been able or are able to perform. I believe this formula is the secret to everlasting life, my love. I know it is hard to believe, but you must believe me. Marci, there is so much you need to know about this formula and my way of life. I know that you may never believe me, but my love, I will never die. I will never physically die or physically grow old, according to Lewis's research. I know you don't believe me, but that is the truth. I know this is a lot for you to take in, but do you have any questions so far?"

Marci sat there looking at me in a strange way. She was mesmerized by what I had said. I was expecting her to burst out laughing in disbelief. Finally, she spoke. "So, you mean to tell me that you will never die or age?" She then smiled at me as she quickly cocked her head to the side and said, "That is impossible, Garrison."

I said, "I know it is difficult to totally comprehend. At first, I didn't believe it myself. But if you have been privy to the things I have witnessed, you would believe what I am telling you."

Marci said, "I just don't understand, Garrison. You are not making any sense."

I continued by saying, "Well, there has been some incredible developments that have happened to me in my life, and there have been a few drawbacks as well. I have so many difficult and hard to explain situations to tell you about, I just don't know where to begin. See, Marci, my birth parents are still alive. In fact, they are quite old, over a century old. Lewis met them when he was in Germany conducting his research years ago. I am one of their offspring. They left me in the woods to die, but I was found by the local authorities. I was taken to the local orphanage where my parents, Trevor and Adelle, adopted me when I was just a few months old. They brought me back to America, but the story does not end there."

I paused to make sure everything I had told Marci up and to this point had soaked in, and by the look on her face, I think it had at least surprised her. She just sat there looking at me without blinking for a long period of time. I continued my story. "There are many drawbacks for me that I have to live with regarding this formula. Not only do I have to life forever and never age, but the heightened level of my senses is very difficult for me to live with at times. I hear, see, smell, and taste everything in my environment, which many times is very unpleasant. The other area in my life is very strange and you will find greatly disturbing. I hate to tell you this in fear of frightening you off, but I must be truthful. I am not asking you to understand or accept what I am about to tell you. I just ask you not to run from me, but to at least try to understand my rather unusual endeavor."

Marci looked very concerned and said, "You are scaring me, Garrison."

I said to her, "I am sorry, I don't mean to scare you, but I have to tell you this." I paused for a few seconds as I took a deep breath and said, "One of the greatest desires in my life is my rather strange eating habits. You notice that I don't eat much, right?"

Marci said, "You don't eat much. Are you okay?"

I said, "Yes, but my diet is rather abnormal. You see, most of my life I have eaten meat, raw meat, live... raw... meat."

Marci looked at me with a puzzled and shocked look on her face and said, "So, you eat live, raw meat? What do you mean?"

I said, "I prefer to trap wild animals. I usually take them back to the house in the basement and I bite into the live animal. I find the muscles and tendons of the animal and devour them as some child would attack their birthday cake. I have been doing this over the last decade, half of my life. Now, I am not a cannibal or anything like that, I just prefer to eat live, raw animal meat, no human meat of any kind. It is one of the side effects, at least it is for me, to the formula."

Marci sat there and was astonished by what I was telling her. She didn't believe me; in fact, she nervously laughed at my story. She playfully said, "Okay, Mr. animal eater, why don't you prove this to me right now, if you care to demonstrate."

I looked at her and smiled. I said, "Do you really want a demonstration, Marci?"

Marci looked at me with the beautiful smile she always had on her face and said in a devilish and playful way, "Yes sir, Mr. Garrison Seawick, make me believe that what you say is true. Prove to me by action and not word," then laughed. She didn't believe me. My angel did not believe what I was telling her. I thought to myself, *What should I do now?* Carolyn was sitting in the chair across from us, not believing what she was seeing. I was now more scared than I was when I started this conversation. My love thinks I am making this story up. I knew that I could not back down now and had to prove what I was telling her was the truth.

I smiled and took her hand gently, and together we walked outside toward the forest. Carolyn was far back but following us. I knew she couldn't believe that I was going through with a demonstration. She stood back and just waited to see what I was going to do. I excused myself from Marci and went and got a golf club, a pitching wedge, and a small basket of golf balls. I walked back to the ladies and placed the balls down along side of me. I told them that I was going to hit the ball and it would hit my brother's tombstone about 130 yards away. I placed the end of the club down by the ball, pointing my feet toward the target. I swung the club about three quarters of the way back then brought the club toward the ball. When the club met the ball, a most beautiful sound was produced as the club head went through the grass and picked the ball up from the earth. As I finished my follow through, I watched the ball take to the air.

I quickly moved my eyes to my Marci. I saw her lovely eyes staying glued to the ball flying through the air. As the ball descended, it hit the side of Adam's tombstone. I repeated the same procedure and produced the same results. The second ball hit right on top of the tombstone and bounced high into the air, landing well past the grave marker.

I then chipped a ball out about one hundred yards. I said that I would place five other shots around that ball in a five-foot circle. After I took my shots, all but one made it within five feet from the original target. The stray landed about eight feet from the target. Marci was quite impressed. I gathered the remaining balls and pointed to targets around the back of the estate. I threw a golf ball to those predetermined targets. One was a tree, one was a water fountain, and the other was a large sunflower in full bloom. I hit all three of my targets, and after each successful hit, I smiled at my lovely Marci. She looked at me every time and smiled back at me. She was enjoying the demonstration.

We walked toward and entered the front of the wooded area of the estate. I picked up a small rock that I found lying on the ground. I told Marci I was going to hit the branch over in the distance. I pointed to the branch and threw the rock as hard as I could. It hit squarely on the object of which I was aiming. I then picked up another rock and pointed to another branch and hit that branch without fail. I continued with this minute demonstration six additional times, and I only missed once and that was by an inch. Marci was not only impressed but was laughing hard after every successful hit. She was having fun watching this amazing display of hand-eye coordination.

I had her stand in one spot then walked a good 100 yards from where she was standing. I told her to gently whisper something to herself with her back turned toward me. She was still enjoying the demonstrations and didn't know what to expect from this one. She continued to laugh and roll her eyes, and after a few moments she softly spoke the words, "You are out of your mind, my love. I cannot believe you hit those branches. That was crazy." I then repeated the words back to her. As I did, she quickly turned and looked at me, but this time she was not laughing or smiling.

I told her to say anything, anything at all, even if it didn't make sense. She turned and started to say a bunch of random words. As she spoke them I repeated them back to her as fast as she could say them. After ten or so words, she abruptly stopped and looked back at me with a stern but surprised look on her face. Now her laughs were completely mooted.

I said, "Do you see that rock by your left foot?' Marci looked down and didn't say a word. I told her to pick up the rock and throw it at me. She didn't want to at first. I insisted, so with unwilling hands, she bent down and took the small marble-shaped rock and threw it at me as I was walking toward her. The rock was about seven feet to my right so I ran to the spot where the rock was headed, reached out my hand and caught it. I told her to throw another rock and she did, this time the rock was off to my left. I caught the rock in midair.

Marci said with a laugh, "There is no way you caught those rocks." I walked up to her with my hands out as I showed her the rocks. She was shocked and very surprised. She was not laughing anymore and her smile quickly changed to astonishment. She kept asking me how I could hear what she was saying from such a far distance and how I could catch such a small object thrown to me from such a long distance. She was now slowly starting to believe what I had told her. My senses were on fire during these small demonstrations, and I loved the fact that I impressed her. For the first time in my life, I felt like a real man impressing a young girl. Playing a musical instrument or having great knowledge of boring subject matters like history, math or science does not truly impress women, at least that is what I thought at the time.

We walked deeper into the forest and I visited one of the traps and found a small visitor. It was a small, gray fox whose population had been increasing over the past year. Marci stood there and didn't move a muscle as I opened the cage and reached inside. After a few bites and scratches, I showed the fox to Marci after getting control of both the neck and back legs. I could sense my Marci was very frightened. I looked at her and said, "I will not continue my demonstration because I sense great fear in your soul." Marci then reached out and placed her hand on my arm. This was very surprising to me because I sensed so much fear inside her. I could smell the terror oozing from her body, but she was not running from her fears. This impressed me so much at that moment that I knew forever more that she was mine. I said, "Are you sure you want to witness this because I don't want to lose you from the shock and likely disgust from my actions."

Marci said, "I asked for a demonstration, so please don't disappoint me. Show me what you normally do to these animals."

I had to admit, I was in great lust at that moment. I could have ravished her right there in the forest if she would have allowed me to act upon my most basic animalistic sexual desires. I swear, even to this day, that if it were not for Carolyn looking down at us, I believe she would have allowed me to have my way with her at that very moment. As she was saying these words, she looked down at my cock inside my pants then looked back up at me as she gently moved her shoulders back and forth. Her large breasts swayed from side to side with the motion of her shoulders, but there was a slight delay when they swung with her body movements. Marci always wore loose fitting bras that made this action possible.

Without notice, I sank my teeth into the middle of the fox. It let out a loud scream as my sharp teeth entered its back. After several bites, I smelled the increasing fear from the fox and from my Marci. When the fox expired, I took my fingers and roughly ripped through the meat as I separated one long piece of strong muscle from the fox. I ate part of the muscle, trying to be as clean as possible. Marci's breath was extremely heavy. I noticed her breasts moving up and down. Without any hesitation, she unexpectedly moved her hands up and down on her hips and upper thighs.

I calmly threw the dead fox's body away from me. I wiped my bloody mouth with my red stained hands. I told her that this was my daily habit. "I love the fear the animal gives off and the dominate feelings that races through my system. I feel like a god when I bite into my capture, and at that moment where life turns into death, that very moment is what I desire the most."

Marci was in total lust as she looked at me with a desire that only an animal has toward its unsuspecting pray. She said to me, "I desire something, Garrison." She walked closer to me as I heard Carolyn say in the far distance, "Stop, Marci, stop." Marci looked at me with lust-filled eyes as she went to kiss me. I stopped her because I didn't want to give her any diseases from the animal that I just killed. She slowly bent down, grabbed my manhood, and squeezed it roughly. Carolyn turned away quickly and started to run toward the house.

Marci's smile widened as she started to rub her hand on my cock hidden under my clothing. She unzipped my pants and pulled them down around my ankles. She released my manhood from my briefs and placed it inside her mouth. After several moments of this intense pleasure, she released her hold on me. She brushed her hair toward her back as she leaned back and placed her back on the cold ground in front of me. She was wearing a floral button-down shirt with a solid white skirt.

Without taking her eyes off me, she raised her skirt up and slowly removed her panties. She allowed me to ogle her moist vagina. She slowly unbuttoned her blouse and released her breasts from her bra. There I saw the most perfect, erect nipples I had ever seen in my life. This most sexy and beautiful creature said, "I want you, Garrison, I have always wanted you. Just fuck me hard and long."

I bent down and raised her hips to my mouth, with her assistance. I orally pleasured her with my long tongue. I first began to slowly move it along the length of her pussy, darting my tongue in and out of her hole. As I licked every ounce of the juices that flowed out of her cunt, I guided my eager tongue over her asshole. The texture from her soft, pink pussy lips to the less smooth skin was exhilarating. I moved my body up toward her, and as my fingers discovered her pussy, I began to softly play with her. As she became more wet, I inserted two fingers inside her. After several pleads from her, I placed three of my thick fingers inside of her. I moved my fingers in and out of her, slowly at first, but after several minutes I had to increase my rhythm. I whispered in her ear the entire time how much I loved her and how I was going to fuck her. This further ignited her sexual desires.

I slowly got to my knees and seductively positioned her hips and raised her legs. I wanted her to see my magnificent length at full erection. My cock was pulsating as I saw what I was about to enter. The dripping wet and warm pussy was begging for me. I quickly placed the head of my cock on her pussy lips. I moved myself up and down, mixing my precum with her vaginal juices. I reached down and inserted my thumb inside her warm hole. I raised her clit up as I slid the full length of my cock inside of her. Each inch that went deeper caused a higher octave of moans coming from deep inside the soul of my Marci. I slowly massaged her clit as I went deeper. When I couldn't go any deeper, I placed my wet thumb on her lips. Without hesitation, she sucked on it as hard as she could.

I wanted her to never forget this moment, so I made sure each stroke was only for her extreme pleasure. I smelled her sexual perfume as I listened to her make beautiful music after each thrusting movement I made. I fought to hold back, but after thirty minutes or so of a fantastic sexual experience, I needed to have release. I pulled out and released my built-up fluids. I shot my first load onto her large, sweaty breasts. The second load hit underneath her chin while the remaining smaller loads fell upon her muscular stomach. Marci entertained herself during my performance. As I finished my orgasm, she was just starting hers. After several moans, her body tensed up and she squirted her juices on me, from my chest all the way down to my cock. When we were finished, I collapsed alongside my girl. We held hands as we attempted to catch our breath and recover.

After several moments of cuddling, we finally got our clothes on. Marci said, "I love the way my nipples feel as the wind blows on them."

I said, "I apologize for this location being our first time as lovers, but this feeling just came over me and I had to have you at that moment."

Marci said, "That just means we are meant for each other. Anyway, I don't care. I would make love to you anywhere and at any time."

In that moment, I knew she would never leave me, no matter what I would do to any animal or human. We went back to the house. Carolyn and Lewis were sitting in the great room waiting for us. They had disgusted expressions on their faces. I sat down with my Marci and continued my story. I told Marci what happened to my parents and their transformations. I also told her about my brother, Adam, but I used the more condensed version of how I tortured him. Marci was glued to everything I was saying to her. I reiterated about my original birth parents and how they were still in Germany, but I included now how evil my birth father was, or still is for that matter.

Lewis joined in the conversation and told her about my father's many experiments on animals and humans he had conducted through the years. He talked about our own experiments on animals from the forest area.

Marci made it clear to us that she was interested in seeing the transformations for herself. Instead of her being disgusted or totally turned off by this, she was rather intrigued with what she was hearing. Lewis and I went into detail about the transformations of the different species of animals that we had been experimenting on over the past year or so. I was astonished that Marci was not squeamish over the information we gave her. She was generally excited about the news she was hearing. Although I think at the time, not all information was being processed completely. I think she was still in a state of shock, not only from the family news, but from our lovemaking that was still lingering as an afterglow in her innermost thoughts.

I told my love about how the formula made me into what I am today. I told her about my senses, the hand-eye coordination, and the fact that I had never been sick in my life. I shared with her that in the future I wanted to recreate and then mass-produce the formula. I wanted to market this product for the betterment of man and womankind, not to mention the possible financial benefits of such a discovery.

Lewis and I continued our conversation on the problems with this kind of thinking. We told her how the formula changes both man and animal physically, as well as mentally. We told her that the changes were not pleasant either to experience or to accept when the transformation was complete.

I told Marci everything, I held nothing back. I was afraid of losing her if she caught me in a lie. I sensed she was not totally against what we were telling her and seemed to be generally interested. I was rather amazed because even though she has had a difficult life, she was a woman that was gentle, soft, and caring. Her personality was of such a nature that the very mention of these types of facts would totally disgust and make her leave me on the spot. I was hoping within that as I pushed more information in her face, I would not push her away permanently. My situation was such that I felt if I would piece-meal the information bit by bit over weeks or months, it would have a negative effect on the way she viewed me. I wanted to leave nothing out, to display everything to her so she could pass judgment on me instantly, not have it change throughout the following weeks or months.

Imagine if your mate was hiding something from you that was significant, like they were having an extramarital affair. I think it would be better for them to tell you everything at the start, like how many and how often they cheated rather than to tell you little by little. I believe if you withhold any part of the truth, you are lying to the person you are expressing your thoughts to. I think it's wrong to hold back any material information that could tear down trust that is established at the beginning of any relationship.

I reluctantly told Marci that I currently had two homeless inhabitants locked in large cells in the basement. She was very concerned over this at first, but I explained that they would end up dying anyway and that I needed them. We needed to experiment on them to see what would happen when a mutated animal bit a normal human. These types of experiments had never been conducted in any area of science.

Lewis and I attempted to answer all Marci's questions. Much to our surprise, the questions were more in the form of trying to learn about our end results instead of being in total disgust or trying to talk us out of these experiments. In fact, not once did Marci say anything negative or judgmental about our experiments or studies. The only negative remark was basically saying she could not believe we are attempting such a fate.

After our discussion, we headed toward the basement. Carolyn stayed upstairs because the very idea of what we were doing repulsed her and made her sick to her stomach. Carolyn knew, as I did, that Marci was not leaving anytime soon. Carolyn lost this battle and she knew it was in her best interest to fade away from the idea of pushing Marci away from me as quickly as possible.

We took Marci into the basement and introduced her to the lab more closely. Next to the lab Marci saw the human specimens in their individual cells. The specimens bothered Marci at first, but I could sense that she was in total understanding as to what we were doing, she just had to come to grips with the situation. The specimens were pleading with her to release and help them. Johnny was the only one of the two that made sense. Mary just mumbled and was nearly screaming. I had to ask them rather harshly to be quiet because all their noise was upsetting Marci.

Lewis pulled up some research footage on the computer and played back some of the tapes that were made of my parents. He showed her their rather quick transformation in a time-lapse sequence on the computer screen. Marci seemed to be very upset when she first viewed the footage, but she began to grow used to the different stages of the transformation. This was a lot for anyone to fully accept and comprehend. I asked her repeatedly if she was tolerant of the state of affairs and she told me that she was fine with the situation.

We then showed her our videotapes of the different kinds of animals we had experimented on, and that seemed to really interest her. We even showed her some live subjects and she just laughed and thought it was incredible to see what this formula could do. What was really freaking her out most was that all these changes were caused by a certain cell structure that I possess in my blood. Marci thought that was rather amazing and she kept looking at me in admiration. Marci said that she knew something was different about me, but in a good way. She just couldn't put her finger on it as to how I could be so intelligent and be such a violin and piano virtuoso in such a short time. She told me she always wanted to have things come easily to her like it did for me. Ever since I told Marci the truth, her attitude toward me was more of a worship mode than a judgmental one.

While we showed Marci all our little secrets, we impressed upon her that we needed for this to remain a secret. Marci was very humbled that we trusted her enough with these secrets. I could sense that she was not going to tell anyone about these experiments because, like she said repeatedly, who was going to believe her anyway? Marci seemed to understand why I kept all this a secret from her. Much to my delight, she didn't hold any of what we told or showed her against me. In fact, I could sense she wanted to be a part of this operation.

At the end of the day, I kissed my love goodbye and she went home. I told her that our sexual encounter was the greatest pleasure I had ever experienced in my life. That was one hundred percent true. I remember turning to Lewis who looked at me and shrugged his shoulders as if to say, *Well, what is done is done.*

I called Marci the next morning and she acted as if nothing happened the previous day, she was the same Marci. Her attitude, in fact, was even better toward me than before. I kept questioning her about what we talked about and she was rather convincing when she told me that our secret was safe with her.

The next few days Marci called me but didn't come back to the house. I was very stressed out. I thought she would be fine with the situation that she found herself in, but you always have doubts. From all that I gathered and what she told me, the experiments, my past and my current situation did not phase her one bit. I had some concern that she wouldn't show up again after she last left, but she was so wrapped up with school and her course study that she just didn't have the time. She assured me that was her reason for not showing up over the past few days. I had to admit that I was worried that I might have scared her off.

The next time I saw Marci she acted like it was no big deal to her. In fact, many times she asked if she could help us with our experiments in the future. I felt as if I was living in a fantasy world. She told me that she loved me so much and that she never wanted to lose me. She did have some concern that she might get hurt by one of the subjects, but I assured her that if she took precautions and as long as I was there to protect her, nothing would happen.

A few weeks went by and our relationship got stronger by the day. Marci was doing well with her college studies, but she remained in constant frustration regarding her struggles to grasp school as quickly as she would like. Many times she got extremely upset with her violin practices, especially when she made mistakes that she thought she shouldn't have made at this juncture of her career. She desperately wanted to be a part of the Louisville Orchestra, but with her current talent level, she was not going to achieve her goal.

On top of this, having me as her significant other didn't help the situation. She continued to marvel at my ability to play with such ease and was astonished with the fact that I never made mistakes. I told her that I had practiced for many years to achieve the playing level I was at and reminded her that I was aided by the formula. This did not satisfy her because she had been playing the violin a lot longer than I had and she has had more lessons than I had ever had. This bothered her greatly. She was not jealous of me, she was just envious of my talents and wished that she possessed the same greatness. One day she was so frustrated that she wanted to stop playing all together. She wanted to give up the violin. She was at a point where the more she tried to play perfectly, the more she struggled.

Marci never held my perfection against me, but she always overly admired it. She admired me to a point where she openly worshiped me, which bothered me to no end. I told her on countless occasions that she could not compare herself to me. No one can compare themselves to me. I couldn't help it, the formula in my blood made me superior at every endeavor I attempted, I was not normal. Marci was the normal person in our relationship. I always encouraged her to have self-confidence and gave her all the support I could possibly give, but she allowed her personal loathing of the fact that she was not going to be perfect to stand in her way of success. I could never rid this imperfection from her constitution. I always attempted to keep her from comparing herself to me. That was so unfair; neither she nor anyone could compare to my skills or my knowledge, other than maybe my parents. I had met some people that were very brilliant and came close to my intellect on a few subject matters, but they seemed to struggle with the vast array of knowledge that I possess. Marci is very smart, but a genius she was not, and that was okay with me, but down deep this was not acceptable for my love.

We had many emotional talks during our courtship, but one of the most emotional talks I remember as if it were yesterday. We started out talking about god and she was blaming god for not blessing her with great skills to master the very instrument she so loved or a great mind for certain subject matters that drew her interest. All she wanted to do was play the violin at its highest level, but when she played, as soon as she would reach a certain point, her concentration would break and she would miscalculate a note here or there. Most people would never catch the miss, but in her mind, everyone heard it and that mistake would anger her to her wits end.

Marci once said to me, "Garrison, I envy you so much. I wish I could play like you and be able to think and reason as you can. Ever since I first saw you, I have admired you. Your presence was god-like the first night I saw you on stage. It was like god sent his private angel down from the heavens. There are limited people on this earth that I admire or respect. My parents left me when I was a baby and no one wanted me during my younger days. No one wanted me as a baby or as a child. I was always left behind. To this day I don't understand why I was never wanted.

Then I saw you on that stage, and I followed your different career paths in the paper and on the Internet. Then, like a miracle, you came after me. You approached me first and you never left me. You care about my feelings and my well-being. This is something I am not used to. To me, you are someone god sent down from the heavens to help people. They stay on this earth to do their work, to help their fellow man. God chose certain people to be the best at something that is good for mankind, in general. These people are expected to have many accomplishments throughout their lives. They accomplish many feats that bring glory, honor, and recognition to themselves, for being able to create or make something from nothing. Some even control their creations for a short period of time while they are still alive. This is what god does with his creations. But you, my dear Garrison, are the rare creature that defies even god. You laugh at his threats when others cower. Your heart, your mind, and your soul are his equal. You are his main competition."

"Garrison, you are a man confused by your genius, as most geniuses are troubled by their gifts from god. God gave you a talent that you developed at such a high level. In fact, you were creating and developing such beautiful music that even god had to be envious. And your intellect is unlike anything this world has ever seen. Your command over your senses is nothing short of astonishing. What god would not be envious of their own creation that went beyond the boundaries of his work, and possibly god's own understanding of how his creation could bring a small glimpse of heaven to earth? This cannot please god. Your existence can't possibility please god, and so help me, I am in lust with the power you possess in your soul. You laugh at death, you treat it as if it doesn't exist and, of course, it doesn't for you."

"Death is meaningless to you because it does not affect you. You have the knowledge to understand that death is the only way we mere mortals can experience never-ending life. Death created god, or the god idea, into a more powerful entity than even he could imagine. Then, through repetition, the fear that others have of him is more powerful than any action he could perform."

I was very taken by her words because I felt the same as Marci. It was as if we shared the same mind and soul. She then spoke about Mozart. She viewed me as the modern-day Mozart, which touched me greatly. She went on to say, "I believe god killed Mozart because he was jealous of his perfection. Garrison, you are what Mozart was like when he was alive. You are a brilliant man, and a prodigy like no other. You are a man that everyone worships. God stole Mozart from us. The thought of what could have been is painful to comprehend. God teased us with a small amount of his perfection that he displayed in Mozart's music. Throughout time, god has only allowed one man, that being Mozart, a glimpse into the Garden of Eden. Mozart saw and experienced paradise in his mind. He then created that vision onto paper so the less fortunate could see and feel the paradise that he experienced."

"Mozart was getting too close to revealing the complete and total picture of paradise, and maybe that is the true punishment that every man and women must suffer. My love… you are the next Mozart. The next creation that god had to be envious of to a point that he wants you destroyed. Do not let that happen. You can live forever. Imagine what you can do… you have so much time. My love and my all, I want to share this with you. I want to experience this with you. I want to live forever with you. Please let me be by your side. Take me, my love. Make me into one of you. I never want to die as long as I can love you. I want to be perfect as well. I want to share in the powers that you possess. Take me, Garrison. Take me and I will serve you forever as your lover and as your wife."

I raced over to her, then we kissed passionately as Lewis and Carolyn quickly made their way out of the room. As we kissed, I slid my hand down her back and to her backside. I caressed her ass with my right hand as my left hand slid up to the back of her head. I gently pressed the back of her head as her beautiful face melted into mine and I explored her mouth with my tongue. We were beyond caring as we undressed each other in the great room. I got down on my knees as I tended to her firm and heavy breasts. I pushed her onto the sofa, parted her legs and pleasured her for a long time as her entire body writhed from her intense bliss. My large tongue knew how to please her. I could sense what she wanted from the sexual experience. Marci didn't have to say a word; I just sensed what she wanted. Her smell was intoxicating and her body scent changed as the gratification increased.

I ran my tongue from the top of her clit to the bottom of her anus as my hands caressed her breasts. I gently squeezed and played with them as I toyed with her nipples. I then mounted her as her legs wrapped around the lower part of my strong back. As I was in her wet opening, I pressed roughly to go as deep as I could. While she thrusted toward me, I held her back with my arms. With one hand on the small of her back and the other behind her neck, I stood up with her in my arms. I began to move her up and down in a pumping motion. I loved the way her breasts felt on my chest as my right hand ran down her back and onto her ass. I held then firmly squeezed as I made my strokes in her longer and harder, especially at the end of each long stroke. I turned my body and gently sat us down on the sofa, moving Marci on top of me. She rode my manhood for what seemed to be ten to fifteen minutes. She orgasmed twice, but I did not allow her to stop. I then pulled out and pushed her face onto the sofa and pulled her backside toward me. I entered her roughly and pounded away for a good twenty minutes. I did not stop. I was exhausted, but I couldn't stop pounding her because she felt so good, warm, and tight. She was screaming in ecstasy.

I could hear Carolyn and Lewis through the house, as they thought it was terrible that I was making love to my girlfriend so openly. I knew they were in the other room and didn't want to disturb us. Lewis was trapped. He wanted to go into the basement but had to go through the great room for that to happen.

I continued to make love to my Marci's love channel. I needed my release and pulled out of her, but she hurriedly slid down between my legs and took my manhood into her mouth as I emptied my fluid into her. She moaned and moaned, and after what seemed to be a never-ending climax, I had to stop. I collapsed on the sofa as Marci lay on my hard stomach, still playing with my manhood. After a few minutes she mounted me again. She moved her body from side to side, frontwards and backwards, trying to capture as much of my manhood as she could inside of her. This lovemaking continued for another half an hour. When our loving making was complete, we laid on the couch together, with her beautiful body on top of mine. She was so warm and sexy, I had to fight back the animalistic urge to ravage her once more. I had to rest because I was exhausted. We both were totally spent, emotionally and physically.

As the night grew late, Marci got dressed and left the house. Lewis ended up leaving because I sensed our lovemaking was making him horny. I assumed Carolyn went on to bed long ago. I got myself dressed as well and sat on the couch, still enjoying the feeling of the afterglow from our lovemaking. I savored Marci's scent that permeated the entire room. I was never so happy as I was that night.

As the weeks went by, our love for each other grew stronger. We had a healthy sexual desire for each other. We made love every day and explored not only each other's bodies, but what we both wanted in our relationship and in our lives. I told her that I could never let her into my disjoined world, it would create her into a monster and I couldn't do that to my love. Marci understood, but was disappointed in hearing the news. She wanted to be perfect.

I made sure that Marci, no matter what, would complete her education and her violin, of which she agreed. I didn't want her to stop chasing her dreams. Over the last few weeks, Marci had a renewed sense of life about her and she found the energy that she had before her momentary lapse. I comforted her as much as I could, but I was also honest with her. We talked about how she would never achieve or come close to perfection. No one ever would. I told her that she couldn't compare herself to me because that was unfair to her, or anyone for that matter. She still insisted that she wanted to be like me at any cost. I told her she wouldn't like her new lifestyle. She disagreed with me but understood that I was only trying to protect her, which made it a little easier for her to accept.

I had many college professors that I knew at Harvard that were as smart as they come, but I became smarter than them. It might have taken me a while, but eventually I gained more knowledge because of my retention abilities. I cannot explain it, but I never forgot or became confused by any information that came my way. It seems to get better the older I become. Lewis and I considered this a phenomenon and I hoped to see if our experiment on the human subjects would produce some sort of a secret in the DNA. If somehow we could find this secret and isolate it, we could improve the intelligence of the human race. Not only would this benefit mankind, but just imagine the financial potential.

CHAPTER 11

Transform

*O*ur human subjects in the basement were finally completely dried out. The man, Johnny, was a little bit of an issue. He was in serious withdrawal, whereas Mary seemed to coup well with her abstinence. She was still not there mentally, but she seemed to be more with it once the drugs left her system. She still didn't want to talk and only mumbled a few times here and there. After analyzing our subjects, we decided that we would start our experiments on Johnny over Mary. Our thought process was simple; Johnny was stronger than Mary and we could communicate with him better than we could with her. What we wanted to do was to have an infected animal bite our human subjects.

Lewis and I debated back and forth about which animal subject we should use on Johnny. According to our studies, the formula did the least physical change with our rabbit and squirrel subjects. We didn't want to use the smaller insects because the structure of the formula changed too much for our liking, so we decided to use a rabbit that we had changed a while ago. The rabbit was not happy, but we still antagonized and kept the thing hungry. We had to control the deformed rabbit so we could at least capture and manage it for our experiment. Lewis and I planned it out rather well. Johnny heard our conversations and knew we were going to use him as a guinea pig for some experiment, which made him irate, to say the least. We injected a small dose of tranquilizer into our rabbit since we wanted to be able to control the mutated rabbit, not knock it out cold. The issue we were having was how to get the rabbit to bite him without Johnny hitting it or, worse yet, killing it before the rabbit could bite him.

Lewis came up with an idea. He pulled the chain, which was around Johnny's neck, closer to the wall by way of the pulley. He made sure Johnny's neck was about six inches from the wall, which forced Johnny to rest his ass on his cot. He was flailing his arms and legs around, trying to get loose. Lewis and I went inside the cell and forcefully roped Johnny's legs. I tied his hands with one end of the rope then tied the other end to the bar of the cell. The goal was for the rabbit to bite the subject on the leg. I ripped his pant leg to expose the lower part of his leg. He was in a rather awkward position, but we didn't want Johnny to kill the rabbit before he bit him. Johnny was not a happy camper. He pulled and yanked so hard that I heard some of his joints pop. It looked as if he would dislocate his shoulder from all the pulling, jerking, and moving about, trying to release himself from the ropes.

With special thick gloves, we moved the mutated rabbit's cage inside the cell with Johnny. Johnny was going crazy and saying, "What is that thing? Get that thing away from me. What are you sick fucks doing?" I stood inside the cell while Lewis stayed outside. I placed a rope around the rabbit's neck and carefully opened his trap door. The rope was attached to the dogcatcher's-type pole. I sat in a chair inside the cell with the rope tightly around the rabbit's neck. I gently slid the distorted rabbit out of its cell and onto the floor in front of Johnny, then waited for the rabbit to regain full consciousness. I attempted to calm Johnny, but he was scared.

We wanted him to be fully awake, so we didn't want to put him under. We wanted his adrenaline to be up, as well as the rabbit's. After an hour or so the rabbit came out of his loopy trance. I made sure he was well awake before we started the experiment.

Lewis had a loaded tranquilizer gun just in case the rabbit got loose from the rope. The rabbit was strong and pulled hard. I wanted the thing to be mad, so I jerked the pole sideways rather hard and quick. The rabbit let out an eerie, loud-pitched growl, and its yellowish eyes now had some red in them as the blood flowed through the rabbit's translucent veins.

The rope was a little too tight around the neck of the rabbit, so I had to loosen the hold. I told Lewis to hold the rope that bound Johnny's legs as tight as he could. I forcefully walked the rabbit, by way of the pole, over to Johnny's exposed leg. The rabbit was moving his mouth up and down rapidly, flicking its long tongue out between bites. I forced the head of the rabbit onto Johnny's moving leg. After several attempts, the rabbit finally bit down. Johnny yelled and attempted to jerk his leg away from the bite. Lewis had a firm grip on the rope so the movement was not too great, but it was enough movement to loosen the rabbit's bite.

I kept my pole near Johnny's leg and the rabbit bit down again, this time he didn't let go. Johnny was screaming and it looked very painful. The long and sharp teeth went deep inside his leg. I moved the pole so the rabbit would release its grip, but that was not happening. The rabbit continued to bite down so I pulled hard on it. As I tugged on the pole, I could see skin being pulled about an inch or so from Johnny's leg. He was not letting go. I jerked back as hard as I could. After a blood curdling scream from Johnny, the rabbit was free from the leg. I looked down and saw blood gushing from his leg. The rabbit's sharp razor-like teeth went through the skin like a knife.

While I drug the rabbit toward the trap, Lewis got as close as he could to the rabbit and shot the tranquilizer into its thick skin. Within a few moments, the rabbit collapsed, asleep as soon as his body hit the floor. We placed him back in the cage, closed the trap door and made sure it was secure. Lewis raced over to his lab and got his first aid kit and began to tend to Johnny's leg.

Johnny was not happy. He was nervous, worried, and angry. He kept asking questions about what was going to happen to him. Lewis tried to calm him down, telling him he would monitor him to see if any changes took place. This seemed to frighten him even more. Johnny knew enough from overhearing our conversations that he was probably going to change physically, and this scared him to death. Lewis told him to tell us immediately if he felt any pain whatsoever. Johnny didn't like what was happening to him and emotionally broke down and cried. We tried to keep him calm, but we didn't want Johnny to take any pain medicine, sleeping pills, or any other form of medicine because we didn't want any foreign drug to counteract or disturb the formula in any way. Over the next couple of days Johnny's pain was very intense.

The first notice of discomfort, outside of the pain from the bite, came on day four, which was much sooner than what my parents had experienced. Johnny had full body pain, mostly in his legs, arms, and the sides of his ears. We found it very interesting that his ears had pain. He was relatively calm, for the most part, during these periods of discomfort. I think he was just too scared and tired from the pain and emotional exhaustion to display much outward emotion. Lewis took blood samples daily to monitor any changes. We documented everything on videotape, computer, and numerous charts.

Over the next three or four days, the subject had rapid hair growth, in addition to new hair follicles growing where hair hadn't grown before the bite. According to the blood samples drawn, the structure of the cells were different than the earliest blood samples taken from my parents, although the blood samples from my parents were a good month or so into the transformation. We knew we were not comparing apples to apples in this case study.

After a week and a half, the changes became more noticeable and intense. After the second week of being infected, the subject was starting more physical changes, other than just the hair growth. The pains in his legs were mostly coming from his knees and fibulas. He was always complaining and either holding or rubbing his knees. The subject was having trouble walking and was bedridden by the end of the second week.

There was a noticeable deterioration of the kneecap, as if the kneecap was dissolving into the leg. The fibula in both legs continued to grow at a faster pace than the rest of the legs. The feet grew to twice their normal size. During this transformation, the skin of the subject was very irritated due to the stretching and pulling that occurred with the increased length. We were concerned that the skin, and maybe the muscles, would rip and the subject would die. This happened quite often, according to Wolfgang's experiments, but that was during the time of the creation of the formula. It seemed, in this case, the formula was just powerful enough to cause extreme stretching with little splitting.

In this case study, the skin never broke, but it looked terrible. When we touched the skin, immediate bruising would occur. Most of the skin issues were in Johnny's feet and upper leg area. We kept in conversation with Johnny through this process, but he was in such intense pain that he couldn't speak on many occasions. Many times he would pass out, sometimes for long periods due to his severe suffering.

After a few days, Lewis inspected the subject closer and found that the skin had repaired itself. Lewis probed, pushed, and squeezed on the subject's feet and legs, noticing something rather odd. He discovered the muscles were growing more in the back of the leg and knee. He found that the kneecap was completely gone; somehow it totally dissolved into the subject's system. The knees were bending in the opposite direction of a normal human. The legs looked more like a kangaroo's in shape, looks and movement.

As the days progressed, Lewis noticed new kneecaps were forming at the back of the knees. While this area was transforming, the feet were going through a metamorphous of their own. The feet ended up growing about twice the length as their previous state. We measured Johnny's original feet and they were about four inches in width and ten and three-quarter inches in length. After the mutation, the newly sculpted feet were seven inches wide and about nineteen inches in length. The toes were long and somewhat thin for the total size of the foot. All this mutation really upset Johnny, but after a few days, he was forced to accept his newly shaped legs.

After an additional week went by, the newly formed kneecap had more than tripled from its previously discovered state. The legs and feet seemed to have gotten stronger and their appearance looked better than they did a week ago. We tried to get the subject on his feet and walking, but he had many problems with his coordination. After a couple of days, he finally learned how to stand on his new legs. It was truly amazing seeing the legs transform as quickly as they did. The muscles in the upper and lower parts of the leg grew rapidly; they nearly doubled in size almost overnight. As this was taking place, hair developed quickly over the newly formed legs and feet.

While the legs and feet were going through this incredible change, the arms grew about four inches in length. The growth seemed to be in total proportion, not just isolated in one area of the arm. Just like the legs, the skin was red and looked extremely irritated. The biceps and the triceps really developed, and from our measurements, they expanded a good seven inches in circumference. As the arms grew, so did the hands. Johnny's hands grew longer, but not wider. The hand length went from roughly eight and a quarter inches to eleven and a half inches. The bones in the hand grew not just quickly but were disturbingly pronounced on the backside of the hand. The bones of the back of the hands were visibly seen and were raised a good half an inch from the base of the back hand. When the growing seemed to stop, we saw hair starting to form on the entire arms. The developed hair covered the entire fingers, hands, wrists, and up to the shoulders.

The spine area of the subject grew about three inches in height and the chest widened and got thicker, almost tripling the thickness of his previous form. Just like the legs and arms, the skin was red and seemed to almost be stretched to the point of splitting. Hair developed over the front of the chest and back. The hair was about six inches long over most of his body and continued to grow through the process.

According to Lewis's blood samples, the structure of the cells in the subject's body was far less human than in my parents' bodies after their transformation. We immediately had a clear understanding that unless we wanted a more hideous transformation, we could not have mutated animals biting humans. The transformation seemed to be on the backside of completion.

The next largest change came in the head of the newly forming creature. The nose area of the head extended about four inches further from the face than previously. During this process, much pain seemed to be endured by Johnny. At times you could hear a popping sound coming from his face while the nose was growing. This greatly disturbed Johnny because most of the time during the change he felt the nose growing out from his face.

The ears on the subject fell off about two and a half weeks into the transformation, about the same time the front kneecaps were disappearing. There was very little blood, but in the next few days, a large bump on both sides of the head developed. The subject obviously had some trouble hearing during this part of the mutation. With the nose growing out and the loss of hearing, the subject felt very alone. In just two days we could see the formation of the ears, and at times, we could see their growth. It was amazing to witness. The growth would suddenly stop then a few hours later the growth would start again.

Throughout the transformation, the growth pattern was extremely unpredictable. One moment there was actual physical growth that you could see with the naked eye, at other moments the growth would ease to a complete standstill.

After a few days, the ears appeared to have stopped their growth. They were extremely long and measured about seventeen inches from top to bottom. The ears were hairless until the end of the transformation. They were pinkish in color and had small bumps that covered the new ears that grew upward and over the crown of the head. After the complete mutation, the subject was able to control the movement of the long, bumpy ears.

The eyes of the subject transformed into an oval shape and were located more on the sides of the head, which grew pointier and thinner than their original size. The head looked as if the sides were in a vice being tightened, and looked compressed. The larger part of the oval-shaped eye pointed toward the back of the head. The pupil turned to a reddish-brown color with what looked like a glossy film over the entire pupil. Large, hairy eyebrows grew on the greatly protruding bones that developed over the tops of the eyes. Hair started to form over the entire head, and after a couple of days the hair was completely covering the head, nose, and ears of the creature.

After what seemed to be the end of the transformation, the mutated man had trouble speaking. After a few days, he finally got his speech under control, although it did have a little bit of a lisp. In fact, during these few days, the subject seemed to be in total control of its newly formed, mutated body. The transformation process seemed to go very naturally, as if the process didn't need to have any assistance whatsoever from outside sources. Like any animal in the wild, in just weeks or even days the newborn animal could walk and communicate, unlike humans which need to be nurtured for years before they can function on their own.

After additional blood samples were taken from the subject, Lewis confirmed that the cell structure of the formula was absolutely changed after the transformation was completed, explaining why the change was so different than my parents' mutation. By comparing the blood samples from Johnny and my adoptive parents, it was clear that Johnny's blood makeup and Formula L was completely changed. After the mutation process was fully completed, Johnny's pains went away and, according to him, he felt great. No pains, but some disorientation from time to time. We believed that was the mind working with the senses, trying to get a handle on his newly formed body.

Lewis and I had many discussions about where we should go next with our experiments. We concluded that at this point we simply could not continue with more experiments outside of the specimens that we already had in our possession. If Wolfgang was telling the truth, he had already made all the necessary changes that were going to be made on this formula in its current form. We were maxed out to the point that we had to conclude that we could not alter the formula to a point where the physical metamorphous would not be so invasive. We did have additional insights for the history of mankind which we know of: a mutated animal biting a human being, and it was all well documented. This kind of information and the video evidence that we had would be priceless to science, but the issue was that most people wouldn't agree with experimental procedures on human beings. That was the paradox that existed and stood in our way of promoting this wonderful event. Society was just not ready for this type of medical experimentation.

In the meantime, Mary witnessed all this action from her cell across the room. She still hadn't said a word over this past month. In fact, she had very little reaction to what was taking place. We made sure she was coherent, but to be honest, it was hard to tell. For Mary, some days were better than others. Lewis would run as many tests as possible on her to see if her brain was able to function normally. The testing showed that she had a large delay in her reaction time, but she knew what was going on around her. Lewis thought all the drugs, especially the alcohol, had just ruined her mind throughout the years. I thought about getting another female subject, but Lewis was strongly against it and didn't want to take that risk. We had to make do with Mary as our female subject. We just wished that she was more reactive and could speak properly.

My love, Marci, was keeping abreast of everything, but I did not want her to see the specimen, Johnny. I thought I might lose her because he would be quite a shock for her. With great concern, I told Marci in detail about his transformation. I didn't leave any of the facts out and, to my surprise, she didn't seem to be too shocked. In fact, she was very interested and even wanted to help. She insisted that she wanted to help us out in the lab and really wanted to see the freak show. She pushed both Lewis and I hard on wanting to see Johnny in his new state. I was not for this decision, but I knew Marci well enough to know that if she wanted something, she was going to get it eventually.

After days of debate, Lewis and I agreed that we had to bring Marci down in the basement to satisfy her curiosity. If we waited longer, we were afraid that she would break into the basement to see for herself. This concerned us because of the potential dangers not only with her safety, but to the specimens.

We took Marci into the basement for a viewing. I could sense that she was very nervous. I stopped her several times to make sure she wanted to continue with the viewing. She made it clear to us that she wanted to see them. I held her hand as we walked down the stairs to the basement door on the right. Lewis slowly opened the door and we stepped inside the lab. We heard Johnny talking and asking who was coming down the hallway like he had numerous times before.

As we made our way around the corner, Marci saw the subjects. I took Marci to meet the male subject. When Marci saw him, she squeezed my hand hard and covered her mouth with her free hand. She stopped to look at the freak behind the bars. I said, "Marci, this is Johnny, the one that was bitten by the infected animal."

Johnny rose to his feet and stood about six feet eight inches in height. He looked at Marci and said in a very low voice as a tear formed in his eye, "Help me, Miss. Please help me. Please save me from the monsters that did this to me. Please run for help, please."

Marci was very upset as she released her grip on my hand and placed that hand to her mouth. I looked at Marci and before I could look away, she cast her eyes on me. I said, "Are you okay? Would you like to leave?"

Marci shook her head fast and hard to gesture no. She breathed heavily and said, "This is the most incredible thing I have ever seen in my life. I am sorry, but it takes ones' breath away when you see it in person. How hideous this thing looks and to think he was once a human."

The male subject seemed to be very upset and started to react by saying loudly, "Missy, I am still a human. These fucks turned me into this... this... whatever I am now. I can think, eat and sleep just like a human, you bitch."

Johnny's words seemed to shake Marci out of her shock. She got very angry, "Look, you fucking freak. Don't you ever, ever call me a bitch, do you understand..."

The specimen interrupted with, "Shut up, bitch! Are you part of this evil, sadistic plot? Are you fucking both sadistic fucks as well?" Marci ran toward the specimen, and I held her back, but not before she spat on the thing. The specimen let out a loud growl that no one, including us, had heard before. The growl was powerful and forceful to a point where the noise shook the metal bars of the cage.

Marci was a little frightened, but to my surprise, she was even angrier than before. Just then, for the first time we heard something come out of Mary's mouth. She started screaming, yelling, and talking very fast. She gripped the bars and shook them violently. To my surprise, Marci went over to the lady and said, "Shut up, you freak!"

It was evident that Mary was upsetting Marci with her screams and actions. Mary didn't listen and suddenly Marci started to yell," Shut your fucking mouth, you dirty, retarded whore!"

I stepped toward Marci, making sure I didn't lay a hand on her and said, "My dear, Marci… Marci… she is crazy. Don't let her or the freak upset you."

Marci looked at me then back at the specimen and said, "What's in store for these freaks?"

I replied, "After several more weeks of observation, we will conduct another experiment when the time is right. But this must remain a secret until the experiment is over."

Marci said, "When you are ready, I want to be a part of the next experiment… do you understand me, Garrison?" Marci took her eyes off the specimen and looked at me with a set of demanding eyes that I had never seen from my love before.

I smiled and said, "If this is what you wish, you will be a part of the experiment, but it might not be pleasant." Mary started to calm down. She finally stopped shaking the bars of the cage. She just stood there and began to cry softly. Johnny's growl upset her, but she seemed to regain control over her body at that moment.

Marci smiled as she looked back at the freak and said, "I don't care, and I want to be a part of your experiments, my love." She slowly walked out of the room as the freak was yelling at her and calling her not so pleasant names.

I walked up to the thing and said calmly, "Shut up and sit down now. I want to tell you something. That lady is my love and I do not appreciate you yelling at her."

The creature interrupted me and said, "Fuck you, you piece of shit. Just come here so I can kill you." With that, Lewis appeared with a tranquilizing gun. I took the gun from him and pointed it at the creature. He was very pleading now and saying, "Please, please don't shoot me." I shot the gun and hit him below his stomach. He fell to the floor and went to sleep. Mary again started yelling and shaking as she gripped the bars of her cell. I walked over to her and shot her in the leg with the tranquilizer.

Marci witnessed everything, looked at me and said, "Garrison, what you have done here is just amazing, unholy, but amazing. The power of the formula that you possess is just incredibly special and, in fact, wonderful. You have the ability to change people's lives, not only through your music, but through your blood. You can bite someone and it can change their lives forever. That is extremely powerful and very sexy, my love. Very sexy and hot. Maybe one day you can allow me to share this power that you possess."

I said to her, "The formula is not perfected yet. We don't know its structure or understand how to reproduce it, but the side effects are… well… just look at that freak. If I could ever get this perfected to where there are no physically altering changes, you will be the first to know, my love."

Marci smiled and walked out of the basement. I stared at her backside as she walked away from me. Her walk was intoxicating. She moved in all the right spots. She had total command of her movements and I sensed her need for sexual fulfillment. We had a date later tonight and I knew from that look and walk that we were going to have some very entertaining sex.

CHAPTER 12

Inhospitable

eeks went by as we tested Johnny on an array of experiments with a multitude of results. Johnny had developed a very high intelligence and his hearing was incredibly sharp. He heard things that only I could hear. No human could come close to our hearing. It was incredible. His coordination skills were extreme and fast. He could move at a high rate of speed in very short distances. His eyesight improved daily until it became almost equal to mine. For example, he could read a dictionary from fifteen feet away.

Johnny was shocked and amazed at how his mental and physical being had changed. His drug and alcohol addiction literally vanished. He had no interest in drinking or taking drugs, even with a lot of encouragement from Lewis and myself. He was getting comfortable with his new physical state of being.

Meanwhile, Mary was still rather out of it, but at least she was speaking now, just not in fully and completely developed sentences. The years of drug and alcohol abuse to her system were too much for her mind to completely recover from. She would only say a few incoherent words. We assumed that she had been this way since her addiction to drugs many years ago. During her entire stay, she never once smiled or had a normal reaction to us outside of being upset from something that Johnny said or did.

Since Johnny's mutation seemed to be complete and Mary had seemingly reached her maximum state of normalcy, the time was right to take the next step in the experiment – for the couple to mate. I wanted to see what would happen if an infected animal that had been infected by a mutated animal would mate with a non-affected subject. I wanted to see what kind of offspring would be produced and how the formula was going to change chemically. I wasn't sure how we were going to accomplish this feat. The subjects didn't seem to be very attracted to each other, especially from Mary's point of view. During those rare moments of coherence, we believe she found Johnny very repulsive. We thought about putting Johnny under and taking sperm from him and injecting it into Mary.

I brought Marci into this discussion to see what her thoughts were on the subject. I know her judgment was somewhat clouded because she didn't like Johnny, but I wanted to include her in our experiments. I wanted her thoughts on how we were going to get an animal like Johnny to mate with a human like Mary when neither were interested in the act.

Lewis stayed out of the decision making for as long as he could. He was totally against what we were doing and about to do. At the same time, he knew he couldn't refuse our wishes. He had to go along with what I wanted and now he had to succumb to Marci's wishes as well. He knew that his opinion meant nothing anymore. I took twisted pleasure in seeing Lewis in his private hell.

After days of discussion, Marci and I decided they should mate on their own. We thought this would be the easiest and most effective way to start this process. Marci and I had a plan as to how we were going to go about making this idea into reality. I went over to Johnny while he was sitting quietly in the cell and whispered to Johnny, "If you would go over to Mary's cell and have intercourse with her and get her pregnant, I will help find the cure to change you back." Of course, there was no cure in changing one back, but he didn't know that, so hopefully I could use this promise to get Johnny's help.

At first, Johnny didn't want to engage in such an act, but I could sense that down deep he was pondering it. The other problem I was running into was that Johnny liked the way he felt. There was a part of him that didn't want to change back, for many reasons. He felt great, he liked his new-found intelligence, and he loved his newly formed senses.

He was astounded with his amazing ability to perform on such high levels.

On the other hand, Johnny knew he could never go out in public again looking the way he did. He knew he was a freak. He was scared. He wanted to go home and back to the world he once knew so well. Johnny wanted to be normal again, and the possibility of me turning him back to his old appearance was too great for him not to accept my offer. Therefore, I knew down deep that he had no choice but to follow my wishes.

After going back and forth with the idea, he concluded that he would follow through with my plan. I made sure he understood what the ground rules were; he needed to impregnate Mary or all bets were off. I told him he may have to service Mary more than once. He understood and agreed to my terms.

I walked over to Mary and flatly told her to take her clothes off, but she refused. I then encouraged her to remove her clothes or she would be tied up and tortured. After some pondering, she decided to follow my instructions and removed all her clothes. Her body was not attractive, but for some reason Johnny seemed interested in what he saw. I knew he hadn't had sexual intercourse in a long time, therefore, any sex would have been okay for him. I also knew that in line with the formula's characteristics, the formula carries over as well as develops certain obvious and noticeable traits from the infected carrier. In this case, Johnny's change would be more on the side of the traits from the rabbit than another animal. I used this fact to my advantage. I believe the traits of a rabbit's sexual desire were rearing its head in this situation. Formula L's tendency was to bring out the hidden qualities of the subject. This was one of the main reasons I chose a rabbit.

I unlocked both cell doors to allow Johnny to go over to Mary's cell. The chain was long enough that he could reach the end of her cell. I locked the main door that joined the two cells together so Johnny couldn't get out of the caged area. Johnny hurried over to Mary and started to touch her, but she didn't like to be touch. He continued his aggressive behavior, but she continued to push him away. She moved as far to the side of the cell as she could. Johnny stepped closer and finally decided to attack her. She fought him off as long as she could. She started screaming, kicking, and throwing her arms about, hitting Johnny in the head, ears, and shoulders, and he was getting very upset. He finally controlled her, and started to kiss and lick her face, which repulsed Mary. She yelled, telling him to stop. He didn't stop; in fact, he increased his groping. Johnny, who remained naked after his change, was getting worked up over his encounter. His penis grew extremely long and hard during this one-sided struggle. He roughly moved Mary onto her cot and swung her around. As he pushed her head into the cot, he raised her ass up and inserted his penis. After a few moments of thrusting, he finished empting his semen inside of her. He pulled out and gently walked toward his side of the cell. Johnny left her crying uncontrollably. Marci witnessed all this with me, but Lewis had to leave the room in the middle of the performance. He got sick to his stomach and went to the restroom to vomit.

As Johnny walked to his side of the cell, I used the pulley to slowly retract him to his cot. He kept asking me in a quiet voice when I was going to start to change him back to his former state of being. He didn't seem to be remorseful of his sexual encounter with Mary. He kept asking me when I was going to turn him back. I lied to him and said as soon as possible, but first we needed to make sure Mary was pregnant.

I think Johnny enjoyed his lovemaking because he looked at my Marci and showed her his penis. She laughed and said, "I would never fuck a freak like you."

Johnny said, "Oh sister, you will. I am going to fuck you hard when I get out of here and leave you so hurt and bruised, you won't be able to move." I was not happy to hear this so I quickly pulled the chains as far as it would go into the wall. I wanted to kill him right there, but mostly I wanted him hurt, although his hand-eye coordination was equal to mine. It would have been difficult for me to land a clean punch through the bars of the cell. Subsequently, I let him be for the moment.

I locked both cell doors and continued to listen to Marci and Johnny exchange verbal insults. I kept telling Johnny to shut up and stop talking, but he had lost control of his mind and actions. He was threatening to kill me. I went to get the tranquilizer gun, calmly walked over to him, and shot him in the stomach. He collapsed hard onto his cot. Marci was still very angry, but I insisted she calm down because we had a lot of work to do. Meanwhile, Mary was still crying hard with her face buried deep into her pillow. She didn't move an inch during our episode with Johnny.

A couple of days had gone by since the sexual encounter and Mary started to feel sick. In her limited way, she told us she was very upset and concerned about having the freak's baby. She had enough sense and was coherent enough to process that information. It seemed that she was getting better mentally.

Lewis started the pregnancy test and she tested positive. The next week Mary started with severe abdominal pains. The pains would come and go throughout the day. We didn't give her any medicine to help with the pain because we didn't want to contaminate the results of the experiment.

Marci had extra time on her hands since her semester had ended and she was on summer break. She was a constant fixture at the house from morning till night. She was extremely interested in our experiments and was particularly interested in how Mary was functioning while being pregnant. Johnny learned not to be so disrespectful to Marci, and most of the time they got through the day without any drama. One thing I learned through this experiment was that Marci was a strong woman and couldn't be taken advantage of, which was a huge turn on for me. Her assistance was limited because she didn't have the knowledge that Lewis and I had. This didn't set well with her. She desperately wanted to help instead of being so limited in her role as an assistant. We taught her as we progressed through the experiments. She asked many questions, but sometimes she didn't understand the answers we gave her.

Marci was a great help in comforting Mary through her pregnancy. Marci would get mad at me sometimes because I treated Mary as an experiment and not as a human being. I made Marci fully aware that there was a very high probability that Mary wouldn't survive after the birth of the animal.

Lewis administered countless ultrasounds on Mary so we could keep track of the newborn. After the first week, Lewis made a startling discovery during one of the ultrasounds. Mary was carrying more than one animal inside her. In just days, the fetuses grew at a rapid pace. We found as many as five separate fetuses inside Mary. This information really upset her, but Marci was there to help settle her nerves. We couldn't understand why there were five fetuses instead of one. Why five of them? Why so many? From the ultrasounds, each one was of the same size. We thought the DNA of the rabbit was the obvious reason we had so many fetuses. What was also very odd was that all five were the same size in both length and width.

The fetuses' growth rate was astonishing. They doubled in size during short periods of time. The pain Mary was having was almost unbearable. She screamed constantly for hours on end, and on several occasions, she lost her voice. After many conversations, Lewis and I decided to give her as much medication as possible without harming the little animals. I was not in total compliance with Lewis on this issue because I was afraid the medication might somehow interact with the formula, producing false information in the experiment. But we were concerned that Mary might have a heart attack or die from the pain alone. If Mary died, that would be the end of our experiment.

The formula, or some form of the formula, was making Mary better. Her speech, hearing and mental status improved. She was able to communicate with us to a point where we understood what was hurting her.

The newest ultrasound showed the fetuses were not human in form. We thought the form would be of that of a rabbit, but that would not be the case either. It was difficult to see what the form resembled because of the lack of room inside the womb. The five fetuses were packed in the womb tightly. They constantly pushed and shoved each other, which increased Mary's pain. Marci was interested in what was happening. She had never seen anything like this in her life. I told her that we hadn't experienced anything like this either.

Although Marci didn't lead on that these experiments or the screaming bothered her, I knew that at times she was upset. She continued to help in the experiment without any disruption from Mary's audible distractions.

The next few weeks were very unsettling for Mary because her stomach was growing larger each day. The stretch marks were getting worse, along with the pain. Mary would scream as loud as she could many times throughout the day. She was losing weight in her arm, leg, and shoulder areas. She lost over half of her hair as well. The five fetuses were taking the much-needed nutrients from her body, and even with all the medicine and vitamins being pumped into her, her body still required more food and nourishment. Despite all our attempts to help her stay alive, she was slowly dying. It seemed there was nothing we could do about it. I was concerned that if she died, the fetuses would die with her, so keeping Mary alive was our main priority.

Around the seventh week of the pregnancy, Mary's life was hanging on by a thread. Her belly was stretched so badly that the entire area was turning purple, and at times the skin would split and bleed. You could see the stomach move and stretch from what was inside trying to get out. From the ultrasounds we saw the fetuses all moving toward the belly, not toward the vaginal area. Lewis told me that he didn't think the fetuses would come out naturally through the vagina because of their size, but mostly because of their shape. The lack of room made the positioning of the fetuses virtually impossible to have a normal exit.

Meanwhile, Johnny's mutation had stopped and there had been no change over the past few weeks. He was feeling wonderful and, in fact, seemed to be very healthy. He was learning, and I let him read some of the chemical textbooks I had in my library. He was more accepting of his fate and I could sense he was enjoying his new way of life. He was becoming more intelligent and was feeling great physically. He was reading textbooks that he had never read or seen before, and after a few moments of reading, he was beginning to understand complicated formulas and concepts the books were trying to convey. At times I would test him on what he had read, and amazingly he was getting many of the answers correct. He was feeling very good about his mental capabilities, but if truth be told, he would have preferred his previous physical appearance. One certainty that was made abundantly clear was that he wanted out of his cell. What captivated me was Johnny's interest in the animals inside of Mary's stomach. He cared about the offspring and asked question after question about their progress. He showed little attention to Mary, but he always asked about the offspring's status and condition.

Later we strapped Mary to a hospital bed. One strap went under her breast area while the other strap held the back of each leg just behind the knee in the stirrups. I made sure the legs were spread wide enough for the animals to leave her body if they decided to come out there.

Mary let out an abnormal scream that shook the bars of the cell. She was breathing heavily and moving around on the cot in great pain. Marci just happened to be in the lab at this time. She desperately wanted to go inside the cell, but I kept her from entering. I didn't even allow Marci to hold her hand like she had done so many times before, fearing what might happen to my love. For weeks Lewis and I had been debating what to do when this moment, the delivery of the quintuplets, arrived.

After many hotly debated discussions, we decided not to be in the cell with Mary. Lewis wanted to have someone by her side during the delivery, but I felt it was unsafe for anyone to be in there with her. I felt strongly that we didn't know what to expect and out of fear of our safety, we were going to have her deliver the fetuses on her own. To be honest, we thought she would die before that happened. One of the main areas of concern was how large the fetuses would be and if they would be able to run after they were born. If they could run immediately, how would they react? Would they attack or would they be docile? Depending on their size, we thought the cell bars were close enough together that they wouldn't be able to escape, but we didn't know for sure their exact size or how mobile they would be once out of the body.

After approximately two hours of constant pain and screaming, the situation was getting to Marci. I told her to leave, but she didn't want to go. This was something Marci wasn't used to, and it upset her greatly. To make matters even worse, at times Johnny would yell at us to do something for Mary. He was also worried about his kids. Mary was pleading for us to kill her, but I couldn't bear to do that because, in the name of science, I wanted to see what was going to happen next. What I didn't want to do was kill the offspring, and I was afraid that just might happen if I were to take Mary's life. During these moments of waiting for the birth to take place, there was intense anxiety for everyone in the room.

We waited patiently yet nervously for whatever was going to happen next. Our wait didn't last long. Suddenly Mary, who had almost totally lost her voice from screaming, let out a semi-silent yet violent scream. Her head and entire body shook violently, and without warning her stomach started to split open. The split started just below the belly button then continued to spread in both directions, toward her vagina and toward the under part of her chest. As the split continued, out came what looked like rapidly moving arms and legs, mixed with dark red blood.

Mary was still alive, but she couldn't catch her breath. She was in intense pain as she moved her arms and head around as if she was reaching out and asking for much needed help. As the ruptured area of her stomach started to grow, she finally expired under the physical stress of being ripped open and split down the middle from the inside. She looked as if she had been totally gutted.

The fetuses made a very odd sound as three made their way out of the confines of the open wound. The other two seemed to lie on their backs and cry, or that is what it seemed, in the carcass of Mary's opened body. The three that escaped from the belly fell onto the floor. They were obviously covered in blood with a purple slime-like substance that blanketed their bodies. The newborns were in the shape of a rabbit's body, but the heads seemed to be more human-like in appearance. Their legs were shaped like a rabbit's and they kept moving them rapidly as if they were attempting to run. The ears were smaller and shaped differently than a rabbit's but larger than a human's. Mary's eyes were wide open as she seemed to stare at the ceiling above. Her arms were outstretched and hanging on each side below the cot, her legs were dangling at the end of the table as they lay limp in the stirrups. Blood was everywhere on Mary, the hospital bed, and all over the floor.

Marci was about to be sick and had to excuse herself from the room. She ran into the nearest bathroom, bent over the toilet, and threw up. Lewis ran and got the five small cages, and I helped get them near the cages. Thankfully the newborns were large enough not to be able to escape from between the bars of the cell. Lewis and I used special gloves that were bite-resistant. The newborns seemed to be crying and confused, as best as we could tell.

I opened the main door of the cell and told Lewis to help me with the small cages. After all five cages were in the main cell door area between the enclosed cells, I told Lewis to stay outside. I opened the cell doors and took two cages inside with me. The newborns didn't seem to be bothered by my presence while inside the cage. With my gloves on, I proceeded to pick up one of the newborns. The newborn was about fifteen or so inches long, with a body shape of a rabbit, especially below the waist. It was hard to see with all the blood and purple slime, but the rear legs looked just like normal rabbits, but the front legs had a more human arm appearance. These appendages were lower on the torso, closer to the back legs and away from the head more than a normal human's arms would be. The arms were totally covered in long hair, but the arms of the newborns bent outward, in the opposite direction as normal. The hands, or paws, were like a human hand, but with lots of hair and only three fingers and one thumb. The head was like a human's, but on a smaller scale. The nose was very pronounced and seemed to have more of a pig-like snout. The nostrils were large and opened wide as it breathed. The openings of the nostrils were in the front of the face, not below or under like a human's nose. The eyes were small and longish in shape with red pupils.

I hurried and placed the first newborn in its cage and then went over to pick up the second to place him in his safe haven. I got the third newborn and placed him in the cage, but before I went for the other two, I noticed they were still in Mary's open, bloodied belly. Somehow one of the newborns got turned around and must have drowned in the blood of his mother's insides. The last newborn was still lying in the upper part of the open wound. I went to reach for the fifth newborn as it started to get up.

It made a sudden movement to get away from me and as it did, it slipped and was headed toward the floor. Impulsively, I reached out and grabbed it by the neck. With the thick gloves I had little feeling and I pressed my hand around its neck too hard. The newborn found itself struggling to breathe. I believe I broke its neck in my attempt to keep the animal from escaping my grasp. I said to Lewis, "Lewis, I think I broke its neck."

Lewis replied, "Well, bring him over to me and let's see what's wrong." I brought the newborn over to Lewis as his body rested in my gloved hands. The newborn was struggling to survive and as soon as I reached Lewis, the newborn stopped moving.

Johnny was witnessing all this from his cell. He watched everything without making a sound. When I looked over at him, at first he was very sad, then became very angry. When our eyes met I said, "There was nothing I could do. Three survived and the other two did not."

Johnny said, "You killed them. You killed my children. You murderer!"

I tried to ignore him. Marci saw everything after she emerged from the bathroom. As she was wiping her mouth with a towel she said, "Garrison, you did everything you could. It is not your fault."

Johnny yelled, "Liar! You woman, are a lying bitch! Of course, you would take up for that bastard of a boyfriend of yours."

Marci turned around and gave Johnny an evil look. I told Johnny to shut up, and asked Marci to stand down and leave Johnny alone. She looked at me then quickly back at Johnny with a hateful look on that perfect face of hers. I walked over to Mary's body and gently laid the dead newborn by her side.

We cleaned up the three living newborns. Johnny was still upset with me, but it was not my fault the child died. I attempted to explain this, but he wouldn't listen to me. His anger really upset Marci and they got into many shouting matches after I asked them to stop fighting. Not long after this, Lewis shot Johnny with a tranquilizer again so we could get some work completed. Now the difficult part came – the cleanup and deciding what to do with the bodies.

Lewis and I wheeled the bodies over to the cremation machine I had bought many months ago. We unstrapped Mary and placed hers and the two newborns' bodies inside the machine. I stepped out of the way so Lewis could close the door; he locked the large door and turned the machine on. After a few moments, the basement got extremely warm and soon became uncomfortably hot. The bodies burned in no time and soon were nothing but a pile of dust. We had a massive ventilation system built in the basement when we installed the cremation machine, but the venting system only reduced the temperature inside the basement by a small amount.

I cleaned the cell floor with industrial soap and washed the blood and water down the large drain that was in the basement floor. Marci helped with the clean up as best she could. Before we knew it, everything was cleaned up, and the surviving newborns were locked away in their individual cells. We decided to start taking blood and observing them right away since we didn't know how long they would live. They seemed to be content and all three seemed to be as normal as normal could get in this unique situation.

Johnny wasn't happy with the way we were treating the newborns. He wanted them in his cell. He thought they needed to be treated as 'normal' babies, but as I attempted to explain to him, they were anything but normal. We simply couldn't predict what their behavior would be nor could we take a chance on how they would react. We didn't want them to roam free inside a large cell.

A few days passed, and the newborns grew rapidly, as expected. It appeared their blood type changed from hour to hour, like what happened in my body as well as my parents'. The formula was certainly diluted in the newborn's body, to a point where the formula was not recognizable in its current state. But the blood type was unique to anything on record, including mine, my parents', or any animal we had experimented on in the past.

This new species was changing by the hour both internally and in their outward appearance. All of their extremities were getting longer and larger, more pronounced, and better defined. At this point, no new appendages were forming, only the existing features were developing. Lewis and I concluded that the reason the blood type was changing was because the physical body was changing so rapidly. We assumed this was just part of the process of the formula and its effect on the subject.

It was the nature of the formula to affect the blood type chemically. The formula changes the chemical makeup of the host that it invades. It constantly mutates throughout the lifespan of the host. Our theory was that the formula allowed for the host to be immune to any form of disease or infection, thus it effectively stopped the aging process of the host because of its constant mutation. The formula was constantly refurbishing, both in form and chemically, the internal and external form of the host.

We monitored and studied the newborns closely during this time of their lifecycle. In just the first couple of days the newborns already had all their teeth and were ready for solid food. We fed them raw meat during this part of the process and they seemed to really enjoy this. In addition, we fed them heads of lettuce and cabbage, as well as carrots, green peppers and squash; you name it, we fed it to them. They seemed to eat in amount more than they should in conjunction with their physical size. When they ate, they nibbled like a rabbit. They didn't have the eating tendencies of a human where the food would be bitten off then chewed up into more of a mush, making swallowing easier. The subjects displayed the eating characteristics of a rabbit rather than a human.

Marci assisted in trying to communicate with them in hopes they would be able to speak or show some signs of intelligence. From all indications, they had the ability to speak, but their intelligence level was still a large mystery to us. We attempted to read to them, but that didn't capture their attention one bit. We gave them toy cars and trucks, and even stuffed animals to play with, but they totally ignored them. We even showed them how to write, but they were not interested in learning from us. They seemed to have developed personalities and traits more from a rabbit than a human.

Meanwhile, Johnny was very displeased with the fact that he couldn't see his 'children'. He wanted to see them, touched them, and show affection to the newborns that he helped create. On many occasions we had to silence Johnny because he either got too angry or too loud in his cell over this issue. He would constantly needle Marci, and before we knew it, they were in heavy arguments with each other. They didn't get along, to say the least.

After several weeks went by, the newborns had more than tripled in size, which put them about forty-five inches in length. We had to permanently move them into the cell they were born in so they could have more room to move around. They were bipedal, standing on two legs, at this stage of their development. They moved slowly around the floor of their cell, but their walk was awkward, at best, yet at the same time they were very sure-footed.

They were now attempting to speak, but no words were formed. All we heard were regular animal sounds. Meanwhile, Johnny continued his cause for wanting to see his offspring up close. I was not for this idea because I didn't know what he would do to them. I was afraid that he might attempt to kill or hurt them, and that was unacceptable during our experiment. As the days passed, we concluded that we had done all we could do with the newborns' development. Therefore, Lewis and I made the decision to allow one of the newborns to enter Johnny's cell. Using the long pole with the rope at the end, like a dog catcher's, I placed the rope around one of the newborns while outside the cell.

Lewis didn't want me to get inside the cell with the three of them out of fear of what they might do to me. I carefully moved from one opening in the bar to another as I held the pole from outside the bars of the cell. I walked the newborn over to the entrance of the cell door. This area had two main cells and in the middle of these cells was a third cell. This area had three cell doors, one for each of the adjoining cells and the third cell entrance that led out into the room. I had these cells installed this way as a safety precaution in the chance that if one of the main cell doors broke, we would still have another entrance that would secure the opening of the lab.

I went inside the third cell. On one side housed the newborns and the other side held Johnny. I opened the newborn's cell door and led him inside the third cell. I closed the door of the newborns' cell and opened Johnny's cell. I led the newborn inside and after I closed the door, I released the newborn from the rope restraint while still outside Johnny's cell.

At first the newborn seemed to be a little unsettled. Johnny kept calling for his offspring to come to him, but the thing was noticeably scared. After a few hours, the newborn walked over to Johnny who was chained up close to the wall. Johnny put out his hand and the newborn touched it and finally they held hands. Johnny began to weep. He seemed to be genuinely happy and joyful to see one of his offspring. The two quickly bonded and seemed very happy with each other's company.

I asked Johnny if he could teach his son how to speak. Johnny immediately went to work on getting it to speak. Johnny talked to his son for hours each day to no end. Finally, one day the newborn, which Johnny named Jake, spoke a word. He called his father 'Daddy'. This was a big moment for everyone concerned. We documented everything on tape through the many video cameras we had up throughout the lab area. After several days Jake seemed to learn many words, and although his diction wasn't very good, you could still make out what he was saying.

Lewis tested Jake on stacking and lining up blocks. He tested him on catching and throwing a plastic ball, balancing on one foot, and taking a stick and hitting a moving ball, among other activities. The results from these exercises were mixed due more to Jake's lack of coordination, which surprised us to some degree. The major theme in all the experiments and experiences that we have had in the past would seem to indicate that motor and coordination skills would already be advanced at this stage in the mutation process. In all other subjects, after Formula L was introduced into their system, their coordination skills improved dramatically. With the newborns, for some reason this was not the case, and we didn't understand why. The only possible answer was that the formula was diluted and maybe this was a part of the formula that got left out during the transfer from one host to the other.

The other two newborns that were kept separate from Jake and Johnny developed at a slower rate than Jake. The obvious reason is that more attention was shown to Jake. The other newborns were purposely not taught and all they had was each other to learn from. At times, they seemed a little curious about Jake and what he was doing with Johnny, but as soon as the interest peaked, something would catch their eye and they were back to playing games and ignoring their more learned and matured brother. The isolated newborns seemed to play and get along well with each other, but they didn't seem to get along with anyone else.

Lewis and I decided to continue to keep the two together for a while and let Johnny teach Jake for the time being. We wanted to see if the formula would allow the untrained subject to gather knowledge unassisted as compared to the trained subject that was receiving assistance. Johnny hated us even more than he did over the isolation of this other sons in this part of the experiment. He attempted to reach out to them through the cell bars, but the newborns rarely paid any attention to their maker.

Jake was far more advanced than his two brothers. Consequently, at this point we had to make the conclusion that just like in the real world, children that are helped by their parents tend to do better than children that are ignored. To extend this thinking further, in this test, the formula didn't make the child smart automatically, it just helped the child who was being taught become more intelligent. In our findings, the formula is a seed, whereas the teaching is the water and the soil. In this experiment, we concluded that the formula doesn't make you intelligent, it just allows you the opportunity to develop faster and at a higher rate or level than before the formula was introduced. Lewis and I thought this was an important finding on many levels.

CHAPTER 13

Nevermore

My personal life was moving along splendidly during the time of the experiments with Johnny, Mary, and their offspring. Marci and I continued our courtship and would play the violin together for hours on end. I also explained as much as I could to her about cell biology and what we hoped to accomplish with all the experiments we were conducting, attempting to explain my reasoning for the experiments in layman's terms. I told my love everything about the past experiments that we had performed. In addition, I told her about the experiments that my birth father attempted when he was under Nazi rule. I read to her Lewis's notes taken on his trip to Germany and his surprise meeting with my birth father.

The Johnny and Mary experiment was something my birth father never experimented with because his subjects were not allowed to be kept alive long enough. At the time, I thought I really needed to have someone else look at our data and see if we had missed anything. Also, I wanted to tell someone about what we had uncovered. This was incredible news and if presented correctly, Lewis and I would win the Nobel Prize over these findings. The problem was who were we going to tell? We had to be extremely careful not to trust anyone because we could end up being charged with murder, in addition to being charged with cruelty to animals and humanity.

We had to keep this a secret for as long as possible, if not forever. Most people are very short-sighted and would have a very strong opposition to what we had been doing and what we're attempting to do in the future. Religious fanatics wouldn't look too kindly on us tinkering with god's creations and attempting to make them better. A part of me understands this type of thinking, but the other part of me believes that if we can change this formula so it can make humans better both physically and mentally, that would be a positive thing for mankind.

Moreover, imagine having the opportunity to live forever and never age or feel the effects of growing old. This formula and our experiments added to my excitement and passion. I needed to at least speak with someone that had as much knowledge as I did that could think and reason objectively. I knew of no human alive that I had met or knew by name that even closely resembled this, but I did have someone in mind. The only living individual that would at least understand my issues, my questions, and even my answers, was my father.

At first, I was reluctant to tell my love that I wanted to attempt to find my birth father. I needed to tell her that I believed Lewis and needed to fly to Germany to seek out my parents. I knew Lewis would strongly be against any such thought or notion. This was a very difficult subject to negotiate.

One night after we finished our work in the basement, I had both Lewis and Marci sit down in the great room and listen to my idea. I started by speaking to my love. "Marci, I love you very much, but there is something that I need to do, something that I have to do in the name of science, or maybe I should say in the name of my sanity. I need to speak with someone about this formula and what I have uncovered thus far. I need to speak with someone that I trust, someone that understands my logic, and someone that will not call the authorities on me and what I am doing regarding my experiments. I need to talk with someone of my intellect and maybe our two minds can uncover some sort of answers to the formula's secrets. What I have to tell you is not going to go over well."

Just then Lewis interrupted me by saying, "Garrison, whatever it is you're thinking about, just stop right now."

I continued my conversation with Marci while completely ignoring Lewis's outburst. I said, "Marci, I never want to keep anything from you. I want to tell you everything that is on my mind so I can be honest with you. I must talk to my birth parents in Germany. I have to go and find them."

Marci stopped me quickly and said, "No! No… that is just too dangerous, Garrison." She didn't want me to go and I wasn't convinced that it would be in my best interest to leave either at the time, but I had to take the chance.

I said, "I understand, but I need to speak with my father and see if he can share any information that would help us." I looked at Lewis who was just sitting there shaking his head. I said, "Lewis, I know you did all you could when you met with them years ago, but I am their son. They may be more open with me. They may want to share more information with someone like me than with some stranger like you. I know you were scared for your life. I understand, but this is something I must do. I know you are against this idea and think I am crazy. I know, but I need you to help me find where they live – that is, if they still live there now. You would be a huge help to me by telling me at least the direction of where to go and how far in this forest you spoke of on your trip there years ago."

Marci stood up and said, "I don't like this idea and I demand that you not pursue this, Garrison."

I said, "I understand this is something you are against, but with all due respect, my love, I am going no matter what." I looked into Marci's eyes and she knew I was going and there was nothing she could do to stop me. I looked toward Lewis and said, "I need you to help me, Lewis. At least think about it. You would be doing me a great favor and will be doing a great service to the quest of this venture." With that said, Lewis looked at me with a blank expression on his face and quietly left the room.

A few days went by and not one word was said about our conversation. We all went about our business. One day Marci, Lewis and I were sitting together in the great room talking about the newborns and how love can change and nurture not only those creatures, but people in general. Marci was referring to how well Jake was doing compared to the other two newborns, and she brought up another potential idea to this experiment. How does love and nurturing factor into this equation? I began to think about this notion for a moment with them. Normally children that come from good and stable homes or settings typically do better in school than those that are not as fortunate. Also, the more experiences you encounter through life tends to make you a more well-rounded person, and this especially goes for children. Children are influenced greatly by their environment at a very young age. The nicer or richer the environment, the more conducive it would be for them to want to learn. If your environment is made up of drugs, crime, and uneducated people, unless the person is exposed to the contrast, they will have a higher probability of taking on their environment's personality or be persuaded to act according to what their environment has requested of them.

Our conversation morphed to our views on the basic instinct of love. You can debate the true definition of love from now to forever, but the truest and most basic definition of love is an extreme caring for someone or a material item. At least in my opinion that is how I would define love. As I talked I went into more depth on the subject. I said to my love, "In many cases, love can be viewed as basically giving someone your attention and caring for that person in a special way. What is love, really? Is love something you just fall into or does it have to be nurtured at first and then, through time, the attention turns into love? In my opinion, one must act out love instead of just speaking about it. You must prove your love constantly and not just let your loved one assume love is in your heart."

Marci looked at me and said, "Well, I knew that I loved you from the moment I saw you on stage. I kept it bottled up in my heart all through these years."

I said, "Yes, and the same with me. When I first saw you, my heart stopped for many moments. I thought about you, or I should say your image. The image of an idea of what I thought you were without ever actually knowing who you were. That image, the desire that I created in my mind and in my heart, was the foundation for the love that

I have for you. When I finally met you, the building blocks were being laid in rapid-fire succession, one right after another. Each look you gave me pulled me closer and closer to your heart. Then we spoke, and I was hooked forever. I could never let go. Why? Because throughout the years and through all my life experiences, I have built up in my soul what I desire from a woman's love. All the expectations that I have had regarding my loved one manifested itself into a certain likeness. An image of what I thought my love would look or be like in reality. When we finally met, everything was perfect and the feelings I had for you started to multiply because I knew from years of experience that you were the one that I had been looking for all my life. Whether it would have been by physical contact or verbal contact, that first interaction I had with you helped bring out the love that I had pent up in my soul throughout the years."

"I think love must start and be created by the individual. That is what makes love so hurtful and complex. You don't just fall in love. You first fall into infatuation and then love is developed through time. A person cannot truly care for someone unless they get to know that person. People can say they care for someone they don't know, but people tend to care more about people they know over people they don't know. I believe love is built the same way. Love is first created on current and past experiences that you have of the world, then you take those experiences and play them against what your imagination has pre-developed in your mind. One plays off the other, and your conclusion is the byproduct called attraction."

"The reason I say this is that to be happy and find love in the world, one must feel the emotions that those experiences give off. Again… it is called attraction. You must have some kind of attraction to someone before love can enter the equation. This attraction develops into emotional feelings toward a person. Hopefully these emotions will trigger something inside the observer to reawaken the processor of these emotions to an experience they had or had not experienced before in their life. This new familiarity is pleasing to the receiver because this experience or multiple experiences gives a certain type of excitement to the person. The experience that person feels is special to them, and they will never get those exact same feelings with another person."

"They don't want to lose the opportunity that has made them feel so special, so unique. It gives insight to a subject that was unexplored by the human being until that moment hit them. Thus, consciously, these new experiences or feelings help create in one's mind a comfort zone that the person feels at home with, and they don't want to lose what makes them feel so happy. When explored further, they discover additional feelings and experiences that they like, sometimes even more than the original feeling that attracted them in the first place. As these feelings compound upon one another, the person then starts to sense a level of comfort that he cannot live without, and this level of feeling is pure love."

"When we experience something, that experience will give us new experiences and hopefully we will learn from all of them. In my opinion, this is what love is or should be about in one's life. One must feel the emotion of those experiences in their soul first, and through that emotion one relates past and present experiences to gain a better insight of you, and that hopefully will translate to the desired individual that one is infatuated with. Through that insight one will have the chance to find love or pure love."

"So, at that moment when I finally met you, I had to act on my instincts or, as some would say, had to act on impulse. I felt at the time that you were the one, so I had to prove my love for you by first expressing my feelings to you. When that interaction took place is when my love was developing for you by the minute, especially when you were responsive to my actions."

"I think love must be felt and this is obtained through giving someone or something attention in the beginning of an infatuation period. Love must find its way to the individual and not the individual finding love. If you are looking for love, you will find false or non-true love. Your mind will trick you into thinking the person that you 'picked' is in love with you. You start wishing the person is the one for you because you desire to be wanted or you desire to want the image of love that you have manifested in your mind over the years. This is the way love is played out in most people's lives. That is why I think divorce rates have been so high over the past centuries. People pick their partners out of convenience and not out of love. They pick their partners because so many people have told them they need to find someone during a certain period in their life. They follow orders to the letter without actually thinking about answering the most important question... are you really in love with the person you picked?"

Marci said, "I agree because I have often wondered how a handsome, classy, well-to-do person can fall in love with a poor, uneducated and untalented person of meager means. I guess the answer is simple. The idea of love that you just described is operating. See, I believe that love is what you find in your heart and not in materialistic goods. I like to think of the heart as the center of your body. It keeps the blood flowing. All that blood in your body must pass through the heart. The heart also symbolizes god, if it exists, where our veins and arteries are. Like the veins are carriers for the heart, we are the carriers of god's love. No matter how you look at it, the blood is always in some contact with the heart. The heart is what keeps the blood moving. The heart is strong, rhythmic, pure, and gentle; therefore, it represents love. Love must be experienced through the heart for it to be pure. You find this insight through experience, the experience of nature, music, literature, and being alone with yourself. You experience this pure love through death or by any materialistic or naturalistic item or force."

"The ultimate love is god, and no love anywhere can match, equal or better that love. Most human beings love each other through their minds instead of their hearts. In other words, the mind is what governs and controls the heart. It can increase the blood flow, and decrease it whenever the mind chooses."

"The mind is based on experience and reasoning, and pure love has no reason. It is just there. Most humans create their love, and even pure love is created, but it is controlled by no one. You, through your heart, create it, but you cannot destroy it, whereas the mind can. I said that the mind controls the heart, but the heart is what keeps the mind operating and controlling."

I said to Marci, "Well, I don't know about this god angle, but you have brought up some very interesting points. For the record though, I fell in love with you the moment I saw you and I didn't care about your education, financial means or how talented you were. Again, the idea and how I created that thought in my mind of what you would be like and assumed what you were like is what kept the fire burning in my soul."

"When I met you, you performed certain acts for me that proved to me that you were the perfect one for me. These acts were already established in my mind from the very beginning. If you didn't perform the simple acts that I had pre-manufactured in my mind, then you would have been a disappointment to me and I would have simply left you alone and gone on about my business. Conversely, if I did not live up to your expectations, you would have never accepted my invitation to go backstage with me and you would have walked to your seat in the auditorium and resumed your enjoyment of the orchestra without even the slightest thought of me."

"Now I wonder what those two newborns are thinking right now. Johnny's soul is reaching out for a child that he didn't want or expect. He had five, and two died. Of the three living, I allowed him to see, touch and speak closely with only one of them. Have the other two newborns already come to premature conclusions that their brother has left them and they will not be able to share in what he is experiencing at this moment? Have the two newborns bonded with each other over their brother, and because of one simple action like me picking which brother to go to the father, has this totally and completely changed their lives forever before they even had time to think of their fate? If you stop to think about this for a while, how often does this happen to all us in a lifetime?" I questioned.

"To take it a step further, do we just constantly make do with what is given to us? Can we change our fate? If we have no control over our fate, then how can we change it or do we want to change the preset direction our lives have paved for us? When I look at our current experiment, I have basically forced a child on Johnny and thus have forced the child to have Johnny as a father. By design, I have purposely confined Jake's two brothers from as much social interaction as possible. The other two were conveniently left out by my choosing, not theirs. Or was it? Maybe one of the others should have sensed what I had planned for their future and maybe one of them should have been more proactive. Maybe one of them should have anticipated what I was going to do. What if one of them would have stepped in front of me to make sure he would have been chosen and not one of the others? Would that have changed their fate? On top of this, would that have been a smart move on their part? Maybe he didn't want to be with his father; maybe he thought he was better off without him."

I continued. "It is a very interesting dilemma. We might think we don't have choices, and for the most part that is true, but there are times in our lives that the choices we make today effects our future for tomorrow. When I look back on my life, I never had a choice about this formula flowing around in my system. It was just given to me by force. Of course, as I have gotten older, I have grown to view this as a gift. But either way, this has been forced on me and thus it is my fate."

My eyes looked deeply into Marci's as we both smiled, knowing that after reviewing an experiment of the ages, we had just expressed our love for one another. Lewis looked down at the floor and a smile, for the first time in a while, developed on his face. Down deep he knew that what he was doing was not morally right, but he didn't have a choice. He knew he couldn't leave, especially now. I know because I could sense that he believed I would kill him if he tried to leave.

Lewis was forced into this situation and had to make the best of his fate. Like what Jake, Johnny, or I, for that matter, must deal with regarding what fate has dealt us, Lewis thought that maybe down the road, if he had an opportunity to leave, he would make a break toward freedom, but until then he had to do his job and see the experiments through to the end. Of course, in the back of his mind he always thought about the great wealth that would come his way if we could control this formula's makeup to reduce the physical mutations. Hence, he was still with me, and I felt that my partner would never leave me.

Young Jake grew at a fast rate and was getting larger by the day, and so were the other newborns. Jake was at the beginning stages of speaking, but we had no expectations of him speaking well if he was going to speak at all. Looking at his x-rays and upon the multitude of examinations, the voice box was abnormal so we knew that verbal dialogue would be limited.

The other newborns learned from each other but were more playful than Jake. The reason was because Johnny didn't always play with Jake. He was more in the mood to teach and love him, whereas the other newborns didn't have that available to them. They seemed to be slower than Jake and were not advancing as fast as the brother that was receiving love and attention. This was very interesting to us because it does seem that our environment shapes us educationally as well as socially.

As time passed, Johnny was getting more upset with us about not letting him closer to his other sons. Obviously, our relationship with him was beyond strained. We could even tell a difference in attitude from Jake towards us as compared to the other two newborns. Jake disliked us and, of course, had developed this trait by way of his father. As part of the experiment, I purposely made sure Johnny and Jake would overhear my conversations with Lewis and Marci about the other two newborns. I openly expressed that I saw no reason to keep the two newborns alive. Of course, this made Johnny extremely upset.

We did not train or instruct the isolated newborns. I wanted them to learn from each other and see if their innate senses would take over. The only potential problem with this was that they were part human and, as any human newborn, they needed to be nurtured and taken care of by an older human or they would die. Animals throughout the world learn extremely fast, hours after birth, to at least take care of themselves. Many animals learn how to walk just hours after birth, and many learn to fend for themselves in just days. This is obviously not the case with humans.

The newborns made terrible messes on the tile floor, they were not neat when they ate, and they were not developing like I had hoped. Johnny was very upset over these facts, but he knew better than to make a scene. He knew that we would take Jake away from him in a second, so he knew we had control over him. Most of the time I think Johnny just ignored our conversations because it was just easier for him to accept the unknown instead of trying to guess what would happen to him or his sons in the future. He was scared, but he didn't want us to know.

Over time, I told Lewis and Marci that we had an over population of specimens. We had gathered as much data as possible at this point, especially with the isolated newborns. Jake was taught by his father, so he was not an issue at this point. In fact, our attention was totally on Johnny and Jake at this juncture of the experiment. The way I saw it was that we already had two subjects and we didn't need four. Marci agreed with me, but Lewis didn't. I told Lewis that we had learned all we could from the newborns and mentioned that we could dissect one of them while disposing of the other. Lewis was beside himself. I don't know what disturbed him the most – my ideas or Marci agreeing with them. He told us that he felt dirty, sinful, and remorseful about all that he had participated in to this date. He said that the further he went along, the deeper he went against his God. For me, that was just pure nonsense.

I sometimes wondered why Lewis even became a doctor. He had a faint heart, and what he had gone through over the years had almost broken him. I sensed he was about to give up, but I also sensed that he was afraid of me. I kept that fear alive in him and used it to my advantage. I needed Lewis more then he needed me, but now with Marci coming into the picture, I was becoming more comfortable with Lewis's stubbornness at times.

The main problem was that Lewis had the education and the knowledge of science, whereas Marci didn't. I found it very odd that

Marci was so accepting of what she was being exposed to. Most people would not only be totally repulsed by our experiments, but they would be running to the police for them to put a stop to what we were doing. I sensed nothing from Marci that would suggest her doing any of that to us. In fact, Marci wanted to do more around the lab and to assist more in the experimentations.

Like clockwork, after many discussions and having some time to mull things over, Lewis reluctantly agreed to my wishes. Lewis did have a different point of view; he wanted to wait to kill the newborns until they were fully grown. The only problem with that line of thinking was that I didn't want to wait on them to grow to full maturity. I was only interested in perfecting the formula, and the newborns were certainly not providing any answers toward that goal. Also, I just wasn't interested in the lesser of the new species. I did decide to let the newborns live for a while just to see what would happen to them physically and see if they would improve mentally.

After a couple of months, it seemed to us that the newborns had all stopped their growth. They didn't grow to the length we thought they would. When we extended the hind legs fully and measured them from top to bottom, they measured to be about five feet in length, and stood about three and a half feet in height when they were not extending their legs. What we found very interesting was that the two isolated newborns were shorter than Jake. They also grew less hair, and had smaller arms, legs, and heads. This was really strange, and we couldn't understand why the physical differences between the three newborns. We could understand the difference mentally, but why the physical difference?

In fact, the isolated twins took on more rabbit-like features than Jake did. To be quite honest, the changes were striking between the two brothers and Jake. The differences between the three brothers were very entertaining and astonishing. Jake ended up having thicker, healthier hair. He also was bigger, about a half foot longer and taller than his two brothers. The blood work was the same, but we were at a loss as to the reason for the different sizes and appearances between the brothers. We could understand the intelligence being greater for Jake because Johnny taught him and took care of him, whereas the other twins were basically forgotten. For the life of us, we could not explain the differences in the physical factors of the newborns.

Jake did end up being able to speak, although it was very difficult to understand him. He couldn't form certain words, which made communication very difficult since the voice box wasn't made for human speech. Also, their tongues were very long and thick which greatly affected the process of speech. The isolated twins, outside of grunting and making strange animal sounds, didn't speak or even come close to speaking. After taking numerous samples of their blood, hair, and skin during their growth periods, we decided to terminate the two isolated brothers' lives.

Lewis had a lot of trouble preparing himself to kill the isolated brothers, so I had to be the one to end their lives. I was going to place Johnny under so I didn't have to hear his cries and threats, but like Marci told me, we were going to hear him bitch about it eventually, so why bother. The two brothers were always calm and they never seemed to be aggressive at all, but I didn't want to take any chances with them. I loaded the tranquilizer gun, planning to put the two under and then drag them over to the cremation machine and dispose of them. I had Marci there with me who was going to help me carry one of the bodies to the cremation machine.

For most of my life, I had never liked animals. Even when I was a young child, I never really liked them outside of a dog, and even then they would always run from me. On a few occasions I was taken to the zoo and all the animals either ran from me or growled. This behavior really bothered me because I wanted to see them and study them, but they wouldn't allow me to view them long enough to satisfy my curiosity. My adoptive parents never allowed me to have a pet and I knew after the dog incident that I would never have a dog as a pet. I never liked cats for some reason.

I loved to watch the deer as they pranced around the back of our yard. I would watch the squirrels, birds and raccoons run or fly around the house, but I never got the chance to get too close to them. They all seemed to run from me. Of course, for me, these little species were and are my food preferences, so logic would dictate that would be the reason animals ran from me.

I went over to Johnny with the gun in my hand and I said to him, "Johnny, I am sorry for what I am about to do, but these animals cannot be allowed to live any longer. They are not as advanced as Jake and they serve no purpose to me."

Johnny said in his growling and deep voice, "Listen here, you fucking bastard. If you hurt my children, I will kill you. Do you understand me, you son of a bitch?"

I said, "Johnny, you didn't want to impregnate Mary from the start. You followed my instructions and soon I will let you go."

Johnny quickly retorted, "You will not let me go. Just look at me, you sick fuck. I know you just told me that to keep me calm. Look what you did to me. I am a freak. On top of this, you bring your little whore down here for her sick, sadistic pleasure to watch you screw with human life."

Marci then chimed in our conversation, "First of all, I am not a whore. Second, yes you are a freak and I have been trying to tell you that for months. Mr. Seawick made you better than you were before your transformation. You were a drunk, a loser, a parasite to society. You owe Mr. Seawick everything. He has given you a better life."

With that, Johnny started growling and snorting angrily. He paced the floor of the cell, keeping his eyes on both of us, but especially Marci. Jake was noticeably scared and found his way under his father's cot, just lying there shaking in fear in a rather large pool of his own urine. I told Marci to ignore him and help me with the other newborns.

I knew Marci never liked Johnny from the get go and I don't know why. Sometimes people just don't get along for some reason.

I thought about what I was going to do with the bodies and how I was going to carry them from the cell to the cremation machine. They were not tall, but very thick, and because of this wide girth they weighed more than what they appeared. I didn't want to be messy like I was with Adam. I didn't want to cut them into pieces and take each piece to the cremation machine. I thought it would be too much of a mess and I didn't want to disturb Marci with all the blood and loose body parts.

I decided if I could get them to walk most of the distance and then shoot them with the tranquillizers, I could drag them into the machine or, if I was lucky, they might stumble inside with some encouragement. I decided this would be the best way to handle these animals. The only issue I had was the fear of one of them, or both for that matter, getting loose. They hadn't shown any aggressive behavior patterns in their short lives, but I was still concerned about the potential of them escaping. They were very strong and if one decided to run, it would be difficult for us to stop them.

I placed the rope around the neck of one of the newborns and had Marci hold the pole from outside of the cell. The newborns were very docile and had been that way since their birth. I placed the other rope around the second newborn's neck. I ordered Lewis to hold the other pole as I went into the newborn's cell. I took hold of both poles then gently walked the newborns out of their cell. Lewis took his tranquillizer gun in hand and had it pointed at the newborns during their walk.

Johnny was screaming and growling all this time and his behavior was upsetting Jake. Jake had never seen this side of his father and it was upsetting to him. Johnny was so upset that he was taking items in this cell and throwing them at me, which upset Marci. She was afraid it would upset the newborns and cause them to harm me in the process. Marci quickly yelled at Johnny to stop throwing items and keep quiet. Just after Marci stopped speaking, Johnny picked up a book and threw it at Marci when she was not looking. The book hit her sharply on the side of her face, hard enough that she grabbed her head with both hands and fell to the ground. I heard the book sail through the air and before I could say anything, I saw the book hit her.

I was very angry and yelled at Johnny to stop throwing things and to control himself. I saw Marci hit the floor and knew she was in pain. My anger reached a fever pitch. No one hurts my Marci and gets away with it without repercussions. This was the first time I had ever experienced someone hurting Marci, and obviously I didn't like the feeling. So many loved ones in my life have been hurt by others. I vowed that with Marci, this would be different.

I couldn't express my anger when I saw my love get hit in the head. At first, I did not know if she was knocked out or not. I knew the object was a book, but I didn't know if the book hit her in the temple, the eye, the ear or where on her head. I looked at Johnny and said, "You fucking bastard. That is my future wife you just hit. You will pay dearly for your actions, you fucking freak."

I looked at Marci and she signaled that she was okay. I took a stronger hold on the pole and jerked it hard as I was walking the newborns to the cremation machine. I told Lewis to follow me. Marci was getting up and I asked her if she was okay. She told me she was fine and that the book hit her just above her ear.

I roughly led the two newborns to the oven while Lewis opened the door. Johnny was enraged. He slammed his chest, shoulders, and forearms on the thick bars of his celled home. He kicked, pulled, and pushed the bars. At one point, I thought he just might break through them. I told Lewis to keep an eye on Johnny and make sure he didn't break out. Johnny was so upset and yelling so loud that he was not making sense. It was as if his animalistic senses were now taking control of his human senses.

Lewis took one of the poles from my grasp as I had asked him to. He was so nervous that his hands were shaking quite noticeably. I strongly pushed one of the newborns inside and had it sit down in the chamber of the cremation machine. I released the rope on the newborn and as I did, I poked as hard as I could at the newborn's stomach to make him move toward the back of the machine. It made a horrible grunting sound as it bent over, holding its stomach from the pain. I took the other pole from Lewis as he was busy guarding me from both newborns while keeping an eye on Johnny. His gun was moving rapidly from the newborns to Johnny.

I pushed the second newborn inside of the machine as the first one was still captive on the end of my pole. The second newborn didn't want to go past the entrance of the machine. His small right hand stopped himself from going inside, its fingers gripping the side of the entrance. As I pushed the pole onto the back of his neck, his left arm went up and he placed it on the other side of the entrance. I was worried for a moment, but I quickly told Lewis not to shoot with the tranquilizer. Lewis was arguing and yelling at me that he was going to shoot the thing in the back so we could get him inside. I was becoming aggravated with him because he wasn't listening to me.

I moved the pole back about a foot and a half and with all my strength, jammed the pole as hard as I could in the back of his neck. He didn't budge an inch. I quickly told Lewis to give me the gun. I needed something to force the second newborn into the machine. After my second request, out of the corner of my eye I saw Marci attempting to get the gun away from Lewis. I yelled the order for the third time, finally getting his attention as he loosened his grip on the gun and let Marci take possession. Before I knew it, Marci took the gun in her hands and raised it over her head. I could hear her breathing heavily and could sense her fear and the extremely high level of anxiety. She used the blunt end of the gun and struck near the middle of the newborn's forearm. The arm broke in two, causing the newborn to lose its grip from the side of the oven. The newborn instinctively moved his head to see what happened to its arm. She quickly raised the blunt end of the gun again and landed the hit on its temple. As contact was made, I simultaneously pushed the newborn forward and he finally fell into the chamber.

While this was taking place, the first newborn got up and looked as if he was going to come out. I had the second newborn in the chamber, but his legs were sticking out of the entrance. He was moving his legs rapidly, and I was having trouble getting control of its thick, fast-moving legs. Marci got behind the door and told me to watch out. With all her might, she attempted to close the door on the legs of the newborn that was lying on the oven floor.

Marci's body was tall and thin and she was not that strong. When the oven door hit the leg of the newborn, he hardly moved. I still had the pole around his neck and was franticly trying to loosen the rope. I was yelling at Marci to stop so I could get the rope off its neck. After the first attempt, I used one quick motion and freed the rope from the neck of the newborn. I swiftly lunged with the pole and hit the first newborn who was trying to come out. It stunned him somewhat and he stumbled backward a foot or so. I moved the pole down between the legs of the newborn and then moved the pole upward. The body of the newborn moved quite easily and I finally got his legs cleared from the entrance. When I moved back, Marci suddenly closed and locked the door as fast as she could.

Marci turned to Lewis and she said, "Thanks for the help, Lewis! I would suggest the next time you listen to Garrison and follow his orders."

Lewis said abruptly, "Listen, don't tell me what I should or should not do. I have been doing this type of work a lot longer than you, little girlie."

Marci quickly interrupted and said, "Little girlie! Look here, you fucking bastard, we needed your help with these freaks and you stood by and did nothing. What if one of them got loose? What if one of them would have bitten Garrison? Is that what you wanted?"

Lewis walked toward Marci with his finger pointing at her and I quickly stepped between the two. I grabbed Lewis's index finger and bent it back until I heard a crack. Lewis fell to his knees as I still had possession of his dislocated finger. I sternly but softly said, "Lewis… Lewis… I would suggest two things to you, my good man. First, never come after Marci again in a threatening manner. Okay?" Lewis was kneeing before me, shaking his head in agreement as additional perspiration developed on his forehead. I continued, "Second, when I ask you to do something, I need for you to follow through with the task. Is that understood?" Lewis nodded quickly, hoping for some relief from the pain. I released my grip and Lewis quickly bent over onto the basement floor, holding his finger as he was trying to pop it back into socket. I looked up and saw Marci standing there smiling at the scene. She was loving every minute of it. I could sense the sexual excitement from what she had witnessed over the past few minutes. Marci raised her sultry eyes as she studied my body from my feet up to my eyes. When our eyes met, she slightly opened her mouth and her pouty lips mouthed, "I want to fuck you."

This tense moment with Lewis and Marci was disturbed by the newborns lightly making noise inside the chamber. They were hitting the rounded glass window

Meanwhile, during all this action, Johnny was making a mess in his cage. From the time we got the newborns out of their cage up to me dislocating Lewis's finger, Johnny had picked up his cot and was banging it against the bars of his cell. The bars were very strong and could withstand all kinds of abuse, but I still had some concern over whether the bars could hold up to such force. He was so angry that drops of sweat were flying in all directions from his large body. He loathed the fact that the bars were keeping him from protecting his two other boys. Jake was now getting more upset and was behind him, mimicking his father's behavior.

Marci's hatred for Johnny grew after he hit her in the head with the book. She so desperately wanted to be the one to turn the machine on. She requested this in front of Johnny and made sure he heard. She was smiling at him the entire time she waited for my answer. Of course, I could never say no to my Marci, so I showed Marci how to turn the machine on. The machine didn't take long to heat up, although some take a while for the burners to produce enough heat for the burning process to begin. I instructed Marci to turn the temperature up as high as it would go from the start.

As Johnny and Jake were making growling and hissing noises, Lewis was busy attempting to move his finger back into socket. As the finger popped into socket, he let out a loud moan. As he collected himself, he immediately started looking for the tranquilizer gun. I had kicked it out of the way of the cremation machine while I was getting one of the newborns inside the chamber. Lewis was very upset and wanted to at least put Johnny and Jake out with a sedative, but I refused. Lewis wasn't fond of burning the two newborns alive, but I was beyond caring what Lewis thought at that moment in time, and I wanted Johnny to suffer from hitting my love. Johnny was about to lose his mind. I could see his arm bleeding from the many times he had smashed his arm into the bars, trying to get to us and save his children.

I wanted Johnny to witness Marci burning his sons alive, and I know Marci would have it no other way. She was so excited, and I could sense the hatred filling her soul each passing moment since she closed the chamber door. This was a side that I was not familiar with from my Marci. A part of me wanted her to remain nice, pure, and sweet, but this side had significantly peaked my interest. She was becoming more like me. This was exciting for me because her hatred was a sexual turn on. I sensed a sexual attraction from the scent her body was giving off. This newly discovered sensual place that Marci found in her personality was strange and scary to her, but in a bizarre way she felt comfortable in this mindset.

Marci and I were quickly connecting on a spiritual level. No words needed to be said between us. Her actions were speaking for both of us. She wanted to please, assist and defend me, and this experience with the newborns gave her a sense of worth. She felt that she interconnected with me for the first time since we met. I believe it brought back fond memories of when she first saw me and had followed me through my career.

I sensed that Marci created a fantasy world in her conscious mind. In her world, she viewed me as a perfect man, a man that she controlled throughout those many years of adoration. As anyone who has ever fantasized before knows, you create the fantasy where you always win or you always get the cherished prize at the end. You create the scene that plays out to your benefit to please and make yourself feel as the victor in your fantasy. You make sure you are in control and are the king of the imaginary world that you created.

I believe that when Marci first met me, she didn't feel that she measured up to me on any level. I could sense this, and it saddened me.

She knew her violin and piano skills or intelligence level couldn't match mine. She felt as if she was not worthy. I didn't feel this way toward her, but that didn't matter. What mattered was what she felt and believed in her heart and imagination. Now she had discovered a couple of subjects that, in her mind, we could relate to on a higher level; those being sex and excitement for the macabre. This was her finest personal discovery because now she felt she had something that we could relate to with each other and that made her feel wonderful and needed.

I peered through the circular window of the steel chamber door. The newborns were now moving around inside the tightly confined space. I saw Marci turn the machine on, but instead of turning the temperature button on the highest setting, she only turned the temperature knob half way. She wanted to make the newborns suffer, but more importantly, it was to get back at Johnny. She wanted to torture his sons for what he did to her. I could sense the anger and hatred in Marci. Her body was giving off this incredible and indescribable scent that I had never inhaled before. It was a mixture of anger and extreme joy, and somehow this mixture produced a scent that was intoxicating to me. I knew Johnny had to notice the odor as well. That was probably why he was so upset with her because he sensed what she was going to do to his offspring.

When Marci increased the temperature in the chamber, the newborns were visibly upset with the sudden change of heat and airflow. They pushed, shoved, and tried to climb over each other in the attempt to get out. One of them looked out of the window and moved its mouth. I knew it was asking for help. Suddenly, the newborn was pushed out of the way and the other one shoved its face in the window.

After a few moments, I could hear the screams they were making and so could Johnny. Johnny pressed his body against the metal bars. Part of his arm and shoulder were still bleeding from repeatedly ramming his body against the bars of the cage. His anger had been replaced with heartfelt pain and anguish, knowing that his sons would soon die and suffer a very painful death.

On the other side of the room, I could sense that Lewis was extremely nervous as he witnessed all this before him. He was the type of person that wanted to be liked, and he didn't want to have to worry about creating an enemy and have the fear of that enemy coming after him later. He was yelling at Marci to stop, but he knew full well that he could not stop her, knowing I would have stopped him before he reached her. I knew Marci was enjoying the scene. I wondered why situations like this didn't bother her but bothered everyone else in the house. I think it is because of the love she had for me.

I looked inside the chamber and saw their skin turn light black for a moment and then suddenly they both burst into flames. It happened in a manner of seconds. They were yelling and running into each other and the walls of the enclosed chamber. Suddenly, they stopped making noise and moving. Their bodies were engulfed in flames as I had to step back from the steel chamber because the heat was so intense. As I stepped back, Marci turned the heat up to the maximum temperature so their bones would completely burn. Johnny was in tears as he witnessed everything unfold. He stood there with his body pressed hard against the bars as if they had grown into his body. He felt the most helpless feeling fall upon him. I could sense his hurt and longing for his lost children. What made the situation worse for him was that he never had an opportunity to even touch them; he only saw them from across the room. When the cremation was nearing the end and he suddenly knew it was all over, his sorrow turned back to anger. He looked at me and my love and vowed that he would kill us all.

As the newborns continued to burn, Johnny was crying and telling us how he hated us and was going to kill us. I looked at my love for what felt like hours but was only a moment, until her eyes met mine. She stood there with that half smile that I had grown quite fond of. It would form on her beautiful and flawless face whenever she would do something naughty or if she had an impure thought. Her mouth was open just enough to allow her heavy breath to escape from her luscious body. She stood there as if she were posing for a sexy magazine photo.

That sultry, sexual look of pure womanhood pierced through me like a well-drawn dagger.

As Marci stared at me, she would occasionally look over at Johnny. Her smile widened after every glance. She would then look back at me and that wide smile would hastily turn back to the sultry look. She slowly walked over to me with a grace that a queen would be envious of. She stopped a foot from me, then moved her head over to the right and looked inside to see the two bodies on fire. She looked back at me and said, "That was incredible. You know, if you would have told me a month ago that I would have done something like this, I would have laughed at you. I don't know what came over me, but I had this rush, this passion inside of me that I just had to push that button. I know I just committed murder but… god help me… I loved it and would do it again."

I said to Marci, "You killed two animals; you did not kill any humans. You killed two things that we created with an unknown formula. You did this in the name of science. We could have not kept them alive anyway."

Johnny started to mouth off and while crying said, "Animals? They were not animals, you sick bitch. They were my children."

I quickly said, "Shut up and quit calling her a bitch." With that, Marci took my chin with her left hand and roughly moved my head toward her. Before I knew it, her mouth was caressing mine. Her tongue snaked its way inside my mouth while her right hand touched my cock.

Lewis said, "Marci, stop that. What is the matter with you two?" I raised my hand up as if to say, 'mind your own business.'

Johnny was even more upset now with this spontaneous act of passion before him. Marci unzipped my pants and inserted her hand inside. She sternly pushed me, by way of my manhood, down onto the floor of the basement. She pushed me back as our lips parted and she took her free hand and pushed me to the floor. My ass crashed onto the floor, and in one splendid movement, Marci pushed my shoulder back with her foot as she reached under her skirt. She peeled her panties away from her vagina and pushed them to the side. She slowly moved her pussy closer to my penis. A couple of times she looked directly into Johnny's eyes. Johnny was upset and banging on the bars of the cell so hard that small amounts of blood were being splattered onto the floor in front of him.

I felt the head of my penis being rubbed across a silky wetness, and suddenly a slow warmness developed over my manhood. The pleasure was very intense as my love slid as close to me as she could. She attempted to take all of me and then retreated about half way back. Slowly, she pushed her body onto my manhood and again went as deep as she could. The strokes added up, but her pace remained slow and steady. She was now possessed and I could sense that she had never felt so alive.

As we continued our lovemaking, Johnny was moving around in his cell, trying to find a way out or to find something to throw at us. I saw Lewis quickly grab the tranquilizer gun off the floor and shot Johnny in the chest. Then a second shot was released and the tranquilizer went into Jake. I was glad because I was growing tired of their idle threats and sadness over their sons' and brothers' deaths. The complaining got on my nerves and I had more important business to attend to at that moment.

Lewis lowered the gun and looked over at us and said, "You two disgust me. What is wrong with you? You just killed his sons and then you make love in front of him. I have never in my life been more appalled than what I am right now."

Marci muttered, "Shut up, Lewis. You enjoyed it as much as I did. You are just upset that I am not fucking you." Lewis was pissed and walked over to his lab table, pitched the gun onto the table, and walked out of the room. Marci and I finished our lovemaking and my love slowly dismounted. She moved her panties back into place and adjusted herself. I slowly got up and with a smile said, "Well, that was unexpected." Marci walked out of the room without saying a word and I started to clean out the crematory machine. I didn't expect what had happened to become reality. Marci was turned on by the excitement of not only the unknown, but the intense stress and adrenaline rush of killing something. These feelings Marci experienced were new to her. Most people would run from this situation, but she not only accepted it, she indulged herself in the moment. I had never felt her love so strong.

When Marci went upstairs, she engaged Lewis while he was nervously sipping on some of my finest brandy in the great room. Lewis didn't look at Marci when she spoke. Marci said, "Lewis, I am sorry for the way I spoke to you, but I was in another world. Garrison makes me feels so… so different, so alive, and so special. I never did anything like that in my life." With that, a smile came over her face as she allowed a small giggle to escape her satisfied body.

Lewis lowered the drink from his lips in total amazement from what he had just heard. He got up from his chair and said to her, "Did you just hear yourself, Marci? You just killed two little boys in front of their father and their brother. You fucked your boyfriend in front of them. What the fuck is wrong with you?" The uncontrolled anger quickly built up inside of Lewis as he looked at the childlike glow on her face. Her attitude and smirky smile was an all too often annoyance to Lewis.

Marci saw the look on Lewis's face and felt his disapproval, which quickly sent her into a rage. She stepped toward him, forcing him to step back abruptly as she said, "Look, I am not proud of what I did down there, having sex with Garrison in front of you and those things, but I had this feeling that I had never felt in my life come over me and I just lost control of my mind. He is the only person that has ever truly loved me."

Lewis interrupted and said, "See… see, that is what I am talking about. Garrison is dangerous and is controlling you."

Marci quickly said, "Oh no, he is not controlling me. I am fully aware of what I'm doing."

Lewis said, "Marci, you have to go. You need to leave this place. He is not sick, he is just demented. He is going to hurt you someday if you don't break it off with him."

Marci said, "I will never leave him."

I heard most of the conversation, and as Marci ended her sentence I stepped into the room. I quickly asked Marci, "My love, why are you so different from the rest of the people in this world? I mean, I love it that you are different and that is one of the many reasons why I love you so much. You don't pass judgment on me. In fact, you embrace my actions and thoughts. I can sense the passion that you have towards me and I admire your attitude and desire. Why are you the way you are, my beautiful Marci?"

Marci looked at me and said, "For some strange and unexplainable reason, I enjoy your experiments. I think it is awesome what you are trying to do for humanity. The thought that people will never grow old, never get sick or to have all their illnesses disappear is nothing short of something god would discover. You hold the secret of everlasting life, Garrison. You and you alone are unexplainable. You are the only one in this world that is like you. You are the mold of which all mankind wants to be like, what they strive to be. Oh, how I wish I could have just a fraction of your intelligence or of your ability to play the violin or the piano. To imagine for just a second that you will live forever is such a turn on because no one else in this world could say that but you. I knew from the moment I saw you that something was special about your persona. Now I know your secret. I want someday to be you. I want you to make me perfect like you. I want to play like you, feel what you feel, hear, smell and taste what you experience. I am totally, absolutely, one hundred percent obsessed with your complete, total makeup. You have what I desire physically, mentally, and spiritually. Garrison, if there is a god on earth, I would swear it would be you."

I continued to look into her eyes and I could sense that she was telling the truth. I said to my love, "Marci, you know I could never infect you with the formula, not until it is perfected and that might not be in your lifetime."

Marci said, "I don't care, Garrison. If I knew that my changed looks would not repulse you, I would want you to infect me now."

Lewis interrupted quickly and said, "No! This can never happen. Garrison, you need to talk some sense into her."

I said to her, "You know you would change into what my parents changed into, right? As you can clearly see, I could never do that to you. But if I would ever find the final solution to this formula, I would be more than happy to… correct… you so you could live forever by my side."

Marci said, "What happens if you don't find the answers until it is too late for me?"

I looked down at her feet and said, "I don't know. That is why I need to learn as much as I can as soon as possible. That is why I am conducting these experiments."

Marci walked over to me, took my hands in hers and said, "I think it is time for us to get married. I never really cared for marriage growing up, but you have changed all that for me. I need to share my soul with yours. You make me a better woman. I have never felt this way about anyone or anything. You know, for me, when two people are in love it is all about wonder and new experiences. The problem is that people are so concerned about what others think that they just go ahead and rush into marriage. I never wanted to be that person. Marriage should be based on endless, uncontrolled, undisciplined, maddening, obsessive love. Marriage is a bonding forever, it acts out the beginning of a relationship that unites two people into one. But as I search my heart, I have found that my love for you first started out as a fascination with you, your life, your command of the violin and, of course, your intellect."

"Then over time, that fascination developed into love. That love has been created and formed through my past experiences and from those experiences I know I have met my true soulmate. For that fascination to be true, pure love, one must go beyond oneself. The two must be in unison with one another. Not on the outside just to prove to their friends or to themselves that they are in love, but on the inside, in their hearts they must be one. They must learn to work and love together. One must experience this first and when one does, they will know if it is that true and pure love that we all are striving for. I believe I have arrived at this stage of our relationship."

I found those words to be very comforting as Marci revealed her soul to me. I happened to be in full agreement with her premises on love and how love is developed between two people. I told her, "My love, I agree with you and what you told me melts my heart. I personally believe that a couple must find each other interesting at first, and then allow it to develop into love. Like I have said before, I knew you were special the first time my eyes rested upon your body. You were and are still so beautiful. I have not experienced a lot of love in my life. The love from my mother is the closest thing I had until I met you. You stirred my heart into chaos until I found my center. After I recovered, I knew from the get-go that you were the one for me. I had to have you, both sexually and spiritually. The love I have for you has reawakened all areas of my heart that I closed years ago. Throughout our relationship, I have found newly discovered areas of my soul that have been exposed. At first those areas were frightening and intimidating to me, but I have learned to accept them and allow them to educate me so I can be a better man for you. This newly found education has bonded my love even stronger than ever before."

"This energy that I have felt since the beginning of our love affair, I knew was something special. If a person were to ever miss the feelings and the passion that we have spoken about today, then that person is not in love or practiced pure love. Now we will always have doubts at times and I believe that would be normal, but I have never doubted my heart or the feelings that I have for you because true love is never doubted or questioned. My love is present in my heart and my eyes. The eyes are the most important of your lover's body because the eyes are the windows to their soul and heart."

After we expressed our love for each other we embraced. I looked over at Lewis and he just shook his head. I could feel what he was feeling. I knew what he was thinking. I could sense his thoughts and feelings so readily, it was crystal clear to me. He was afraid of me and my family. He never wanted this life for himself and now he saw a lot of himself in Marci. He could not understand why anyone would volunteer for this life willingly.

I wanted Marci to graduate from college before we got married. She worked too hard not to follow through on her graduation. She agreed and we put the wedding date off until she took and passed the necessary courses needed to get her degree. My fear was that if she didn't get a degree now, she probably never would.

Marci was really improving on her violin studies. Since we had known each other, she had improved by great lengths, but in her eyes, she was not perfect. I don't know how many times she told me that her goal was to play the violin perfectly like me. She had spent a good part of her life striving for that goal to turn into reality, but no matter how many times we spoke about this unattainable goal that she set for herself, she just could not accept the fact that her skills would never be perfect like mine. I did everything I could do to teach her. I spent many hours with her myself, as well as had private lessons from others in the Louisville Orchestra conducted at my house. I tried every angle to help improve her playing, but she just didn't have the talent to be a flawless violin player. In fact, she would probably struggle to make it as a member of one of the lesser known orchestras in smaller cities. This fact was just unacceptable to her and I felt her pain and frustration. The only recourse I had was to try and perfect Formula L and somehow stop the horrible physical mutation process. In doing so, it would provide an opportunity for my love to be as perfect as she wished and it would make her live forever and never age just like me. Then we could literally be together forever. This was my primary goal at that moment in my life.

CHAPTER 14

Grueling

ewis and I ran as many tests as we could on our newly formed subjects, Johnny and Jake. After we collected as much data as we could, I decided that I didn't have any need to keep them alive. Truth be told, I was growing more concerned with each passing day that one or both would escape their celled world. I felt Johnny's intense and disturbing hatred toward me and my Marci. I believed that he despised Marci the most. I knew I had to end his life because we had run all the tests that we could, and from all indications he was finished with his growth. We thought about not exterminating Jake's life for the time being; we wanted him to grow up and see what kind of changes he would undergo, but after we thought about this issue more, we decided that it would be in everyone's best interest to end his life as well. These experiments were not getting us any closer to the underlying root of the issue, therefore, keeping Jake or Johnny alive only wasted our time and resources.

I believed at the time that the specimens sensed their ending. I felt they were plotting their escape which, if they were to escape, would be a tragedy, not only for us but for mankind as a whole. It would be unacceptable if they would have ever escaped. That would be the end of our experiments and probably the end for us all. I could not have this creature and his son roaming the city uncontrolled. He could infect anyone and, like a virus, the formula would be transferred to multiple hosts, and in just months the situation would be out of control. This could never happen. Now, all three of us were getting paranoid with the idea of the worst-case scenario developing, so we had to decide when and how to exterminate the subjects. We decided to have Marci help us with the killings. She would never forgive me if I didn't include her, so we had to make her a part of the end of this particularly long experiment.

With careful thought, I wanted to test an issue further before we had the subjects exterminated. At the beginning of this part of the experiment, I wanted to see how long it would take for the subjects to live. From all our data, we concluded that they would probably live forever.

I wanted to conduct experiments on their immune system, but as with anything, time has a way of changing your goals. I would say that Lewis was surprisingly willing to go along with the experiment in the beginning. This was a perfect opportunity for us to at least test his immune system, to see just how much the system could take from outside sources or influences. It was well documented and proven that the infect host's body could take an extreme amount of abuse and still survive.

I wanted to run a test on Johnny by giving him large doses of poison, and we decided to use arsenic. Lewis placed a high dosage in Johnny's food and drink. After several days, there were no visible or physical signs of the poison affecting him. We took a few blood samples and the poison was in his system, but it was not affecting Johnny. In fact, under the microscope, Formula L seemed to be attacking the poison, almost isolating it, and over several hours the poison seemed to slowly disappear. It was amazing to watch all this unfold before our very eyes. After further studies, Lewis and I came to the conclusion that any noncorrosive poison would not affect the Formula L host.

For the next experiment, I wanted to see how quickly they would heal after a cut or a burn. From my own life experiences, I have noticed that after I receive a small cut or a scratch from an animal, within a few hours the cut or scratch would completely heal. The cut in the skin would close within a few minutes by healing from within. After a matter of hours, there would only be a blemish and then before I knew it, the blemish would be gone. The same injury would take most people as long as two weeks to be completely healed with no evidence of a prior injury or tear in the tissue. The deeper the cut or injury, the longer it would take, but again, the speed of the healing on my body would take a fraction of the time it would for a normal human to heal. I wanted to see if this was also true for Johnny.

One day, while Johnny was sleeping near the cell wall, I quickly took a large knife in my hand. I quietly made my way toward Johnny and with one quick and decisive slash with my knife, I made a large, deep cut into his arm. Johnny woke up in obvious pain. I retreated from the bars of the cell as fast as I could. He was upset and very annoyed by my actions. The blood was forcefully dripping from his arm. I quickly went to the lab table and took a highly corrosive acid that I had poured into a beaker from Lewis's lab.

I told Johnny, as I was walking back toward him, that this solution would stop the bleeding. I quickly flung some of the acid at his face. As the acid hit his face, he was in immediate, intense pain. He moved around the cell, practically tearing up almost everything. After a day or so, the deep cut from the knife had completely healed. The acid burns on his face took about the same amount of time to entirely heal. Some of the acid got into his left eye, but after several days his eye and eyesight were back to normal. Again, further proving what I had already known – that the formula protects and nurtures the host.

Throughout this experiment, I toyed with the thought of wanting to see how much physical abuse these subjects could physically and mentally undergo. I recalled the physical torture of my brother and what he had endured. He lived through some of the most intense torture methods that I knew of at the time. I sawed off his arms and legs and went very deep into his torso with the saw, and he was still living at the very end. Obviously, the formula causes the body to maintain life no matter how catastrophic an injury the body endures.

These facts concerned me because I knew the longer I kept these creatures alive, the better my chances of potential danger existed to me, Lewis and, more importantly, my Marci. I also had concern about all living life, plants, and animals. The purpose of this experiment was to learn more about the formula which, at the end of the day, we learned little more than what we already knew. The formula's makeup was too complicated for us to figure out. We felt there was no way we could determine how to recreate the formula, much less learn how to manipulate it so the physical mutation would not take place. We were back to where we started. There were some interesting tidbits that we discovered through this experiment, but nothing that would lead us to our desired results. We just confirmed a lot of information that we, and especially I, already knew.

We were now beyond the point of experimentation on Johnny and Jake. Their services were no longer useful. Keeping them alive served no purpose outside of watching them as if they were a freak show at the circus. Lewis and I pondered about how we were going to exterminate them, and we wanted it to be clean and quick. We planned this event carefully. We wanted to shoot both with tranquilizers and then I would move one of the bodies to the crematory machine. Lewis thought it would be a good idea to have two guns just in case something went wrong. We decided that Marci would have the other gun in her hands, away from us, while Lewis would have the other gun on the one that we got out of the cage. We talked it over numerous times and finally it was time to end the experiment.

As expected, Marci wanted to assist in the extermination process. She arrived in the early morning hours. The three of us proceeded down to the lab. Lewis walked to his lab and next to his desk was a large cabinet. He opened the cabinet doors and took out two tranquilizer guns. Immediately Johnny started to mouth off, asking a bunch of questions about what he was going to do with the guns. Lewis handed Marci her gun and showed her how to fire it.

Johnny knew we were up to something. We made sure not to talk about what we had planned in front of him so he would not get more upset. We decided to fully load the tranquilizers. I doubted if that would have killed them since Formula L had the ability to combat any manmade or natural medicines from killing the host.

Without looking, Lewis went over to the cell and raised the gun. Johnny quickly moved back and before he knew it, Lewis had fired the gun and hit Johnny twice. He quietly reloaded and shot Jake twice. The bodies fell to the floor and were out cold. Marci was instructed to shoot Johnny twice with her gun. She did as instructed, then reloaded and shot Jake twice as well. Lewis told Marci to reload and when Lewis and Marci were finished, I went inside the cell to make sure they were out as Lewis and Marci kept the two at gunpoint. When I was inside the cell, I kicked Johnny's foot and he didn't move.

I knew Jake would be out because of his size and how the four tranquilizers would have a major effect on his consciousness. In theory, it should keep him out for a long time. But as we discovered while using the tranquilizers on them in the past, their recovery time was much shorter than Adam's recovery time had been. We thought that maybe the formula was more diluted in Adam's system than with the two subjects, but that remained a mystery to us. Lewis and I found this to be quite puzzling.

We thought in the beginning that possibly the tranquilizers might not be as effective because Formula L tended to work on any foreign substance, and for the most part it did on the tranquilizer medicine. What should keep a normal animal the size of Jake down for a night, it seemed the affected time would only be a couple of hours. When I shot Adam many times with the same tranquilizers, I thought it would keep him out for at least twelve hours and it did. With our current subjects, the time limit was much less.

We thought maybe Formula L would mutate on its own from one host to the other and might learn from each of the different hosts; in other words, in this experiment, as the formula went from my mouth to an animal subject. Then that subject passed it along to another host. When that happened, that host passed it to Johnny. In this case, it was passed along from four different hosts which included, me, the container that collected the formula, the rabbit, and finally to Johnny. We concluded that in theory the formula mutated and learned, if you will, from each of the hosts. The blood samples we took were so complicated to figure out that we thought it was impossible to even attempt to isolate this part of the theory, and therefore it was impossible to distinguish if this was the case.

I drug Johnny's body out of the cell first while Lewis held his gun on him the entire time. Marci, armed as well, viewed the action from the far corner of the lab. I struggled mightily with the body, but I finally slid the large animal to the entrance of the crematory machine. With a lot of extra effort, I pulled the body inside the machine. I stepped over the body, got out, closed and locked the door. We were all very nervous because we didn't know when Johnny would wake up. I went back to the cell and picked up the other creature and carried it to the machine. He was easy to move since he was so much smaller. I did find moving the bodies very repulsive, not only because of their deformities, but because of their smell. They had an indescribable sulfur smell from an oily substance that excreted from their bodies.

When I approached the door of the cremation machine, Lewis looked inside and saw that Johnny was still out. He quickly opened the door and I placed Jake on top of Johnny and locked the door of the machine. We were still nervous because we thought if Johnny woke up he might be able to bust through the door. Marci made her way toward us. I went over to the controls and turned the heater on. For some reason, there was a strange silence in the air. Marci and Lewis remained eerily silent during this process, like they were at a funeral. I expected Marci to say a few words, but she didn't utter a sound. I could sense that she was very scared, not only for her own safety, but for mine. It was risky moving these two from the cell to the machine. If they would have woken up and either Lewis or Marci would have missed, it would have been very dangerous for us and mankind.

I stood there and waited for the furnace to heat up and then we suddenly heard something from inside the chamber. Lewis and I looked inside and saw Johnny moving about. He woke up from the heat that was now getting dangerously hot. He was quickly moving around and appeared to be disorientated. Then without notice, he pressed his large face onto the glass window. He was mouthing, "Let me out of here," as he was taking both of his arms and slamming them on the sides of the window. I was concerned that he might break the glass or even the door. I heard the burners starting to fire up to maximum capacity. The burners were now at full power, so I knew the heat inside the chamber had to be at a level that would soon not be able to sustain life.

Jake suddenly woke up and started to panic. Both subjects were moving around from one side of the chamber to the other, trying to find a way out. Suddenly, without any notice, the specimen's bodies caught on fire. I heard their cries outside the machine. I stood about ten feet from the fiery chamber as I saw Johnny with a sorrowful and scared look on his face. I saw smoke around his head and he looked very red. His hair caught on fire for a second and as the hair burnt, the flames went out. I watched as his skin began to lose its moisture and took on a darker look, and before I knew it, his entire head was totally engulfed in flames. He pressed his burning head against the glass window while brownish-black pieces of flesh and blood smeared on the glass. We watched the blood as it cooked and became a solid substance.

As we continued to view the show, the next event was a deep orange glowing hue from inside. I walked toward Lewis who was still holding the gun in his hand and I gently took the gun from him. He was in a small, trance-like state and suddenly he mumbled, "We cannot ever do this again, Garrison."

I smiled and looked over at Marci. Marci didn't say a word as she just looked at me as I walked toward her. I gently took the gun from my lover's hands as she offered it to me. I walked over to the area where Lewis kept his guns and placed them inside the cabinet. I closed the door and turned around. I noticed Marci walking over to the chamber, staring at the window. She was looking at the large smudge on the glass from the bits of burnt skin clinging to the window. Both bodies were totally engulfed in flames. The two bodies laid on top of each other in a pile of burnt flesh which quickly was turning into a pile of ashes.

I broke the awkward silence that dominated the room and said, "Well, guys, this chapter is over and we learned very little from the experiment. I believe we need to discuss what little we know with one other."

Lewis broke out of his trance and said, "What! What did you just say? Garrison, no one can ever find out what we just did. We would be arrested."

I said, "I know, I wasn't talking about speaking to someone new on this subject matter, but someone who already has experience dealing with this."

Lewis said, "Garrison, no! Absolutely not! I forbid you to go to Germany. You are not going there and I am not going back there. Your father will kill me." Lewis was almost to the point of tears as he said, "I promised him that I would never come back or even tell anyone what I found in that forest."

I said to Lewis, "Oh, come on, Lewis. Do you really think my father knew you wouldn't tell anyone about them? Of course, he knew you would tell Trevor everything. That must be the only explanation as to why he didn't kill you. I think you peaked his curiosity, to be honest with you. If he is what you say he is, then you know he needs help on this issue. You know he desires his formula, which he created, to be perfected. If he is as badly disfigured as my father was, then he is trapped, concealed by the forest and its treed walls. Maybe he knew you would come back someday with me or with more information."

A very nervous Lewis walked over to me and said, "Garrison. He is dangerous. You were not there. He is a very evil man."

I said, "Well then, maybe he just needs some tender loving care."

Lewis shouted, "Damn it, Garrison, you don't understand! Don't take this lightly. He will kill you, but you might not have to worry about that because I just might do the job myself after what I witnessed with this last fucked up experiment of yours."

I raced as fast as I could toward Lewis. I grabbed his shirt with both hands and pulled him up off the ground about a half a foot. I sternly said, "Look! Do you see that beautiful woman standing over there? Do you?" Lewis was shocked as he looked over at Marci. I continued, "Now let's get one thing straight, you piece of shit. I will not rest until I can make sure that I have not left any stones unturned in my quest for the chemical makeup of this formula. See, what you obviously have failed to comprehend is that while I will continue to live forever, the love of my life will continue to grow older by the minute. At some point, she will die and that is just not acceptable to me. On top of that, I want to find what is behind this formula. It is my obsession, and while I have more than a few lifetimes to figure this out, my love does not. I would strongly suggest that you do what I ask you to do. I need for you to show me that spot where you found my birth parents. You do that, and I promise you this will be the last thing I will ever ask you to do for me again, unless you want to help me. I need to find my parents. I need to talk with them just to see if I am missing anything. Maybe, just maybe, if we put our heads together, we might find the answers. What about it, Lewis? Are you with me or against me on this issue?"

I lowered him, but still maintained eye contact with him. Lewis said, "Fine! I don't have a choice, now do I? I will take you there, but this is the last of it, Garrison. This is the last of it!"

I said, "I will tell you when it's the last of it... got it? Oh... and never threaten my life again, you son of a bitch or I will end your life. Is that understood?"

Lewis nodded, and I immediately asked loudly, "Is that understood?"

Lewis said angrily, "Yes, yes, Garrison, it is understood."

I pushed his body away from me while I had him suspended in the air and he came down on his feet but fell backward after his landing. I suddenly stopped and noticed how strong and good I felt. I had the strength of many men inside of me. I was very surprised that I possessed that kind of strength.

Marci then spoke, "Garrison, my dear, please don't go. It sounds very dangerous to me."

I walked over to my love and said to her, "My dear, don't you worry. I need to speak to my father. Hopefully he will tell me something that I don't know or I can show him what I know. Maybe we can discover something that the other had not thought of regarding the formula. This is just something I must do, not only for me, but for us. Hell, even on a much larger scope, for humanity." I turned away from my love, walked past Lewis and said as I walked out of the door, "Lewis, we will talk more about this tomorrow, first thing in the morning."

As I walked out the door I heard Marci race over to Lewis and help him up. I stopped just outside the door to the basement. My senses were still on fire. I could hear everything around me. I heard Lewis tell Marci, "He is crazy, Marci, just crazy."

Marci said, "No, he is not, Lewis. He is just dedicated to his work."

Lewis quickly said, "He loves to torture. He loves to create these freaks and then he loves to kill them. I am very concerned for your safety, Marci."

Marci said, "I don't appreciate people talking about my Garrison behind his back. He is a special man. He is unlike any man or person that I have ever met in my life. I stand by my love. I know he would never harm me, but if he did then it would be something that I provoked."

I heard Lewis walking over to his desk and as he sat down he said, "Just don't provoke him, that is all I am going to say." I was so proud of my love for standing up for me. I hurried upstairs as quietly as I could and got prepared to retire for the night.

The next morning Lewis and I called Sonja in Germany. Sonja was my adoptive mother's sister. I hadn't spoken to her in years and felt a little bad that I hadn't maintained contact with her. When we got her on the phone, she was very excited about our visit and offered for us to stay with her. I politely declined and said that we were going to Germany on business but would like to see her along the way. I told her that we preferred a small house or cottage that we could rent for a while, located near the forest area. She told us of this small but very upscale bed and breakfast type of inn located near the forest.

After our conversation, Lewis and I deliberated what we needed to bring on our trip. I planned to stay in Germany for as long as a month. I wanted to get to know the village Lewis talked about where the people seemed to never have any major health issues and where the villagers seemed to age at a slower rate than most. I found this area of the world to be fascinating for the fact that if the villagers did live longer and were healthier, then why had no one investigated the reason? Lewis said that the uniqueness and isolation of the village is why no one had really investigated.

I had heard of small villages buried deep in the jungles of Africa or deep in the Russian wasteland where people lived longer than the average person elsewhere. Many say the secret might be in the water they drink or the regional food they ate. I know that in America, there are places where cancer is of a higher rate compared to other parts. It is amazing how our environment plays such an important role in our existence on this earth.

On Lewis's trip to the forest years ago, he discovered this rare and strange moss plant during his hiking adventure. There was something about the chemical makeup of this moss plant that had both of us wondering about the high health rates of this small community. He discovered that the people that lived near the forest hadn't complained or contracted a cold or flu for decades. In fact, many of the inhabitants of this community were extremely healthy and had few medical issues compared to the average person.

This moss plant was unlike any other type of moss normally found next to a stream or near a tree. The moss grew in a small area of the forest. Apparently, this area had a small stream of water that was under or near the moss. The moss plant had a large carrot-shaped root on the bottom of the primary part of the plant. As the plant grew, long stems grew out from the main stalk. As the stems matured, moss developed on the plant itself and would grow out onto the ground or on anything that was around the plant. The plant's root that Lewis had pulled from the forest floor was wet from water. Lewis believed this moss plant was the main ingredient in Formula L. Lewis's theory was this root somehow excreted a chemical that, when introduced to the human body, caused the aging process to slow and increased the immune system. Lewis had done very extensive research on the moss plant and had a bottle of the chemical that had been extracted from this plant. The chemical makeup is so strange and complicated that it couldn't be correctly identified.

On top of these amazing facts, Lewis told me he had conducted many experiments with his own blood after his return from the forest. He would draw his blood and use it as part of his experiments. The chemical, much like Formula L, changed when it interacted with human blood. In addition to this, he believed the chemicals from the moss plant would have a different and more active reaction if adrenaline was introduced to the substance. As for Formula L's reaction to blood, we knew that the formula seemed to only work when it connected with the warm blood from the host. The warmth of the blood due to a certain body temperature, as well as adrenaline, seemed to fuel the formula's effect. We believed that as with the Formula L in the blood, the same case could be made with the chemical excretion from the moss plant. The chemical by itself isn't effective until it joins with warm blood and adrenaline.

Lewis conducted a few experiments on his own when he got back from his trip to Germany. After many tests and investigative work on his part, he sought out some local animal shelters and bought a small dog, a cat, and a hamster. He made sure each subject had injuries. The dog had a broken leg, the cat had a few broken ribs, and the hamster had a large bite mark from the owner's dog who had bitten the hamster and threw it across the room. When Lewis got the three animals home, he put them in separate cages and injected them with the unknown chemical from the moss plant.

After a week of observation, the animal's injuries seemed to be healing well. Not long after the injection of the unknown chemical, the animals improved rapidly and faster than they would have normally. He consulted a few local veterinarians on how long it would normally take them to recover from these types of injuries. Most of them told Lewis it would take about twice as long for recovery as Lewis's subjects experienced.

When Lewis told me these stories, I was very intrigued. I knew that somehow the chemicals that the moss plant produces or a combination of its excretions mixed with other chemicals, was the key to Formula L.

That moss plant was still alive in Lewis's lab through all those years. It lived basically on water alone. Lewis and I studied this information and the only possible answer to the German locals living longer and better lives was the chemical from the moss plant, which had been carried down through the forest and into the village via water. That was the only explanation we could come up with at the time.

There I was, at another dead end. Every time I got close to a solution, I got turned away or something was blocking further information from coming forth. That is why I needed to see this village with my own eyes. I needed to ask questions and see if I could stumble on any useful information. With me staying here in the States, I was not getting the job done, I was just confirming what I already knew either from my own discoveries or what Wolfgang relayed to Lewis on his trip to the forest. I also knew deep down that I wanted the opportunity to see my birth parents. I needed some type of closure about being abandoned as their son. I needed closure for me personally because I couldn't live forever with the knowledge of what might or could have been. I just hoped my father knew something I didn't. I hoped that if I got the chance to meet him, he would allow me to show him the knowledge I had collected over the years.

Marci didn't want me to go to Germany, but she understood my situation. I told her that I might be gone for a while, so we made the most of our time together. I asked her if she would move into the estate with me. At first, she was somewhat against the idea, but after some thought she decided it was in her best interest to live with me. She understood my position on the issue. She had a long commute from her apartment to my house. With her living on the grounds, she would obviously be closer to me, and would also have someone else to do laundry and cook her meals. I also wanted her to really get the feel of the mansion.

After several weeks of constant encouragement, she finally moved in with me and quickly got used to living a different life. Marci continued with her studies, and her violin playing was rapidly improving, but as always, it was never good enough by her standards. I felt bad that she felt this way. Many times, I went out of my way not to show off my intelligence, musical skills, or my other special abilities, but Marci knew I was trying to hide them and was very upset with me for keeping them hidden from her. She even threatened to call the whole wedding and relationship off if I were to ever dumb myself down again in her presence. This was a shock to me, but I just never wanted her to feel inferior, although I knew, and certainly she knew, that she was not my equal. No one is. It is not my fault that I was born this way. I am not perfect, but when I practice performing any action or actions, I tend to excel and perfect them in a short amount of time. Marci understood this and in the future she wanted to be able to do the things I could presently do. The only way for this to happen was for me to somehow perfect that damn formula. She loved my special talents because it was exciting for her to see someone complete or demonstrate abilities that are not humanly possible.

I took the chance of a lifetime when I courted Marci and chose her as my girlfriend. I could sense that she loved me from the first time I met her. Although I perish the thought, I knew she was the perfect specimen for me as a mate. She had no family and if she was not too understanding or cooperative or would have done something ill-advised, I could easily explain her disappearance. I loved her with all my heart and could not bear anything to happen to her, but my life, my money and my work are the most important things in my life.

I am going to live forever unless someone murders me. I don't believe I could be poisoned or have any disease that would kill me. I have never been sick a day in my life, and from all the research we have conducted, I believe I will never succumb to disease or physically grow old. I chopped my brother into a puzzle and he was still alive at the very end. I think the only way to exterminate my kind is through the brain. I kind of feel like someone out of the 'Night of the Living Dead' movie.

My Marci joked about that with me since she found out about my situation. If I allowed myself to dwell on this issue for longer than a moment, I tended to become rather uneasy about my lot in life.

While my situation is complicated and extremely rare, I do like who I am. I am comfortable and accepting of the blessings that have been bestowed upon me. My own personal nightmare that I found myself experiencing more throughout the years is everyone that I met will grow older. While I am growing older as well, at some point I will stop growing old and time will stand still for me. This is unsettling for me to think that I will never die and, at least in theory, the decades will turn into centuries, and the centuries will turn into millenniums for me. To make matters more complicated, all this is still based on theory. I have only one story and one eyewitness report, that being from Lewis, on any kind of proof that this is true. Only Lewis has witnessed my birth parents, and if they are who they say they are, which I don't doubt for a moment, then I must conclude that I will live forever. But will I? It is all based on theory and not cold hard facts, at least not enough facts to totally convince me this is an absolute.

CHAPTER 15

Longing

$\mathcal{L}$ ewis and I packed our clothes and equipment for a planned stay of a month or so in Germany. We only brought the essentials for clothing, but we took many items from the lab. I had these items sent over before we left the States. I made sure Lewis and I had all the necessary chemicals, new lab notebooks and testing equipment that would be available to us in our small villa in the foreign land. I copied most of the information on as many disks and thumb drives as possible. I made sure the batteries for the computers were all fully charged and we had many extras in reserve. I brought two very expensive laptops as well as many cell phones and other media friendly devices with us. I wanted to make sure I could be reached, if needed, for two reasons; one being for business, the other is in case of an emergency, I could either be reached or I could reach someone for help.

After a good night's sleep, Lewis and I prepared ourselves for our long trip. Carolyn and Marci drove us to the airport. We said our goodbyes to the ladies and boarded our plane. Marci was not happy about our decision to go, but she understood why we were going. It was very hard for her to let go, and she was very emotional that morning. I kissed her goodbye and held her tight, telling her I would be back and not to worry. I don't think that helped ease her concerns, but it was the best I could do. I told the ladies that I would call as often as I could, but I clearly instructed them not to call us. I told them I didn't know what we might encounter and that I would have the ringer on my cell phone off so I wouldn't disturb anyone or anything that might be lurking in the dark.

Lewis and I boarded the plane in a very emotional scene. My Marci was crying uncontrollably, as was Carolyn. As the women left our sight, we found our seats and prepared for the long trip to my homeland. Lewis and I usually traveled well together. Lewis was an interesting and well learned man. During our trip, we spoke about everything under the sun, but mostly about his life prior to meeting my father. I always admired him as a person, but at the same time I felt sorry for him. He was a slave to his own quest for greatness. He wanted to be known as a great man when he passed from this earth. He took the job for my father so he could gather additional money for the new lab he wanted to build. He then became a slave to my father and now he is basically a slave to me as well.

Lewis was a person trapped between a man wanting to run for dear life to get away from this very strange and awkward world that he found himself presently enslaved to, to a person that wanted the answers to the age-old desire of eternal life. He found the potential to discover the perfect immune system, to cheat death, to heal faster than any human could imagine, and to be able to create like god was too great of a temptation to walk away from.

Lewis was torn between the killing or allowing the killing to take place and not preventing them, to the potential riches that would be beyond comprehension. He became a tragic figure the moment he was introduced into our family, a pawn in the Seawick family from day one. He was treated and sometimes viewed as disposable by the family, but at the same time he was someone that could potentially be so powerful. If he wanted, he could have brought the family down like a house of cards. Our family was very lucky that not only Lewis, but the others like Carolyn, Loren and even Marci hadn't contacted the police or authorities. I was very careful, just like my father, to always make sure nothing would get out to the public. Our inner circle had to be strong. Lewis stayed and never opened his mouth to any of the local authorities because down deep in his soul he was interested in fame and fortune. After he met me as a young boy, he knew he was onto something that could change the world as we knew it in potentially the not too distance future.

We landed in Germany and Sonja greeted us at the airport as we got off the plane. Sonja had seen only pictures of me throughout the years, but none recently. Sonja never visited the States because of her extreme fear of flying. I knew that on many occasions my adoptive mother offered to pay her way to the States, but each time she refused. I assumed that with all my issues plus my father's issues after I bit him, she never wanted or couldn't go back to her homeland.

Sonja was quite excited to see me in person. She had followed my life not only through Adelle's phone calls and instant messaging, but also through my career as a violinist. Apparently, I am a superstar in Germany. The locals loved my story of being found in the woods, being adopted and then word got out that I was this high-level genius as well.

I worked and spent a lot of time studying the German language about a month before our trip. I told no one about my studies. My accent was off, but I spoke to her in German when we first met. She was very impressed with my command of her language. Lewis was at a loss for words when I first opened my mouth. As he stood there listening, a large grin came over his face because he knew what I was capable of when I studied a subject. I could sense his admiration, as well as his jealousy. Lewis had always been envious of my abilities, but he would never admit it to me or to himself for that matter. He was always outwardly resentful of my abilities, but I knew that down deep in his soul, he strongly desired the gifts I possessed.

Sonja and I spoke for a while and reminisced on many subjects, especially Adelle. It was a very emotional moment we had together. I could see just how much Sonja loved Adelle. I heard the despair in Sonja's voice with the fact that she didn't make it to the States for the funeral. I helped ease her troubled soul with kind words. I told her that she shouldn't feel sorrow or guilt for not being there in person. After our conversation, I felt I had made her feel somewhat more at ease with her haunting.

As we finished our chat, Sonja told us that the airline had packed the supplies we had shipped about a week ago into a large truck, then Sonja had the supplies delivered to the small cottage we had rented out. She oversaw them placing the supplies inside the cottage and, as per my instructions, they kept everything wrapped in the boxes. I had Sonja make sure there was enough space in the cottage for us to spread out in case we needed to conduct any experiments. I also had a car rental company have a small car waiting for us to drive when we arrived at our lodge. Sonja went out of her way in preparing everything we needed for our stay. She was even prepared to stay the night with us to help us unpack, but I told her that wasn't necessary.

Sonja led us to her car then drove us to our cottage. The trip was long and the roads to our cottage were curvy with lots of hills to negotiate. The area that surrounded the cottage was that of a picture-perfect postcard. Everything was green, had a most natural scent to the land, and the air was as pure as it could be for that time of year. The weather was getting colder and rain was present in the air. The weather was cool enough for most to wear a jacket. I had to play the part and place a coat on my shoulders although I never experience the cold unless the temperature is well below zero, and even that is comfortable for me. The coat that I wore was making me very warm inside the car, but I needed to play the part as I was so accustomed to doing throughout my life.

The cottage was small but nice for the two of us. Sonja showed us the inside of the cottage and made sure we had everything we needed. She took the liberty of fixing us a small meal before she left us for the night.

The next morning Sonja showed up early and took us on a small tour of the village. The village was just as Lewis had described it from memory and through his notes from years ago. It seemed to be very quiet, clean and it had an old world feel. We walked the small area of town and visited many of the small shops. People didn't often visit this area outside of the locals. At first, many of the people we met were nice but distant. I sensed they didn't want to be caught speaking with us for an extended time. They were nice enough but seemed to be in a hurry for some unexplainable reason. I sensed fear, not from us, but from us being in their town. It was a strange feeling that I was sensing, a feeling I couldn't put my finger on at the time.

I asked many of the patrons of the businesses that we met, which was only a few, why there were such few visitors. To my surprise, each of their answers were basically the same. They didn't want to talk about it and told me that everyone liked to keep to themselves. Most all the locals were born in this small town and had never left the area nor had any intension of leaving.

Lewis and I were standing outside of a small hardware store with the owner and two other local store owners. One owned a small neighborhood grocery store and the other owned a gas station. I was told by the three gentlemen that most of the inhabitants of the town worked at the large mill house that was located on the other side of town, opposite the large and dark forest area. As we spoke, I noticed the gentlemen started to warm up to our presence. We spoke about everything under the sun, but the longer our conversation lasted, the more serious it became. They started to talk about strange happenings around the community, which really peak my curiosity. This subject, I was quickly discovering, was a local legend.

I listened to every word of the many stories they were telling. The main storyline was an encounter that happened many generations ago. As the legend goes, one night many decades ago, a large creature was spotted coming out of the woods in the nearby forest. This creature would stalk the small town at night. Sometimes it would leave evidence that it was there by leaving footprints, uprooting a shrub or, on some rare occasions, breaking a door, window or tearing down part of a fence. The common theme with this creature was that it seemed not to want to be seen. The creature had been spotted by some through the decades and was described as extremely tall with long arms and legs. It walked like a human and had human features except for the face, which resembled more like that of a wolf.

Lewis and I looked at each other and knew it had to be my birth father, but of course we laughed this off as a fairy tale. The three gentlemen telling the story were a little put off that we seemed not to believe the tale. We were told these tales were so heartfelt and strong that none of the villagers would even think about entering the forest. They made sure we fully understood that these tales were not made up; in fact, they were real… very real.

The forest near the village was large, dark and went very deep. There were trails made here and there, but they only went short distances. Legend had it that one day in the late 1940s or 1950s, this creature spoke to a handful of hikers that were hiking outside of the village and told them to never enter the forest again. The legend grew through the decades and only a few brave hikers had entered the forest since.

Time after time, every hiker would have the same story to tell. As the hikers would get to certain points in the forest, strange happenings would begin to surface, and out of fear they would retreat. The happenings included rocks, sticks or small pieces of dirt clods either hitting them or near where the hikers were standing. On other occasions, hikers heard voices and some even heard screams.

Over time, the forest had grown, but mostly in denseness. The plants that were native to the area grew to enormous sizes. Trees and brush grew taller, wider, and thicker than normal. The trees grew so large and thick that the sun would be totally blocked out in many areas of the forest. In addition to these strange growing patterns, even without the proper sunlight on plants like flowers, bushes and vines, they would still grow as if they had more than adequate sunlight.

The legend of the forest grew amongst the small neighboring towns and after so long, the locals just accepted leaving the forest alone. The outlying area from where the forest started to approximately a quarter of a mile inside was hiked often by the same hikers in and around the local village. They knew about how deep they could go, then when they got to that certain point – and many said the forest would let them know when that point was – they would stop and turn back. There was, at least in theory, only one area where the trees hadn't grown together, which was near a small stream in the middle of this area. This piece of information spiked our interest. Sonja whispered in my ear that this was the place where the hikers had found me when I was a newborn. Out of basic curiosity, amongst other obvious facts, I was very interested in seeing this place for myself.

After our visits we came back to our cottage, and Sonja left us to go back to her home. Lewis and I sat in our new temporary home and looked at each other in utter amazement. Lewis said, "Garrison, this place has not changed one bit since the last time I was here. The same people are still at the same small businesses and they look the same today as they looked over a decade ago. There is something odd about his place. The stream we talked about flows downhill toward this village. They use that stream's water for many things, like well water. My theory is that whatever chemical the moss plant excretes, somehow has gotten into their well water. They even told us that all their water comes from the well."

I said, "You are onto something here, Lewis. Good find. I think we need to really investigate this area of your discovery. Now aren't you happy you came along with me on this trip?" Lewis looked at me with a crooked smile and just laughed.

We had reservations about drinking the water or even taking a shower. The absorption into the skin might be another way the water got into a human's system and affected the immune and aging systems, so we decided to refrain from taking showers and drinking the water. What we couldn't understand was that the locals had to know they were getting healthier and aging slower than their mothers, fathers, and grandparents before them. This was one part of the many pieces to the puzzle that was just not making sense to us. You would think that some forward-thinking people would at least try to profit from this idea of a miracle of the fountain of youth. The locals had to understand they were not getting sick or aging like a normal person would, so why didn't they question this? We both just stood there shaking our heads at one another, trying to mull over this quandary.

The next morning, Lewis and I went back to visit one of the store owners. We went to his place of business and he was surprisingly happy to see us. He was there with three other gentlemen who were there apparently just to visit with the owner. I went to them and spoke in English since they said they could speak my language. I asked them why no one in this village got seriously ill. I also asked why the lifespan of the villagers seemed to be longer than the average lifespan. At first, they ignored me, but after my constant barrage of questions, one of the gentlemen had to say something to break the awkward silence that had developed over the men in the room. This gentleman motioned for Lewis and me to come to the back of the store with him and his friends. I didn't know what they were up to or what they were going to do, so we cautiously followed them.

The gentleman had a small office in the back of his store. After several uncomfortable moments, he allowed us inside. He closed and locked the door after everyone made their way inside. He knew we were nervous and told us to relax. I remember him sitting down behind his desk while the other men sat in chairs off to the side of us. He offered us a seat in front of his old, dusty desk. He said to me in rather high-quality English, "Sir, you have come a long way to find the truth of this town. We find that to be very odd. We don't understand how you've come to know about this place. We usually keep our business to ourselves and we don't like to tell outsiders about our community, for obvious reasons. But we have discussed this with the others in our village and believe that we need to let you guys in on our secret, for our own protection. So, here are our secrets and we hope this stays in this room."

"I have lived a long time inside of a body that should have grown older. I cannot explain this nor can anyone explain it. I feel that it is in God's hands and we should not question this blessing. Some of us experienced pain and suffering many, many years ago, but today those pains and health issues are gone. Oh, don't get me wrong, sometimes we have an occasional ache or two, but it usually goes away quickly."

"There are few of us, to be honest with you, less than fifty villagers, to be exact. Let me tell you a story, Garrison." He sat back and became very sad. I could sense what was about to come as I was slowly putting two and two together. "See, we had, at one time, a small but thriving community here in the early years, which dates back to World War II years. Many of the native German Jews escaped while the Holocaust was going on. They would hide out in this town, but eventually the Nazi party would find them and took them back to the work camps. As time went on, especially after the war, some of our people started coming up missing. It was said that many of the missing people ended up moving away, and some of them far away from this town. At first everyone accepted the stories, but after what had happened through the 1920s and 1930s, most of us had our doubts. As time passed and more people started to leave or, in many cases, just ended up missing, we started to get concerned. Over time, many of the older folks in this community started talking about seeing some large human-like monster that would linger around the village at night.

Many people said this monster came from the deep forest area, but most of us just ignored these tales as folklore. There were many rumors but... I personally didn't believe until, well..." His voice stopped and he looked away. I knew something was wrong and I had to find out what.

I asked the old man, "What? What happened?"

The old man looked at me and got very serious. He was almost mad at me and said, "One night I was outside my store locking up. I turned around to leave and saw something out of the corner of my eye. It was a large figure. I asked who was there and got no reply. I then walked around the side of my business and noticed footprints in the dirt area up near the house. It looked like very large, almost human-like feet in the dirt, but the feet were too big for it to be a man. As I looked down I had the feeling I was being watched, and I looked up quickly and saw this large figure. It must have been eight feet at least, because the overhang of the roof was at least nine feet high. It moved very quickly and disappeared on the other side of my business. I was frightened at the thought of this humanoid monster."

"I hurried to get to my car and before I could get there, I heard this gallop of some sort, a heavy and hurried gallop that sounded like a horse. I was scared out of my mind. I quickly turned around, and I remember I was in a defensive stance. I didn't know where or how close this thing was, but I knew he was going to attack me. I know this sounds rather hard to believe, but I swear to you that I am not making this up. As I turned around as quickly as I could, I saw this large figure come at me, but as I turned, it slowed down. I lowered myself and raised my arms up to my head to protect myself. I was never more shocked in my life. I heard its large, bare feet slowing down as it approached me."

The ground was somewhat dry, and to this day I can still recall the cloud of dusty dirt around its feet as it stopped near me. It had total control over its body and it seemed to stop very quickly. I felt the wind that his body created when he stopped. It had an odor of the forest mixed with some rotten smell that was very repulsive. I found myself face to face with this monster. It was a half man, half wolf-like creature. Everything on this creature was huge. It was hairy with large hands, large feet, and no shoes. I didn't know what he was going to do, but I knew I was dead. I just knew he was going to attack me. He then spoke to me as he moved closer. I couldn't believe this monster could talk. He had this growl that had an undertone to his voice, and his breath was terrible. It had this out-of-this-world kind of smell to it as it spoke. His face was a foot from mine as he backed me up against the front of my car. My heart was about to come out of my chest it was beating so hard. I had never been that scared in my life."

"He started to speak to me as his unusually long finger pointed toward my face. He had my back bent over the edge of my car. He opened his mouth and as he did, some of his saliva fell out of his mouth and onto my chest. His warm breath was so terrible I could hardly stand it, but I was so afraid I couldn't look away. I was preparing myself for a very painful death."

"The creature spoke and told me to stop having people come into the forest. He told me it was his forest and not for us villagers or anyone outside of this community. I was so frightened. I just nodded in agreement and kept saying, 'Yes sir, yes sir.'"

The old man stopped and looked down to collect himself. He was visibly upset. He had to stop and get control of his emotions before he could continue with his story. "This creature told me not to let people go past the lighted area of the forest. This area had been well known for decades. Legend had it that this area was the only area of the entire forest where the trees don't touch each other to block out the sunlight. I asked him how I could keep people out. I mean, I have no control over people and what they do. He told me to tell as many people as possible about this encounter. He put all the responsibility on me. What was so odd about this exchange was that he did not threaten me or tell me he was going to kill me if people did go into the forest. It was more as if he wanted me to be his messenger."

"Before I knew it, he quickly ran toward the forest and disappeared as he rushed to get inside. He ran with amazing speed and agility for a monster that size. I never saw anything move that fast in my life, either human or animal. I just stood there, scared out of my mind. I fumbled for my car keys and as I did, I dropped them. I thought I was going to have a heart attack the moment the keys hit the dusty parking lot. I quickly reached for the keys and after what seemed to be an eternity, I got in my car and drove home as fast as I could."

"Every meter that I drove, I was sure I would find him running alongside my car, but I saw nothing. That night when I was home was one of the worst nights of my life. Every noise I heard, I thought was him. Every shadow I thought it was him standing there, getting ready to kill me. I didn't sleep a minute that night. When the morning came, I went outside and looked everywhere. There was fog around the village, which made for an eerie feeling. I went back to my store and as people started to walk outside of my shop, I did what he told me. Obviously, at first many did not believe me, but I showed them the footprints at the side of the building. I showed them the footprints next to where my car was parked when he confronted me. It was as if the creature wanted people to see that he was there, and he left proof that would add credence to my story."

"Some of the villagers even ventured inside the forest in groups. Nothing happened to them, but many people that tested their nerve and ventured deeper into the forests seemed to get a little spooked. Nothing happened to them physically, but it seemed with more regularity that when people went beyond the lighted area, they were turned away by something that scared them. No one saw anyone or anything, but they experienced rocks being thrown at them or noises that didn't seem to be natural. As time went on, some brave, stupid folks would go past the lighted area and over half of those poor souls were never seen again. The ones that made it out of the forest were visibly shaken. They would come out as if they had seen a ghost. From all the reports, none saw the creature, but they heard it or other strange sounds that really scared them. For those that made it out, almost all left town and never came back. I knew a couple of those people and even to this day, the ones that are alive never want to talk about what happened inside of that forest."

"Throughout time, many of the townspeople left the village. Our population decreased rapidly and hardly anyone new to the village showed their face. It was so strange that few went to the authorities over the issue. The ones that did were laughed at and basically dismissed. From time to time we would see a police officer stop by, but they would never go inside the forest. They would look around and question us, but we never told the true story of what happened here."

"We didn't want to excite the creature. As for as the people that stayed, life was actually very good here because the mill paid well and there were a small number of people here competing for jobs. We had a specialty that few businesses had in this part of the country. We had access to a lot of lumber from the forest. It was and still is today, a seemingly endless supply of trees. In many of the areas around town, the trees grew at a rapid pace. As time went on, we tended to just take the hasty tree growth for granted. The mill got a tremendous reputation for not only producing Grade A products, but for the wood being extremely strong and heavy. Other types of wood used at other mills would split or easily dent in places over time from people dropping heavy items. The wood from our town's mill would not split or dent over time as much as the other types of wood. Even to this day we have a steady stream of orders that creates a good life for us all."

"We also have great access to food. Our food grows faster and larger than places around us. Throughout the years we stopped buying food from outside of the village because we had enough food here at a cheaper price. As we continued to eat our own food, it seemed that everyone started to feel better and were healthier. In the past, the local people that worked on farms and ate the food that grew on their land seemed to be healthier than the people who didn't."

"During this time, we didn't have a clue as to what was happening, but we started to realize this was a healthy place to live. After many town hall gatherings and small meetings at church or a chance meeting at the market or shop, we discussed these odd events. Many of us didn't want to leave, but some wanted to leave out of fear of the creature from the forest. To remind you, only a few have seen this creature, but many of the local farmers have seen evidence from tracks that he would leave. Many times, a chicken or two or a dog would be missing, or food from the field was taken; not much, but some disturbance was discovered from time to time."

"There was not a whole lot to do about it, to be honest with you. Many of the locals just gave up trying to catch the thief or the creature. Many didn't want to attempt to catch him out of pure fear of what he would do. You need to understand that after a while, the number of people being killed or lost was decreasing. Over time, there came a point where no one came up missing. I cannot tell you the last time we had someone get mysteriously lost in the town."

"It became common knowledge that if we stayed away from the forest, the creature would leave us alone. None of the authorities would believe us because nothing would happen when they were on their stakeouts, so we had a choice to either stay and live with the creature or move. For some of us, moving was just not an option. During World

War II, the economy throughout Germany was not good so why would anyone leave a good thing for a bad thing? Many did though because they were afraid for their lives. Most of the people that are in this town today are respectful, but not necessarily afraid of the creature anymore."

"Well, anyway, with all this in mind we figured that to lose a dog, a cat or a farm animal here or there seemed to be a small price to pay for not losing a human life. Some people started to leave food out for the creature, and some even supplies. Most days nothing was touched and then unexpectedly food or supplies would be gone. Many of the locals that practiced this believed that if they put out some of their food or supplies they would be protected. That was a popular belief and one that seemed to ring true. As time went on, we didn't encourage strangers in our town, fearing they may make life worse on us by their actions. Not a lot of people live here anymore, but we had enough to keep the mill going and some of our small stores. I must say that you guys being here is not necessarily welcome. If I may ask this question which is on the minds of everyone here, why are you here? What brought you to this place?"

I looked over at Lewis and spoke. "Many years ago, about a quarter of a century, there was a report of a baby boy found in the forest area. Some hikers found this young one and took him to the local orphanage. Have you heard this story?"

The men in the room all nodded and said they had heard the story. The gentleman spoke up and said, "We wondered what happened to that baby. I think someone adopted him."

A second gentleman spoke up and said, "I heard he became a famous musician."

I smiled and looked over at Lewis. I said through my smile, "Well, I can assure you that young boy is doing fine and well today. That little boy was me."

The room grew very quiet. All you could hear was the men's body movements as some leaned into the guy next to them. I was a little surprised they hadn't heard of me or what had happened to me, but like the gentleman just finished explaining, few people leave or visit the town.

I told the gentlemen in the room the complete story of how my adoption took place. I told them about my parents and how they raised me. I told them I was a scientist and was visiting my aunt. I said, "I heard rumors about how the locals have an immune system that is very strong. I was wondering why that would be the case. I also have always wanted to visit this part of the world considering that I was apparently born here. I want to see the area where it all started for me and to at least see the town."

The guy behind the desk was lost for words. He finally spoke and said, "So you are the lost boy, huh? I never thought I would meet you. Well, you were the talk of the town at that time. Like I said before, we don't get too many visitors up here and no one from this town was missing a small, newborn child at the time. I remember many police officers and investigators hit this area hard, but found nothing. It was a mystery from day one. We still don't know who put you there. Did you ever find out who your natural parents were?"

I quickly said, "No, sir." I changed the conversation to the fact that I wanted to hike the forest for a few days. I wanted to explore the forest and see where I was found and see if I would experience anything out of the ordinary. The old men were totally against the idea, but I was persistent. I told them I wanted to take some samples from the forest, but I wanted to ask permission first. That really went over well with the older gentlemen. I sensed they all liked me and even though we had just met, they trusted me enough to allow me to take samples from the forest. All they asked was that I not disturb the creature.

Many of them said they understood my feelings. One of the gentlemen said as far as he was concerned, the forest was mine as well as theirs, but they all voiced concern about my safety and, most importantly, their safety. They were adamant about me not venturing too far inside the forest where it seems no one comes back. To be honest with you, they were getting into my head. I looked over at Lewis and could sense this was the last thing he wanted to do, but I needed him on this.

After our meeting with the gentlemen, Lewis and I went back to our cottage and I told him we would set out first thing in the morning. We packed up some supplies, enough for a good two days of hiking. From what Lewis told me, he had hiked about six to eight hours, if not longer, when he met my father. I didn't believe him at the time. I could not imagine Lewis hiking, especially mostly uphill, for that long of a distance and over those long hours. Lewis was and still is in good shape, but to hike that long seemed strange to me, but he was not the type of person to make something like that up. Nevertheless, Lewis was focused on the task at hand.

CHAPTER 16

Insufferable

The next morning, we started out as early as possible. As we were making our way to the forest, one of the store owners stopped and pleaded with us not to go. I could sense that he was more concerned about the town than us. I knew he didn't want the creature upset and for him to take his anger out on the town.

I had some concern that maybe the town would get together and form a human barrier to keep us out or worse yet, hold us at gunpoint. That issue never arose so I was pleased that we didn't have to encounter that obstacle. I spoke with the gentleman at length and assured him that I was not going to upset the creature. I just wanted to collect some samples from the forest. To my surprise the old man allowed us to go without any further delay. Little did he know that it was my full intention to meet my father face to face.

As we walked to the edge of the forest I sensed someone was watching me. I looked back and it was one of the other older gentlemen. When I looked back, he raised his old, chipped coffee cup and mouthed the German words for 'good luck'. I also saw a couple of additional store owners and then a handful of locals come out of the stores. It was like they were all saying goodbye to us as we left on our trip.

We proceeded inside the forest area. Lewis was very nervous, and he told me repeatedly that he thought this was a bad idea. He kept repeating that my birth father told him to never come back and never bring anyone into this forest. I was concerned as well because I did fear for my life. I remember what my father looked like before he died and how tall and ferocious he looked. From Lewis's accounts, my birth father looked even worse and also was an evil man. My legal father was not an evil man, he had a lot of good in his heart, but my birth father apparently was or is not a very kind-hearted man.

As we proceeded about one hundred feet into the forest, the vegetation was so thick it blocked out over half the sunlight. We hiked through the thick vegetation growing all around us. Our hike was mostly uphill, but at times we had to walk down some large hills as well. From what Lewis and the locals told me, the deeper you went into the forest, the higher the elevation. We traveled the pre-made paths of overgrown vegetation that was starting to take over the small pathways.

As we made our way through the forest, we slid a few times on the green, leafy vines that grew under our feet. I told Lewis that if he needed to rest we could stop anytime. Since I needed only two or three hours of sleep a night, I could travel a long way through the night. Lewis looked very worried, but the search for the truth and potentially great financial reward was too much for him to overcome. This was the driving force behind his desire to keep moving forward. He paced himself and kept up with me early on in our journey.

The deeper we went, the darker our surroundings became. I looked up and there was this somewhat large area over our heads. It was like I was walking in this invisible tree-lined dome that only allowed the trees to grow together at the top of the highest point. Inside of this natural dome, the lower parts of the trees didn't have many branches. The tree trunks looked as if they grew straight up, pushing the branches higher than normal. At the top of the trees, the branches and leaves were so deep and thick that hardly any light passed through them, even with the wind present. Everything around us was in this dark, greenish-gray color. The smell of the forest was thick with a musky woodland smell that radiated every inch surrounding us.

As we moved forward, I suddenly noticed sunlight peering through the trees just ahead. I raced to this area and saw the small stream of water that flowed toward where we had come from. On the other side of the steam was a rather large area of dirt. No grass, moss or plants were growing in this area. I assumed this was the place where my birth mother placed me after they took off to their home in the forest, wherever that could be. Lewis finally caught up with me and confirmed my belief. This part of the forest is where most people would stop and turn back. I looked up and sure enough, there was a rather large opening in the trees. I could see the clouds. It was like this area was so different from the rest of the forest area. It was a surreal moment for me considering this area is where my parents left me to die. I once laid on this cold and hard ground and was left without protection.

I looked straight ahead and saw a path that was not recently traveled. I took out a large knife and cut our way through the thick vegetation as Lewis and I entered this area. After a couple of hours of non-stop hiking, Lewis was tired and had to stop. I knew we were in possible danger from all the stories of the past, so I forced myself to have an adrenaline rush. This caused my hearing to improve greatly. I heard everything the forest had to offer as I took in the area that was teaming with life. Birds, which seemed to be larger than normal, were everywhere making very loud sounds. Like Lewis had said in the past, everything about this forest area was oversized, even the animals – from bugs to birds, all were larger than normal.

It was about mid-morning and I wanted to be careful not to push Lewis too far and to keep my bearings about our location. I was focused on how long it took us to get to where we were and how long it would take to get back to the edge of the forest.

We continued our hike. According to Lewis, the small trees, which now had grown to an immense size, seemed to have really taken over. Of course, that was a long time ago, but I noticed how large the brush was in many parts of the forest. The floor of the forest seemed to be getting thicker with plant life.

As we walked I kept my ears and eyes opened. The terrain under our feet changed more and more the further we went. We had to stop more often than I would like because Lewis had to rest from all the uphill hiking.

Lewis needed another rest. During his respite, I walked about one hundred feet from him. He called for me not to leave his sight. I obviously could sense his fear of the unknown and the possibility of meeting my father again. My heart was pounding inside from fear as well, but more from being anxious that I might have a chance to meet my parents.

Thoughts entered my mind about the possibility that they had moved deeper into the forest since Lewis's visit. Lewis said that he highly doubted they would have moved deeper into the forest considering how they had everything they needed and had been living in the cave for about one hundred years. He also said we were getting close to their location.

I stepped up onto a large rock formation. Everywhere I looked, I saw nothing but trees and brush. It was also hard to see because of the lack of sunlight. I noticed that I was experiencing a harder time breathing because there was hardly any fresh air, and a breeze was just non-existent. I listened intently and heard nothing but the sounds of a wooded area.

I jumped down and began to walk toward Lewis then heard something move behind me. I stopped to take more of this sound into my ears. I turned to see what it was, but as soon as I stopped, the sound never repeated itself. I slowly walked back to Lewis and told him about the sound I had heard. I told him, "I swear I heard someone speak in German." Lewis was noticeably shaken but we forged ahead. We traveled up a rough hill that was laid with small rocks peppered with heavier stones making their way out of the soil. In some places we used these stones as leverage to help us get up a steep incline.

A couple of hours passed, and Lewis looked as if he couldn't take another step. It had been a while since he had had this much physical activity, plus he was much older than he was when he first made this trip. It was about midafternoon and I was prepared to set up camp and stay the night. I could sense that Lewis needed a good night's rest if we were going any further into the forest. We found a small area which was perfect for setting up camp. I moved the leaves around as best as I could with my hands and feet, then pulled up the small plants to clear as much space as I could for our campsite. I was getting tired myself since I was carrying most of the load, so I also needed to rest.

We had some food to eat, but I was going to live off the land. We got most of the supplies out and I gathered some branches for our fire. Lewis took out his GPS to see our exact location. It was amazing to see how far we had come. I walked around our camp, familiarizing myself with the surroundings. When the sun went down, this area was going to be pitch black so I made sure we had enough firewood for the night. We brought special logs that would burn for long hours through the night. They were not very large, but at least they would stay lit for a while so we could add firewood to the existing flames. The temperature was not the problem since it was warm that day. The forest's temperature seemed to remain constant. The trees all grew together and the warmth of the forest seem to stay trapped under the blanket of trees.

As the evening wore on, I started to hear movement in the forest. I understood that as night approached, many smaller animals would start to come out, but this movement didn't sound like a small forest creature such as a squirrel or a deer. The sound was very faint but from my judgment, the noise sounded like it was coming from some unidentified animal. The noise I heard had a heavy sound to it and then it would stop. After so long, it would start up again. Whatever was making this sound, it didn't sound like an animal to me because it had a rhythm to the sounds that would resemble something with two feet instead of four paws or hooves.

As the evening grew into dusk, I noticed the sound was getting closer. Lewis didn't hear a thing, but I could. I could sense something was coming our way. I attempted to smell whatever it was, but we seemed to be downwind. It didn't matter because we didn't have that much wind to deal with anyway since the massively thick and tall trees blocked out any wind that attempted to penetrate the forest floor. At times, I could hear the strange noise getting stronger, but I couldn't pinpoint what or who was making the noise. I had a feeling it was someone or something that wanted to get close enough to investigate us but didn't want to get too close.

The night was long and stressful. The fire that we lit cast a flickering glow around the trees that protected us from the night above the treed dome. If not for our fire, I don't think anyone could see a hand in front of their face. The forest had no moonlight or allowed any natural light to shine. I was fortunate to have excellent night vision, so I could see things that others couldn't see. Although I kept an eye out from all angles, I never saw anything out of the ordinary, but I kept hearing strange noises throughout the forest. The noises were as if there was some sort of disturbance in our private, treed jail. It was driving me crazy and I became more nervous.

During the night, I noticed something strange about the native animals of the forest. They all acted as if they were running from something. Most of the animals walked past us and away from what lie ahead. Every leaf or branch movement increased my pulse in anticipation of the unidentified. All my senses were on high alert due to the possible encounter of this unknown creature. This was also working against me getting my dinner for the evening. The small animals were all jumping from one tree to the next, making their capture most difficult. I was fortunate to hit one small squirrel with a sizeable rock, it fell to the forest floor, and I was fast enough to capture it before it ran away. I devoured the little creature as fast as I could while keeping my eyes open to my surroundings. I tore into its flesh, savoring the taste and smell. I hadn't eaten in a while and the taste of the squirrel was different from what I had tasted at home. It was more gamey and tougher. I assume the reason for the change in taste was due to the forest diet.

As the morning approached, Lewis woke from his sleep. I could tell he hadn't slept well because he was still very tired. We packed up the campsite after breakfast and moved deeper into the forest. At every step we took, I became more convinced that we were being watched. Before it was just a feeling, a sense that we were, but now I knew for sure that something or someone was watching us. My heart raced when I thought that my birth father or mother might be the ones watching. So many thoughts were invading my mind at that point so my senses were lit up like a Christmas tree. I sensed everything around me. I heard and saw every move. I wondered to myself if my parents and I would meet, would they sense that I was their son at first or just some human that was trespassing on their soil?

I carried a small pistol in my backpack and I was willing to use it, but only if our lives were in danger. Of course, if I would meet my father face to face, I doubted that one of my bullets would find my father's body. I obviously had to assume that he would be even more advanced than I, and his reflexes and natural instincts would sense any unwise movements that I would make. In the back of my mind I knew it would not be in my best interest to even draw my pistol, but just in case I was glad I had brought it on our trip.

Ahead, I saw a large hill that looked as if it led to higher ground. I waited until we got to that spot then told Lewis to stop and sit down. I was now sensing that we were very close to whoever was watching us. My natural animal instincts were totally taking over my senses and I was in full protection and awareness mode. I could also sense that Lewis was becoming more afraid and even he knew something was around us.

I put my backpack on the ground and raised my voice and said, "Who's there? I know I am in your forest. I know I am trespassing on your soil, but I am here in peace. I wish you no harm and I hope you wish me no harm." I then said the same words in German.

After I spoke, Lewis was whispering to me saying, "Garrison! What are you doing? Do you hear something? Do you see something?"

I told Lewis to be quiet. I stood as still as I could and ordered Lewis to do the same. I stood there for many minutes and the sounds that I had been hearing for almost a day now seemed to stop. I looked all around the forest to see if anything looked strange or if anything or anyone would appear. Nothing happened. I continued yelling, "Please don't hurt us. We will be moving forward, so if we get too close for your comfort, please don't hurt us. Just let us know where or when you want us to stop. I would like to see you so we can talk. I have some interesting information for you about Formula L that I believe you will find very intriguing."

I started to repeat these words in German, but after saying the first couple of German words, I heard something move deep in the forest. It was not very plain, but it was a strange sound. I sensed that whatever was in front of us wanted us to continue straight ahead.

Lewis was now extremely concerned because he knew it was Wolfgang. Of course, I knew this as well because a random animal didn't make those sounds; they had to be made by a humanoid creature. I wasn't sure where the sounds were coming from, but since we had been on the higher ground of the forest, I had heard something on two legs make shuffling and running sounds.

I again spoke loudly saying, "Wolfgang! I need to speak to you please. I come only in peace and I will leave in peace, but I need to speak with you. I have something very important to not only tell you, but to show you as well regarding some experiments I have been conducting in the United States."

With that I heard something quickly moving toward us. Lewis was frightened, and so was I for a few moments. Then my fear changed to anticipation since I had never seen my own true birth father. I knew something or someone was going to make its appearance. I heard something coming toward us as if it was half way running or jogging. It sounded as if it were dodging trees and plants. The sounds it made were massive as the branches from the small plants made a distinct sound as they were moved by this seemly large object that moved with ease.

Moments later, my heart stopped for a second as I could see the branches dance as they were being moved and then... I saw it. Large in stature, tall and wide in girth, it was a massive being. Bigger than my adoptive father ever was. It was Wolfgang. The man that wanted me dead at birth, the man that married my mother, the man that was a monster in many ways, but he was my creator, my birth father. The formula that he created was in his blood, in my mother's blood and thus in mine. There stood before me the creator of the formula that had made me powerful and special. There stood the man that did not understand what pain and burden he had unknowingly bestowed on me and my family. All I wanted was to speak with him about what he knew about the formula that he created, and hopefully I would be allowed to go in peace.

I stepped down from the large rock that I was standing on and slowly walked toward my father. Lewis was in the background and said, "Garrison, be careful." I walked slowly toward my father and stopped about thirty feet from this awesome figure before me. I said, "Good evening, sir. My name is Garrison Seawick and I am from America. Do you speak English, my friend?" The creature looked at me and as he squinted he cautiously nodded his head yes. I continued, "I believe you are the man that created Formula L. I had my good friend, Lewis here, tell me about you and your wife. I am not here to cause you any harm and I certainly don't want to disrupt your way of life. I am here mostly for informational purposes. Likewise, I have some news that I think might be accurate. I was told a while back that, well, sir... I believe I could be your son." I sensed he knew this already.

I knew he was studying my every move, like some animals do just before they attack. At that moment I knew we had much in common and I felt the immediate connection as our eyes met. I sensed the creature knew I had this special formula in me before I told him. I said, "I would like to sit down with you and discuss some issues with you in detail. Lewis and I just completed some rather interesting experiments on not only animals, but humans as well, and I would like to share the results of what we found with you."

My father moved his massive shoulders back and puffed out his large chest. I could sense he was either going to attack me or was trying to intimidate me. I tried to force myself not to be scared, but of course that was a failure. I sensed he was impressed that his appearance did not scare me off. My eyes never left him. My heart felt as if it was going to pound out of my chest. I then notice he opened his mouth and let out a large growl. Lewis yelled immediately and said, "Garrison! Look out!" I stood there looking at him, scared out of my mind. He knew I was scared, he could sense it; I knew he could sense it so there was no reason to try to hide the fear.

What I didn't want to do was run away because if I did that, it would probably mean instant death to both me and Lewis. With all the gumption that I had in my resolve, I took a few steps toward him. I said, "Now, was that to intimate me or are you about to attack? Let's get one thing straight; although I am afraid of you, I have had experience with your type before I bit my adoptive father on the wrist and he turned into a creature that closely resembled your stature and facade. So, even as daunting as your appearance is to me, it is not like I haven't seen this before. I have your formula in my blood. I have grown up with it all my life. I am the smartest person I know, until today. I have amazing reflexes. I have never been sick a day in my life. My body has been on a rapid growth acceleration since birth. I have mastered playing the violin in a fraction of the time that most virtuosos take fifty years to accomplish, and most of them don't even come close to my talents. I learned the German language in less than a week. I am being told by my doctor, Lewis, that gentleman standing over there that you met a long time ago, that I would never die a natural death. I am in love with a human woman that will die a normal death."

"All I want is three things in my life. One, I want to keep my love young and alive forever. In other words, I want the eternal fountain of youth for my love. Two, I want to control this fountain of youth, and three, I want to change the formula so the mutation, like yours, does not happen. I have used this formula on countless bugs, cats, dogs, birds, frogs, and other animals. I have used this formula on human beings. I even had a mutated human mate with a non-mutated human who got pregnant and had five babies that were horribly mutated. After all our tests, we killed them by fire, and burnt them alive so there would be no evidence for the authorities. I have everything documented to back up what I am saying. Now, can you help us? If not, then I would like for you to let us go. If you can help, I would like to show you what we have discovered so far."

My father stood there breathing heavily. I could sense that he was not used to being spoken to in such a manner and I knew he could sense my fear of him, but I was not backing down. I believe this impressed him.

The massive creature cleared his throat and with a strong, thick German accent he looked over to Lewis and said, "I thought I told you to never come back and never bring the authorities to this area."

Lewis was so nervous he could not stop his hands from shaking. He said, "Forgive me, but I didn't have a choice. Garrison is my boss and he forced me to bring him here to meet you."

Wolfgang shouted, "Lies! All lies you tell me. You had a choice. You broke a promise to me. You lied to me. I trusted you." Wolfgang quickly looked at me. His large, yellowish-red eyes looked me up and down slowly. He then snorted at me, raised his right index finger and said to me, "You should not have come here." He looked back at Lewis, "Both of you should not have come here."

Without warning, Wolfgang quickly ran toward Lewis. His large body looked as if it slithered through the air with the speed of a bullet leaving the barrel of a gun. His swift movement was most impressive to see in action. As he ran, his hands hit the woodland floor and his stride was long and fast. Lewis tried to run, but my father was too quick for him. He grabbed Lewis by his right arm and pulled him up so his feet were off the ground. Lewis pleaded with my father to spare his life. My father looked at Lewis and said, "You grew weak, old man." He looked back at me and was surprised that I only moved a foot. I could sense he was surprised that I would not come to the aid of the doctor.

I had anticipated that he would attack Lewis first. I knew my father's quest for knowledge was my key to staying alive. He could sense what I was thinking. He was impressed with the control I had over my physical body and my mental state of mind. Wolfgang looked at me as he lifted Lewis off the ground even further. Lewis continued to plead for his release. I stood there and said nothing, which seemed to momentarily puzzle my father.

I was not used to having someone read my thoughts and my body movements as my father had accomplished with such ease. I was in the presence of one of the few people that could fully understand me. He was obviously my father. I felt it and if I was feeling this, I knew he was sensing this to be fact as well. I would guess living with my birth mother for almost one hundred years helped him perfect the art of anticipating someone else's moves, especially one that possesses the formula. Although I was new to this game, I was prepared like no one he had seen outside of his wife.

My father said, "I will make a deal with you. Your life or your friend's?" I looked at Lewis with his pleading eyes. He was scared out of his mind. I felt his fear. I smelled the disgusting scent that his body gave off whenever he was frightened or angered. It was a smell that I had become all too accustomed to despising.

I sensed my father's eagerness to end someone's life at this very moment. He loved to kill. I felt his desire. I sensed his longing to extinguish a life, and I understood how good that felt. I knew he was used to killing and I knew he would probably take Lewis's life instead of mine. My father knew what I was thinking. He already knew the decision was made before he even attacked Lewis. This ability, or as I call it this gift of being able to fully sense, to be able to read someone else and to anticipate what actions other people or animals will take, is truly a strong weapon to have in one's constitution.

I knew my father wanted to know what we had discovered. I knew he was not going to kill me or Lewis; certainly not at this point. I could almost read his thoughts. I sensed he was fascinated that I had survived and what I had grown into as a human being. I was his son, but more importantly I was a byproduct of his formula, his creation. He had never tested any subject over such a long span of time. Time had tortured him through the decades, coming up with the same answer to the same question time after time. This I understood all too well, for I had the same experience as he had had.

We understood the power of Formula L, but most importantly, we understood its hidden powers. The chemical gives you countless advantages, but at a high cost. To live with this gift is difficult. To hear, see, and sense everything that others don't hear, see or sense is sometimes difficult to comprehend and impossible to explain.

I don't know how it is to live like a human because I was born with this blessing, whereas both my birth and adoptive fathers were born normal then in the middle of their lives they made the crossover. In the beginning stages of their transformation, it had to be difficult for them, but in different ways. My birth father wanted to change, whereas my adoptive father did not, but later accepted the gift and cherished it closely.

I stood admiring my real father, although I still had conflicting feelings. He wanted me dead at birth; he gave me up, he did not want me, but I had become used to this throughout my life. I never felt that Trevor wanted me from the start either. The only person that had truly accepted me in my life was my Marci. Loren was a close second, but even she waivered some at the end, just before her acceptance of her upcoming death. My adoptive mother only loved me for a few years until I grew into something she did not understand or wanted to accept. Oh death, an undiscovered friend to humans. Death is something I will probably never experience. I am only allowed to experience this phenomenon through other human's feelings and experiences.

I watched my father holding Lewis by his arm. The doctor was in obvious pain, but his fear was his greater adversary. I stood my ground and I didn't answer my father's question. Again, he asked, "Your life or your friend's?"

I said, "Why must I make a decision? Why do you have to murder one of us? We have not caused you any harm and we have no intention of causing harm to you."

Wolfgang said, "I told this man not to speak of me or my forest to anyone. He did. I told him not to come back or bring anyone back. He did anyway."

I said to my father, "But Father, you cannot blame Lewis for telling me about my long-lost Daddy."

This upset Wolfgang and he shouted back at me, "How do I know you are my son? I wanted you dead! Why in the world would I want to see you after all these years?"

I said to him sharply, "Listen, I have been trying to tell you since we met. We share something that only a few have shared in the history of mankind. I have seen both of my adoptive parents experience the transformation, I have seen countless animals go through the process, and we have injected a man with the formula from my body. I watched him transform and he mated with a non-infected human. She got pregnant, had five babies that were all mutated. I have all this documented on paper, on tape and on video. I want to present this knowledge to you and see what discoveries you have made in the past. I want to compare your notes with mine and hopefully we can duplicate Formula L without the mutation process, market this chemical, and make billions upon billions of dollars. But my main concern is not with money because that I already have. The main reason for my presence before you is twofold. I want to discover the secrets of the formula that gives us the fountain of youth and the ability to achieve perfection. I want to play god. Do you fully and completely understand that or do I have to explain myself more clearly?"

This retort further angered my father as he bent his head back with his mouth open and let out a growling yell of frustration. The growl bounced off every leaf, branch, and tree in the forest. He apparently was not used to others speaking to him in such a tone. After his display of territorial marking and the failed attempt at intimidation, he stopped, looked at me and said, "Does this Lewis hide information from you about your experiments?"

I said, "No. Not to my knowledge. We share all information and discoveries together. Lewis is my friend and I have known him my entire life."

Wolfgang was still holding Lewis firmly by the arm. He looked at me and said, "Then this one is mine now. Come. Follow me."

Lewis screamed, "No! No! Please let me go!"

Wolfgang took his right hand and grabbed Lewis by his jaw, pulled it toward his face and said, "Shut up, old man or I will end your life in the most unpleasant manner." Lewis was now crying as Wolfgang lifted him up and placed him over his shoulders. Wolfgang walked toward me and said, "Come."

I followed my father with Lewis draped across his left shoulder, dangling like some oversized stuff animal. I followed them deeper into the forest as the terrain became denser and steeper. I struggled to keep up with his pace. We walked for what seemed to be an hour and finally came upon my parents' home. I noticed some large figure standing in the entrance of the cave. This was obviously the cave that Lewis spoke of and now I was seeing it firsthand. I continued to stare at this large figure and I knew it was my natural birth mother. I did not hesitate for a moment during my walk toward the cave. I felt and sensed that, for the time being, I was going to live through this experience.

I walked up to the huge female figure who had a surprised look on her face. She looked at Wolfgang and then her eyes darted back toward me. I noticed her eyes developed tears as her extremely large and thin hands went up to cover her mouth. Suddenly, she moved with amazing speed, thanks to her long and powerful legs, toward me. She stopped just a couple of feet from me and quickly looked back at Wolfgang and said to him in broken English, "This cannot be. Is it our child?"

Wolfgang said, "They said he is. I believe this to be truth. You can sense it, can't you, Zelda?"

Zelda? I thought to myself, *What a beautiful name.* My mother's name, for any son, is one of the sweetest and most comforting words a son could hear. I was overcome with emotion and said in a quivering voice, "Mom. Are you my Mom?"

Zelda moved her large head and looked at me. She immediately broke down and fell to her knees in front of me as she wrapped her arms around my waist. At first, I thought she might hurt me. I lost control over my senses and mistakenly allowed my emotions to take control. I quickly put myself on high sensory alert and regained control. Her massive arms and shoulders hugged me with great strength. I instantly smelled an odor that was not to pleasant to my senses. My mother, although not dirty, had this very strange odor to her skin, a musky odor that one would experience being around a wet animal that had been running a long distance. That musky animal smell was not pleasant, but I have smelled worse on many an animal that I have feasted on during my lifetime.

Zelda could sense I was afraid and she said to me, "Don't worry, my son, nothing will happen to you here. I will not harm you. I cannot believe it is you." She stood up and said, "May I see something on your head?"

I was confused, but I sensed no harm coming to me so I said, "Yes. What is it? What is wrong?"

My mother said, "Nothing. I want to see if the mark is still there on the top of your head." Her large hands moved my head downward so she could see the top of my head. Her long, thin fingers went through my hair and suddenly she started to cry again. She said to Wolfgang, "It is really him, Wolfgang. Our son that I did not kill had a mole on the top of his head. It is still there. It is on this boy." Wolfgang didn't say a word, but he didn't need conformation as to who I was; he already knew. I believe he knew I was his son the moment I walked into the forbidden zone of the forest.

Wolfgang went inside the cave and placed Lewis down at the table rather rashly as if he had placed an oversized sack of potatoes on the ground. My mother held my hand and walked me inside. I thought this time would be a perfect time to say something, so I said, "I want to apologize for intruding on you like this, but like I told your husband, I came here to learn more about Formula L. I am very glad that you have accepted me into your home. I mean you no harm. You are my parents and I would never do anything to harm you in any way. I am not here to disturb your lifestyle, I just want to learn something if you could be so kind. Please, don't hurt my friend, Lewis. He was just doing what I ordered him to do. He didn't want to come here, and he kept you guys a secret from me for many years. But as you know, more than anyone would, he knew that I could sense that he was keeping something from me. He had to tell. He had no choice."

Wolfgang spoke abruptly, "He had choice. He is weak. He should have followed my instructions." There was a long and uncomfortable silence that hit the room then Zelda broke the awkwardness by insisting that we stay the night. Wolfgang agreed as he looked at me and said, "I want to see what you have for me now."

I nodded my head and pulled out everything that I had brought. I started at the beginning and told them my story, at least the part that was told to me by Lewis. I showed Wolfgang and Zelda my laptop. They were amazed that such an invention was created. It was hard for me to comprehend how far behind the times they were, especially from a technological perspective. They knew of the inventions that took place, but they had never seen many of these inventions up close. Before we even got into the video clips of my experiments, I had to show them the computer and the Internet. At the time, they were more interested in viewing the basics of what the Internet provided. I showed Wolfgang the Internet, and live music and videos. I showed him clips on Hitler, his former boss, and the last days of the Nazi reign. I could tell it disturbed him greatly, but both were very interested, although at the same time they were absolutely floored and speechless after my very long presentation of the computer and Internet. I even let them use and experiment with the computer; both were very grateful to me for showing them this new world.

As my computer and Internet demonstration ended, I continued to reveal everything that we had discovered about the formula. Zelda made us dinner and offered us water. The hours went by quickly as we ate, drank, and continued our discussions. Wolfgang was very interested in many of the discoveries that we had made. Most of the discoveries he already knew, but some parts of the experiments surprised him. He made many mental notes as I could see that these experiments really caught his attention.

Wolfgang was very impressed with my knowledge of the chemical and biological makeup of the human body. He was especially interested in my knowledge of genes and cell reproduction. He seemed to have great knowledge in that field and admitted this was his favorite area of study. I told him of my days at Harvard and went on a long litany of subject matter that really impressed him. I could sense the great pride that he was feeling, even though I was the son that he didn't want years ago. The night was getting long, and Lewis was exhausted. He fell asleep on the table and we ended up moving him to the couch in the cave. My parents were like me in that we did not require much more than a couple of hours of sleep a day.

I covered the many animals that we had injected with the formula and I discussed in excessive detail about Trevor's condition. Wolfgang was very interested in Trevor because he had never seen any of his subjects last that long after the formula was injected. The Nazis would kill off the subject before the transformation was fully completed.

Wolfgang was most impressed with my decision to infect homeless people. He was enthralled with that idea and said that he always wondered what the reaction would be if an infected animal would bite a non-infected human, then to have that infected human mate with a non-infected human was an interesting twist. Even he hadn't thought about conducting that kind of experiment.

Wolfgang watched all the tapes and read the notes that I had brought regarding this experiment. We also looked at the other experiments we had conducted. After a small respite, we noticed it was morning and the sun was coming up. The forest was still dark, but you could tell the sun was coming up by the way the beams of light would pierce through small openings of the leaves. The beams of light that made their way through were large and noticeable. These pillars of light looked as if they were supporting the overly large, thick trees, then suddenly they would disappear and others would reappear. If one would have any imagination at all, one would recall something out of an outer space movie script where laser beams would shoot from the sky and land on the ground.

I continued discussions with my father as he gave me a tour of his lab. Inside of his laboratory, some of the plaster had fallen off the walls, exposing the inner layers of the cave. He showed me live specimens that had mutated sitting in cage upon cage. I looked at each species that was on display. They had a look of great despair on their newly deformed faces.

These numerous experiments and mutated specimens were impressive, but what was a disappointing fact to me was that he never discovered the complete makeup of Formula L. Wolfgang could not come up with the correct change in the chemical makeup to stop the severe physical metamorphous from occurring. He told me he had conducted thousands upon thousands of experiments yet had never perfected the old formula; in fact, through all his experiments he saw worse results. To make this more maddening to my father was that he was never able to reproduce his most perfect batch of the formula.

When the Allied Nations were invading Germany, his lab in Berlin was badly damaged and most of the notes were burnt or buried. To make matters worse, this lab and mission was so top secret and sensitive that Hitler ordered the lab to be blown up. Wolfgang, to this day, believes that he and his wife got of the lab area just minutes before the lab exploded. He also wondered if Hitler, the man that he followed and admired so much, also ordered the bombing for Wolfgang's death. My father told me this is what had haunted him every day since the bombings.

Wolfgang did manage to save a few gallons of the formula, and luck would have it that he took those samples into the forest with him. He apparently buried the samples throughout the forest and only he knows where they are buried. Of course, access to the original formula meant nothing to me because I already possessed the original formula in my body. But the danger of having that formula hidden away in some container, the fear of someone taking possession of it is unthinkable. They would not have a clue as to the horrible side effects that formula would bestow the accepting hosts.

Wolfgang said that for the life of him he could not remember the exact makeup of the original formula. He tried many experiments to get this information, but had failed. Either way, he said it really didn't matter because in his view, the formula would never stop the mutation process from happening. The only way to get the mutation process to stop is for two infected subjects to mate and produce a child. This is what happened with me. My three other brothers were all physically normal human beings like me. Obviously, that is where the secret is hidden; inside of the hosts.

My father's life and countless experiments were an amazing tale. I wanted him to come back home with me to the States, so I asked him if that interested him. I told him I would charter a private plane to assist him, but he flatly refused. My father wanted, maybe even more than I, to find the answer to the mutation problem, but he wasn't comfortable with the idea of coming to a strange land and time at this stage in his life.

We grew close during our conversations. I greatly impressed him with my intellect of which he was a large proponent of throughout his life. He was most awestruck with the fact that I was willing to experiment not only on animals but on humans, and that the thought of killing them or torturing them didn't really bother me. He saw himself in me and this is what was keeping me alive. I feared that Lewis might not have built up as much goodwill and was concerned that he never once asked Lewis questions about the experiments. I knew Lewis was afraid for his safety, but I believed he just accepted his fate when he finally agreed to come along on this trip.

I decided to stay for another night. Lewis wanted to leave immediately, but there was so much I needed to find out before we left. We were all getting hungry and my father went out to hunt for dinner. I asked if I could come along. We took Lewis with us, along with a bow and some arrows.

Years ago, Wolfgang had brought many weapons to the cave, and one of those weapons was a bow and arrow set that was specifically for deer hunting. Wolfgang hoisted the bow and arrows on his large back and we went into the forest to find our food. It didn't take long for us to find a deer. In the distance, we saw a small deer behind many large trees. Wolfgang carefully took the bow off his back and loaded it with an old semi-rusty arrow. Meanwhile, I looked down and saw this oddly shaped rock. I slowly bent down and picked it up. I carefully and slowly moved into position and when I got a clear lane to the deer's head, I slowly drew back my hand and arm. I studied the deer for a moment and, based on my senses, I picked the exact perfect moment to throw the rock at the deer. I'd had so much practice at this over the years that this had become easy for me to do.

I threw the rock as hard as I could without making any sound outside of my arm whipping through the air. The rock moved at a fast pace and before we knew it, the rock hit the deer in his head and it fell to the ground. The animal was stunned for a second. Wolfgang wasn't expecting me to throw a rock at the deer, so I heard the arrow moving quickly through the thick forest air. I saw and heard the arrow go through the deer's neck, up toward its head. We ran toward the animal and we all just watched the animal moving around on the ground, trying to get up. Wolfgang looked at me and smiled. He was very impressed with my throw. He quickly bent down and twisted the deer's neck to kill it. He hoisted the carcass onto his shoulders and we headed back to his home.

We went inside, and he flopped the deer down on the table. Wolfgang and Zelda stopped and looked at us. I knew this was one of the many tests that my parents were giving me, so I quickly went over to the table, sat down, and pulled the deer toward me. I opened my mouth and plunged my teeth into the chest of the deer. I hadn't eaten anything in over a day and I was quite hungry. As I was eating on the side of the deer, Wolfgang let out a vociferous laugh that filled the room. I swear that I saw some of the pots and glasses shake from his deep laughter. He sat down across from me and started on the back of the deer, then Zelda sat down next to me and started on the belly. I assume we all had our favorite spots on the animal.

Lewis stood there like a fish out of water. He went over to his backpack and brought out some food. Wolfgang just laughed even louder as he pointed to Lewis as to make fun of him. From that moment on, I felt and was accepted into their family. My family. Wolfgang told me in his loud, deep voice with broken English, "Garrison, you are one of us. I like you." We continued to eat, and even though the trip was not necessarily a success on understanding the formula any better, I had found my original birth family and that made everything worthwhile.

My parents wanted me to stay one more night with them, rest up, and head back to town in the morning. I was happy to accept their offer. This additional time was well spent. We sat for hours on end discussing the formula. Wolfgang told me repeatedly that in his opinion the physical transformation was inevitable. He could not explain why, but this formula, when mixed with human adrenaline or when the body hit a certain temperature, the formula changed. He didn't think there was any way around this problem.

Wolfgang had shown me documentation and pictures of the different chemical changes that he would administer to his human and animal subjects. Usually the result was the growth rates of the limbs were too fast for the tissue to recover in time, resulting in open sores caused by the bone lengthening too quickly. The muscles and tendons surrounding the bones could not grow fast enough to keep up with the bone. Many times, a complete tear in the tissue would result and would cause pain and permanent damage, but most of the time the subjects would bleed out and die. All these complications developed from only a slight change in the makeup or mixture of the chemicals in the host's body when mixed with the formula.

Even body temperature had a major role to play in the development of the host. This made a lot of sense to me because I often wondered why the formula seemed to be almost dormant when the blood cooled. We ran tests on Adam's blood after he died, finding the chemical composition of the cold blood was vastly different from the blood when it was warm. This obviously explained why, under a microscope, the blood type and chemicals in the blood changed day to day, even hour to hour. This was the reason many of my past doctors, including Lewis, were so dumbfounded when they viewed my blood under the microscope. Basically, to find the absolute and most perfect chemical makeup of the formula is damn near impossible because the variables are constantly changing. For the formula to react properly, you must have the perfect amount of adrenaline to secrete from the adrenal glands and the blood must be a certain temperature.

When the formula is mixed with the body, somehow the formula mixes the perfect amount with the host's blood. The mixture between the two substances works perfectly in the mutation process. If you disturb one of these natural processes, then the effect of the formula is changed dramatically. Wolfgang described this process as someone chasing and attempting to capture a certain design in a puff of smoke. The slightest movement or change in the wind affected the design because the smoke design is in constant motion, like blood or any liquid. It is impossible to isolate the moving parts. It would also be difficult to change its design in any way because if you change an area of the design, that disturbance affects other areas. The moment you disturb the design, you alter the look of the design. The same premise is working regarding Formula L.

CHAPTER 17

Forbidding

The next morning, I packed our belongings for our trip out of the forest. This trip was very educational for my mental health, but not so much in my quest in getting any headway on changing Formula L's mutation. It was a pleasure to be able to visit with my parents and get to know them. It was nice to have something in common with someone that you could share experiences with that you couldn't share with others. I had a lonely life until I met my Marci. Before her, I felt as if I was just going through the motions in life with no purpose or goals to achieve.

I didn't feel lonely in my parents' cave, I felt at home. I finally knew what it felt like to have a family, a real mom and dad, not just some strangers that were afraid of you or didn't want you. Oh, don't get me wrong. I loved my adoptive mother. She will always have a place in my heart. I felt so sorry for her in what she had to endure throughout her life after she adopted me, and I felt responsible for her death. I wish I could have done something that would have prevented her from killing herself.

I grew close to my father at the end of his life, albeit for only a handful of months. We were at one time best friends, but when I look back on that time in my life, I wonder if he was more interested in my condition instead of being interested in me as his adopted son. He only grew close to me when he was going through the transformation, and we were closer after his mutation was complete. For the first time in his life, he finally understood me and what I was. I tried not to think about this too much because it tended to make me angry. My entire life I had always been told to control my anger, mostly from people that did not understand and was afraid of me.

Lewis hadn't slept well since we left the States. I knew he was looking forward to going home and getting away from Wolfgang and Zelda. He hardly said a word during our entire trip in fear of upsetting either one. I could fully understand his concern and I felt sorry for my lifelong guardian. We had been so close throughout my earlier life, but ever since I left for college our relationship had changed. He always seemed to be so judgmental of me and my lifestyle. He had been that way with me since I could remember, but this attitude of his had increased since my college years. I knew he didn't like me as he did when I was younger. I always felt that he looked at me as a subject and not as a friend. When I needed a father figure in my life, Lewis was the closest friend I had until I left for college. I guess like most things in life, we just ended up drifting apart.

I think the many years of dealing with this abnormal subject matter might have taken its toll on his limited understanding or willingness to understand me or my condition. He had told me years ago that he wasn't comfortable with the experiments we were conducting. I knew he was totally against all the experiments on humans that we had conducted.

Lewis was a very smart man, but his internal struggle between reality and his faith was hindering our pursuit of our goals for Formula L. Lewis wanted to be famous, special, and well known across the medical field. He needed that attention to make himself feel important. For Lewis, working all these years on Formula L projects was slowly killing him emotionally. He couldn't share his findings with anyone outside of just a couple of people. He was feeling that he had wasted a good part of his life on a subject that had no final, absolute answers.

This trip was the final straw for him. I could sense his emotions were getting the better of him. I attempted to keep him as calm as I could. I knew if he lost his temper on this trip, his life would end almost immediately. My father would not hesitate to kill him in a matter of seconds.

Lewis should have known that if I could sense his innermost feelings, so could my parents. I had spent most of my life controlling my feelings and thoughts, and had been constantly disappointed in Lewis for not doing the same. He should have learned from me. I know he found himself trapped in a situation that he never wanted or dreamed to be a party to.

Lewis was a rather tragic figure in my life. He stepped into a socially emotional case where a child did something that was highly abnormal. He discovered a child and his situation that was so unusual, no one in the history of mankind had ever faced it. He was trapped in a web of greed. The potential of having his name immortalized in history and medical books for eternity dominated his being. He saw a financial windfall like no other.

I knew what he was thinking because at one time I saw and felt the same. The only difference between Lewis and me was that I was living our experiments. Lewis wanted what I had; money, fame, fortune, and knowledge. He was even jealous of my relationship with Marci. He was always jealous of what I possessed physically and intellectually. I sensed it after the first year we met. Other times, we just grew apart all because of his resentment toward me and my many possessions. He also hated parts of my lifestyle and my personal thoughts on humans. He was a humanitarian of the utmost level. I am as well, but the difference between us is that I am willing to sacrifice a few to save the whole.

As Lewis was busy packing his bags, I could sense something was not right with him. I sensed Lewis was disgusted by what he saw, read, and heard over the past couple of days. He had not spoken but a few words to me since we met my father in the woods. He was not only avoiding me, but was ignoring me all together. I knew something had been brewing inside of him the past several days. I didn't want to encourage too much spoken dialogue between us because of the high probability that Lewis would say something that might get him killed. Lewis and I both knew Wolfgang was just waiting for the right moment to engage Lewis. I was keeping an eye on this situation.

When Wolfgang stepped into the room and walked over to Lewis, I knew we could have an issue on our hands. Lewis was visibly shaken when Wolfgang walked over to him. Wolfgang looked at Lewis and said, "We disgust you, no?" Lewis was forced to look at Wolfgang. When he realized he had made eye contact, he quickly looked down at his bag while he continued to nervously pack.

Wolfgang stepped closer and said, "Answer the question, little man!" Lewis looked around, not wanting to anger him further. Then in a blink of an eye, Wolfgang took his long arm, grabbed Lewis's backpack, and threw it in on the floor violently. Wolfgang said, "Why aren't you answering me?"

Lewis had great fear in his soul, but he was pushed to the breaking point and suddenly let his true feelings out. Lewis shouted, "Of course you people disgust me. You people are not human." Wolfgang showed his teeth as this retort angered him. Lewis continued, "You started all this, you and your Nazi friends, a century ago. You people were not scientists, you were murders. You loved to mutilate and cause suffering. Because of you, you brought that thing standing over there into my life. It all started when he ate a dog. A fucking dog! At first, I thought he was just a kid going through some awkward phase in his life. Then as he grew up he did things that no human had ever done. His IQ is at limits no man has seen before. He went to college and studied with the smartest professors in the world and he basically taught them before he was a teenager, for christ sake. He hears and notices everything. He learns at an inhuman pace. He learned German in less than a fucking week. How is that possible? He damn near mastered the game of golf in less than a few weeks. He hits birds at 100 feet in the air with a fucking rock. Who does this? He bit his father, and he turned into a monster just like you. A hideous creature that should have never been allowed to manifest into this... this state of evil. This state of half human, half animal is against everything God wanted or had envisioned for mankind."

"Then I am forced to come here, not once but twice, to find a secret to some fucked up formula that you somehow stumbled upon. No one understands or can remotely change its chemical makeup without it totally killing the subject because the bones grow too rapidly for the muscles to keep up. This is beyond any form of understanding. I couldn't even attempt to explain this without someone locking me up in some insane alyssum a minute into my discussion of this issue. I am totally trapped and have been for over a solid twenty years. I wish you never existed, I wish that boy of yours never existed. I wish this whole experience gone wild never existed. You are twisted and evil and your son might be worse than you. He does not have any feelings for any animal or person, and on top of it his fucked-up girlfriend wants to be like you people. All of you disgust me."

Wolfgang stood there, furiously breathing heavily. I must say, I was incensed as well. I knew Lewis never approved of my lifestyle, but I never sensed this much hatred toward me or my condition. I thought the pent-up anger was more for Wolfgang and not me. As I listened to him profess his hatred of me as much as my father, it greatly disappointed me. To be honest, what bothered me more was when he brought Marci into the conversation. Considering all the years we had been together, it was difficult to stand there and listen to this man speak of me in that way.

All the thoughts of not being wanted by my birth parents and my adoptive father were all now attacking me from all angles. I didn't like what was coming out of Lewis's mouth. His words hurt me deeply. Maybe I had sensed it through the years, but chose to ignore it because the thought of being alone was not pleasant.

I had to acknowledge Lewis's thoughts as my father listened. I said, "So, you think we are animals, huh? Maybe you are jealous of our talents. Maybe you are envious of what we can do mentally and physically."

Lewis said to me in a hateful voice as he pointed to Wolfgang, "No! I am not jealous of you or it." Wolfgang immediately reacted with cat-like reflexes. He grabbed Lewis by the throat with his powerful, large right hand. He raised Lewis about a foot and a half from the ground with his face just inches from Lewis's face, "Listen to me, you inferior, stupid little man. I am what you envy. I am what you seek. Just admit it, fool. That is why you came back to my home, not once but twice." Lewis couldn't speak because he was being choked to death by a man that had haunted him for years. Wolfgang continued, "You judge me without knowing me or having knowledge of the many burdens that I carry. You disgust me, little human. Maybe you need to walk in my shoes for a bit before you start passing judgment on me."

Without notice, Wolfgang took his free hand, grabbed Lewis's right arm, and extended it out from Lewis's body. As fast as he did this, he opened his large, wet, and malodourous mouth as wide as he could and bit into Lewis's forearm. Wolfgang continued to bite down on the arm until the bone in his forearm broke in half, continuing to hold Lewis by the throat with is other hand. Lewis was surprised and shocked beyond all belief.

I studied Lewis's face while my father was biting him. I saw a face filled with horror. I saw a man's worst nightmare unfold before his eyes. He was terrified and shocked. At first, I sensed that he didn't feel any pain from the horrific bite, but after a few moments passed, the pain started to increase its intensity. Wolfgang continued to bite hard. He moved his head from side to side to make sure his teeth were deeply imbedded into Lewis's broken arm.

Lewis cried out in tremendous pain. Every pulling and yanking motion sent sharp pains throughout Lewis's arm and shoulder. Throughout the continued bite, he could feel half of his forearm as it swung freely. Wolfgang then allowed Lewis to pull his arm out of his large mouth as he threw Lewis to the ground by his neck. Lewis was totally stunned, and after he collected himself he looked down at the open wound on his bent and broken arm. He started to yell as he grabbed his throat with his uninjured hand and said in a hoarse voice, "Nooooooo!"

Life can be cruel, unfair, and filled with great irony. What revolted Lewis the most, he was now on the boundary of becoming. He knew from the moment my father embedded his teeth into his arm that his worst nightmare had just began. While he laid on the floor of the cave, Lewis attempted to cradle his broken and bent forearm with his good arm. With some hesitation, he moved the limp part of his hurt arm to a straight position. He screamed out in pain as he held his forearm together. The pain started to set in even more as the shock of being bit was now wearing off. Blood was pouring out of the massive area in his arm.

Wolfgang turned his large, angry face to me and looked for my reaction. I stayed as calm as I could. He knew I was scared, but my lack of reaction surprised and pleased him. Lewis was looking at me with the most painful and horrifying look on his face as tears developed in his eyes. I looked at my former friend as I tried to imagine how much pain he must be feeling. I took inventory of my emotions and discovered that I no longer felt any emotional connection to him. My eyes moved to my father and back toward Lewis. I knew I had to say something, not for my personal safety but what I felt in my heart. I said while looking at the human, "It serves you right, Lewis."

I removed my eyes from the broken human and said to my father, "What did he call us? Oh yes, animals." The sides of Wolfgang's mouth rose, exposing long, sharp teeth. A growl from the pit of his stomach came from this most perfect specimen. I looked down at the human and said, "Now you will be an animal like us."

My father smiled widely and a hard laugh escaped his mouth. I walked over to the pathetic human who now was busy looking at his arm. He didn't know what to do. He kept observing his bitten and broken arm. The pain was so intense. The constant fiery feeling coming from his injury was so concentrated that it was taking his breath away. My father and I could almost feel his pain as it trumped all his thoughts. He wanted the pain to cease, but he knew that was not going to happen. He looked at us with the most perplexed look. He kept moving his eyes from us to his arm; he was speechless from the pain he was experiencing.

I bent down and said, "Well, at least you know what is in store for you, unlike my father who had to experience the transformation all on his own. You need to learn to keep your mouth shut, Lewis. I know you didn't ask for this in the beginning, but remember what I told you after my father died and I killed Adam? I sat down with you, Carolyn and Loren, and I told you all that if you wanted out, you could get out, but if you stayed, I needed your total devotion. You saw dollar signs and, quite frankly, I did as well, but this is beyond that for me now. Now I want to discover the truth. I want to possess the knowledge of what is behind the secrets of the formula. I want to be god. I want to have the ability to cheat death, time, and disease. But I also have another incentive in my life, Marci. I want the love of my life to experience centuries upon centuries of the love that I have in my heart for her. I want her to be perfect because she wants to be perfect. She looks at me and she envies me, she wants to be like me. Do you know how hard that is for me to deal with? I expected you to be on my side, not against me. I expected your support, not your opposition."

All Lewis could say was, "I am bit. He bit me."

Wolfgang quickly said, "Yes, old man, I bit you and I want you to think about that every day of your pathetic life. You will now be, what is it you call us? Oh yes… a monster, an animal like us."

I looked at my father and said, "What, it would take about two to three months for the transformation to be complete?"

Wolfgang smiled and said, "Yes, maybe two months. You know, I don't think he is healthy enough to travel back to America. Maybe he needs to stay here with us until he… gets better."

I nodded my head and said, "I think that is a good idea and the best for everyone involved."

Lewis was scrambling around on the floor with his legs and his good arm, trying to get up. Every move he made sent sharp, shooting pains up and down his arm. When he used his good arm to help himself up, the injured arm bent downward and dangled. Lewis let out a loud scream, which amused my father. The pain caused him to fall to his knees as his entire body shook violently. His red face was covered in sweat. It took all his might to get back on his feet. As he held his bent arm close to his body, he ran toward me and said, "You bastard! You cannot leave me here with this monster."

Wolfgang let out another loud growl and in one quick motion he rushed toward Lewis and grabbed his good arm at the wrist, causing his broken arm to fall out of place again, producing more extreme pain. Wolfgang took Lewis's hand and extended the unbroken arm from Lewis's body as he placed his large palm behind Lewis's elbow. In a matter of seconds, Wolfgang pushed the elbow in while holding his arm down in a locked position, thus badly hyperextending the elbow. The elbow made a loud cracking sound that resembled a walnut being cracked open by a hammer. Wolfgang moved the forearm upward toward Lewis's head for a complete dislocation of the elbow. Wolfgang bent the arm backwards, forcing Lewis's hand to touch the back side of his own shoulder. Wolfgang released the hand as the whole arm fell, drooping to Lewis's side. Both of his arms were bent in so many directions it was rather difficult to look at.

Lewis seemed to be in more shock than pain. Now both arms were at a point where he couldn't move them. Never in his life had he been in so much agony. Suddenly, in one quick motion before Lewis's body was about to hit the floor, Wolfgang guided his hand up to Lewis's upper arm area. Lewis was very unstable and was falling from the burning pain that Wolfgang had caused him. Wolfgang quickly placed his right hand on Lewis's shoulder and with one swift movement, there was an additional pop and cracking sound. Lewis's right shoulder was out of socket. Lewis couldn't breathe while in this mind-numbing pain. His head fell back and his knees hit the floor. Wolfgang released his hold on Lewis and allowed Lewis's body to fall hard onto the wooden floor. He looked like a pretzel lying on the floor.

I don't believe I showed any emotion during this torture process. My heart was numb to his pain. I finally came to the realization that Lewis was not with me, he was against me. This not only angered me, but it greatly disappointed me. All the thoughts about our relationship came to my mind at once. Most of my life I thought he was on my side. I thought he was my protector, the consistent father image that I never really had in my life. I believed he was a man that I wanted to be like when I grew up. But through the years I began to realize that I was the better man, both physically and mentally. I gave my fallen co-worker credit; I believe, from a humanitarian point of view, that Lewis was the better man. I never really adopted the view of caring for my fellow man. We viewed the world differently and at times our desires and beliefs intersected. When that happened, we worked well together, but when our views crossed the paths of discontent and disagreement of principle, we had problems.

As I looked at my once close friend lying on the floor in unimaginable pain, a cold and crass feeling attacked my being. I said to my new adversary as he was gasping for air, "You never loved or cared for me. You never cared for my family. You just feared my father. You feared the unknown. You never embraced me as a friend. You just tolerated me along the way. After I grew up, you thought you could control me, but when you found out you couldn't, you started to fear me. That fear turned into disgust, didn't it? I cannot continue to work with someone that is disgusted by me. Hell, even Marci, a woman that I have known for a fraction of the time that I have known you, accepts me and my lifestyle fully and completely."

Lewis interrupted me and said with a painful and breathless retort, "That bitch is just as fucked up as you are, you evil, sadistic bastard."

My anger got the best of me and something within me had to outwardly express itself. The feeling that came over me I had never experienced in my life, at least not to this level of pure hatred. I was blinded with hate and instinctively felt that I had to lash out at my adversary. I let out a growling sound that came from the pit of my stomach. This was the first time I had made that horrific sound. I saw and felt nothing but pure hate, rage, and anger. This rage and anger was so blinding that I lost all control of my senses. I remember jumping toward Lewis without any control over my physical body.

Suddenly, in the middle of my attempted attack, my father stopped me with his large hands. They landed on my shoulder and arm as he stopped me from attacking my once close friend and father figure. I turned my head toward my father and let out the same growl at him.

He copied my retort and I immediately backed down. I did not appreciate the fact that my father had stopped me. I wanted to kill Lewis. I wanted to tear him into pieces as I did to my brother, Adam, but this time it was an uncontrolled anger that dominated my being. I could not see straight I was so angry. Never in my life had I experienced such anger. Lewis had always taught me to control my emotions, and for most of my life I had subdued my angry feelings and thoughts, but not this time.

My father pushed me back and I fought with him momentarily. I could sense he liked my anger and at that moment, I could sense he understood me. For the first time in my life, I finally found someone that understood me and felt what I felt. It is difficult being different. What is more difficult is not being able to understand others and for those not to understand you. That is extremely hard to accept.

Before I knew it, I found myself not being able to control my movements. My father held onto my shoulders with his large, powerful hands. Suddenly, my father's right hand was around my neck while his other hand was still on my shoulder. He shook me rather hard and rapidly during my restraint. I started to get my wits about me as I finally noticed that I was being choked. At the time I didn't care, but after a few moments my senses came back to me and I stopped struggling. As soon as I stopped trying to attack Lewis, my father's hands released their grip on my neck and I fell to the floor, coughing and trying to catch my breath.

After several long moments, I regained control over my breathing and cough. My father said, "Calm down, Garrison, get control of yourself." I was suddenly scared like no other time in my life. I had never felt this way before. I then noticed a small amount of blood was coming from my mouth. I placed my hand up to my mouth and when I moved my hand back, I saw more blood. My tongue brushed up against something in my mouth. I moved my tongue around and discovered something felt different. As my tongue moved along my teeth, I felt four of my teeth had changed in size. Two teeth on the top, my lateral incisors, and two on the bottom had grown about a quarter of an inch.

Wolfgang noticed the blood and came over and said, "Did I hurt you?"

I responded, "I don't think so, but my teeth... they seem to have changed... they... grew."

Wolfgang took his massive hand and cupped my chin and gently lifted my head toward him. He said, "Open." I opened my mouth and I could tell something had his interest. He said, "Your teeth, your incisors, top and bottom, were they always like this?"

I felt my teeth again with my tongue. I then used my finger to explore the new growth. I quickly said, "No. They changed. They grew. I swear to you they grew." Wolfgang released my chin and helped me up from the floor. He asked me to sit down for a while until he got back. He told his wife to keep an eye on me and for me not to attack Lewis. I told him I had regained control over myself and I was not going to attack.

Lewis stared at me with a look that I had never seen before. He was totally terrified of me. He was so frightened that he forgot about his badly wounded arms and horribly dislocated shoulder. I told him, "Don't say a word to me, Lewis."

Lewis struggled to say through his pain, "Your teeth, what is wrong with your teeth?"

Before I knew it, Zelda came stomping toward Lewis and kicked him in his dislocated shoulder. Lewis screamed and about passed out from the pain. He was moving about on the floor like a fish out of water. He was in unadulterated pain. Almost simultaneously, Wolfgang returned. He flopped a large bag down on the table, opened the bag and told me, "I need a sample of your blood."

I wanted to know what happened. I wanted everything to be documented. My father drew some blood and said, "Follow me." Without hesitation, I followed him downstairs to his laboratory. His equipment was very outdated but better than what I had carried with me.

My father and I spent about an hour of highly intense studying of not only my sample of blood but my body as well. We checked every inch of my person. We wanted to see if there were any other changes. We checked my face, hands, and chest. I stripped naked in front of him to see if any part of my body had changed. Nothing else seemed to be different. My eyesight and hearing were the same as before. After careful analysis, besides the growth of my four teeth, we found no physical changes. In fact, I felt fine and had no soreness. This phenomenon perplexed my father to no end. He had never seen anything like this before, but then again, he never had a subject like me before.

We thought about every possible reason this might have happened. Wolfgang came up with a theory. He believed that my adrenaline was at such a fever pitch that somehow it reacted with the formula in some unique way, causing the physical change in my teeth. These are the same teeth where the formula comes out to inject into my prey. Wolfgang asked me many questions, and after another hour of being interrogated, I told him that I had always kept my emotions in check as far as I could remember. The only time I was not under total control was the day I ate a dog named Snowy, and that was when I was five or six years of age. My father and I concluded that this was the only answer. We discovered something new about the formula. Four of my teeth grew from my uncontrolled anger. So now, I had even more questions than before.

One of the unanswered questions we had was what would happen if I lost control again in the future. Would my physical appearance change or would something else change in my body? Although I didn't feel any different physically, I didn't want to change physically, I wanted to keep my current appearance. With all due respect to my father and mother, I didn't want my physical appearance to be altered. I wanted to be able to have the freedom to fit into society and not have to live in isolation like they had to for decades. For the first time in my life, I feared this newly discovered nuance of the formula.

Even Wolfgang wondered about himself. He had always controlled his anger to some degree because he knew that the adrenal glands were the main basis for the degree of reaction to the formula. He kept his temper at a certain level in fear of what might happen if he didn't. Through the many decades of living with the formula, he knew about what level he could push his anger to without any repercussions.

But what happened to me surprised and jolted Wolfgang. He admitted to me that he had always prided himself in keeping calm because he didn't want to lose full control out of fear of the unknown. Now he was more worried about himself. He thought that maybe one day this type of physical change might happen to him as well.

During these long discussions, a thought suddenly came to me. I went for my laptop and searched for the video of the homeless guy. When Marci and I were upsetting him, I wondered if he somehow changed physically. Wolfgang and I looked for any clues and we found nothing. I told him that I had more tapes at home and would research them to see if anything happened. I rehashed what I did to Adam and told my father that I didn't notice any physical changes during the torture of my brother. Not to him or to me. I told my father that he was quite upset, but also angry with me at the time. I told him that before torturing him, he was very angry with me when my father was alive, but to my knowledge he didn't have any additional physical changes to his body.

Lewis documented everything about Adam, Trevor, and Adelle daily. Through the years he had documented everything he could about me from age five to when I was a teenager. Wolfgang listened to every word I said. He took notes as fast as he could physically write. At the end, we were still stumped for answers.

I happened to glance at one of the few creatures that Wolfgang had in his old cages. My eyes quickly looked at my father. He suddenly smiled at me, knowing what I was thinking. We didn't have to say a word to each other and, like two adolescent school kids looking at porn for the first time, we went over to a transformed frog that had been alive for quite some time. Wolfgang took a long stir stick used to stir chemical mixtures in beakers. He proceeded to poke at the frog in hopes of angering him and seeing if the thing would transform further. After many attempts, nothing physically happened to the frog. We just looked at each other in bewilderment.

For the first time in my life I was truly scared. I told my father that in all due respect, I didn't want to transform into what he was or how Trevor transformed, for obvious reasons. I wanted to be able to function in my world. Wolfgang understood my concerns. What was now disappointing, but exciting at the same time, was that we now had another issue that needed exploring regarding the formula. Of course, I knew what to do; just don't lose control over my emotions like I did with Lewis. I had been angry before but for some reason he angered me to a place that I had never visited before. I had a blind fury that was so animalistic that I lost all control over my human self, and in that small moment of time, I had the emotions of an animal. I discussed all my feelings with my father and he found this amazing and something else he didn't have solid scientific answers to.

Meanwhile, Zelda was upstairs with Lewis. Zelda was a very large and strong woman who had a kinder heart than her husband. She had always been a faithful, loving wife to Wolfgang and she followed and supported his every endeavor in life. She respected his intelligence and, like so many people of Germany during the Nazi reign, she was obedient and loyal to her country and its leader. For Zelda, her love for my father transcended everything. She adored him and fully embraced his love for science and zest for knowledge. She loved my father so much that she was willing to change her body into a look that was completely unaccepting to humanity, just so she could share her life with the man that she loved for centuries on end. She wanted to be able to live forever with the man of her dreams, her protector, and her lover. It was an incredible sacrifice that she had made, not only for my father but for their relationship. For obvious reasons, I see a lot of my mother in Marci.

As my father and I were downstairs, Zelda walked over to Lewis who was lying on the floor whimpering like a baby. She positioned herself appropriately and adjusted his shoulder back into its socket. She had two long sticks with a large roll of tape. She knelt beside his hurt arm and quickly moved the arm and elbow back into place. Lewis's screams could be heard throughout the cave.

Zelda placed the two wooden splints on each side of his arm, in addition to the wooden sticks, and wrapped him with the tape to keep his arm as stable as possible to prevent any painful movement. Zelda picked Lewis up and placed him in a chair at the dinner table. Lewis was in terribly agonizing pain, but he was grateful that he was getting some help. Zelda tried to be as careful as she could with Lewis, but his injuries were very severe. In the past, she had been trained as a nurse, so she knew what kind of pain Lewis was in and knew how to address his injured limbs.

Lewis knew he was in trouble. He knew what had happened to him was his fault. Many thoughts went through his mind at the same time. The pain he was experiencing was extreme. He knew he was bitten and that he would have a rough couple of months as he went through the transformation. He knew Wolfgang wanted him alive or he would have killed him by now. All he wanted now was to just die a normal death because his greatest fear was coming true. The greatest fear that he'd had since he first discovered the formula was that he might turn into one of 'them'. He also knew beyond any doubt that Wolfgang wanted to torture him for his own amusement. The best thing for him was to die or be killed, but he was in no position to kill himself and he knew he couldn't convince them to kill him.

Finally, Zelda spoke up in her broken English and said, "You are unlucky man, Lewis. Unlucky to be alive. I fear that you might not like your stay here. You do know that you will never go back home, no. Wolfgang will never allow that. It seems you have been replaced by my son. Wolfgang once liked you. He thought you had promise. That is why he allowed you to live years ago when you visited. But you failed him, and he does not accept failure well. You wanted to stop the experiments whereas Garrison continued them. Garrison reached out and experimented and you were against them. You called us animals." There was a long and uncomfortable pause as she looked at him closely for any type of response and then she said, "I will try to make your stay here comfortable. You will learn our way of life, if he does not kill you before you learn."

Lewis knew he was in his own private hell. He knew what to expect regarding his fate. For the past twenty or so years he had fought off the worries of becoming what he feared the most, which was becoming one of them. Becoming a monster that comprised of half human, half animal that was in constant battle with both sides the human world verses the animal kingdom. This strange realm of continuous schizophrenic conflict of what is human and what is animal requires the victim to constantly balance their emotions. It forces one to merge the two worlds so the one can exist in peace. Once this is mastered, a special unknown world is revealed, and the victim becomes blessed. The only price one must pay is an altered physical appearance and the knowledge that the blessed one will outlive all that they met throughout their existence.

For these unnamed beings, the experience of death will become one's most frequent incident that they will share only through the eyes of others, but will remain the most distant and unknown companion through the journey of the unidentified. Sometimes in life, death for some beings is the only way to total freedom. For the blessed, they will have no description for this state of being that is placed on this rarest of species. Death will be a strange and unchartered concept to their personal world.

Lewis thought about all that he once had that had now vanished. He knew death was the only answer, but would Wolfgang be so kind as to grant him this option? Lewis had spent almost half his life searching for answers to something that apparently didn't have retorts to his questions. There is no cure; there is not an antidote to this strange metamorphic transition from one commonly known world into a dark, demented underworld where only a handful of beings existed. He was at the threshold of a world that had no hope for normalcy. He was entering a world that, for him, was frightening, a place that was dark on so many levels. But what confused him the most was that the few occupants of this dark and seedy world viewed this form of life as a wonderful and lovely place to exist.

This concept was lost on Lewis. He could not accept or understand their way of thinking. How could one cope with such restrictions on one's destiny? He didn't want this 'blessing'. Thoughts of suicide went through his mind, but this window of opportunity was only open for a few months. After this window was boarded up, he knew he would never die once the transformation was complete. Forever is a lonely and powerful word for the victims of despair.

We went upstairs and found Zelda sitting down at the table with Lewis. Lewis looked rough and was obviously in terrible pain. He was mentally and physically exhausted from his pain and injuries. Zelda told us how she popped his shoulder back into its socket then taped and set both of his arms. Lewis looked at me and when our eyes met, he quickly glanced away. He wanted to speak to me but after all we had gone through, he thought twice about it. He was also in so much pain that to speak would cause him more pain throughout his body. He wanted relief from the acute pain, but there was not going to be any relief from his injuries.

I approached my once longtime friend and for a moment I felt sorry for him. I sat myself down in a chair next to him. Lewis began to weep uncontrollably, but his tongue remained silent. I said, "Lewis, again, I am sorry for attacking you. I want you to know that my incisors grew about a quarter of an inch, but no other physical change took place. I was in a blind rage and now I am totally convinced that I must always keep my emotions in check. I need to thank you for forcing me to stay in control of my feelings since I was a small child. You always told me to keep calm and keep my emotions reigned in."

"Do you know of anything that would cause the physical reaction that happened to me? Did this happen to Trevor or Adelle? Did this happen to Adam or to any animal that we experimented on at any point in time?"

Lewis looked at me and began to speak in a frightened voice, "I don't know, Garrison. I do know that when your father, I mean Trevor, was alive, when he got angry his personality seemed to change to a more highly aggressive state. My theory is it all rests with the adrenaline and somehow when it mixes with the formula it has a reaction."

I said to Lewis, "But did Trevor have any permanent physical change to his body when he got angry?"

Lewis quickly said, "No. Not to my knowledge. I have saved all those tapes which you need to go over and see if you can notice any physical alteration. Of course, I never would have thought to look at his teeth, but Trevor never complained or commented on any physical change on any part of his body. Maybe you hit a certain level of anger that somehow triggered a chemical change in the formula."

With that said, Lewis quickly started to show panic in his voice and his body movements as he said to me, "Garrison, I am so sorry for what I said. I didn't mean to hurt you in any way. I hope you can forgive me."

I walked away slowly and said, "Well, Lewis, these have been difficult times for us and especially you. I just wish you would have thought differently about our problems. We are human, we are not animals. An animal is something that does not think. They only react to their environment. We have a brain that is highly advanced. To even remotely suggest anything differently is a complete insult to us."

Lewis said, "I understand."

I continued, "I am sorry for what happened to you. It didn't have to end this way. You should have kept your mouth shut. I don't understand your new-found feelings toward me or my family. I thought you were my right-hand man. I knew years ago that you never asked for any of this. No man in his right mind could have imagined this would have turned out this way. You were my friend, one of the very few true friends that I had in my life before Marci. I knew we had grown apart the moment I left for college, but I always thought you would at least have some respect for me and my relationship with this unknown formula in my veins. Lewis, I cannot take you back to America. I need to leave you with my parents. You must stay here. I have no choice in this matter. I will keep in touch with you when I can."

Lewis knew I was going to keep him there from the beginning, but he had hoped for a small chance that he might escape Wolfgang's world. After all Lewis had gone through over the past few days, all the emotions swelled up inside of him. He cried out, "Garrison, please don't leave me here. I don't belong here. I am so sorry for what I said."

I interrupted him with, "This is not about what you said. It is what you believe and it's your thoughts about us. I gave you an option a long time ago to either leave or stay. You chose to stay with me. At the time, I thought you loved me and wanted to stay for that main reason. But you wanted fame and fortune. You wanted to be immortal in the medical history books. Through the years you began to conclude that you would never be able to crack the code of the formula, thus I believe your sentiment towards me grew poorer. Then we started our experiments. A part of you loved it, but the other part of you despised what we were doing. Your sad devotion to your religious beliefs gave you doubt to our mission. You wanted to understand the formula, but you were not willing to sacrifice a few of your precious god's subjects to get to the root of the issue. Thus, all the conflicting emotions you were experiencing had turned you against not only our cause but me. So, I support my father's wishes in keeping you here. He will take good care of you."

I got up from my chair and walked over to my father. I extended my hand to him and we shook hands. Suddenly, he pulled me close to him and we embraced. For the first time in my life, I sensed what it meant to be loved by a man called your father. We patted each other on the back then parted. Wolfgang turned away and walked toward the large fireplace that was in the middle of the room. I walked over to my mother whose eyes were filled with tears. I reached out and hugged her with all my strength.

For a moment, I felt like I was back home as a child and Adelle was holding me. I longed for those days. Oh, how I missed my mother. I knew my birth mother felt my emotions as she held me tight for a few moments longer. I didn't want the embrace to stop, but all good things must end. We gradually parted as only our hands continued to stay in contact with each other. I told my mother that I would like to come back someday.

They both told me that I would be welcomed anytime. Wolfgang was especially proud of me and told me directly. He was proud of my continued research into his lifelong dream. He knew that I was his only way to ever find out the true chemical makeup of the formula. His lab and resources were so limited because of their age and lack of any sort of updates. My father had already exhausted all possibilities years ago to ever finding the secrets of the makeup of the formula.

We left each other with the knowledge of what both Lewis and Wolfgang thought to be true years ago — that the secret to this formula was somehow linked with the human's adrenaline and its effect on the formula while inside the body. My parents sensed that I didn't want to leave, and I think it made them feel good. Even my father and I had grown close in these past several days. This was the same man that wanted to kill me when I was born and the same man that killed my three brothers. While that thought still lingered in my mind, knowing that I was not wanted, all those unpleasant thoughts of yesteryear disappeared during this moment. For the first time in my life, I felt wanted by both of my parents, not just one of them.

Just before I left, I was given a picture by my mother. It was an old wedding photograph of my parents. It was one of the few they had. I knew deep down inside of my heart that she truly loved me, and during this trip they came to care about me. Like all humans and animals, the mind plays tricks on the user. You can trick the mind into believing anything. Even the strongest and most intelligent mind can be swayed to any one side of a subject. There is a fine line between someone being a murderer and someone who is not.

I had tears running down my cheeks as I picked up my bags and walked out the entrance of the cave. I looked back and saw my mother crying while my father was holding back his emotions. I could sense his emotional struggle with letting go of his new-found offspring. What a conflicting, emotional ride it must have been for them both.

When I was leaving, I heard Lewis repeatedly cry for me not to leave him. As I walked away, I heard him scream. I didn't stop nor did I look back. The man should have learned from his past mistakes. From that moment on, I knew Lewis's life would never be the same. He was probably going to be nothing more than a permanent test subject for Wolfgang to experiment on as long as he allowed him to live. As large and gruesome as my parents were now, at one time these two physical monsters were once all human, just like Trevor and Adelle was at one time. They are still human to me, but better than anyone I had ever met. They were so perfect. They were both so in tune with their environment, like they were one with their surroundings. They heard, saw, and felt everything around them. I was the only one that I had known for a long time that experienced this phenomenon. My adoptive parents had this talent, but one didn't live long enough to understand its power and the other was just starting to enjoy its advantages. To visit and speak with a couple that have had over a century of experience with such a pleasure was exhilarating.

While I walked from the cave, I was mostly walking downhill. I kept a close eye on my compass. My father told me to walk in a southeastern direction and I would eventually find my way out of the forest. I remembered most of my steps and I saw evidence of where I had been several days before. It was a long way out of the forest, but I'd had a good night's sleep. Since I required little sleep, I knew I didn't have to stay the night in the forest.

When I hiked back to town, my thoughts were with Marci back home. I had not called her for days and I was sure she was worried about me, but I didn't want to call her until I got out of the forest. I had a feeling that my father was probably either watching or listening to me while I left the area. Although I knew he would not attack me or prevent me from leaving, I didn't want to push the issue whatsoever. As I walked further, I thought about my life. A life without Lewis was going to take some time getting used to. I wondered what my love would think about the story that I must tell when I saw her. Those days in the cave changed my life forever, and it changed three other people's lives as well. I was anxious to tell my love all about my experiences. Now I felt for the first time in my life that I had both parents that loved me and to some degree wanted me to stay. It was a twisted relationship, nevertheless it was a relationship that I had longed for all my life.

CHAPTER 18

Egress

After what seemed to be forever and a day, I finally came upon the lighted area of the forest. This was the same place where my mother had laid me as an infant with the hopes of someone finding me. I stopped and knelt by the stream and started to cry. I cried hard, sobbing like a newborn. The colossal amount of stress and strain had finally taken its toll on me. I normally kept my emotions in check, but I allowed myself to cry. Part of my emotional outburst was self-pity, part of it was the built-up stress, and part of it was a sense of completion. I finally felt complete for the first time in my life. I felt normal.

I reached out and placed my cupped hands in the water and brought the water to my face which was wet and dirty from the humidity in the forest. The water felt so cold and pleasant on my face. I just knelt there for a while, looking at the area which I believed was the area where I was first discovered as a baby. Imagine if I would have died during those hours or days or however long I was lying on the forest's floor. How my life had changed so many others, some for the good and some for the bad. I got on my feet, picked up my gear, and headed out of the forest.

When I walked out of the forest, the sun was falling from the sky. I had an hour or so before the sun rested for the night. I was very tired, and my legs and feet were hurting from the long hike. I made my way to where the bed and breakfast was located. I struggled to the front door and as soon as I stepped inside, I was ready to crawl into bed. Even though I don't require much sleep, I was mentally and physically exhausted. I needed time to myself for relaxation. I walked over to my bed to lie down on the soft mattress. I must have slept about three or four hours. When I awoke, it was dark outside.

I laid in my bed, thinking about coming up with a story about what happened to Lewis. As dawn broke, I called my love and told her that I would be home later that night. I knew Marci really missed me and was very nervous throughout the entire trip so when I called her, she seemed to be very relieved. I had never sensed so much love from one's heart to another being than through Marci's passion. She is a very special person and one that I cannot live without. Marci said that she had missed me terribly and wanted to know if I was doing well.

I told Marci that I had met my parents and was doing fine. I could sense that Marci was shocked that I got to meet them. She was busy asking me a thousand questions a second and I had to tell her that I would answer all her questions when I got back home. We said our goodbyes and I started to pack up our belongings.

After my conversation with Marci, I called Sonja and told her that I was back from the forest. I made up a story about Lewis deciding to leave Germany early, and that he flew out on an earlier flight and was going to meet me in the States.

I asked Sonja to make some plane reservations for that day, and luckily I got on the first flight leaving Germany for the United States. Sonja seemed confused at first with Lewis's quick and silent departure. She asked numerous questions about who picked him up and took him to the airport. To keep Sonja from asking too many questions, I kept her busy with a small but steady to-do list. Sonja sent people to pack up my gear, suitcases, and equipment. She told me they would place my belongings on another plane and deliver them to my residence in a couple of days. I wanted to tour the area, but I decided that I needed to get back home instead. I missed my Marci and I had some unfinished business to take care of regarding the explanation of what happened to Lewis. I said my goodbyes to Sonja and thanked her for all her hard work in organizing and planning our brief stay. Sonja had to think this set up was very odd, but she played along and didn't ask any more meddlesome questions. I drove myself to the local airport and boarded the plane for the United States. The plane ride was long and boring. I thought I would never get home. I had to change planes in New York City and from there I had a direct flight into Louisville.

When I arrived in Louisville, my beautiful Marci, along with Carolyn, was there to greet me at the airport. As soon as I left the checkout area, Marci and Carolyn were waiting for me. Marci couldn't wait to see me as she ran as fast as she could and almost knocked me down as she jumped into my arms. Her legs wrapped around my hips as we engaged in a long, passionate and heated kiss. Carolyn gave us our space then after a few awkward moments she said to us, "Okay, you two love birds, you do know you're standing in an airport, right? Garrison, where is Lewis?"

Marci continued her deep kiss as her tongue was as far into my mouth as it could go. I had some explaining to do since I was one partner short from the trip. I sensed that Marci didn't care, but Carolyn was quickly becoming very concerned. I gently but begrudgingly pushed Marci from my lips, then carefully pushed her thighs down from my hips. She still held onto my neck as she was now standing in front me as she moved her hips into my groin area. Her eyes were filled with a lust-filled, longing desire. I looked at Carolyn and she knew something was wrong. I knew that someday she believed something bad would happen to Lewis. Carolyn's face turned completely white as she stared into my eyes. She knew something had happened to him even before I said a word.

Carolyn then spoke as her eyes started to swell up with tears, "He is dead, isn't he?"

I looked at her sorrowfully and with a heavy heart I said, "No. Lewis is not dead. He is alive, but not well. He is with my parents."

Before those words escaped from my mouth, Carolyn broke down and sobbed uncontrollably. Marci was in shock as well, but she handled the news better than Carolyn. I stepped closer to Carolyn, but she backed away as if she was afraid of me. I told her, "Carolyn, I am so sorry, but my father bit him, thus he couldn't come back with me."

Carolyn interrupted me and said, "He bit him?"

I continued, "My father wouldn't allow him to leave with me and, in fact, I was very fortunate that I was allowed to leave." I looked around the airport to make sure no one was overhearing our conversation. I said, "This is not the place for this conversation. I will explain everything to you when we leave. I will drive us home and then I will explain everything in great detail to you both." I went over to Carolyn and this time she didn't back away from me. I gave her a hug and attempted to console her. Carolyn couldn't stop crying.

I sensed more than fear in Carolyn's heart and then it hit me – I believe she was in love with Lewis. I was careful not to say anything about what I had discovered on my own. When I thought back, Carolyn was adamantly against us going to Germany. Now I know why she was adamantly against the trip. She was in love with Lewis. I wondered if Lewis was in love with her as well. I wonder if they had a secret affair right under my nose. I never sensed there was anything between the two, and it surprised me that I had possibly missed that fact.

We walked to the front entrance of the airport and our car awaited us. We got inside, and I drove off to the estate. Carolyn was seated in the passenger's side of the car as Marci was in back. I started telling them what had happen almost immediately after driving off. I told them, in detail, what had happened on the trip. Marci was still stunned over hearing the tale. She couldn't believe Lewis was bitten and was still alive.

Carolyn was in deep mourning and could not stop crying and shaking during our drive home. I reassured Carolyn and my love that I had no choice in what had happened. "I knew Lewis didn't want to go on the trip, but in the end he wanted to find out the truth. I promise nothing like what I experienced will ever happen to either of you as long as I am alive. In the future, I will make my way back to Germany and check up on Lewis and my parents."

Marci bluntly said, "I never want you going back to that place again."

Carolyn was beside herself. She was in such an emotional turmoil, unlike anything she had experienced in her life. She didn't want to tell us that she loved Lewis, at least not in a romantic way, and I had no intention of leaking her secret. Carolyn and I'd had some good times in the past and she was with me for years while I was at Harvard. She kept to herself and she allowed me the freedom that I so desperately needed at that time in my life. I knew she wanted my Marci to leave me and pushed her out the door many times, but I understood her motives. Carolyn was a loving woman and she cared for others more than I could ever imagine. I know full well now that she was just trying to protect Marci when she told her to leave me a while back. Now I know why she did what she did. Carolyn didn't want Marci to fall into the trap that she fell into, which was to love a man that was driven and possessed with an impossible and disgusting obsession. Carolyn had to know that Lewis was headed for an eventual disaster and she could not bear to witness his potential destruction like she had witnessed so many times since she had become a member of my household.

After what seemed like hours, we finally got to the estate. I pulled into the driveway and made my way to the garage. When I stopped, Carolyn got out of the car as fast as she could and ran to the door of the garage. She tried to open the door, but of course it was locked. She fumbled furiously through her purse until she found her keys. She nervously tried to find the right key and in doing so, she dropped the keys on the step. She then broke down as she took her left hand, made a fist, and slammed it onto the locked door. She slowly slid her grieving body down the side of the door. She finally came to rest on the step in front of the door going into the house.

I went over to assist her, and before I got to her she spoke through her cries, "I loved him! He was the only man that I ever loved!"

I turned away from her for a quick second to look at Marci. I wanted to see her reaction. She just stood there shocked as she looked at the broken women in front of us. Marci's eyes darted back and forth from me to the grieving old woman. Marci's beautiful mouth opened slightly as she looked at me and mouthed the word, "What?" She then had a devilish smile that developed on the most stunning face that man has ever seen. She placed her hand up to her mouth to hide her snickering. I quickly shook my head to tell her to stop making fun of the situation.

I went over to Carolyn and before I could reach out to her, she started to scream as she pressed her face up against the door, then she pushed her head and shoulders into the door. I gently bent down and picked up the keys and said, "Let me get the door." Carolyn nervously moved to the side as I unlocked the door. I opened it and helped Carolyn inside. I looked back at Marci who was trying hard to hide her amusement.

I suggested we make our way to the great room and I would go more in depth into what happened to Lewis and my experiences on the trip. I started telling my story from where I had left off in the car, and the ladies were listening intently to my story. I was very honest and held nothing back. Carolyn was overly emotional through the entire story. I sensed that she was angry with me for leaving the man that she loved there to basically die, but she understood that I had no choice in the matter. I could also sense the diverse arrays of feelings that were attacking Carolyn's soul.

The ladies were worried when I told them about my teeth growing after I became very angry. I tried to explain the entire theory behind what happened, and I felt that they understood to the best of their abilities. What we experienced on the trip was impossible to explain.

When I completed my story, Marci spoke up and said," I am so glad that you found your parents, but I am happier that you came out of the situation alive."

Carolyn seemed to accept what happened after I explained everything. I told her that I was sorry for her apparent loss. I'd had no knowledge that she was interested in Lewis; this was a complete surprise to me. My senses never once noticed the fact that she loved him. I asked if they were ever romantically involved and Carolyn quickly said to me, "No. I don't think he even knew I was interested in him or that I loved him. From the first time we met, I fell in love with him, but I kept it to myself. I never wanted to make a fool of myself, especially sense we were all under the same roof. I needed this job, and throughout the years I have fallen in love with this place and, of course you, Garrison. I couldn't risk my relationship with you over some infatuation that was obviously one sided. I am sorry for being so emotional and to have made such a scene in front of you guys but... well... it was just very emotional for me. What will happen to Lewis?"

I looked away from her sad eyes and stared at the floor. I said, "I honestly don't know. What little I know of my father, he will probably keep Lewis alive, at least until he changes completely. The complete transformation will probably take two to three months. From there, I just don't know. I assume a lot of experiments will be conducted on him. Beyond that, it is anyone's guess. Lewis did not want to change, so death would be his best option. It would put him out of his misery, but Lewis really upset my father with some very harsh words, so I fear that he might suffer for quite some time."

Meanwhile, Marci was getting restless sitting on the couch. She was smiling and winking at me the whole time I was explaining my story to them. Her fingers played with her hair, twirling it around her long and elegant fingers. After several minutes they found her blouse. She rubbed her fingers across the edge of the silky fabric just below her shoulder. Suddenly and without notice, her fingers found her lips as her long fingernails would brush the corners of her pouty, moist lips. I knew Marci was glad to have me back home. It had been a long time since we showed our love for each other. Carolyn apparently had perceived her playful actions and politely excused herself from our company.

When she left the room Marci said to me, "Thank god, I thought she would never leave. Garrison, I have missed you so much. I was so worried about you, but at least now you are safe and here with me where you belong. Please don't ever leave me again."

I said, "I cannot promise that I will not go back to see my parents again, but I will promise that I will always love you. You will always be a part of my existence, if you wish."

Marci said quickly, "I will never leave you. I love you and I find you and your special gifts to be such a turn on. I want it, Garrison. I want what you have. I want your gift. Do what you need to do. I really don't care what the consequences are, I just want your gift of perfection."

I reluctantly said to her, "I can't, my love. I could never live with myself, making you become one of them. I have tried to find the cure to the physical transformation process but Lewis and I nor my brilliant father have figured that out yet. We must have patience. I want you to spend the rest of your life with me. There is nothing in this world that I want more, but I need more time. I know that I can figure this secret out. I just know I can."

Marci looked at me and said, "But, Garrison, time is not on our side."

I looked down at the ground as my lips pressed hard together. I shook my head and uttered the words, "I know."

My love slowly knelt before me. She studied my entire body in front of her. She looked down at my groin and eagerly started to unfasten my belt. She then reached inside and pulled my cock out of my pants. Soon I felt her wet tongue licking the length of my shaft. I felt those soft lips sliding down on me until I felt the head of my penis on the back of my lover's throat. As she gagged, she quickly moved off my cock, but after she composed herself, she repeated the action. As she continued to suck on me, she removed her blouse and bra.

I took my shirt off and stepped out of my pants. As Marci rose, I removed her shorts and small panties. I forcefully spun her around and laid my cock between the cheeks of her ass. I could feel her asshole and pussy lips as she moved her body up and down on my manhood. I moved my hands up and squeezed her large beasts. I could feel her body getting warmer as the blood raced through her veins. I heard her heart rate increasing with a mixture of sexual moans of pleasure. I moved my hand down her muscular torso until my fingers found her wet pussy. I gently rubbed her clit until it was fully erect. I slid two fingers inside of her, and as I wiggled them in opposite directions, I felt her entire body tense up.

Her loud cries of passion were music to my ears. I not only wanted to give my love pleasure, but I felt obligated. I kissed the side of her neck while I mixed in several licks of wanting desire on the back of her neck and across her shoulders.

While her ass muscles were milking me, I brought my hands up to her shoulders and bent her over the couch in front of us. I placed my cock on top of her ass and the small of her back. As I looked down I wondered how all of me was going to fit inside of her. I ran my hands up and down the sides of her powerful legs and then up to the cheeks of her ass. I slowly moved up the small of her back. My cock leaked a rather large puddle of precum in the middle of the small of her back. I took my fingers and wetted them with my juices then quickly moved my wet fingers across her pussy lips. The sounds of my wet fingers and her lips made for an insane sensory pleasure to my ears. As I again inserted two fingers inside of her, I moved myself around so I could move my fingers in and out with a jack-hammering motion. Marci could barely catch her breath. My hand moved so quickly that large drops of her womanly juices were splattering out of her lovely hole.

I continued to pound her as she orgasmed on my long, thick fingers. When she was finished, I moved in front of her. I bent down and picked her up with my hands holding her ass. She wrapped her beautiful legs around me for support. With one hand, she guided me inside of her. As my head entered her, she threw her head back, and I had to move my hand up the middle of her back, then slowly pushed her ass toward me with my other hand. The feeling of her wet cunt sliding down my cock caused a great strain on me from not releasing inside of my love. As I quickly controlled myself, I knew I could only go so far inside of her. I began to pump slowly and as the moments raced by, I began to increase my thrusts. After several minutes, my love was experiencing her second orgasm. When her pleasure started to decrease, I placed her on the couch and slid myself out of her, causing her to moan even louder.

I knelt in front of her then moved my fingers across the lips of her pussy. As I brought my face closer to her, I spread her lips open with my thumb and index finger. I made my tongue wide and slowly ran it up the length of her pussy. The taste of silky honey mixed with her womanly scent was driving my animal instincts to the point of complete obsession. My tongue lapped up her wetness like a thirsty dog to water. As I slowly went down her lovely vagina, I discovered her asshole and paid close attention to that part of her body. I brought my hand around her waist and while I caressed her perfect breasts in my hand, I took the liberty of sliding two fingers on each side of her clitoris. I ran my tongue across her lips then I would momentarily slip it inside of her. Her moans of passion were so pleasing to my ears. My cock was becoming as hard as it had ever felt in my life.

I positioned her on the couch so I could take my love with full force. As I entered her, I immediately began to pump as fast and hard as I could. When I looked down at my beautiful woman, I could barely contain my seed from leaving my penis. Her breasts moved in an upward and downward motion, making perfect rhythm and timing with my thrusts. Marci moved her hand down and started to finger her clitoris as I continued to fuck her. When I decided not to hold back any longer, I pulled out and shot my load all over her stomach. Some of my seed hit her face and breasts. At one point, I thought I was going to pass out. It had been so long since I had felt the inside of my lover's cunt.

That night we continued to make love for many hours in the great room. Our cries of passion had to be heard throughout the house. I could tell that Marci had missed me and was glad that I was home where it was safe. At the end of our session, Marci collapsed on the couch and passed out from the exhausting lovemaking that we created. I went and retrieved a blanket and wrapped the most perfect body up while she slept on the soft couch. I got dressed and went over the bar and had a much-needed drink. I looked back toward my love while she was sleeping.

A tear formed in my eye, knowing that someday that perfect vision would grow old and die while I would remain ageless and alone. What used to anger me now only frightens me. The formula was so complicated, so perfect, so ever changing to its environment that I highly doubted I could ever change its complex chemical structure.

I went back to the bar and poured a large amount of Kentucky bourbon into my glass. So many thoughts were going through my head as I took large sips of my drink. So many thoughts lingered in my mind about my once dear friend Lewis and how much he had sacrificed in these past decades, not only for himself but for my adoptive father, me and now my birth father. The pain that he was experiencing now is beyond what any human or animal should be able to endure. My father would further increase his suffering after the change was complete. I knew this to be a fact. To attempt to grasp all that had happened over the past handful of days was something that even for me was almost completely incomprehensible.

I walked outside and strolled through the backyard. For a moment, I glanced at the four tall, healthy trees that were now fully grown. Just like the trees in the forest in Germany, they kept getting larger and thicker. I thought to myself that at least my dead brother was good for something. Being fertilizer for those trees is about the only advantage that freak of nature was good for. I walked over to the gravesites of my adoptive parents and grandfather. I gazed at their resting sites and after a moment I remembered that Loren's body had been added to the collection of bodies just a short while back. I thought that one day my dear Marci would be laid to rest amongst these tragic figures in my life. This, of course, was unacceptable to me. I wondered how many more would be added to this site throughout my life, a life span that would continue forever. I raised my head and looked across the valley of trees as I thought about the concept of forever. Forever is where time is everlasting, continuous, and unrelenting. It is a concept of life that I found unsettling because to me, forever is a long time to be alive and alone.

About the Author

$\mathcal{K}$ evin C. Popp was born and raised in Louisville, Kentucky, graduating in the early 1990's from Bellarmine University with degrees in Business Administration and Accounting. After working a couple of jobs after college, in 1997 he found a great company in the Financial Securities market, working in the finance department.

Kevin grew up as an only child, living modestly. His parents saved every dime they made, but when it came to Kevin's basic needs, he wanted for very little. His parents were much older than most of his friends' parents, thus his grandparents were older as well. His mom and dad spent the majority of his youth taking care of their parents, so his entire youth was surrounded by grandparents' illnesses, hospitals, nursing homes and eventual pending deaths.

One of Kevin's childhood memories was a struggle to find time to be alone. He felt strongly that he needed that time to himself, even for short time spans. He would regularly take long bike rides through the neighborhood, ultimately taking him through a park that his neighborhood bordered on. At times he would think to himself about money, politics or the concept of God.

Kevin took up golf at an early age and played the game well, but not to the level that he desired. He always admired people that were great at something, venerating intelligent, athletic, wealthy and attractive people, both young and old.

Kevin had many obsessions growing up, including golf, stamp collecting, money, stock market and numbers. He grew up thinking he was poor, but actually the opposite was true. He always saved more than others. At the impressionable age of twelve, he invested in the stock market and quickly enjoyed making money.

Although very intelligent, Kevin never liked school, and constantly daydreamed, thinking about things that never occurred to others. His mind, even to this day, continuously ponders and worries about everything, planning out numerous courses of action for every situation that he attempts or is forced into doing.

As an adolescent, Kevin was starved for attention so he attempted to be the class clown, only to find himself a colossal failure in that role. One area of his mind that was not a failure was his imagination. His mind worked continuously, exploring many subject matters. The one motif that kept his attention was horror. He loved watching 'monster' movies, and found that he could stomach the most ghastly scenes that included demonic possession, dismemberment, and torture at a young age. His mind was fascinated with the macabre, both real and imaginary, trying to understand the complicated relationship between life and death and how God played His part between the two.

As the years passed, Kevin could no longer find any outlet to whet his appetite for this strange, dark world resting in the innermost parts of his brain. One day at work, he decided to write a book, and began creating an outline. Before he knew it, he had over five typed pages of notes. Creation, he loved that word! So he began creating a story, not about anyone in particular, but a story that he created from his imagination alone. He quickly found that he could create something by writing down what was in his mind.

Although certainly not the twisted, heartless monster that you see in his books, Kevin says he sometimes has a dual personality, especially when he writes. While busy typing away, he loses himself in an imaginary world of a multitude of sadistic renderings, and his hope is that he is talented enough to bring his imaginary world into focus for all to see and enjoy. It is his goal, as the writer of this series, to disrupt not only your cognizant state of mind, but also your unconscious realm simultaneously. Like any great composer of music, artistry or writing, as you read his books, he wants you to experience what is in his mind and soul. He wants you to understand his repulsion and loathing for a portion of the human race, as well as the pursuit of perfection that is inside his being. He doesn't want to just scare you, he wants to firmly implant horrific torture scenes in your memories that will haunt you daily. He wants you to question the human race and the many gods they pray to. He wants to dominate your thoughts and force you to feel others' pain.

www.ingramcontent.com/pod-product-compliance
Lightning Source LLC
Chambersburg PA
CBHW020244200626
46816CB00001BA/125